Barefoot in Pearls

The Barefoot Bay Brides #3

roxanne st. claire

Barefoot in Pearls

roxanne@roxannestclaire.com
www.roxannestclaire.com
www.facebook.com/roxannestclaire
www.twitter.com/roxannestclaire

Cover Art: Robin Ludwig Design
Interior Formatting: Author E.M.S.
Seashell graphic used with permission under Creative Commons CC0 public domain.

ISBN-13: 978-0-9908607-1-6

Published in the United States of America.

Critical Reviews of
Roxanne St. Claire Novels

"St. Claire, as always, brings a scorching tear-up-the-sheets romance combined with a great story: dealing with real issues starring memorable characters in vivid scenes."

— *Romantic Times Magazine*

"Non-stop action, sweet and sexy romance, lively characters, and a celebration of family and forgiveness."

— *Publishers Weekly*

"Plenty of heat, humor, and heart!"

— *USA Today's Happy Ever After blog*

"It's safe to say I will try any novel with St. Claire's name on it."

— *www.smartbitchestrashybooks.com*

"The writing was perfectly on point as always and the pace of the story was flawless. But be forewarned that you will laugh, cry, and sigh with happiness. I sure did."

— *www.harlequinjunkies.com*

"The Barefoot Bay series is an all-around knockout, soul-satisfying read. Roxanne St. Claire writes with warmth and heart and the community she's built at Barefoot Bay is one I want to visit again and again."

— *Mariah Stewart, New York Times bestselling author*

"This book stayed with me long after I put it down."

— *All About Romance*

Dear Reader,

Welcome back to Barefoot Bay and another romantic interlude with the Barefoot Bay Brides! As her two best friends settle into their happily ever afters, destination wedding designer Arielle Chandler is beginning to wonder if the promise of "The One"—one true love, meant only for her—is merely folklore passed down from her Native American grandmother. But when a mysterious man nearly mows her down on a hill overlooking Barefoot Bay, the legend of destined love suddenly feels very real. That is, until Ari learns of Luke McBain's plans to demolish a piece of land she believes is sacred.

While their immediate and potent attraction grows complicated, Luke and Ari discover the hills of Barefoot Bay could be hiding something far different—and even more valuable—than ancient art or graves. They are determined to discover the truth, but that will come at a cost. Will they risk their chance at once-in-a-lifetime love to uncover secrets that could change the landscape of Barefoot Bay forever?

As always, a crew of incredibly dedicated and talented professionals stand behind me as I write these love stories. I simply couldn't bring these characters to life and get them in readers' hands without the help of my amazing backup team. A million thanks to my editor, Kristi Yanta, whose talented touch brings the best out of my writing. A million more to copyeditor and proofreader Joyce Lamb, who polishes every page to perfection. More love needs to be showered on the formatting team at Author E.M.S., the artists at Ludwig Designs, my super enthusiastic Street Team (let's hear it for the Rocki Roadies!) and, of course, my tireless assistant,

Maria Connor. And last, but never least, my deepest gratitude to my family for their constant patience, support, and brainstorming over every meal.

Like every book set in Barefoot Bay, this novel stands entirely alone, but why stop at just one? All of the books and series are listed in the back. There are plenty of opportunities to go barefoot and fall in love! Check out my Web site for a complete list, and while you're there, join my mailing list for monthly updates and release news. In addition, check out the Roxanne St. Claire Street Team Page on Facebook if you'd like to join the fun with other Barefoot Bay fans.

Have fun in the sun!

— *Roxanne St. Claire*

Barefoot in Pearls

roxanne st. claire

Dedication

Dedicated with love and appreciation to
Toni Linenberger, one of my most enthusiastic readers and a
Street Team member with style!

Without readers like Toni, writers would be lost!

Chapter One

Arielle Chandler never prayed, not in the classic head-bowed, hands-folded, beg-for-help kind of way. Despite the fact that her father was a Bible-thumping Oklahoma man of God, Ari's spirituality came from the other side of her family, the Native American side that her shaman grandmother had nurtured and tended during long summers they spent together, communing with nature. So when Ari needed help, she headed outside, under the sun, next to the trees, close to the earth, where "the universe" could provide assistance.

Or maybe she just needed fresh air, a practical, skeptical little voice whispered in her head. Maybe she just *imagined* that nature delivered answers. She'd never been one hundred percent certain that Grandma Good Bear had known what she was talking about all the time, but everything the dear woman said had *felt* right.

So today, when things didn't feel right at all, Ari had escaped to one of her favorite places in Barefoot Bay—the only hill on a flat, tropical Gulf Coast island. The rise took her closer to the sky, and sometimes, when the universe smiled, she'd see an osprey with golden eyes and gray-tipped wings nesting in the tall palms.

She liked to imagine that regal bird was the spirit of her departed grandmother, soaring overhead to remind Ari to trust the universe and everything would work out as it should.

Even when it felt like nothing was working out as it should.

She checked the sky to gauge the time, certain she had a few hours, maybe more, before she needed to be in the Barefoot Brides dressing room. But this afternoon, the event wasn't work, as it usually was for Ari and her two bridal consultant partners. Today, one of those partners was the *bride* and not the consultant, and Ari wasn't just the event designer, but one of the two maids of honor.

And she needed every minute of that time to figure out why she felt so *unsettled* today. Was it the wedding? The love that seemed to permeate the lives of her closest friends...but not hers?

"I'm happy for them," she said out loud, as though she needed to be sure the universe understood that she really *was* happy when best friend number one is about to say "I do" and best friend number two just fell hard for the man of her dreams.

Nearly at the top of the hill, Ari looked out to the horizon, the sun glittering bits of gold on the indigo Gulf of Mexico, a commanding view sitting on pricey—and abandoned—real estate. Still, *someone* must have lived here once or owned the land, because there was a dilapidated old bungalow at the bottom of the hill, missing most of its roof and all of its windows.

The old house looked as hollow and empty as Ari felt.

"I just want to know what it feels like to be complete," she whispered, thinking of Willow's ethereal joy and Gussie's never-ending smiles since the two women had each found their true loves. Until then, Ari hadn't realized just how much she wanted that kind of joy for herself. "Just how much I want to find…"

She closed her mouth, purposely silent. The universe would laugh at her. Like her friends tried not to do when she told them that Grandma Good Bear convinced her that there really is *one and only one person* meant for everyone on earth. They said they were laughing at her grandmother's adorable Miwok name, but Ari knew they thought she was nuts for believing her grandmother and promising to wait for him…wait in every imaginable way.

Two years had gone by since Ari had made that vow to her dying grandmother, and sometimes it felt like she'd been celibate for so long that she was practically a virgin again. There had been a time when Ari thought the idea of "The One" was just folklore that Grandma made up to justify how Ari's half-Native American mother had ended up happily married to a Presbyterian pastor. It did explain Ari's parents' bizarre, yet wildly successful, union.

But over time, during those spectacular summers spent alone with her Grandma in Northern California, Ari had realized that the old shaman truly *believed* in the concept of a single real love, meant only for you. And, no surprise, Ari became a believer, too.

Grandma had said that Ari would recognize her "one true love" by the way her heart would feel like it was literally expanding in her chest when she met him, because it was "making room for love that will last a lifetime." She'd said Ari's spine would tingle, sending sparks out to her fingertips that wouldn't stop until she touched him. Grandma had talked of white lights that would go off in Ari's head and a numbness that would spread over her whole body. She might not be able to breathe.

The whole thing sounded like what happened when a person got shit-faced drunk, which, come to think of it, might be the optimal way to get through tonight's wedding.

The truth was, Ari had never met anyone who'd made her feel things like what her grandmother described. *How do you explain that, Universe?*

The flutter of bird's wings pulled Ari's attention. She hoped for the osprey, but instead, menacing black wings beat the air, and an evil red face and predatory eyes gazed down at her.

A *vulture*. Didn't see a lot of vultures in Barefoot Bay. She ducked instinctively as the bird swooped low then ascended high and mighty, like a poor man's eagle. But not before it dropped a dollop of poop.

"Eww!" Ari backed away in disgust. Is *that* what the universe thought of her dreams and longings? Bird doo all over...

What *was* that? The bird dropping had landed on something white, shiny, and long that looked like an ivory-colored snake curled under a pygmy palm tree. Ari stepped closer and leaned over to examine a string of tiny misshapen stones curled along a section of dirt.

Were those...*pearls*?

Leaning over, she squinted at the row of at least a dozen stones, the droplets of bird doo still wet on the ridged surfaces. Reaching into the pocket of her shorts, she fished for a tissue or receipt or, much more likely, a candy wrapper, but came up with nothing that could wipe the stones clean.

So she'd have to man up and touch the stones, because they were absolutely stunning. Kneeling closer, she squinted at the bluish-purple color of the largest pearl. Wiping her hand on her shorts, she extended two fingers gingerly toward the end of the strand.

These were not your basic jewelry-store freshwater pearls. These had an ancient, handmade look, the string between each stone clumsily knotted and frayed with age. A memory slipped through the edges of her mind, barely more than a wisp of smoke, but Ari closed her eyes and drifted back to a Native American festival she'd attended with Grandma Good Bear.

Pearl necklaces had been among the artifacts found there…artifacts discovered in *Indian burial mounds*.

She gasped, blinking at the punch of realization. What if this hill—on an island that had no other hills—wasn't a *hill* at all?

What if—

A rhythmic pounding broke the silence, but not a bird's wings this time. The sound was steady, strong, a drumbeat of…feet.

Ari whipped around to see a man jogging—no, seriously *running*—full speed toward her, bare-chested and bronzed.

She blinked as if the sun were playing tricks on her, highlighting the glistening muscles of his torso and abs, the powerful thighs as he took each stride, the tanned, sweaty shoulders held straight and strong as he powered up the hill, directly at her.

He had earbuds in, short, dark hair, and a mouth set in a grim line. He wore sunglasses, so she couldn't see his eyes, but he made no effort to change his path as he barreled forward.

It happened so fast. With no time to stand, she threw herself back with a shriek to get out of his way, but he stumbled over her foot and barked a black curse. The sunglasses went flying, and he hopped to get his balance.

"Whoa!" He fought to stop his own momentum. "Where the hell did you come from?"

Her? What about him? "What do you think you're doing?"

"Running up a hill. What are you doing here?"

"How did you not see me?"

"My eyes were closed." He practically spit the words at her, popping out his earbuds, his chest heaving with shallow breaths.

What?

"I was in the zone," he added, as if that explained why anyone would run with eyes closed and ears plugged. He reached for her hand to help her up. "You okay?"

"I'm fine." She started to wave off the help, but he clasped her wrist, wrapping huge, masculine fingers around her, giving her an effortless tug that brought her to her feet. She still had to look up at him and still needed to squint, but not because of the sunlight.

He wasn't handsome, at least not by male model-type standards. This man was rough and dark, with heavy whiskers over a jaw that looked like it might have met a few fists in its day. His nose was a little off-center and maybe broken once or twice. His chest and shoulders dwarfed her, no tattoos, no chest hair, but tanned, sweat-dampened skin covering rolling, ripped muscles.

"Really sorry," he said. He scanned her face and made no effort to unlock his grip on her wrist.

She should yank free. She should step away. She should stop staring. She should…breathe.

But right that minute, bathed in sunlight and pinned by a green-gold gaze the color of oxidized copper, Ari Chandler couldn't do any of those things. Because her whole body was kind of tingling and buzzing and sparking, like she'd stuck her entire arm in an electrical socket.

"You sure you're okay?" he asked. "'Cause you look like

I rang your bell."

He rang something. There was no other explanation for how lightheaded she suddenly felt.

"I...I'm...I think..." Words failed her. No chance of a coherent sentence.

His brows pulled into a frown as he turned her arm and placed a thumb over her pulse, which hit warp speed.

"Whoa. Your heart's racing faster than mine and I've been running." He started to lower her back to the ground. "Sit down. I have some water in my truck. Let me get it."

"No, no, I'm fine." But Ari let him guide her down, sitting on the grass as he crouched in front of her. She searched his face, trying to decide if she'd ever seen him before. No. In fact, she'd never seen anyone quite like him.

"Who..." Are you? She swallowed the rude-sounding question since he seemed to be considerate, at least. "Who runs with their eyes closed?" she finished.

"I was trained that way."

"For what? Suicide missions?"

"Something like that." His voice, low and charged with mystery, sent another cascade of chills down her spine, a shocking feeling that had no place dancing over her in the heat and humidity of the end of August in Florida.

"Really, what are you doing here?" she asked. "Not very many people on Mimosa Key even know about this place." Only dirt roads led to this acreage, which was marked at the perimeter as Private Property.

He glanced around. "I'm checking it out."

"With your eyes closed?"

He almost smiled, just enough to hint at dimples and straight white teeth. Just enough to take the edge off his face and turn it into something arresting. She needed to look away, but all she could do was blink at the white lights flashing behind her eyes.

Had she hit her head or...or...oh, no. *No.* This wasn't possible.

"No," she murmured.

"No...what?" he asked, leaning in closer. "It's okay, I can check the place out. I have the owner's permission." He narrowed his eyes, scrutinizing her. "Do you?"

"No, this isn't...you can't be..." But he *could* be. This *could* be the universe answering her plea...or the handiwork of a wild imagination. Which was it?

For one long, suspended second, the world around her crystallized, making her hyperaware of every color, scent, and sound. Everything was magnified. Like the slow roll of a bead of sweat trickling over a scar on his temple. And the flecks of color that somehow mixed to make his eyes a haunting blend of emerald and topaz. Even the timbre of his voice, baritone and sweet, and the rhythmic huffs of his breaths as the run caught up with him all sounded like music to her ears. He smelled like sunshine and the sea, and his hand, still wrapped around her wrist, was like a hot brand of man against her skin.

Everything about him was...*right.*

"Miss?"

She tried to nod at him, letting the very real possibility of what was happening sink in.

"Hey." He snapped his fingers in front of her face, making her jump. "Do you know your name?" he asked sharply.

"Arielle Chandler."

"Place of birth?"

"Sacramento, California."

"Husband's name?"

"I don't have one."

His eyes flickered. "Phone number?"

She didn't answer, but not because she couldn't remember the number. But because his smile went from *almost* to *full force*, and the impact actually hurt.

She could practically hear Grandma Good Bear describing exactly these feelings.

"No way!" She shook her head, still not believing it.

"Hey, it was worth a try." Still smiling, he leaned back on his haunches. "Since you're coherent enough to turn me down, you must be okay, Arielle Chandler from Sacramento, California." Then he let his gaze drop over her. "Yeah, you're fine."

And all those dancing cells in her body tripped and flatlined.

After a few seconds, he scooped up his sunglasses and stood. "And, by the way, if you don't have the owner's permission, you won't be able to come here when construction starts."

She looked up at him, digging deep for some semblance of sanity and cool, when all she wanted to do was grab his jaw and stare into his eyes and figure out if he was her future…

Wait a second. "Did you say construction?"

"That old hovel that got messed up in Hurricane Damien? It's history, along with this hill, which the owner said would block his water view when he builds his house. Well, when I build it for him."

Another, different kind of buzz hummed through her head. "It's history?" Her gaze shifted to the right, to the string of pearls not an inch away. Yes, it *was* history. Ancient, hallowed history. "How can you get rid of a hill?" Especially when it might not be a "hill" at all?

He lifted one mighty shoulder. "With a backhoe." He

wiped some sweat from his brow and shifted his gaze to the water. "I wish we could put the house up here for the best view, but there are crazy-strict rules about how close you can build to the shoreline."

And rules about protected land, rules she'd heard about a hundred times from her grandmother. "You can't just *backhoe* this hill."

"One of my subs will, and soon." He angled his head and looked closely at her, his stare so intent her heart ached like it was…expanding.

Expanding to make room for the man who wanted to destroy what might be sacred ground? What would Grandma Good Bear have to say about that?

"You positive you're okay?" he asked.

No, no, she was not okay. Not at all. "Yes," she lied glibly.

"Maybe I'll, uh, run into you again." He winked and slid on his sunglasses. "Next time I'll have my eyes open."

As he took off, she stared at his physique, the back every bit as mouthwatering as the front. Her fingers brushed the pearls next to her, and a different, visceral tug tightened her chest.

She'd have to find out the truth about these pearls and this land. And if it turned out she was sitting on a Native American burial ground, this man would *not* bulldoze it away.

Even if he was *The One*.

Chapter Two

When Ari arrived at the Casa Blanca Resort & Spa, the management offices were hushed and dark since Willow and Nick had decided on a Sunday afternoon beach wedding. Ari was headed to the bridal dressing room when she noticed the door to the Barefoot Brides office was open, and that quickened her step and her heart.

Maybe Gussie was in there, and Ari could tell her what happened today. She had to tell someone or she'd go crazy, but she certainly didn't want to steal a moment of Willow's special day by chattering on and on about some mystery man.

She rushed inside and came face-to-face with Gussie McBain, who was dressed in one of the white satin robes the Barefoot Brides provided for members of the wedding party.

"Where have you been?" Gussie asked, a tinge of impatience in her usually bright tone.

Ari froze, not realizing she was that late.

"Why aren't you in the dressing room with the rest of the bridal party, clean, showered, made up, and ready to put our dresses on for Willow's wedding?" She came closer, curiosity and a little frustration sparking her green eyes.

"Why didn't you answer your phone?"

Had her phone rang? Wow, she'd really been daydreaming after meeting him. "I was...out."

Gussie frowned. "Do you mind telling me what is more important than the fact that one of your best friends is getting married and you are a co-maid of honor?"

"I had to go somewhere," Ari said, suddenly realizing that Gussie was right—their best friend was getting married, so this might not be the best time to go into details about the stranger she'd met.

But Gussie looked extremely curious. "Where? Tell me."

Definitely not the right time to get into it. "Not important."

Gussie huffed out a breath at the vague answer, her exasperation growing. "I've been keeping Willow calm, assuring her you'd be here, lying for you when I couldn't reach you so she didn't become the freaked-out bride we all swore we'd never be, so yes, Arielle Chandler, you *are* telling me."

Dear God, was she that late or was it just standard wedding stress? A wash of guilt poured over her for being so self-involved on Willow's big day. Suddenly, the story felt a little preposterous.

"I had to do something." Lame, but she hoped it put Gussie off.

"Now? Today?" Nothing put Gussie off.

Ari lifted her hands in surrender. "I had to..." She squeezed her eyes closed. "I think I met him."

"What?" Gussie squished up her features. "You met who?"

"Him. I met...*him*. You know, my one, my only, my destiny."

Gussie choked as if she didn't know whether to laugh or

not. "Ari," she said, clearly working to be an understanding friend, but struggling right then. "You know I think your new-age superstitions are precious and you believe in love at first—"

"No, I don't. It's not love at first sight. It might not be, anyway. It's fate. It's destiny. It's—"

"Hogwash." Gussie scooted closer, sympathy softening her eyes. "You know what's happening, don't you? Willow is marrying Nick. Tom and I are together. That leaves you as the only one of the three of us..." She let her words trail off, as if she felt bad even making the suggestion.

"I'm not mooning over the fact that my two best friends and business partners have found their mates, Gussie." God, she hoped not. Maybe she'd *imagined* all those feelings for that guy on the hill.

"Mates. You make it sound like we're dolphins, for crying out loud."

She shook her head, ignoring the joke. "But there's a problem."

Gussie gave a wry, teasing smile. "There always is. What? He's the wrong sign? His aura is bad? What's his fatal flaw?"

Behind Gussie, out the window, a movement snagged Ari's attention. "I think he's going to hate me," she said quietly, staring at the man crossing the parking lot, obviously dressed to attend the wedding, but...oh, *Lord*.

Gussie made a comment, but Ari didn't hear it because...that was *him*. The same man, the same clipped hair and square jaw and wide shoulders. Even the sunglasses were the same. "Who...is...that?" Ari asked, not really expecting an answer.

"Luke made it!" Gussie exclaimed, almost jumping.

Luke? Luke McBain, the long-lost brother Gussie had

reconnected with in France earlier that month? *He was The One?*

"He's here to…" Gussie started laughing, giving Ari a pat on the back like she could knock common sense into her. "I know, put your eyeballs back in your head and let's go before Willow hits Bridal Defcon 1."

Ari couldn't stop staring as each step ramped up the same symptoms that she felt the last time she saw him. "That's…Luke?"

"So much for the Mr. Soul Mate you just met, huh? I thought you were—"

"You guys!" Willow shot into the room, her voice rising as high as her hair in megacurlers, her own white robe slipping off her shoulder. "Where in the hell are you two? I am officially having a breakdown. I'm getting married!"

Gussie and Ari laughed at the mix of panic and delight as Willow covered her mouth like she just couldn't contain her joy. "I'm so happy and scared and excited and happy!"

Gussie gathered them for a hug that Ari fell into, the mysterious man—who wasn't so mysterious now—momentarily forgotten. She *had* to remember what was important today, and that was Willow's wedding.

As they walked out, arm in arm, Willow was on a cloud and, honestly, Ari had to climb up and join her, because the universe was a strange and magnificent thing.

Luke McBain would be at the wedding, and she'd "meet" him in an hour. Just the thought gave her a swift set of chills. The universe was already working its magic. Now she'd have all evening to get to know him, find out about this "construction" he was involved in, and try to delay it until she figured out exactly what that "hill" in North Barefoot Bay really was.

And what had Grandma always said about meeting The

One? Don't tell him. If he doesn't realize it, then...Ari wasn't going to think about that.

Right now, her faith in the universe was too strong.

There were few things that pleased Luke McBain as much as a good coincidence. Oh, he liked himself an ice-cold Sam Adams on a hot summer day, and he'd been known to nearly kill a man in order to catch even one inning of a Red Sox game on the only television in a Third World country, and, yes, he had a secret collection of Louis L'Amour Westerns that had given him hours of entertainment. But *coincidences* were right up there with wonderful things he deeply enjoyed.

All those people who said, "Everything happens for a reason," could suck it. Nothing happened for any reason, it just happened. Like two days before he was to fly back to France, Gussie had heard that Cutter Valentine, Luke's old high school buddy and a superstar pro baseball player, was planning to move to the little island where she lived and worked. And Cutter needed a house built.

Of course, Luke was all over that. He'd cruised by Cutter's mom's house, got the guy's phone number, and wham, Luke got what he couldn't get before: the chance to start his building contractor business stateside.

And today he ran into—literally—the very woman who *just happened* to be in the wedding party with his sister. A coincidence—nothing more, nothing less.

And not a bad coincidence at all, considering the woman was damn near edible. The minute he laid eyes on her today, he'd wanted...more. He hadn't *needed* to check her pulse, but he sure needed to make some contact. The attraction was raw and instant and real, and totally unexpected.

It had been a long, long time since he'd felt anything remotely like it.

Leaning back on his chair in the last row of friends and family gathered to witness a sunset wedding on the beach, Luke let his gaze rest on the onyx-haired beauty who'd just glided down the sandy aisle. Of course, now that he saw her in the bridal party, he deduced that this was "Ari," his sister's close friend and business partner.

She was barefoot, like every guest and attendant around, wearing a strapless sapphire-blue dress that clung to feminine curves and showcased toned shoulders and a long, slender neck. Her gorgeous black hair was no longer falling out of a ponytail, but swept up, decorated with tiny diamonds that sparked in the light and gave her the air of a magical princess.

A low, slow, powerful burn started in his gut, the heat actually emanating right into fingertips that suddenly itched. He wanted to touch that hair. He wanted to take it down and spread it over a pillow and bury his face in it.

Holy hell, this wedding might be interesting after all.

As she turned to face the audience, her gaze went straight to Luke. Directly, *wham*, like she knew he was there, which seemed impossible since he'd slipped into his seat in the back at the last moment. But the instant their eyes met, he startled slightly, the impact undeniable.

Neither one of them looked away. Even when the bride came up the aisle, flanked by some famous parents and demanding every eye at the wedding, Arielle held his gaze.

Long. Direct. Damn. *Hot.*

She looked away first, forced to slide her attention from him to the bride, if only for propriety, but that lasted less than two seconds before she glanced at him again, this time with a challenge in ebony eyes that reminded him of ancient warrior princesses. Not that he'd ever met an ancient warrior princess, but if he had, she'd look like this woman. With hair glitter.

He accepted her silent gauntlet and tossed it right back with the most minuscule lift of one corner of his mouth. He could have sworn some color deepened the tone of pale skin that contrasted sharply with midnight hair and eyes. Once again, he won the face-off, and she shifted her gaze to the festivities, a young woman kissing her parents in a symbolic good-bye while her man beamed at them all.

Luke didn't bother observing the hand-off from father to groom. The exotic bridesmaid on his radar was much more interesting.

Yes, *exotic*. That was the very first word that had popped into his head when he practically mowed her down, and it knocked around his brain again now. She was nothing like what he usually liked. His whole life—well, since he'd left the country fifteen years ago when he was barely eighteen— his taste ran to the California Girl, like the one getting married, all blue eyes and blond hair, suntanned, freckled. Luke liked the all-American girl next door.

And yet he couldn't take his eyes off those slightly tilted, heavy-lidded, India-ink eyes that locked on his.

Luke shifted in his seat as the official ceremony began, taking a moment to enjoy how his sister glowed in her role as the other bridesmaid. Gussie wore a lime-green version of the same dress, her caramel-colored hair pulled up in a way that cleverly hid the burn scar on the back of her head.

He waited for the pinch of guilt that always accompanied the thought of how his little sister had gotten that scar, but she'd so effectively swept all the blame away in the past few weeks since they'd reconnected. She'd assured him that the accident that had been the catalyst to make him leave the States was well and truly *in the past*.

If only he could put the rest of the things that haunted him in the past. He was trying; that's why he'd moved here, gotten a job, and had a plan. Everything could be buried, right? Memories, mistakes, aspirations, and…people. Buried like land mines that only needed to be avoided to survive.

He shook off the thought and forced his attention back to the compelling woman he'd met earlier in the day. No hardship there. A woman hadn't been in his plan for his new life, but the way she looked at him and the response he felt from head to toe—and plenty in between—made Luke think he could certainly make room for a minor distraction.

He tried to listen to the vows, but he kept drifting back to what else Gussie had said about her close friend and business partner Arielle Chandler. He remembered that all three of the women had traveled together for some wedding consultant organization, then they decided to start their own joint business in Barefoot Bay. They lived in a Victorian house on the south end of the island, each in their own apartment. Arielle was on the third floor, if he recalled correctly, so she'd be one story above the guest bedroom in Gussie's apartment where he'd be sleeping for a while.

So, right on top of him, more or less. He felt the corner of his mouth kick up at another happy coincidence.

The newlyweds kissed, and a cheer went up as everyone stood to celebrate, including Luke, who inched to the side to be sure he didn't lose eye contact with his current target. She was hugging his sister, and then she slid her hand onto the brawny arm of the best man, a Navy SEAL friend of the groom, whom Luke had met before the ceremony started.

The best man seemed to be waiting for Gussie to take his other arm so the three of them could come down the aisle together, since there were no other groomsmen or bridesmaids. But Gussie gave her head a shake and gestured for them to go alone. So he'd have to time this just right to relieve that SEAL of the woman Luke had silently claimed as his, at least for the evening.

Around him, all the guests emptied their seats, heading toward the bride and groom or the bar to start the festivities.

Luke hung back, watching Arielle make her way down the aisle. She stopped to greet or hug a friend here and there, laughing at something someone said, smiling at others. But every few seconds, she ventured a look his way.

And every time, it shot a little more heat into his blood.

Just before they reached him, she and the best man separated. He went off to the left, but Arielle kept coming straight toward Luke. Their eye contact intensified, the ambient sound of laughter and conversation faded, and Luke actually felt his fingers burn again with the need to touch the beautiful woman coming right at him.

Yeah, this was one helluva nice coincidence.

He took a few steps closer to the aisle, his row cleared of people. He timed his arrival at the end to precisely match with hers, stepped onto the sand in front of her, and blocked her way.

She closed her eyes and smacked right into him, the tiny bit of contact sending a small explosion through his body.

"Oh, I'm sorry," she deadpanned, sounding not sorry at all. "Did I run into you? I was merely meandering through life with my eyes closed."

He stayed a little too close as he gazed down at her, narrowing his eyes at the sheer impact of being within touching distance. He had her by a good six inches, and his vantage point gave him an excellent shot of her cleavage, which was curved and soft and inviting.

"Eyes closed is the only way to run."

"Until you hit a tree."

"Or a gorgeous woman."

She angled her head, either to accept the compliment or wind up for another zing. Good God, she was pretty. Blinding, kind of. It felt like heat flashes were hitting his eyes.

"You run like you know exactly what life is going to put in your way," she said.

"I don't know, but I like what life put in front of me today. Twice." As much as he wanted to touch her bare shoulder and linger on her gleaming skin, he inched back and offered a more formal handshake. "I'm Luke—"

"McBain," she finished, her hand almost lost in his. "Gussie's brother."

How did she know that? "And you're Arielle, Gussie's partner. Imagine the luck of meeting you here."

Her eyes flickered and darkened for a quick second as she finally let go of his hand. "Luck?"

"Coincidence?" he suggested.

"I don't believe in either one."

"Ah, a reason-for-everything kind of woman."

She lifted a brow. "Absolutely."

"All right, then. What was the *reason* you spent the entire ceremony staring at me?" Not that he didn't already know. She felt the same physical reaction he did, and she could call it anything she wanted. He called it *hot*.

"I was staring because you're..." She hesitated, clearly looking for the right word, her color deepening as she whispered, "The One."

He inched back. "The one...what?"

With a smile, she slipped her hand through his arm and broke into a wide, bright smile, which catapulted her face from really pretty to insanely hot. "The one who's going to get me a drink, amuse me by gossiping about the guests, dance with me when they play the first slow song, and kiss me under the moon when it rises."

He tugged her closer. "You're right. I am definitely the one."

A soft cheer rose from a few people near the water, where the wedding canopy stood empty. Everyone turned in time to see Gussie being lifted into the air by Tom DeMille, the man she'd been seeing since before Luke and his sister had their unexpected and long overdue reunion in France.

"What's going on there?" he asked.

Tom twirled Gussie, and she let out a shriek, holding up her left hand so the setting sun captured a rock gleaming there.

Ari turned back to him, her eyes sparking like that diamond on his sister's hand. "I'd say your family just got bigger."

He felt his jaw loosen as he shook his head. "Well, I'll be damned. That was fast. Didn't they just meet a month or two ago? This seems a little…impulsive."

"Have you met your sister?"

He laughed. "Actually, only recently, as you know. But, still." He looked back again, feeling a bittersweet happiness for her. "I don't know. They seem pretty sure, but…"

Arielle eyed him suspiciously. "Don't tell me, you don't believe in love, marriage, or happily ever after?"

"Believe in it?" he said with a soft snort. "I just witnessed it. So, what's not to believe?"

"Do you have to see something to believe it?" she asked.

"Why do I think that's a trick question?" he asked, noting

that she looked awfully serious, like the answer mattered.

"I'm simply looking for some insights. Do you need to see something to believe it exists?"

There was no avoiding the question, so he shrugged and gave the only answer there was. "Of course."

She turned her lips down as if that disappointed her, but spun around as Gussie came rushing over the sand to them. His sister held out her hand, beaming with more joy than he'd ever seen on her face.

"Congratulations, Auggie," Luke whispered, hugging his sister and getting a pelt on his back for the hated nickname.

She turned in his arms to reach out to Arielle, who hugged right back, eyes closed, an unreadable emotion etched on her face.

"I'm so happy for you, Gus," Arielle whispered.

Gussie backed up, laughing. "I guess I found The One, huh?"

"Looks like you did," Arielle agreed.

Gussie kept her arm around Arielle, giving her a squeeze. "This is our resident sorceress, you know," she told Luke. "She's all about the woo-woo, like signs from the universe and your mate being fated by destiny."

Arielle gasped softly. "Gussie, I—"

"Really?" Luke asked.

"Oh, yes," Gussie exclaimed. "In fact, I'm surprised you didn't call it when I met Tom, Ari." She glanced over her shoulder to see her new fiancé approaching. "You always say there's only one true love for everyone and you'll know it the very moment you meet him."

Next to her, Arielle smiled self-consciously. "Well, sometimes it's not immediately obvious."

But she didn't argue the fundamental point, he noticed. "So you really believe that?" Luke asked.

"She really does," Gussie answered for her, clearly too over-excited to let Arielle say a word. "She's always going on and on about meeting The One." She added air quotes for emphasis. "In fact, she told me she met the man she'd marry to—"

Arielle's hand slapped over Gussie's mouth. "Shut up."

Just then, Tom came up behind Gussie, wrapping his arms around her waist. "Good luck with that, Ari," he said. "My *fiancée* is too happy to stop talking."

After another flurry of hugs and handshakes, the bride and groom came rushing over to share the moment of Gussie's engagement, the friendship between the three women palpable even to a virtual outsider like Luke.

He had to hand it to Willow. Most brides would go bat-shit if someone in their wedding party borrowed the limelight like that, but these three seemed to be more like family than friends, and it was clear Arielle and Willow were genuinely happy for Gussie.

Luke stepped back to let the small crowd around them grow, taking a moment to drink in his sister's obvious joy. But, after a few seconds, something drew his attention right back to the black-haired beauty who was standing awfully close to the best man, sharing a laugh with him.

Uh, sorry, SEAL.

Luke stepped closer to her and leaned down to put his mouth near her ear and let his lips graze that hair that reminded him of satin sheets. And being in them with her. "I thought I was the one—"

She froze for a second and slowly looked up at him, slaying him with a look of hope and heat in her soulful eyes.

"—who was going to amuse, dance, and kiss you," he finished.

Her lips lifted into a smile. "Oh, you are."

He angled his head toward a table in the back in silent invitation.

"After the pictures," she whispered. "I'm all yours."

For some reason he didn't really understand, those words ricocheted around his chest and squeezed everything into a knot. He hadn't met a woman he wanted so much in...hell, a long time. And the last time...

Well, that was the last time. But right that second, watching Arielle walk away, he forgot every other woman on earth.

Chapter Three

Ari skipped the champagne during the photo session, but she had a buzz anyway. The same fuzzy-brained sensation that started when Luke McBain knocked her off her feet still hummed through her during picture taking, making her a little giddy with anticipation.

After the last shot, she worked her way across the dance floor under the tulle canopy stretched over the cool sands of Barefoot Bay, and the lightheaded, fluttery feeling only intensified.

Was that because the universe had so instantly gone to work to put them in the same place at the same time—oh, how Grandma Good Bear would love that!—or was it because he'd flirted so hard, it made her *think* he felt the same sensations, too?

In other words, were these feelings fact or fiction? Since childhood, Ari had balanced that particular tightrope in life and learned that time would tell. She just hoped that it told her this was real and not imagined. So, until she figured that out, she'd be totally cool and not do something bold, like lean over and kiss him. Or even casually touch the tanned and strong forearm that he'd exposed by rolling up a sleeve.

Luke stood as Ari arrived at the table in the back, pulling out a chair with a smile so easy and sexy she'd have probably wobbled if she weren't barefoot. As she took the seat, she got slammed with a scent that smelled all earthy and woodsy and like the sun had set on his shoulders. And, of course, the minute he sat down, she forgot all her promises to be cool and put her hand right on that masculine forearm.

Which was so not cool—the move or his arm. His skin was warm, with a dusting of dark hair, corded muscles, and one long vein that she imagined pumped very hot blood.

She used the bubbly he'd put at her place as her excuse for what she hoped appeared to be a casual touch. "Thanks for the drink."

"I believe it was on my to-do list." At her questioning look, he added, counting on four fingers, "Drink, amuse, dance, and uh…"

Kiss. He let the unspoken word hang long enough to make them both smile at their first inside joke.

She lifted the champagne to him. "On to number two, amusement. Are you having fun?"

"I'm people watching. And by people, I mean you."

She laughed, the compliment as effective as the champagne. "You don't even know me."

"I know enough; Gussie told me about you."

"Today?" Damn, her voice cracked. Gussie couldn't possibly have had a chance to spill any more beans, had she? She'd been one inch from Ari for the last hour.

"No, no. While we were up in Massachusetts with our parents a few weeks ago. She talked a lot about her business here and, of course, Tom. She told us about you and Willow. And Tom." He grinned and gave a playful eye-roll. "Mostly Tom."

"And now he'll be your brother-in-law. So what did she tell you about me?"

"Let's see." He thought about the question for a moment, maybe mulling over how much to tell her. "You're a compulsive gambler who likes to bet on Milk Duds."

She made a face. "Not Milk Duds! I wouldn't waste a wager on something so pedestrian. And, trust me, your sister's the gambler, not me. But when I do bet her, it has to be rare, vintage, or mouthwateringly delicious candy to make it worth my while."

"I'll keep that in mind. What do you like?"

You. She recovered before the word slipped out. "Nik-L-Nips," she said easily.

He fought a laugh. "Excuse me?"

"You know, the wax bottles with syrup in them you probably drank as a kid."

"That's what they were called?" He curled his lip, which only made him cuter. "Disgusting shit, especially the wax-biting part."

"Ah, the wax bite is an art. I'll teach you."

He lifted an eyebrow. "The only thing that should come in a bottle with wax around the top is good wine. Not blue sugar juice."

For a few seconds, they stared at each other, and Ari heard nothing but that buzz in her head. She could banter with him all night long. "Blue is my favorite. It makes your lips blue."

A dare in his eyes, he licked his lips, and the sight of just the tip of his tongue sent a blast of heat through her. "So, what else did your sister tell you about me?" she asked quickly.

"Let's see..." He tapped the table and notched his chin toward the centerpiece. "That your staging and designs for the weddings are spectacular."

She gave a shrug. "I try. I like things to look a certain way, for impact." She reached out and rearranged the one cheery sunflower tucked into the arrangement of cobalt orchids spilling down to the table. "I balance the expected with a twist. I tell the brides it's what their married life will be like."

He laughed at that. "Good skill to have. How'd you pick that up?"

"I studied interior design, but my first job out of college was as a receptionist at a bridal consulting firm. I took to the business and discovered there's actually a big role for a designer in weddings, so I worked my way up the ranks until I met Gussie and Willow and we started this company."

"Interior design?" Interest and the spark from a torchlight turned his eyes closer to gold than green. "Wow, that's a fortunate coincidence."

She lifted both her brows, not at all sure what to make of that comment.

"Oh, that's right." He snapped his fingers. "You don't believe in stuff like that."

"But if I did, why would that be fortunate or a coincidence?"

He leaned on the back legs of his chair, the fine white linen of his dress shirt pulling across well-developed shoulders. "I might need a designer."

The way he said it, low and sexy and slow, sent all the symptoms she'd been fighting into a higher gear. "Why? Did you buy a house you need to redecorate? Here? On Mimosa Key?" Oh, great. She sounded all eager and hopeful. She covered with a sip of champagne, as if his long-term living plans were nothing but small talk. Which they would be if he weren't…special.

"Actually, I am going to be staying in Gussie's apartment for a while." He let his chair hit the temporary wooden floor with a jolt. "Right under you."

Oh, he was good. Smooth and sexy. "Really. For how long?"

"As long as it takes." He gave a teasing laugh, as if he caught the genuine interest in her question. "I'm working on a project for a while."

A whole different set of nerve endings sparked. A *project.* "Something to do with backhoes and bulldozers in North Barefoot Bay?"

"Something." He rocked back again, eyeing her. "So what's this business about you being, what did Gussie call it, woo-woo? Are you a witch?"

"My father's a pastor, so don't let him hear you call me that."

"A preacher's daughter, huh?" He kicked up a half smile.

"Yes. But my spiritual side actually came from my mother's mother, who was part of the Miwok Indian line of Northern California. All my 'woo-woo,' as you call it, comes from Grandma Good Bear."

"That's her name?"

"Was. She passed. Her real name was Uzumati, which means bear, but I always called her Grandma Good Bear since I was a baby, and it stuck. And she was a shaman, so she could out-woo-woo anyone."

The chair came down slowly, and intrigue tapered his eyes. "So what does woo-woo mean? You commune with clouds and howl at the moon?"

She laughed lightly. "Very little howling. Really, all it really means is I'm a good judge of character and I trust the universe."

"To do what?"

"What it's supposed to do."

Another look skyward communicated his skepticism. "I'm not woo-woo," he said. "But I am a good judge of character. A superior one, actually."

"Oh, really?" If that were true, wouldn't he sense the connection and bond between them? He would if he were what she thought he might be. That was the rule, right? He would know the minute she knew; no one had to be told they'd met The One.

She took a sip of champagne, weighing all the different questions she could ask him. "Gussie's hardly had a chance to tell us much about you," she said. "All I know is you two reunited in France after you hadn't seen her for years and that you were in the French Army."

"That's the abridged version. And it was the French Foreign Legion, which is definitely *not* the French Army." He shifted a bit and took a drink.

"Then what is it, if not the French Army?" she asked when he didn't elaborate, sensing the faintest discord emanating from him. Was it her or the topic?

"Exactly what you've heard. An army of mercenaries who fight wars for money." He sliced her with his gold-flecked eyes, narrowing them until the thick lashes touched. "I don't talk about it."

Okay then. The topic and not her. "Is there a code of secrecy or something?"

Very slowly he shook his head, a vein lightly throbbing in his neck, the thin half-moon scar at his temple white against tanned skin, all playfulness gone. "I simply don't talk about it."

She nodded, as her natural ability to read people hit a brick wall.

He put a single finger over one of her knuckles, the slight

contact like a spark silencing her thoughts. "We were talking about my superior ability to judge character."

A little disappointment tweaked that he wouldn't confide in her, which made her wonder if all these crazy sensations were one-sided. Or, worse—the dreams of a desperate woman.

She slipped her finger out from his touch. "You want to bet?" she asked.

"On what?"

"Anything. Remember, according to your sister, I'm a compulsive gambler."

He gave her a slow half smile. "Would it be horrible of me to make a joke about Native Americans who love to bet?"

"Well beyond horrible."

"You'll bet on *anything*?"

She had to laugh at his incredulity. "Pretty much, and since you're a rookie, we'll make it easy." She lifted her glass and gave a questioning look. "Loser goes to the bar?"

He gave her a sideways look. "It's an open bar, Arielle."

"Everyone calls me Ari."

"I'm not everyone," he reminded her. "And I like Arielle. It suits you. It's..." He eyed her, scrutinizing her face, openly studying her every feature. With each passing second, she could feel heat rising, her dress suddenly feeling constricting around her chest.

"It's rendering you speechless," she teased.

"Arielle is mysterious and deep, like your eyes. What does it mean? I bet it refers to some ancient spirit or the goddess of all living things."

She almost bit her lip to keep from laughing. "You'd bet that?"

"Yeah," he said after a second, inching slightly closer.

"I'll wager there's a profound significance to your name and it has a deep meaning to your parents."

Oh, boy. Like taking Jujubes from a baby. A very sexy baby. "What are we betting?"

"A dollar."

"Fine." She held out her hand, and he closed his fingers over hers, and damn it all if the Fourth of July fireworks didn't explode up her arm. Why did he have this effect on her? His eyes flickered a little, and he added some pressure.

He feels the same way.

The thought made her throat dry, but she gave a hearty shake. "A dollar," she confirmed.

Once again, it took a few seconds too long to let go of each other's hand.

"So, what does your name mean?" he asked. "Elusive jaguar? Midnight sky?" He leaned closer, lowering his voice. "Doe-eyed man-eater?"

"Little mermaid."

He looked skeptical. "Native Americans believe in mermaids?"

"My parents watched *The Little Mermaid* with my older siblings one night, and when it was over, they told them there would be another baby in the family." She fought a smile. "My sister announced I would be named Arielle, and it stuck, with a slightly fancier spelling."

His jaw loosened. "So nothing mysterious or ancient?"

"Only the ancient and mysterious Walt Disney."

"But what about your parents and the universe?"

"My *grandmother* and the universe," she corrected. "My mother did not share that connection. Quite the opposite, in fact." She held out her hand, palm up. "Payment, please."

He reached into his back pocket and pulled out a wallet, sliding out a one-dollar bill without taking his eyes from hers. "I'll add that to the list," he said softly, placing the bill in her hand.

"What list?"

"The list of things I know about you." He started counting on his fingers. "Disney princess, interior designer, sorceress, candy snob..." He reached forward to touch the sunflower. "Twisted."

"Twisted?" She angled the champagne flute, enjoying the playful exchange far more than the drink. "What I said and what you heard were two different things."

"That's how it is for us superior-character judges. Let's bet again because I hate to lose." He swept a hand toward the wedding guests. "Ask me about anyone you know here, and I'll tell you something just by looking at them. If I'm right, I win. If I'm wrong, you win."

She waved the dollar bill. "Double or nothing?"

"You keep that." He put his lips right over her ear, ruffling the perfectly placed curl that Gussie had styled earlier. "This time I wager a kiss. That way, there is no real loser."

About six billion goose bumps exploded on her neck, and Ari actually had to tense up to not give in to a full-body shiver. "Losing is losing, and I hate it, too."

"Then we make quite a pair."

Oh, God, she thought, sanity slipping with each passing minute. They *did* make quite a pair.

"Game on, Little Mermaid." And back he went on the two legs of the chair.

"All right." With her chin propped on the back of her hand, she searched the crowd with a pointed-finger periscope that stopped at Mandy Nicholas. "The blonde right over there. Tell me her story."

Would he guess that the woman who ran the

housekeeping company was once a maid at the resort and recently married one of the über-rich men who'd moved here to start a minor league baseball team? Unlikely.

"Ahh, let me think." He peered at her, pursing his lips, nodding as he thought it through. "Definitely on the bride's side. Maybe a sister or cousin. And she's a neat freak."

True enough, Mandy was scooping up a plate that had held hors d'oeuvres and looking around for someone to hand it to. Someone who worked for her, but would he know that?

"And she's pregnant."

Ari sat up straight. "Really?"

"Look how she's sort of absently rubbing her stomach."

Mandy was indeed giving herself the telltale pregnancy rub with her free hand. "Huh. Who knew?"

"Me." He leaned closer. "I'll settle for a peck on the cheek. Ready whenever you are."

"No way." She shook her head, backing away. "She is not a cousin or sister of the bride," she said, glancing at Mandy as her husband, Zeke, walked toward the table, talking to the groom. "She's in charge of our housekeeping service and married to a billionaire."

"But she *is* pregnant."

"That remains to be seen. Would you have known that her husband is a billionaire?"

"No, but that guy behind him is."

She leaned to the side to see who he meant. "Well, yes, Nate Ivory is a billionaire, but that so doesn't count since his whole family is tabloid fodder, and we weren't betting on him."

He laughed softly. "How many things do I have to get right to qualify for a win?"

If he kissed her, even on the cheek, she'd probably melt right into his arms. Still leaning away, Ari spied Lacey

Walker across the dance floor in the center of the reception area. "You win if you can guess who *she* is."

"Easy. She owns the place. Built it, in fact. Husband's the architect."

Ari's jaw dropped. "How do you—"

He put his finger on her chin, closed her mouth, and guided her face to his. "Forget the cheek. I want the lips."

As if she could say no. Ari inched closer, already anticipating the touch.

"Hi there, Luke. Nice to see you again."

Lacey's voice pulled them apart. So he *knew* Lacey Walker.

"Cheaters never win," Ari mumbled, making Luke laugh, low and sly. They both stood to greet the woman who did, indeed, own Casa Blanca with her architect husband, Clay, backed financially and emotionally by her three best friends from college.

"Hello, Lacey." Ari reached out to give the other woman a hug. "You've obviously already met Gussie's brother, Luke."

"Just before the wedding." They greeted each other with an easy hug. "Say, Clay wanted me to give you a heads up that the mason will be at the job site tomorrow morning at eight. He's apparently anxious to meet you."

"Absolutely," Luke replied. "I'll be there bright and early."

Ari knew a little about building from her interior design classes. A mason would be the contractor who'd prepare the foundation...and level any uneven ground. Her heart tripped, the pearl necklace and its possible significance still tugging at her.

"What are you thinking about building?" Ari asked.

"No one's *thinking* about it anymore," Lacey said on a

laugh. "Clay's architectural firm handled the design for the house Luke's building up on Barefoot Mountain."

"Barefoot Mountain?" Ari and Luke actually asked the question in perfect unison, but Ari sounded strangled, while Luke laughed at the name. "That's a bit of an exaggeration," he added.

Lacey waved her hand. "Oh, you have to remember I'm a Mimosa Key local, born and raised. We used to ride dirt bikes on that hill when I was a kid, and it seemed like a mountain to us."

Dirt bikes? On a burial ground? Ari tamped down her reaction. She didn't *know* it was a burial ground yet. But she had to find out.

"And you really want to *destroy* a…local landmark?" Ari asked him.

"Well, Cutter Valentine does," he said. "And it's his ten-thousand-square-foot estate home I've been hired to build."

"That's what's going there?" Ari almost choked. "A McMansion for a has-been ballplayer?"

They both looked at her, instantly making Ari regret the exclamation.

"He's not exactly a *has-been*," Luke said with a wry smile. "Cutter's retiring from a stellar career and is going to be managing the Barefoot Bay Bucks minor league team."

"And, frankly, it's a godsend that someone is finally building up there," Lacey added. "That land's been in probate and court messes, and no one wanted to touch it after Hurricane Damien hit. But it turns out Cutter's great-uncle willed it to him, and he let it sit because he didn't want it."

"Then the opportunity for him to manage the Bucks came up," Luke said. "It was serendipity."

Which Ari didn't believe in. "Why didn't anyone want to touch it before now?" she asked, her sixth sense sparking.

Maybe someone knew what *Barefoot Mountain* really was.

"Balzac Valentine died during the storm, in the house," Lacey said. "One of the windows blew in and killed him."

"Oh, how tragic," Ari said. "Why didn't he evacuate?"

"Lots of us didn't," Lacey told her. "That hurricane was headed straight north for the Panhandle, when *bam!*" She snapped her fingers and pointed to the left. "It turned and crashed straight into Barefoot Bay with cat-five winds. It happened so fast, most of us had no choice but to hunker down and ride it out."

"Did you?" Luke asked.

She nodded, a frown pulling at her lightly freckled brow. "My daughter and I lived right over there where the main hotel is now, in a house my grandfather built. We spent that night in a bathtub with a mattress on our heads." She closed her eyes on a sigh. "It was a miracle we survived, because nothing else did."

Ari had heard bits and pieces of the story, folklore around Casa Blanca now, but seeing the memory darkening Lacey's amber eyes made it real. Yet her mind went back to the land in North Barefoot Bay. "Did you know the man who died?"

"I'd met him as a child, but he was a recluse after his wife passed away." She nodded, narrowing her eyes to pull up a memory. "My grandfather knew him, though. They were both Mimosa Key founders who claimed land in the forties."

"And left it to Cutter Valentine?" Ari asked, wondering about the pro baseball player and how much he might—or might not—care about sacred ground and making a mental note to sit down and talk to Lacey about her grandfather, and that hill.

"Nobody was more stunned than Cutter when he found out he had a great-uncle who left him part of an island,"

Luke said. "But, then, that's how Cutter Valentine's life goes. Perfectly."

"Who lived there before Cutter's great-uncle?" Ari asked. Maybe someone, *somewhere* kept a record of that land or its history.

"No one," Lacey said. "Before my grandfather and his cronies built a wooden causeway from the mainland, this island was purely overgrown scrub and mangroves, totally uninhabited but for gators and birds, like lots of the keys and small islands along this part of the coast and the Everglades."

"And these settlers just claimed the land?" What if it belonged to someone else? "Is that even legal?"

Lacey gave a dismissive laugh. "Back then? Land acquisition was a free-for-all, according to my grandfather. No one cared about this island off the coast of Florida, so the founders built the bridge and took the land they wanted." She swept her hand toward the spectacular view of white sands that curved in a half moon at least a mile long. "Which is how I ended up with such prime property for Casa Blanca."

But *someone* might have lived here before, Ari thought. Seminole, maybe. Or Calusa. Grandma would have known. An old, dull pain, more like the memory of the ache than the actual thing, pressed around the edges of her heart, but Ari pushed it away. Ari's grandmother would have known and she would have *cared*. She'd have done something about the very idea of leveling a burial ground.

"Anyway, you know Clay is really happy you took the job for Mr. Valentine, since your sister works here at Casa Blanca. It's incredible good fortune that it worked out that way."

Fortune. Serendipity. Coincidence. All the words scraped

over Ari's heart. He was here for a reason, all right. But was it because he was The One for her...or the one she was supposed to stop from destroying sacred land?

Right that minute, Ari had never missed her grandmother more.

Luke's reply was drowned out by a cheer that rose from across the dance floor, where a group of guests surrounded Mandy Nicholas and her husband, Zeke. "And it seems we have even more to celebrate today." Lacey beamed at the couple. "Did you hear Mandy's going to have a baby?"

"I heard," Ari said dryly, sliding a look at a very smug Luke.

"Love is in the air, as always!" Lacey blew them a playful kiss, moving on to greet guests at the next table.

"Pregnant, huh?" Luke turned to her and tipped her chin up. "About my winnings..."

She inched out of his touch, thinking hard. She had to make him understand why he couldn't destroy that hill. "One more bet, Luke."

He gave a pretend grunt. "You really want me to work for it, don't you? All right. Name it."

"I bet you"—she put her hands on her hips and looked up, purposely coy—"don't have the nerve"—he lifted one brow at the words—"to take me to Barefoot Mountain after the reception is over."

He frowned, not following. "Kind of dark and scary at night, especially in a place where a guy died."

"I'm not afraid of the dark or the dead, Luke. I respect both too much." She layered on plenty of emphasis, which she hoped he'd understand later.

"All right, I'll take you," he said. "Which means I won that bet." He lowered his face, then moved his mouth to cover her ear. "I'll collect my winnings up on the mountain,

Arielle."

If she didn't chase him away with what she planned to tell him up there. Until then, maybe she should dial back the banter and remember he might end up disliking her very much by the end of the night.

Chapter Four

The clouds were heavy by midnight, blocking any moonlight and threatening rain, but the headlights of Luke's old-but-new-to-him Ford F-150 lit up the dilapidated house like it was a set on a Broadway stage. Broken windows, missing shingles, fallen fascia, and torn porch planks made the sinister little structure look every bit the part of a place where a man named Balzac Valentine had been hit by debris and killed.

Parking the truck in the expanse of dirt between the house and the base of the hill that separated it from the water, Luke glanced at Arielle in the passenger seat next to him. "You still want to do this?"

"Are you asking again if I'm scared?"

He heard the challenge in her voice and was way too smart to say that most women would be. Clearly, Arielle wasn't most women.

"Just making sure you want to go exploring in the dark."

"Who said anything about exploring?"

Whoa. "So, let's get right down to business then." Except he wasn't entirely sure *what* that business was.

He assumed this was a hookup of some sort, but after the conversation with Lacey, he'd sensed a strange distance from Arielle and a pullback from the flirting they'd both been enjoying. Throughout the rest of the evening, she'd evenly divided her attention among the guests and her maid-of-honor duties and saved a little time for Luke. Too little. He'd snagged a few dances and more conversation, but something had definitely changed, and it wasn't on his end. He was still as attracted to Arielle as he'd been the minute he'd met her.

He hadn't really been able to pin her down until the festivities wound down, when she'd returned from the bridal dressing room in jeans, sneakers, and a simple navy tank top that did crazy things to her curves and even crazier things to his hormones. Then, she'd announced the bet was on, and they were going to the mountain.

She put her hand decisively on the door latch, ready to climb out of his truck with the speed of a woman who really had some business to get down to. "Let's go," she said.

He reached out and closed his hand over her arm, which felt narrow in his fingers, but strong, too. Deceptively strong. "It's going to be very dark out there."

"Then it's a good thing you found your way around with your eyes closed today."

He lingered for a moment, memorizing her striking features in the reflection of the headlights he'd yet to turn off. Her cheekbones were high, her lips wide, her jaw straight. But there was something in her eyes that kind of scared him. Determination. Raw, focused determination. To do what?

"Are you going to tell me why we're here?" he asked.

She gave a very light laugh, absently toying with the pearl necklace she wore. He didn't recall her wearing that at the wedding, and it seemed an unusual choice to go with jeans and a simple top, but what did he know about fashion?

"You seem pretty smart," she said. She pushed the door open, stepping down from the high truck. "You'll figure it out." She slammed the door and disappeared into the darkness.

Okay then.

He turned off the ignition and lights and sat for a second, scanning the dark shadows outside the truck. He'd fought too many wars to follow blindly. He reached into the side compartment and snagged a small but powerful flashlight, slipping it into his pants pocket. Swinging down to the ground, he rounded the truck to meet her. Neither spoke as they got close enough to make out each other's face, and Luke automatically reached for her hands.

"Don't tell me you want to go into that house," he said.

She eyed the building, even the outline of it nearly impossible to see now. "Not now. I want to take you to the hill. I have to show you something."

"In the dark?" He almost pulled out the flashlight, but stopped, waiting to see what she had in mind with this midnight adventure.

"You can feel things better in the dark."

Like...her body? An automatic male response cut through him, getting primed for what he hoped she had in mind, despite her all-business attitude.

With a surprisingly calm demeanor, she held his hand and started walking away from the truck, with an utter lack of...sensuality.

"This isn't about sex, is it, Arielle?"

Her step slowed. "That's why you think I brought you out here?"

"The thought crossed my mind."

She let out something between a sigh and a laugh, carefully navigating over the dirt road that rounded the side of the house and led toward the base of the hill. "I have an apartment, you know."

"Not as adventurous."

She smiled up at him, her white teeth showing in the dark. "I suppose you like adventure, having been in the French Foreign Legion and all."

"Unlike a lot of the seven thousand guys I fought with, I didn't join for the adventure." He heard the flat tone in his voice, felt it in his gut.

"Then why did you join?" she asked as they walked.

He didn't answer while they found the closest thing to a path there was, his brain going back to his run along here in broad daylight. He'd made the trip once with his eyes open, and she hadn't been there. Then he'd repeated the course with his eyes closed, as he'd learned to do in every run drill he'd practiced. That time, he nearly flattened the unexpected visitor.

"Or is that part of the thing you don't talk about?" she prodded to break the silence.

"I thought my sister told you the story of why I left the States."

"I know there was the accident that scarred her and that you felt guilty for your part in it and ran away," she said. "That's her perception of why you left."

"That's why I left the States," he said. "Not why I joined the Legion." For some reason, he wanted to confide in this alluring woman, which didn't make sense, but here, in the deep, dark night, that need felt right. So he went with it.

"You of all people will appreciate what actually happened."

She leaned into him, silently asking for more.

"I made a bad, bad bet and lost."

"What did you bet on?"

"I bet I had the balls to kill a guy for money, and when push came to shove, I didn't, and I had to get the hell out of Dodge before someone killed me."

She slowed down, and his eyes had adjusted enough to the lack of light to see the stunned look on her face, underscored by a low, distant rumble of thunder far out in the Gulf of Mexico.

"Are you surprised I was involved in something like that?" he asked.

"I'm surprised the thing you did after you discovered you weren't able to take someone's life for money was join an army to, well, I assume, kill people for money."

"Trust me, the irony wasn't lost on me. And it really wasn't for money. The Legion doesn't pay enough for that to be the sole reason for joining."

"So, what was your reason?"

Oh, hell. He was all in now. "I was hiding, to be perfectly honest. In the French Foreign Legion, you get a new name, a new identity, and you're completely protected and anonymous." He put a hand on her back to guide her to where the path swerved after the second grouping of oleander bushes.

"What was your name?"

"Ricard Caron." He emphasized the hated French accent.

"Can I call you Ricard?"

"Please don't," he said in all seriousness. "I hate the name." And all the...misery it represented.

"But you're not anonymous or protected now."

"No need. The guy who was after me is dead."

"So you didn't really want to be in this mercenary army?"

He let another distant rumble answer for him.

"Am I getting into the 'I don't talk about this' territory?" she asked, giving his hand a gentle squeeze.

"You're there," he told her. "And speaking of territories, where, may I ask, are you taking me?"

"To the top. To where you plowed me over."

He let go of her hand to put his hand on her back, enjoying the play of tension in her muscles and the undercurrent of resolve that hummed through her. It was sexy. But, then, so was everything she did and said.

"I haven't apologized enough for that?" he asked.

She laughed, but the non-answer felt deliberate.

"What were you doing up here, anyway?" he asked.

Her back muscles tensed. "Just thinking. Getting my head in the wedding game," she said, slipping out of his touch to take a few steps away.

"Hey, no." He snagged her hand. "I don't want to lose you out here."

"You won't." But she tucked her hand back into his, another part of her that was small but surprisingly strong. "So you were saying you hated being Ricard Caron?"

"Mmm." He nodded. "When I left the Legion, I purposely had my name—my real name—pressed into the back of my tags. Except..." He shook his head, laughing. "The guy who did it spelled Luke the French way, L-U-C, so I'm always doomed to have a little of that country hanging around my neck."

After a beat, she asked, "So how wonderful was it to mend fences with Gussie and your parents?"

"Wonderful, but we're still mending," he told her. "That's why I decided to take this job, so I could spend more time with my little sister. Except she seems pretty damn happy without me, but still..."

"Oh, Gussie has plenty of room in her heart for you and her boyfriend, er, *fiancé*," she corrected. She shook her head and sighed softly. "I can't believe she's getting married."

"Honestly? I can't believe she waited until she was thirty," he said. "Gussie always wanted a big family. She better get cracking."

Finally, near the top of the rise, which probably peaked at under twenty-five feet and plateaued for a quarter acre, she stopped and turned to face the black expanse of water.

A distant lightning bolt sliced the sky, a streak of white gone in a blink. Neither of them spoke until after the thunder, about five or six seconds later.

A breeze, powerful enough to flutter her hair, blew over them.

"That storm's not too far away," he said.

She nodded. "I know. I can feel the electricity in the air."

He took a step closer, venturing to put a hand on her shoulder. "Maybe that's not the storm, Arielle."

She didn't move, so he got near enough to smell the remnants of hair spray from the brushed-out wedding hair. He slid his hand from her shoulder to stroke her hair, which was absolutely the most insanely stunning thing he'd ever touched. Not silk, it was more like heavy, thick strands of satin and velvet. He couldn't stop himself from putting his lips on the top of her head, actually wanting to bury his mouth in that—

"Is there any way to stop you?"

He stilled. "I'm sorry—"

"I mean, from...this." She gestured around. "From destroying this hill."

The words were so unexpected, such a complete one-eighty from where he thought they were going or why they were there, he stood speechless for a moment.

"You can't bulldoze this rise," she said. "Not until I am absolutely sure that it isn't sacred ground."

He blinked at her. "What the hell are you talking about?"

With two hands, she lifted the strand of pearls that hung around her neck. "I found this here today, and I believe that this unusual hill might be a sacred burial mound, most likely from Calusa Indians who, according to a Google search on my smartphone, lived here thousands of years ago. Until the proper archaeological inspections and digging have been done, you cannot level this ground."

He tried, really tried, to process it all. But it wasn't easy being drop-kicked from the pleasure he'd expected to...*this*. So, she'd found a necklace someone lost, checked the Internet for the name of an Indian tribe, and deduced that he couldn't go forward with construction because dead people were buried there?

It would be funny, except it wasn't.

"That's why you brought me up here?" Incredulity lifted his voice. "Why didn't you just tell me at the wedding?"

"I needed to get up here again, to...feel it." She dropped her head back slightly and closed her eyes, touching the necklace. Whoa. The woo-woo girl was cray-cray.

"So, what do you feel? Is it the Age of Aquarius yet?" he asked.

She snapped her head up to scowl at him, her eyes glinting in clouded moonlight. "Don't make fun of me."

Kind of hard not to. He shifted his weight from one foot to the other and sighed. "Okay, why don't you start from the beginning? You found that string of stones up here."

She bristled at the words, but nodded.

"You dug it up or it fell from a tree or...what?"

"It was on the ground. A bird pooped on it."

He snorted softly, but realized instantly she wasn't joking. "Are you sure the bird didn't poop it out?"

Black eyes narrowed. "You're hilarious. But that doesn't change what I believe, which is that this is most likely an artifact from Native Americans who lived here long ago. And if they lived here, there's a reason this land that we're standing on is elevated, and that reason could be because the bones of tribe members are buried here, along with art and religious items. That makes this land protected by the government, and you cannot put a bulldozer on it until the proper archaeological inspection has been done and the land is cleared to—"

"That's all been done," he interjected, mentally skimming the three inches of county and state documentation that the former general contractor had filed and notarized before he'd been fired. "Listen to me. There are a half-dozen different pre-construction surveys and inspections, and they've all been done. Boundary, topographic, deformation, geodetic, and location surveys, especially this close to the water with the Army Corps of Engineers breathing down a builder's neck."

"Which of those would dig into this mound and search with the care of an archaeologist?"

None. "Core sampling has to be done if there's restructuring of geography, then—"

"Restructuring of geography?" She sputtered the words. "That's what you call destroying an ancient burial place?"

Irritation churned in his belly. "You found a necklace, Arielle," he said. "For all you know, some Realtor could have dropped it."

"Or it could have been unearthed in the hurricane, along with bones or tools or artifacts from four thousand years ago! You don't know. But I can't sleep until this land has been properly and carefully excavated and inspected. Can you?"

He thought about that for a moment, considering which was worse: pissing off Cutter or a code violation that could blow up in his face. He had only a temporary general contracting license, which Cutter had helped him get by pulling a few strings and using his famous name. One mistake, and that could be ripped away. Lose the temp license and he might never get another one, giving up any chance of staying here and working in the States. Working as a contractor, at least, and that was all he really knew.

But if he couldn't deliver on his promise to Cutter Valentine, the big-ass-deal ballplayer would likely say, *Thanks, no thanks, I'll find someone else.*

Shit, he was in a bind.

"Look, I'll find the paperwork and show it to you tomorrow. I promise it will put you at ease." He hoped.

Another bolt of lightning crackled, highlighting her face for one quick second, long enough for him to see doubt and distrust in her dark eyes. "And they won't start bulldozing tomorrow?"

"There's no bulldozer. They use a backhoe," he corrected, purposely not answering the question.

"So will they start backhoeing?"

Actually, they might. "I'm not sure."

Thunder rolled, the storm closer now.

"Luke, you can't!"

"Look, I promise that all the paperwork has been done already, and I'll—" The first fat raindrop splatted on his head. "We're going to get soaked."

"Promise me," she insisted, not moving. "Promise me you won't destroy the land until you know it's just that— land."

An archaeological inspection could take weeks—even more. To get the job, Luke had promised an estate home ready in five months. When he made that assurance, he knew he was pushing the limits, but it was a job, and a good one, on American soil.

Possibly *Native* American soil. He huffed out a breath and ignored the next few drops on his head. "I'll look into it."

She shook her head, hard. "That's a lackluster promise."

"Arielle, listen to me." His frustration increased with the rain. Why was he standing out here in a pending storm with a crazed woman? "All of the routine inspections are done. If something was wrong, we'd—"

"*Wrong*? I'd hardly call land that was designated as hallowed ground centuries ago as 'something wrong.'"

"I mean if something's not right with the paperwork, then I'll do some digging—"

"Damn right you will." She dropped to her knees and pressed her hand to the ground as if she wanted to start *digging* right then. Barehanded. Even in the dark he could see her color was high as she challenged him. "I have a feeling about this." She looked up at him, her hair spilling over her shoulders.

"A *feeling*?"

She closed her eyes as if he'd hit a nerve. "It's just a feeling, yes, but it's strong and real. To me." She added the last two words with a slight note of apology and just enough self-doubt to touch something inside him.

Very slowly, he crouched down and got face-to-face with her, in exactly the same position, and possibly the same place, he'd taken with her this afternoon. And the same force field rolled off her and damn near pushed him over.

What *was* it about this woman?

Another bolt of lightning bathed them in an instant of searing white light, followed by a loud thunderclap not two seconds later. She looked up at the sky, possibly to gauge how far away the storm was, possibly to commune with someone or something. His whole body reacted with a mix of sexual desire and the urge to…help her. To hold her. To give her claims credence and…God, he wanted to kiss her.

This was *insane*.

He put his hands on her arms instead, trying to pull her up. "Let's go." The rain picked up with the next strong breeze, pelting them.

"Not until you promise me you'll look into it."

Two bolts of lightning cut overhead, so close they both startled. He stood as the ground rumbled under them, grabbing her shoulder with a little more force. "Come on, it's not worth getting struck by lightning over."

But she didn't move, her fingers digging into the dirt as if she could hold on to the ground and refuse to move. "*Make the promise.*"

"Or what? You're going to stay out here and…test the universe?" He spat the last word, and she flinched, making him feel moderately bad, but still ticked off enough to make his point.

The only answer was a crack of lightning so close the hair on his arms stood up. "Let's go!" he said. Without waiting for a response, he swooped her up, clamped her kicking legs and flailing arms, and tossed her over his shoulder like a sack of flour.

"Damn it, Luke! Put me down!"

He ran full-out to the path, using the lightning to guide him to the bottom of the hill since his hands were too full of furious woman to get that flashlight.

The last bolt struck right between the hill and his truck, so he didn't even take a millisecond to think. He tore through the wide-open doorway of the house and practically slammed Arielle's feet onto the ground.

He didn't know which was worse—the deadly lightning or the look of rage on her face. Guess he was about to find out.

Chapter Five

Ari didn't know whether to throw her arms around him or smack his smug-ass face.

Instead, she slammed her hands on her hips to keep herself from doing either one, glaring so hard at him she couldn't believe sparks didn't actually ignite in her eyes.

"You threw my butt over your shoulder like a caveman."

"I saved your butt from getting fried like a steak kabob."

A massive lightning-and-thunder combo lit and shook the structure as rain poured in the doorless entry behind him. "I am not afraid of nature. Not in the least."

"You should be." He gave her a soft nudge deeper into the front room. "Get in that hallway. I'm not sure this house can weather another storm."

She stumbled over something on the floor, but got her footing, letting him guide her to a narrow, dark hallway. He shouldered the first door open and pulled her to him.

"It's a closet," he said. "That means there's no metal and no wiring, so we won't sizzle if the house gets hit." He looked up at the ceiling as if he thought it might collapse any second.

"It's just a little thunderstorm," Ari said, still stinging from being hauled down the hill. "You better man up if you're afraid of them, because we get a storm almost every day for half the year down here."

"Man up?" He snorted softly. "I fought wars in jungles, Arielle. My masculinity isn't in question." He gave her a look like her sanity was, however, up for debate. Then he pointed to the ceiling. "You haven't seen the specs on this structure. It wasn't exactly built to code."

The tiny closet smelled musty and damp, the scents going to battle with the rain—and frustration—she could still sense on Luke. His wet shirt brushed against her bare shoulder, making her shiver despite the airless heat.

"If being built to code is important to you, then making sure you're not breaking the law by building in the first place should be, too."

He sighed softly, his breath ruffling her hair. "Got your point, Ari."

The use of her nickname tweaked her heart a little. Darn. She missed the way *Arielle* rolled off his tongue. Missed the flutter in her stomach when he said it the way he did, with the barest, slightest, *infinitesimalest* whisper of an accent from his years in France.

That was the problem with this guy. All the primal, visceral, physical stuff was off the charts and exactly how she'd been led to believe she'd feel when she met The One.

But why would the universe set her up to meet him only to have a problem of this magnitude separating them? Shouldn't things with her perfect mate be problem free? Wasn't that part of the promise of fated love?

Maybe Ari had dreamed the whole damn thing up out of desperation because her friends were falling in love left and right, and she was still alone. Her whole life she'd fought this battle. Certain of what she felt, uncertain of how right it was. It was as though her practical, rational, non-spiritual mother pulled at one hand and her mystical, supernatural, otherworldly grandmother pulled at the other. And sometimes it felt like she was split in half.

"So, do you believe in ghosts?" he asked in between rolls of thunder, almost as if *he* were the mind reader now.

"Not Casper, if that's what you mean. I don't think old man Balzac is about to jump out of the dark hallway and scare us. But..." She took a slow breath. Talking to unbelievers was hard. She knew she sounded wack to them. But she wasn't going to lie to this man and pretend she was as pragmatic as he was just to impress him. No way.

"I believe there are spirits," she finally said.

"Spirits?" The word was laden with skepticism and amusement. "What's the difference between that and a ghost?"

"Ghosts have bad reputations. Spirits don't bother people or show themselves. They live...on their own plane." She closed her eyes, knowing she sounded like...the woo-woo girl.

But he didn't laugh or tease, not yet, anyway.

"I believe in a lot of things that you can't see," she finally said after a beat of silence. "I don't think that everything that exists is...tangible. Therefore, I put a lot of stock in my feelings, which can't always be put into words, but they are very real."

"I believe in feelings," he said, as if she'd accused him otherwise.

"I don't mean feelings like love and hate and anger. I mean intuition. Gut instinct. The perception that something is real even though it is not...possible."

"And that's what you're basing your request to me on?" he asked. "You want me to throw a huge monkey wrench into this project because of an *intuition* you have?"

"And this necklace." That was real, wasn't it?

She felt him inch back and resented the loss of his warmth. "Fine. Go have that checked out by an expert," he said. "If they say it came from a thousand-year-old Indian jewelry maker, then we'll talk."

"What if it's too late?"

He huffed again. "Get it done fast and I'll do what I can to slow things down a day or two."

A day or two? "Building on native burial mounds is illegal in most states. Probably all." She actually didn't know that for a fact, but it was a safe bet. "So you could be saving your client a whole heap of fines and possible jail time." Again, a guess she hoped sounded authoritative.

"If he looks at it that way."

"What other way is there to look at it?" she demanded.

He crossed his arms, leaning against the wall, the only sound throughout the tiny house the pounding rain and a howling wind through the glassless windows. "He fires me and finds himself another builder," he murmured. "I mean, if you hadn't found that necklace today, then we would have built and no one would have been the wiser."

"Depending on what you found when you backhoed."

"They don't stop and inspect the ground covering, Arielle. They haul it to a dump."

"My point exactly. And I did find the necklace, and I found it for a reason."

She caught the whites of his eyes as he looked upward.

"Don't roll your eyes at me."

"You're a cat who can see in the dark now?"

She let out a sigh, and instantly, his hand found her shoulder with a touch that softened that comment. "Look, things don't happen for a reason, Arielle. They just happen, and then you deal with them. At least, I do."

"Fine. This happened, so deal with it by doing the right thing."

He was stone silent, letting the pounding the house was taking by the storm answer for him. For a few slow heartbeats, they stood less than six inches apart, draped in darkness and the tension of his silence.

"You do respect the dead, don't you?" she asked.

"I have a hell of a lot more respect for the living."

A gust of wind screamed through the living room window, along with another flash of lightning and a deafening crack of thunder. Instinctively, she grabbed hold of him. Strong, solid arms wrapped around her and pulled her close into a chest that felt even bigger than it looked.

"It's okay," he whispered. "Don't be scared."

She wasn't scared, not of the storm. Grandma Good Bear had taught her to love storms. No, she was scared of how much she wanted to press against this man who rolled his eyes and teased her about being a witch. She was scared he really was The One...and absolutely terrified he wasn't.

She tried to draw back, but he held her tight. "I'm not afraid of lightning," she assured him, and after a second he loosened his grip, but kept his arms around her.

"You're different from most females, then."

"Ditto."

"I'm not like any females," he teased, his low laugh somehow sexy and sweet in the dark.

Heat rolled through her, settling low in her belly. This time, she let out a soft grunt of frustration.

"What's wrong?" he asked her.

A better question would be, What's right? "I'm just disappointed that this couldn't be...easier."

He made a tiny circle with the palm of his hand on her back. "Who said it has to be difficult?"

Arielle nearly melted into him, reminding her that she hadn't been intimate with a man for a long, long time. Maybe that was why he felt so right.

"I just wish I'd met you at the wedding, had a great connection, so we could flirt, laugh, talk, kiss, and let nature take the course that nature loves to take," she admitted wistfully. "All this other stuff about the land…"

"Is just stuff," he said, dipping his face ever so close to hers. "Let's pretend it didn't happen."

She closed her eyes, longing for that possibility. "But it did."

He moved one of his hands up her bare arm, leaving chills in its wake. "Right now, in this place, during this storm…" He stopped talking while a rumble of thunder vibrated the walls around them. "What if there isn't any of the other stuff for a few minutes? We're just two people who met at a wedding, had a great connection, got to flirt, laugh, talk, and…what was the rest?"

"Kiss." She barely whispered the word, looking up at him, leaning in as she felt her eyes grow as heavy as the pearls around her neck. If only she hadn't found them…

"That's right, kiss, and what else did you say? Oh, I know." He closed the last inch, his lips a breath away from hers. "Let nature take the course that nature loves to take."

His lips pressed against hers, so light it was more of a tickle than a kiss. The lightning was inside her now, like a shot of fire and need, pushing her into him.

"You're a fan of nature, right, Arielle?" he whispered against her lips.

"I am," she admitted. "Big fan."

As if she had to voice her own opinion, Mother Nature sent down one more bolt of lightning, a freakish flash that seemed to last for three seconds, highlighting Luke's surprised look like a klieg light, accompanied by a cannon boom of thunder that rattled everything, including their bones.

All the hairs on her arms and neck shot to attention and tingled as she clutched Luke's arms.

He tightened his embrace and looked beyond her out the door. "Shit. We got hit."

Confirming that, thunder rumbled and reverberated like an angry drunk stumbling through the house.

He eased her away. "I better check for a fire. The wiring in this place is ancient, and lightning in the system could fry us. Fry us more," he added softly. Suddenly the whole lower half of the closet was bathed in a golden glow that emanated from his hand.

"You have a flashlight?" Ari asked.

"You think I was going to get out of my truck and traipse through the night without one?"

"Why didn't you use it?"

"I was trying to follow your let's-play-in-the-dark game. I thought I might win." He took her hand. "Come with me while I check the damage."

She let her hand be engulfed in his, peering into the beam that shed light on exactly how bad a hovel they were in. His flashlight scanned the floor, the walls, and the main room, highlighting the torn and stained carpet, cigarette butts, and pizza boxes, and two empty whiskey bottles that said old man Balzac's wrecked home had been the place for local kids to party.

Maybe the general seediness explained the shudder that rolled through her. "If I'd known what was in this place, I might have taken my chances to get back to the truck."

"Not with that lightning, you wouldn't have. Demolition is scheduled for next week, but I'd rather avoid the hassle of a fire. Talk about red tape." He urged her along. "Stay right next to me while I find the fuse box."

She hesitated for a moment, still torn between…what was tearing her apart? Heart and head? Body and soul? Right and wrong? Real and imagined? Everything about Luke McBain was a paradox to her. So, she took his hand and let him lead her, intent on figuring out what this sensation was and why it was so powerful.

As they walked toward the kitchen, Luke stopped and touched the walls.

"What are you doing?"

"Feeling for heat. Lightning can travel right through the electrical system."

"I don't think there's any electricity in this house, Luke."

"Doesn't need to be on for lightning to shoot through the wires and start a fire. The box is in here, if I recall." He pushed open a door to what looked like a small walk-in pantry in the back of the kitchen.

Something scampered inside. Ari inched back with another shudder.

"We are not alone," Luke droned ominously.

"Of course we aren't," she said. "A man died in this house."

He turned and threw her a look, his eyes hooded in the shadow from the flashlight. "You're not going to tell me I can't tear this place down, too, are you?"

"It's not the same as the hill."

"Why not?" He leveled the beam on an ancient fuse box hanging out of the wall.

"He's not buried here."

Another look from Luke, this one more cynical than the last. "Would you, um, *feel* it if he was?"

She wasn't sure if he was mocking her or just asking. "I don't know," she answered honestly.

The skepticism in his eyes melted as he patted the walls around the box, sticking his head closer to examine each wire. "Nothing's warm. We may be okay." He flattened his hand against the wall again, leaning into it as he sniffed. "I don't smell smo—"

He suddenly slipped as his whole arm went straight through the wall to the elbow.

"Shit!" He yanked his arm out, and when he did, the whole sheet of drywall came right off with it.

"Oh!" Ari backed up, out of the pantry, certain that half the rodent and roach population of Mimosa Key would come scurrying out at her.

"What the hell?" Luke moved in closer, shining his light on the exposed studs and moldy wood. "At least it won't be hard to tear down."

Ari's gaze dropped low, partially in trepidation that a nest of rats lived in the walls—she liked nature, but not *that* much—and her gaze landed on the top of a wooden crate revealed by the broken wall.

"What's that?" she asked.

He pointed the light on it, showing faded lettering across the top, the gray outline curved across the top. "Rueckheim & Eckstein," he read. "Whatever that is."

"Cracker Jack."

He looked over his shoulder, half-smiling at what he probably assumed was a joke.

"Rueckheim & Eckstein was a candymaker in Chicago that invented Cracker Jack." She inched closer, a frisson of excitement and anticipation prickling her skin. Something was in that crate. Something…important. She could feel it. "Please open it, Luke."

"So you can eat hundred-year-old Cracker Jacks?"

"So I can see what the old man was hiding in his walls."

Without arguing, he crouched down and put his hand on the side of the crate. "It's nailed shut."

"Which makes me want to open it even more."

He laughed softly, handing her the flashlight. "Hold this."

She aimed the light on the box as he bent over and hoisted it up. "Heavy," he said with a grunt. "Not big enough for a dead body. Books, maybe? Buried treasure?"

He glanced around for a tool of some sort but, finding nothing, simply dug his fingers under one side and gave it a pull. The wood snapped up and popped off. Ari came even closer, pointing the flashlight into the box, which was full to capacity with cream and brown—

"Looks like a bunch of seashells," Luke said.

"Are you kidding?" Mesmerized, Ari dropped to her knees, her hand almost shaking as she reached out. "These are not seashells. This is art. This is history. This is the most amazing thing I've ever seen."

Chapter Six

She was freaking nuts. There was no other explanation for this woman with the overactive imagination who saw things that weren't there. Art? History?

They were sticks, rocks, stones, and, mostly, seashells.

He reached toward the box, but she grabbed his hand.

"Don't touch anything!" Arielle ordered. "You could break one."

Half of them were already broken, by the looks of it. "It's just a bunch of seashells, Arielle, which are in fairly plentiful supply around here."

"Can you carry it out? Very, very carefully?" she asked, either ignoring him or not hearing what he'd just said. She aimed his flashlight on the shells, her other hand hovering over the crate like she was instinctively protecting the contents.

"Getting a vibe?"

She shot him a vile look. "That you're being a jerk?"

The accusation hit, and he gave his head an apologetic shake. "I'll drag it to the truck if you want to keep it."

"No, that could damage..." She widened her eyes as though she just realized what he said. "If I want to keep it? Luke, this belongs in a museum."

He looked from her, back to the shells, and to her again, trying hard as hell to take this as seriously as she did. "I'm definitely not seeing what you are."

Her lids shuttered as she let out a sigh and gingerly—as if she were plucking a diamond from ashes—lifted one of the smooth, creamy shell stones.

"My guess is this is an arrowhead," she said, reverence in her voice.

"Really." He worked to sound like it was remotely feasible, when inside, he guessed he was looking at a shell worn into a triangular shape. Obviously, she knew more than he did about this.

She carefully set it down and pointed to another. "And this is likely a knife. That one"—she indicated a round shell with sharp edges—"was probably used to skin fish."

Not very neatly.

She leaned back on her heels. "These are *tools*, Luke. Ancient tools that might date back two or three or four *thousand* years. They belong in the Smithsonian, not the kitchen of a house that's going to be torn down." She gave a little shudder as if the idea physically hurt her.

Four-thousand-year-old tools? He honestly couldn't see one thing in the crate that didn't look like someone simply picked it up during a walk on the beach and stuck it in an old box.

"You were so right," she continued. "Up on that hill today, you said, 'It's history,' and you were so, so right. It is beautiful, glorious, magical history." Sighing again, she actually sat on the floor, clearly no longer skittish about the critters they'd seen and heard. "God, I miss my grandma. She'd know exactly what everything in this box is." She tenderly touched another shell. "Other than spectacular."

But he couldn't share her rapture. Instead, he closed the

box as if tamping down his frustration. Why had she come up here and found that necklace and started all this?

He didn't dare ask. He knew her answer would be kismet or destiny or some great act of ancient gods.

"Okay," he said, fighting to keep any emotion out of his voice. "I'll put them in the truck. And when we demolish this structure, I'll be sure to look for any other boxes of similar buried treasure. I'll double-check the paperwork and assure you that every necessary inspection and survey are complete before we level the hill and landscape the sweeping grounds the owner wants out to the sea." Just saying it made him feel better. "But that's it. That's all I'll do."

She stared at him for a long time. Too long. And, damn it, he could have sworn there was moisture in her eyes. His gut clenched a little, and his whole chest squeezed.

Wasn't she going to say anything?

He looked down at the faded lettering of the Cracker Jack company, mostly to avoid her slicing gaze. Putting both hands on the sides, he started to stand and bring the box with him, expecting her to rise, too.

But she stayed firmly on the filthy ground, staring straight ahead, the flashlight still on her lap.

"Let's go to the truck," he said.

Silence.

"Come on, Ari." He hoisted the box higher. "The worst of the storm's passed."

The one outside, that was. The one in her eyes was brewing pretty hard.

"I promise I'll be careful with it," he added, thinking that was her problem. When she didn't move, he puffed out a breath. "And I'll put it in the back cab, so it won't get wet."

Because God forbid *seashells* get *wet*.

His arms were starting to burn from holding the box, but she stayed as motionless as a statue. All this over a box of fucking rocks!

Giving up, he pivoted and marched through the house, trusting instinct and good luck not to trip, stepping into the night where the rain had slowed to barely a drizzle. He walked to the truck and set the box down—*carefully*—and opened the quad cab door so he could wedge the crate in safely.

Looking back at the house, he peered into the doorless front entry, hoping to see the flashlight as she found her way out. But it was still dark and quiet there.

Damn it, woman. He slammed the door and trudged through the mud to get her. He heard her before he saw her, the sound of pounding and ripping coming from the old pantry. He found her in there, biting down on the flashlight, ripping off a giant piece of drywall.

He stood for a minute, watching her small but muscular frame reaching up to rip sheetrock like a professional. Or a woman on a mission.

"Ari, you don't have to—"

She spun around, ripping the flashlight out of her mouth, the depth of sadness in her eyes stunning him. "I thought you were…" She shook her head, biting back something she clearly didn't want to say.

"I was what? The builder? The contractor? I am and I—"

"The *One*."

He drew back, most from the surprising force of the words she whispered. "The one what?"

Another vicious shake of her head, and she whipped back to her job, sending that curtain of hair swinging over her back. Unable to stop himself, he closed the space between them with one step, taking the flashlight with one hand, placing the other on her shoulder. "The one *what*?" he repeated.

He felt her tense and swore he could hear her clamp her mouth shut. With a furious yank, she finished pulling at the sheetrock, exposing more studs but no more boxes of rocks.

She grunted in frustration. "I'm not leaving until I've been inside every wall."

He glanced behind him, confirming that every other wall he'd seen in here was plaster and lath, as any old home would have. This drywall had been put up much more recently. In fact, he thought as he eyed the structure of the pantry, this whole closet had been added on to a much older home.

"Only this pantry," he told her. "The rest of the house is impenetrable, and probably why the walls withstood hurricane-force winds."

She went to work on the next drywall panel, punching her bare fist into it to make a hole. Granted, it was soft and moldy, easy to break, but the move was still stunningly strong. And, shit, sexy. Jesus, his brain was seriously messed up.

Because she might be cute and smart and all kinds of hot, but she was *nuts*. And that meant it was time to end this interlude and focus on why he'd come to this island.

But before his messed-up brain could disconnect from his mouth, he pressed again, because he just *had* to know. "What do you mean you thought I was the one?" His voice was barely audible over the *fshhht* of wet sheetrock being ripped.

"Forget it. Just help me."

"We're taking down every wall tonight?"

"Who knows what we'll find?" she demanded, yanking off another sheet to reveal…

"Nothing," he said. "Except, who knows with you? Maybe there are *invisible* treasures."

She thwacked another piece of wet wall, making a hole. "Shut up." She stabbed her hand in, then pulled it out with a hiss when she must have scraped herself. Instantly, he put his hand over hers.

"Come on, don't do this now."

"I have to. You could plow the whole thing down by tomorrow."

"I won't take it down tomorrow, and if there's anything worth keeping, I'll give it to you, not the owner."

Undeterred, she stuck her hand in the partial hole she'd made and started pulling. "I don't believe you. And I don't trust you."

The admission pinched way more than it should have.

After a few more pulls, she got the sheet off and tossed it to the side, looking down. "Ew. A dead mouse."

Which, of course, didn't slow her down. "Look, you have my word, my promise, my oath on whatever it is you want me to swear on."

"What matters to you?"

"Excuse me?"

She glanced over her shoulder, her eyes wicked and sparking with intent. "Swear on something that matters to you. Whatever is the foundation of your belief system."

Like he thought: nuts. "I don't…" Have a *belief system*. No holy book, no ultimate power, no faith in…anything. He'd seen far too many horrific things to believe there was much good in the world. "Can't you just take my word for it?" he asked.

"No." She started on the next panel, turning away from him. "I don't trust you."

The statement hurt even more the second time. "You

don't even *know* me."

She tried to punch a hole, hammering the side of her hand hard enough to shake the wall, but not break it.

"Ouch," she muttered.

"Let me do it." He eased her to the side and tapped the wall. "There's a stud there. You're lucky you didn't break your hand." He kept knocking on the wall, but it was as hard as concrete. "We'll need a jackhammer for this one, so forget it."

She shook her head. "I'm not going to forget it, and I'm not going to let you demolish this house and desecrate precious pieces of huge historical and archaeological significance."

"Demo isn't scheduled until next week. I promise you, I will personally rip out every wall and stud and make sure there are no more crates full of..." He hesitated long enough for her to turn away.

"Don't make any remark that you're going to regret."

He put his hands on her shoulders, as gently as possible. "I see that you are a very determined and driven woman who doesn't stop when she wants something."

She angled her head, giving him a humorless death stare.

"So I am giving you my word of honor that I will not allow this building to be demolished until I—*you and I*—have, in broad daylight, examined every single nook, cranny, hole, and hiding place in here and made sure that whatever the former owner was secretly stockpiling is taken out and protected."

Her expression softened, but not entirely. "What about the hill?"

Shit. The hill. "I told you, I'll look at the paperwork, and if there's anything at all that can delay the lot prep and grading until we do some preliminary excavation—"

"Not preliminary. And a certified archaeologist has to be there."

That would take a month. "Whatever it takes. But let's do it right and not here in the middle of the night by flashlight."

She didn't move, hopefully considering his promises and not…conjuring up a spell to put on him.

"We don't want to miss anything in the dark," he added, trying to seal his deal.

A scratching sound at their feet made her inch toward the door. *Thanks, Mickey.*

They drove toward the other end of Mimosa Key mostly in silence, past the four-way intersection in the heart of town toward the three-story house in Pleasure Pointe where Ari lived. Where they both lived now.

Luke cleared his throat, breaking the silence, as he pulled into the driveway, the headlights beaming on the sweet wraparound porch that circled Willow's first-floor apartment. That apartment was dark now, since Willow and Nick were on board the *N'Vidrio*, the yacht that Nate Ivory had lent them for a honeymoon cruise.

"You know, you still haven't answered my question." Luke's low voice was soft and, thankfully, without any teasing edge.

"Which question?" But deep inside Ari knew exactly which question she hadn't answered.

"What did you mean when you said you thought I was the one?"

Yep. She knew it. She gnawed on her lower lip, staring straight ahead, praying—hard—that he wouldn't see through her lie. "I meant the one to help me discover what's under that hill and in that house."

"I'm also the one hired to destroy the hill and the house, or lose the job."

What could she say to that? She certainly didn't want to be responsible for him losing the work, but in the grand scheme of things, what was more important?

She put her hand on the door handle, not wanting to tackle that question with a man who had the shadow of his own determination in his eyes.

"I'm sorry there's no elevator to the third floor," she said. "Can you carry the crate up for me?"

"Sure," he agreed. "With all the TLC I can muster."

Still no real sarcasm there, which she kind of missed. At least when he was joking about her, they had a connection. Now, the only thing she felt was...distance. No doubt he thought she was crazy.

"Thanks," she said softly.

Out of the truck, she waited while he gingerly slid out the crate and followed her up the two flights of stairs that ran along the outside of the building.

Ari peeked into Gussie's darkened kitchen window as they passed the second-floor apartment. "I guess she's staying at Tom's tonight."

"Something tells me I'll have her place to myself while I'm here, which will save me the trouble of finding my own apartment."

"How long are you planning to stay with her?" she asked, no longer satisfied with "for a while," as he'd answered her the last time she'd asked.

He didn't respond. After a moment, she glanced over her shoulder, but his eyes were cast down, looking at the crate.

He reached the top landing and set the crate on the stone step. "Not really sure yet," he finally said. "I guess that depends on you."

"Me?" For a second, her legs felt a little weak. "Why would you...oh." She realized what he meant. "If your project gets killed, you won't stay."

He lifted a shoulder and nodded. And Ari could have kicked herself for thinking he meant anything else by "that depends on you." A longing, a wistfulness, an achy something rolled through her.

She'd blown this. With her...*feelings* and *intuition* and certainty about things other people weren't certain about. Even she, in the dark, empty nights alone in her bed, wasn't sure what she was certain of sometimes.

Sighing, she unlocked her door and stepped inside, reaching to turn on the entryway table lamp and holding the door open for him.

"You can put it on the dining table." She indicated the high-top table with four stools tucked into a bay near the kitchen.

"Well, there you go," he said as he set it down. "I'm certain I didn't break a single seashell butter knife." He turned, looking around. "Wow, this place is so different from my sister's apartment."

She tried to see the small one-bedroom—since the top floor of the Victorian was the tiniest of the three apartments—through his eyes. She'd decorated in shades of cream and white, all earthy and natural, especially compared to Gussie's confectioner's collection of purple and pink, with about fifty satin pillows lying around.

"It matches you," he observed. "Very...real."

Unable to decide if that was a compliment or not, she wiped her hands on her jeans. "Considering I've been sitting on a floor infested by God knows what, I feel a little too real right now."

He nodded. "Then I'll leave."

Something in her heart slipped, something that made her want to say, *No, stay, have a drink, curl up, and hold me.* "Okay," she said instead, reaching for the door. "So what happens next?"

"I'm meeting with the mason in the morning. And I'll go through all the paperwork, present and past," he assured her. "And, you know, while the equipment is up there, we can do a little digging around the area where you found your pearls and see what comes up."

Her pearls. They didn't belong to her. They belonged to...history. She started to tell him that, but stopped and shook her head.

"What?" he prompted, as if he were really interested. As if maybe he didn't really think she was crazy and wanted to run as fast as he could. Maybe if he could understand her a little.

She took a breath. "I was just thinking about my grandmother," she said.

"Grandma Gummy Bear?"

She smiled, happy he was teasing her again. "*Good* Bear. She was a very influential person in my life, and her way of thinking really affected who I am."

He didn't reply, studying her, listening intently enough that she was encouraged to continue.

"But her way of thinking and seeing life, her feelings and...and connection with her heritage and all that entailed, well, that wasn't the only influence on me."

He nodded, seeming to sense there was a lot more.

How could she best explain the conflict in her heart? "You know Alcatraz?" she asked.

"The island that used to be a prison? Of course."

"Have you heard of the Indian occupation of it?"

He frowned and slowly shook his head.

"Between 1969 and 1971, over fifteen hundred American Indians occupied the island of Alcatraz, demanding government intervention and support for the people of all tribes, all across the nation," she explained. "They did this because thousands of tribes and remnants of long-gone tribes lived in poverty and deplorable conditions. And they got change and help and truly revised the course of history."

"Okay." He drew out the word, clearly uncertain where this history lesson was going.

"When she was forty-five, my grandmother left her kids and lived there for a year as part of the protest. My mom was fifteen and furious. Somehow, their family got through it, but my mother was really affected by losing her own mother for a year at that age. She basically chose to disenfranchise herself from anything 'Indian.' She moved away from the culture toward her father's side."

"Your grandfather wasn't a Native American?"

She shook her head. "Irish. My mom's only half-Native American, and I'm a quarter. Anyway, my grandmother felt that the protest was more important than her family, her husband, anything. It cost her, but she said it was worth it." She smiled. "Grandma Good Bear never met a Native American cause she didn't love."

"And you're telling me this because…?"

Because she wanted him to know her. "I'm telling you because I know what it's like to think someone who cares about people who died thousands of years ago is"—she circled her finger around her head—"cuckoo."

He didn't argue, but the faintest hint of a smile gave away that he'd been thinking exactly that.

"I spent a lot of time with Grandma Good Bear, more than my brother or sister ever did, and we were very close." Her voice rose, ready to defend the woman she loved unconditionally. "And I know what she'd want me to do. What she *wants* me to do," she amended. "Because I do believe her spirit is here."

At least he didn't roll his eyes, but he did give a resigned shrug. "I get it."

He didn't, not fully. "My grandmother taught me that my feelings matter. They matter a lot. And sometimes you have to pay a high price and lose someone because those convictions and beliefs aren't, well, concrete."

"I like concrete," he admitted softly.

"You would. You're a builder."

He smiled again. "Thanks for telling me, Ari."

Distance again. She answered with a soft sigh. He mustn't be The One after all, because he'd know it, right? He wouldn't put up a wall, would he? He'd reach out and put his arms around her and hold her close and tell her he got it and they should spend the day tomorrow getting to know each other.

But he didn't do any of that. He just looked at her like he wasn't at all sure what to say, do, or think.

"Well," she said. "Good night then."

"I'll call you after I meet with the mason tomorrow."

She reached up and touched his jaw, purely unable to resist touching him. All the sparks were still flying, the lights inside her head were still flashing, the numbness and quivering…all still there.

So he *felt* like The One but didn't *act* like The One. Grandma never covered this contingency in her tales of a fated mate.

He turned his head enough to put the tiniest kiss on her

thumb. But he might as well have licked her it sent so many lightning bolts through her.

"I don't know what it is about you, Little Mermaid," he whispered. "You've *got* something. You *are* something."

Her only consolation was that he was as confused as she was.

Chapter Seven

Ari blinked into the lavender tones of dawn that slipped through the wood shutters on her living room windows. Disoriented for a moment, she shook her head to clear it, lifting her face from the rough tweed of her sofa, rooting for an explanation as to why she wasn't in her bedroom.

Luke.

Just thinking his name sent a little bombshell of awareness through her, waking her up. Of course, he wasn't there, she thought sleepily, pushing herself up. She'd fallen asleep around three in the morning, alone, after a shower, some tea, and a few hours of sifting through the Cracker Jack box of treasures.

Even in the dim light of early morning, she could see the fruits of her middle-of-the-night labor, rows of shells, tools, utensils, and items she'd classify as art all laid out on her table and the kitchen counter, then onto the floor when she ran out of surface space.

She'd painstakingly lifted each item out of the crate, carefully set it on tissue paper, and taken a photograph to catalog it. With her laptop open, she'd done research on the fly—enough to be genuinely encouraged her find was authentic proof that Calusa Indians had been living there long before Balzac Valentine.

Ari stretched again, eyeing her half-empty teacup, working out a painful crick in her neck. But what about the ache in her heart? She put her hand on her chest as if she could actually gauge the status of that delicate organ through her pajama top.

The state of her heart was...disorderly. Chaotic. A little bruised from the push-pull of last night. She'd met a great guy—understatement of the year—and he no doubt thought she was a lunatic to be avoided at all costs.

The snap of her door latch made her whip around. For a second she didn't breathe, half-expecting Luke to come through the door she knew she'd locked, but it was his sister's green eyes that popped wide when their gazes met.

"Oh, you're up," Gussie said, dangling the master key the three women had made to get into each other's apartments. "I thought if I knocked, I'd wake you."

"No, I'm awake." Not quite coherent, though. She waved her friend in. "What's up?"

"My brother—"

"What about him?" Oh, man. Did she have to sound so breathless and eager?

Apparently, Gussie didn't notice as she dropped the key on the entry table. "He's a milk-siphon, that's what. He drank every drop I had, and I will die if I have to drink black coffee." As she got farther into the apartment, she squished up her face, looking from Ari to the table, counter, and floor and back to Ari again. She lifted one eyebrow in question. "Shell collecting now, are we?"

Ari pushed down frustration. They weren't shells. "Didn't Luke tell you?"

"He was gone by the time I got home, which wasn't even

twenty minutes ago. Left the empty carton on the counter, too, the jerkwad." She grinned. "Have I mentioned how much I love having him here? Because I do."

He'd left for the job site already? Judging by the light, it couldn't be seven o'clock. A little niggle of disappointment wormed around Ari's chest, but she pushed it away. Did she really think he'd come up here, knock on the door, and invite her to go with him?

Yes. But he didn't want her there. "Where's Tom?"

"Working this morning. He had to go over to Miami at the crack of dawn to test the morning light for a photo shoot he has coming up there. He'll be back later today."

"You still on cloud fifteen, Miss Engaged Woman?" Ari asked.

"More like cloud fifty, but, Ari, what is all this?" She took a few steps to the counter and reached out.

"No, don't touch!"

Gussie's hand jerked back like she'd been burned, and she shot Ari a disbelieving look.

"They're not seashells," Ari said.

Gussie pointed to a finely sharpened conch. "Could have fooled me."

"They're Native American tools, every one an ancient, valuable, museum-quality artifact."

"Really?" Gussie eyed them closely, holding up her hands to show she wouldn't touch. "Where on earth did you get them?"

Ari sighed, almost too exhausted to tell the story, but she had to. If anyone could help her figure out what to do about Luke and his building plans, it would be his sister. "Do you have time to have your coffee here?" she asked.

"Of course. Alex just crawled into my bed and went back to sleep," Gussie said, referring to Tom's twelve-year-old niece, who completed their newly formed family. She wandered along the counter that separated the kitchen from the living area, studying each item. "Wow, I'd never guess these things were valuable. They look like stones and shells and sticks to me."

"They would to anyone who hasn't studied Native American art and history."

Gussie shot a brow up. "I know you like all that stuff, but you know it that well to know what these things are? Or were?"

"I'm no expert, that's for sure, but my grandmother was. And there's plenty of online information. What I read last night makes me think these could be three thousand years old."

"Three thousand?" Gussie gasped. "Holy crap, no wonder you don't want me to touch them. You still didn't tell me where they came from."

"Inside the house your brother was going to demolish." And still might, if Ari didn't stop him.

"These were in that creepy old house?" She blinked as what Ari said hit her. "Wait. You were in that house? With my brother? When?" With each question, her voice rose with disbelief and interest.

"Last night, after the wedding."

Green eyes grew wide with surprise. "Spill the beans, baby, and I don't mean coffee."

As Ari made two cups of Nantucket Blend in her Keurig, she told Gussie what had happened the night before. Mostly. She didn't mention meeting Luke on the hill earlier in the day, or that Luke was the man she'd meant yesterday when she'd told Gussie she'd met The One.

Because Gussie would be all over that.

Gussie curled into an oversized chair, holding her mug,

rapt, while Ari finished the story and pointed out a few of the most amazing tools, such as the tapered bone-colored shell so sharp that it had to have been used as a needle.

"Isn't it amazing?" she asked, holding the instrument up gingerly.

But Gussie was looking at Ari, not the needle. "So you basically want to stop his whole entire project because of these...things?"

Ari closed her eyes. "Surely you can understand the historical significance of these *things*. Whole museums are built to house these *things*."

"Cool. So give your shells to the Smithsonian, let them name the exhibit after you, and then let Luke do his job."

"The hill could be a burial mound, Gussie. Weren't you listening?"

"Yeah, but there has to be a way around that. Maybe Cutter Valentine will agree to leave the hill as is and put the house somewhere else so his view isn't blocked. There has to be another solution rather than Luke losing this job." Her voice was tight in defense of her brother, and Ari understood that, but this was bigger than one guy's building assignment.

"The whole place should be sacred and untouched," she said. "It's hugely significant in the history of the Calusa tribe."

"You're not a Calusa."

"No, but there is Native American blood in my veins, Gussie. I appreciate that you don't understand the meaning of that, but you have to trust me, it matters. My grandmother..." She shook her head to fight the emotion. "This...*things* like this"—she gestured toward the table of tools—"were her whole reason for living. Her own children stopped caring about their heritage, but I can't do that. I know it mattered to her, so it matters to me. I have to do everything I can to preserve and protect this land."

Gussie put the cup down on the table with a resounding knock, leaning forward. "Ari, listen. Obviously, the land should be checked before plowing it, but if Luke says that's been done and whoever is supposed to sign off has signed off, then you shouldn't get in the way of his project. If none of that stuff has happened, then you have to trust Luke to do the right thing, along with whatever government agency is involved."

Ari puffed a breath, pushing up to walk around her array of treasures. "The United States government hasn't always been a friend to Native Americans."

"Yes, but Luke can be trusted. Look, I know that your history and bloodline were a huge cause for your grandma, and I'm not saying you shouldn't do the right thing, but if the building project gets put on hold, or worse, *canned*, Luke will most likely move away. There's no work for him in Mimosa Key." Gussie's voice lost all lightness, fading into dead serious. "Then I'd lose him again."

"You wouldn't lose him, Gussie, not now that you've found him again. And why couldn't he just find another job here if he wants to stay?"

"His contracting license is temporary, and once it's lost, it'll be really hard to get another Florida license. That's just how it works in this state. Believe me, he's looked into it. Then he'd have to move, and I don't know where he'd go, but it could very well be back to France where he has a license and a guaranteed income."

"What? Why not just get a license here and stay?"

"It isn't that easy. You can ask him about it, but it has to do with mountains of rules and regulations in this state, because of the hurricanes and bad contractors who swoop in to make a fast buck."

"Luke would never do that."

"Of course not, but his license is temporary and for this one job only. If the job stops and he loses the work, I don't know what he'll do, but it won't be in Florida." Gussie looked stricken, pulling back her honey hair to show the concern on her pixie-like features. "Ari, he's my *brother*. I haven't lived on the same continent with him for fifteen years. I want him in Barefoot Bay. I want him close."

"I totally understand that," Ari agreed. "But couldn't he do something else?"

"He was a builder in France, and he says it's all he knows, though I never expected it would be his career. When we were kids, he wanted to be a cop or an FBI agent, but that..." She sighed. "Didn't happen."

Ari knew the story well enough, and having talked to Luke about what happened after, she understood even more. "If he wants to be in law enforcement, he could go to school to do that now and stay here in Florida."

Gussie shook her head. "I suggested that once, and he totally shut me down. I guess he thinks having been in a mercenary army like the Foreign Legion isn't the kind of thing that impresses the FBI."

And he was probably right, since he left the country and "hid" in the Foreign Legion after not having the guts to kill someone for money. The FBI wouldn't want someone with a questionable background, and Luke had made it sound like that's what Foreign Legion soldiers all had.

"But there are lots of other jobs," Ari said, knowing it sounded weak.

Gussie narrowed her eyes as she rose. "He *has* a job, Ari. One he needs and worked hard to get and keeps him right here in Mimosa Key, which is like we won the brother-sister lottery. Do you really want to screw that up for us?"

She didn't answer, considering it all. Luke shouldn't have

to jump the career track because of Ari's crazy ideas. She could see that, but…

She glanced at the tools on her table.

There had to be an answer to this. She *had* to figure it out.

Gussie reached out and put a hand on Ari's shoulder. "If he loses this job, I know he'll have to go back to France. But he won't be happy. And he won't be near me."

Ari looked at her, seeing the plea and worry in Gussie's eyes.

"I didn't have my brother for fifteen years." Gussie's voice was barely a whisper away from cracking. "Please don't do anything that would take him away from me now."

Ari opened her mouth to reply, but shut it again, backing out of her friend's touch and her imploring gaze.

Oh, this was complicated.

Ari went back into the kitchen, ostensibly to get another cup of coffee, but really to get a moment to think this through.

"Do you like him?" Gussie's question threw her a little.

"What? Well, I mean, yeah. He's…" *Meant for me.* "Nice."

Gussie grunted. "I definitely sensed a spark of something between you two."

"Did you?" She tried to sound as casual as possible.

Gussie didn't answer, and Ari waited, choosing her coffee flavor. While a cup brewed, she looked over her shoulder to see Gussie standing by the window, admiring her brand new shiny engagement ring. She wasn't worried about Ari's—

"There might be something to that mated-by-destiny thing you talk about," Gussie said. "I kind of think I fell in love with Tom the moment I saw him in the Super Min."

Ari swallowed. "Belief that there is one person meant for you, and that you'll know them when you find them, is absolutely *not* love at first sight, Gussie. I don't think there is such a thing. You were attracted to Tom and went to France and discovered great things about each other. Were you destined for each other? I hope so, since you're marrying him."

Gussie turned from the window. "What does it feel like?"

Amazing. Terrifying. Thrilling. Perfect. Treacherous. Wonderful. "I don't know," she said softly.

"Didn't your grandmother tell you how it's supposed to feel?"

"Yes, but…I got the impression it's one of those 'you'll know it when you feel it' things. What does it feel like to love Tom?"

Gussie smiled and ran a hand through her hair, long, natural, and uncovered. Before Tom, Gussie had worn wigs and slathered on makeup. But as she got to know him, she'd grown more confident and even more beautiful.

"It feels incredible," Gussie said. "Like I can't believe I'm going to spend the rest of my life with him. Like I couldn't stay this happy because my chest would probably burst open at some point."

"Like your heart's…expanding? To make room for more love?"

"Yes!" Gussie made a little shriek. "Exactly!"

"And your hands kind of hurt because you want to—"

"Touch him so bad." She laughed again. "Yes."

"Numbness, tingling, and slight dizziness?" Ari asked.

"Like vertigo for days." Gussie sighed and came a little closer. "Is that what your grandmother said?"

"More or less."

"Did you feel like that when you met my brother?"

Yes. "I definitely felt something," she admitted.

"Enough to"—Gussie tipped her head toward the shells on the counter—"let him do what he has to do to stay?"

Ari felt her whole body sink a little. "What should I do?"

Gussie passed her, rinsing her cup in the sink for a long time before she answered. "I think your Grandma Good Bear would tell you to follow your heart."

That was the problem. Her heart was torn in two.

Chapter Eight

Duane Dissick was late. After all his years in the military, Luke had very little patience for delays of any kind, but the fact that the mason slept in or stopped for coffee gave Luke even more time to walk through the old house in the broad daylight, reliving the events of the night before.

He'd come out here with Arielle hoping to get to know her better, maybe make out with a pretty girl in the moonlight, and have some fun. Instead, he ended up with hardly a kiss, a mess he didn't need or want, and a problem that spelled nothing but trouble and delays.

Unless he ignored her insistence that this was some kind of hallowed ground, accepted the reports that had been done, and embraced the obvious: Her box of rocks was not full of valuable treasures.

Couldn't she *see* that?

No, not a woman who seemed to see things that weren't there.

In the kitchen, he examined the hole they'd left in the pantry again, stepping back to see that his original assessment had been correct: This closet had been added on to the house. He wandered through the other rooms, looking closely at what was clearly a dump that had to be demolished down to the foundation, noting there were no other additions made to the original bungalow.

So, surely there were no more "secrets" in the walls.

And what about the hill out there?

What would he be legally and morally bound to do? Tell Cutter, obviously. Then, according to the research he'd done last night, contact the Division of Historical Resources. Which would wrap them all in miles and months of red tape, and implode Luke's plans to get a permanent license and start contracting in Florida. If the project ended, or was mercilessly delayed, he'd have to pay back the advance Cutter gave him, and that advance was all he had.

Luke cared very little about living lean and would, in fact, not give a flying shit about money for the rest of his life, except…he'd promised some. He'd promised a lot. And there was no way he'd renege on that promise. Lives, one particularly precious, depended on him. So, if this project blew up, Luke would have to go back to France, where he had a guaranteed income.

It wasn't only him, and he couldn't forget that.

He kicked a crushed beer can across the living room floor, the tin sound clanging in the empty hovel. Then he heard the rumbling engine of a big work truck, and walking to the opening that once was a front window, he spied a mud-splattered Toyota Tundra slowly making its way around the property and stopping a few hundred feet from the house, next to Luke's equally dirty truck.

After a few seconds, a middle-aged barrel-chested man climbed out of the cab, a thick file folder under one arm, and looked around, obviously searching for Luke.

"Mr. Dissick?" Luke called as he stepped out to the wood-framed front porch.

The other man turned, tugged on a faded Florida State baseball cap, and strode toward Luke, mud slushing under his boots.

"Sorry I'm late, Mr. McBain," he said, extending his free hand as they met. "I stopped by the county zoning office soon as they opened to get the latest surveys for you."

Instantly, Luke adjusted his opinion of the man's tardiness, shaking his hand. "Great. I thought I had the latest."

"I don't think so." His broad face, creased from years in the sun, broke into an easy smile. "Hate to say it, but your predecessor wasn't the world's greatest on filing paperwork on time."

"Paperwork's the bane of this job," Luke said, going for humor but probably sounding bitter. He loathed the mountains of paperwork involved in building, but it came with the territory.

"Still, he sucked at filing anything."

"So I don't have all the surveys and inspections in the files I received?" Damn, that would be a problem.

"You do now." He held out a brown Pendaflex folder nearly bursting at the seams. "I figured if you don't see this now, we'll never get my crew out here to put up the silt fence and start the grading. And time is money, Mr. McBain, as I'm sure you know."

"Call me Luke." He opened the file folder, immediately looking for the survey that would matter to Arielle. "Core sampling done?" That might be enough to appease her. Maybe.

"Shells."

"Excuse me?" He looked up from the paper he'd just pulled out.

"The engineer broke two pipes and finally quit because

that right there"—he pointed to the hill—"is one big mountain of seashells."

Seashells, but not...bodies and bones. A wisp of hope curled through him. He'd done enough Internet research in the wee hours to know shell mounds were common here, and not protected. "A shell mound would be..." The answer to a prayer.

"A sonuvabitch to level," Duane said with a humorless laugh. "Probably cost an extra two grand, which is what I told your predecessor and he told me to fu...forget it." He grinned and lifted his cap bill a little to peer at Luke, as if waiting for the same response. "Mr. Purty had a way with words."

"I'll pay it," Luke said quickly. "If you can prove to me that entire hill is ground-up seashells and nothing else, I'll gladly pay you two grand." Because his troubles would be over.

"I can't prove much until we start moving dirt, but the core sampling is what's been filed as an approved inspection. No need to dig any deeper or look for trouble where there isn't any." He tugged a thin blue paper from the file with the name of a geological engineering firm at the top. "That says that starting at about six feet from the top of the grade, it's solid shell. Not as hard as rock, obviously, but still tough on equipment."

"And nothing else? No...bones?"

Duane looked hard at him for a second, then suddenly burst into a belly laugh. "Scared of the dead Indians, are you?"

So it wasn't completely out of the realm of possibility. "I don't want to start the project only to find out the land is protected and can't be built on."

"Damn, you *are* a better contractor than Jim Purty was,

but, well…" He took off the hat and revealed thinning brown hair and a sweat-dampened brow. "That's the thing that got his ass fired, just so you know."

"He suspected the land is a burial ground?"

"He let all kinds of shit delay the project, and if you want to bring the government in here and a bunch of tomb-raider types who turn this into some kind of 'dig,' then knock yourself out, sir, but you'll be the next general contractor to be fired."

"Not if it's the right thing to do under the law."

Duane scowled at him. "Just who is it feeding you this burial-ground crap? You secretly working for the government or something?"

He considered how much to tell him. "There's a local woman with ties to the Native American culture, and she seems to think it's a possibility. All I want to do is make sure it isn't. Have you run into that around here before?"

Duane snorted out a breath, clearly taking some time to choose his words correctly. "I don't know this as a point of fact, since I've never met the owner, though I've sure watched him play baseball enough, but it's my understanding your boss or client or whatever you want to call him wants this house built, finished, and ready to move into by February one. Am I right?"

"Very right." Luke knew it had been a risk to commit to the tight deadline, but it's what got him the job.

"And this is your project, sir," Duane continued. "If you don't like what I say, you can easily replace the subs Purty hired with guys who'll do whatever you like, whenever you like. You're the GC."

Luke nodded, waiting for what he would say next, already knowing he probably wouldn't like it.

"But, I've been doing grading and masonry in southwest

Florida for twenty-some years and a decade up in Maryland before that. There is always someone who wants you to stop for some farfetched reason. Look, I appreciate you wanting to do this right, and you're correct, but…"

"But?" Luke asked.

Duane paused, turning to look at the hill, narrowing his eyes. "There are big environmental protection issues on these islands, no way around some of 'em. Can't build within fifty feet of the shore, can't tear down certain kinds of mangroves, and God forbid you accidentally kill a damn gator even though the place is crawling with 'em." He gave a low laugh. "And the Indians? Well, shit, brother, I know it's not politically correct, but I can't imagine you'll find much land anywhere in this country where Indians haven't been first. What are we supposed to do? Not build anything at all?"

"No, but we can build in the right place."

"If you can find one. Or not build it at all, or tie the whole thing up in some bureaucrat's file drawer for three years so—"

The sound of a motor revving up the dirt road grabbed their attention, making them turn to see a bright blue subcompact roll up next to their trucks, pulling between the two like a baby stepping between a couple of dirty giants.

The door popped open, and thick black hair swung over narrow shoulders as Arielle looked up at the two of them, then waved.

"Don't tell me," Duane muttered. "Pocahontas."

Luke sliced him with a look, as his frustration at seeing her barge into his meeting dissolved into the need to defend her. "Her name is Arielle Chandler," he said, his jaw tight. "You'd be wise to not call her anything but that."

He didn't bother to see Duane's reaction, instead

watching Arielle navigate her way through the mud puddles on her way to join them, a slender but strong figure who seemed both fearless and vulnerable. For some reason, that combination did something to him. He left Duane's side to meet her.

"Couldn't stay away," she called out with a smile.

Luke couldn't help it; he smiled back. "Why am I not surprised?"

"So, what'd you find out?" she asked, then leaned around him to direct her smile at Duane. "Hello!"

"Ma'am."

"Are you going to find out what the hill's made of?" she asked.

"I found out," Luke said, relieved to be able to say it. "I have the report from"—he opened the file and took out the top paper, handing it to her—"GeoTech Engineering, which did a core sampling and found that this hill is made of shells, nothing more, nothing less."

Duane joined them before she could answer, tipping his hat back to peer up at Luke, who had him by a few inches. "If I can start the silt fencing today, Mr. McBain, I can get my crew here in an hour or two."

"Yes, get the fence complete, by all means, and I'll start going through this file to check against what I have."

"And we can probably start the structural demo." Duane gestured toward the building.

Luke felt, rather than saw, Arielle bristle. "Let's wait on that," he said. Damn it, she was not going to dictate how he did the job, but he wouldn't fight over that in front of a sub.

"This company is in Fort Myers," Arielle said, tapping the GeoTech report as she read it.

"They've been around awhile," Duane said, as if she'd

questioned their integrity. "If they say they found crushed shells, chances are they found crushed shells."

She lifted an eyebrow. "Chances are?" she asked. "Did the firm save the samples from this work?"

"No clue. Why don't you go talk to him?" Duane asked. "The engineer's number is right there."

Duane gave a wry smile of pity to Luke, nodded, and headed back to his truck, cell phone out and to his ear before he got ten steps away.

"Listen, Arielle, I—"

"I'd like to talk to this guy at GeoTech."

Of course she would. "I respect your concerns about this land, I really do. But even you can't think five tons of broken shells that were used to create elevated land falls under protected-land laws."

"If that's what's there, no, you're right. Shell mounds aren't protected. There isn't anything in them of value." She glanced at the house. "But that treasure box came from somewhere."

Treasure box? He bit back his response and tried a different tack. "Listen, I'm willing to bet the hill is shells."

"How much?"

Of course, he forgot she had a gambling problem she liked to deny. He studied her for a second, half-hoping all the unexpected and, frankly, unwanted, physical reactions to her would have dissipated in the harsh light of day. No such luck. She was just as beautiful, and he was just as attracted.

"Seriously, Luke, what's on the table?"

"Dinner." He grinned. "Get it? On the table?"

Against her will, she laughed softly. "Fine. Let's start with this engineer. Give me that guy's address." She pulled out her phone from her back pocket, typing in the street address he gave her.

"I'll call and make an appointment with him," Luke said.

"Can you make it for forty-five minutes from now? I don't see any reason to wait."

"I'm sure you don't."

With a satisfied smile that said she either missed or ignored his attempt at sarcasm, she pivoted, marched around a mud puddle, and headed to her car.

Damn it. Could she get away from him any faster?

He darted after her, getting a hand on her shoulder. "Arielle, we'll go together. Let me call the guy, and we'll take my truck."

She closed her eyes and nodded once, a look of utter misery and defeat on her pretty features. Why? Had she been trying to beat him there? End-run him?

He'd stay with her every minute and make sure she didn't do anything of the sort. Not that her constant company was painful to him. On the contrary, he was grateful for the excuse to be near her. Which was just one more complication he didn't need.

Chapter Nine

Nerve endings tingling. *Check.*

Limbs feeling numb. *Check.*

Heart bursting in chest. White lights flashing in head. Common sense on vacation. *Check. Check. And double damn check.*

Ari yanked Luke's truck door so hard the whole monster shook when it slammed.

She'd clung to the hope that all those physical responses had been her wild imagination or brought on by something else, like sacred hills, or the emotional roller coaster of one friend getting married and the other getting engaged. No such luck.

Not a *single thing* had changed overnight. She still practically swooned at the sight of Luke McBain, going weak at his touch. Even his voice sent hundreds of butterflies soaring through her stomach.

Oh, Grandma Good Bear. Why does it have to be so complicated? Why wasn't it obvious to both of them? Was that because it wasn't real and she merely *wanted* him to be The One?

But Grandma didn't answer, the universe was silent, and the only sound in the truck cab was Ari's slow intake of breath as she peered through dried rain spots at the man pacing twenty feet away, a cell phone to his ear. Why did those softly worn jeans have to hang so low on his hips, accenting a perfect, curved, masculine rear end? And of course his white T-shirt stretched over every impossible muscle, including some in his arms and back she didn't think she'd ever seen on a man before. His body looked carved by an artist...or was that from years of fighting wars?

And his face. He'd never be asked to be a model, but his features were strong, commanding, and dusted by dark whiskers that set off his incredible, ever-changing eyes.

Everything about him made her hungry and itchy and achy and...

Maybe he *wasn't* The One. Maybe he was just *The One She Wanted to Screw Because She Hadn't Had Sex for Damn Near Three Years.*

She couldn't ignore that very real possibility.

Maybe this was raw, unfettered lust that would go away with a good, long bout of wild monkey sex. But if she did fall in bed with him and he *wasn't* her destined life partner, or whatever Grandma called it, would that ruin her chances of ever meeting The Real One? That's what Grandma had said, but maybe that was nothing but a loving grandmother trying to make sure her granddaughter didn't ever have sex again until she was good and in love.

And it had worked.

So maybe Ari should get this needy, achy, *horny* hurt out of her system.

"Oh, jeez." She stuck her hand into her hair and dragged it back, hard, as if a solid tug on her head would pull the thought out of her brain. That didn't work, though. She still imagined those strong thighs straddling her, those tanned, manly hands caressing her, that unkempt jaw sliding between her—

Her throat grew dry as she watched him slide the phone into his pocket and amble over the muddy front yard to the truck, every step like...sex. Easy, slow, confident. Her gaze dropped over his body, settling on the faded jeans, the narrow hips, and the slight rise of his—

Dear God, she was actually trembling.

She blew out a breath, gave her hands a shake, and willed her thoughts into submission as he pulled the driver's door open.

"We're all set," he said, hoisting himself up into the truck that sat a good two feet off the ground. Suddenly, the oversized cab smelled like soap and sunshine, and his sizable body—the one she'd just been imagining naked—was all too close.

He reached forward to stick the key in the ignition, taking her focus to corded muscles and a dusting of dark hair on his forearms. Strong, tanned, masculine forearms that could hold her. Blunt-tipped, powerful hands that would touch her...everywhere.

She looked down, taking a moment to move her handbag from her lap to the floor, anything to keep her eyes off him and corral some cool and conversation.

"And I have good news," he said, bringing the engine to noisy life.

"Really?" Her voice cracked from how parched her throat was, earning a quick look from him.

"They keep the soil, or in this case, shell samples, in airtight containers until after the job site is completed and closed, so you don't have to worry."

"I'm not worried."

One side of his mouth lifted. "You look worried."

Not about *that*. "I just want"—*focus, Ari, focus*—"a solution for this problem we have." She cleared her throat as she grabbed on to the explanation for her worry and nerves and all that dang fluttering in her stomach. And lower. Lots of fluttering *lower*. "That's why I'm here."

Not to, you know, drool over the idea of getting you naked.

Oh, now the word *naked* was in her head. Naked, naked, naked. What would he look like naked, hard, ready for—

"So," he said, drawing the word out to end her thoughts. "You're checking in on me, then."

And he probably didn't like that too much. She looked ahead as he maneuvered over the narrow road, some branches of scrub scraping the side of the truck. "Are you mad at me for coming up?"

"Disappointed in you."

Her heart dropped. "Why?"

"I was sure you'd be waiting for me when I arrived, shovel in one hand, a conch-head hammer in the other."

"You're making fun of me."

"Ya think?" He reached over the high console that separated them and put his hand on her arm, his fingers hot on her skin. "How late did you stay up examining your seashells, anyway?"

"Late." Why deny it? She shifted enough in her seat that he lifted his hand, and she didn't know whether to be disappointed or relieved.

"We should have set up camp together and saved each other a lot of frustration," he said.

Or caused way too much of it. "Why? What were you doing?" she asked.

He threw her a look, his eyes impossible to read, but she tried anyway. "Digging around for information that would help me. You. Us." With each correction, he smiled a little bit. "What did you discover about the shells?"

She was grateful there was no condescension or even skepticism in his tone, just interest. "I'll have to do more work, but I did manage to examine and even catalog quite a bit of what was in that box," she told him.

He slid a glance her way, nodding. She waited for a question or even a joke about cataloging seashells, but he touched a button to lower his window and gestured toward hers. "Do you mind open windows?"

"I happen to love them." Hers went down immediately, and warm wind whipped through the cab, giving her some much-needed air to breathe. After a moment, she remembered the idea that had been dancing around in her brain since Gussie left—before she set eyes on Luke and forgot everything but *sex*—and how she might approach it. The idea, not sex.

"So, I didn't realize that you're personal friends with the guy who hired you to build the house," she said.

He gave her a quick, questioning look.

"Gussie came up and had coffee with me this morning," she added. "And we talked."

"I don't know if I'd classify us as *friends*," he said, after another second's hesitation. "Cutter Valentine is my client, first and foremost, and he's definitely doing me a favor by giving me the job. We hung out together in high school, played varsity ball on the same team, though he was obviously a helluva lot better than I was."

"Well, I would think that puts you in a really solid position," she said. "If, you know, you were to come up with a better place for him to build his house."

He slowly shook his head. "There's no better place, Arielle. All we have to do is make sure that it's a shell mound and you can rest easy."

"And if we don't?"

"We'll cross that bridge"—he pointed to the entrance to the long causeway that joined Mimosa Key to the mainland—"after this one."

Letting it go, she dropped back on the headrest and turned her face toward the breeze and generous sunshine, the water sparkling below like a navy blue carpet sprinkled with diamonds. Just the few minutes of direct contact with the elements invigorated her.

"What else did Gussie tell you?" he asked.

She closed her eyes for a second, remembering snippets of the conversation. "She told me how important it is to both of you that you stay here and work in Barefoot Bay."

"Absolutely," he said without hesitation. "I've missed seeing her grow up and into such a great woman. And now she's getting married." She heard a wistful note in his voice. "So that only makes me want to be here more so I can get to know my brother-in-law."

She sighed. "And you probably think I'm some kind of hard-line activist who would put an end to all that family goodness."

He didn't answer for a minute, then said, "But you have to honor your grandmother's wishes. That's family goodness, too."

There was enough softness in his voice to fold her heart in half, and she appreciated that he at least recognized what mattered to her. She needed to do the same for him, but how?

"I told you Grandma always said that being true to a cause has a cost."

"So if she wasn't close to your own mother, how'd you manage to have such a great relationship with your Grandma Good Bunny?"

She laughed. "Good Bear. We had the power of the universe on our side, or so Grandma said. At first, it was just a series of what *you* might call coincidences that happened during consecutive summers. My parents had to travel, and I got to stay with her when my brother and sister went with other family. Then, Grandma had cataract surgery and needed someone to help her and asked for me. After a few years, it became an unspoken thing—I spent two months every summer with Grandma Good Bear."

She closed her eyes, stepping back in time to remember going to Native American festivals around California, with the rows of crafts and sounds of drums and the sweet, sweet taste of spicy hazelnut relish on cornbread. There were long walks in the woods, late nights of talking to the wind, and learning that faith was really another word for *trust*. "Best times of my life."

"Did it cost you?" he asked. "I mean, are you close to your parents or was your relationship with your grandmother more important?"

She considered the question from a few different angles, including the fact that just asking it made him seem incredibly wise. "I'm fine with my parents," she said. "I did what they wanted me to do, which was to entirely and completely assimilate into a non-Native American cultural existence. My Indian blood is no different than my Irish blood or, on my father's side, English blood."

"Except it is," he said, his voice barely loud enough to be heard over the wind. "And, honestly, I get that."

She studied him for a minute, trying to put all the hormonally charged thoughts to the side completely, appreciating him for the man he was right then. Sexy in a whole different way.

"I lived in another country for almost fifteen years," he

told her when it became apparent she was looking at him a little too hard and long. "I fought wars in many others. I understand cultural battles, internal and external."

As they reached the top of the causeway bridge, high enough that tall-masted sailboats could easily pass underneath, the wind howled through the windows, snapping her hair across her face and filling the car with the brackish smell of the gulf below.

She pushed the strands back and turned to face the wind, absently counting a half-dozen pleasure craft leaving long, white wakes behind them.

It was too noisy for easy conversation, so they drove in silence to the mainland, then headed north from Naples, until he had to navigate the streets of Fort Myers. When they finally reached the address that housed GeoTech Engineering, Ari lost the fight not to reach out and touch Luke's arm.

"I'm not an ogre who wants to separate you from your sister," she said.

"And I'm not the evil builder who wants to desecrate sacred ground."

For a few seemingly endless seconds, they stared at each other, his skin as warm and inviting as she knew it would be, his eyes a deeper, darker green than she'd even remembered, his chest rising and falling with a slow breath.

"Let's go, then," he finally said. "We have a bet to settle."

"That we do."

Chapter Ten

GeoTech sounded a lot more high-tech than it looked. In fact, the place looked more like an abandoned building than the office of an engineering firm. There was no reception area, no sleek office space, not even a mass of cubicles with ringing phones and busy people.

When Arielle and Luke walked in, the smell of burned coffee assaulted them, the "reception area" nothing more than an empty room with an open doorway that led down a barely lit hallway, no sign of life anywhere.

"Hello?" Luke called, stepping into the hallway. "Anyone here? Mr. Waggoner?"

A woman came out of a door at the end, thin and blond, peering at him over reader glasses. "Are you looking for Ken?"

"Ken Waggoner of GeoTech," Luke confirmed. "He's expecting us."

He thought she laughed, but maybe she coughed. "C'mon back. He's in the bathroom."

Luke and Arielle shared a quick look, then he put a hand on her shoulder and guided her ahead of him.

"You with that property down in Mimosa Key?" she asked as they got closer.

"Yes, I'm the general contractor." He held out his hand. "Luke McBain. This is Arielle Chandler." He shook the woman's hand, realizing that she was much younger than she looked from a distance, though she'd done some hard living in her forty-some years.

She gave a tight smile. "I'm Michelle. Come on in. He'll be back. Never takes him more'n ten minutes to do his business." The woman opened a door and led them into another room that was part office, part kitchen, all royal disaster. Papers and files stacked halfway up walls, a desk covered with notebooks, coffee cups, and a pair of headphones dangling out of the computer tower on the desk.

Luke knew exactly what Arielle had to be thinking. *This* was a respectable engineering firm that did a legitimate core sampling? And he could hardly blame her. Who would hire this kind of sub?

He hadn't built a house in the States, but things couldn't be that much different here than in Lyon. The way a person's office looked usually reflected the quality of their work.

And if that were the case, GeoTech was a wreck.

"Here's a chair." Michelle indicated for Arielle to take a straight-backed wooden chair that looked like it came from a fourth-grade classroom. Luke was presumably left to stand or take the chair pushed under the only desk in the room.

He stood while Arielle perched on the edge of the chair, and after an awkward beat, the woman nodded at them, wiping her hands on a pink cotton sweater that barely reached a pair of hip-hugger jeans, revealing a slight roll of extra skin.

"I'll go knock on the door," the woman said.

"No, no," Arielle said. "Let him…we'll wait."

She brushed some hair off her face and sighed. "I'll be right back." Then, taking a cell phone from the top of a file cabinet, she stepped outside, sneakers squeaking on the linoleum as she walked down the hall.

Arielle looked up at him, and he could swear he read admonishment in her eyes.

"Engineers," she said, tipping her head to the side. "Strange breed."

He laughed, appreciating her humor, and gestured toward the mountain of mess behind her. "Not usually so sloppy."

She stood up, rubbing her arms and taking a step toward the other side of the room. Behind some folded-up blueprints, a whiteboard with an annual calendar leaned against the wall. *Last* year's calendar.

"Mr. McBain." A man marched into the office, tall and so lean his chest looked concave. Now *that* was an engineer, Luke thought. "So very nice to meet you, sir." He offered a cool handshake and turned to Arielle. "Mrs. McBain, I presume?"

"Oh, no." She shook her head. "I'm...the historical significance consultant," she said.

Ken blinked at that, and Luke did the same thing. The *what*? But then Michelle walked in and croaked, "What the hell is a historical significance consultant?"

Luke stared at Arielle, curious to learn the answer to that question.

"My role is to make sure the land that's being developed doesn't hold any historical significance to the state or country."

Ken turned down his lips and drew back like he'd been offered a lemon to bite, then chuckled. "Can't say we've ever had one of those, huh, Shelley?"

Michelle didn't laugh. "Do you have a license for that position, ma'am?"

Arielle shook her head. "No, it's really more of a hobby."

"Then don't be sniffing around our records and being a bother," she said. "If you're not licensed, we don't do business with you. Right, Ken?"

Luke stepped in between them, literally and figuratively. "We want to go over the core sampling you did for the North Barefoot Bay property on behalf of Jim Purty, the former GC. And I'm licensed," he added.

"Temporary license," Michelle shot back.

How did she—

"Michelle, let me handle this," Ken said, heaving a sigh as he walked to his desk. "I know where that file is..." A stack of papers began to topple, but Ken flattened a seasoned hand on the top, averting disaster before he pulled out a drawer stuffed with more papers.

"We really can't do business with someone not licensed," Michelle said, still eyeing Arielle. "You'll have to—"

"She's also a designer," Luke said quickly. Both woman looked at him, one with mud-colored eyes narrowed in suspicion, the other with ebony eyes wide with surprise. "And I assure you she is licensed and contracted as a certified interior decorator." He underscored the bluff with his own expression of confidence, which worked. At least enough for Michelle to nod slowly, then excuse herself and return to the hallway.

While Ken paged through paperwork, Luke winked at Arielle, getting a quiet smile of gratitude in return.

"Oh, here it is. Purty, James S., general contractor," he read aloud, pulling a slender manila file from the drawer. So slender, in fact, that when he opened it, there was nothing but a business card that floated to the ground. "Oh," he mumbled. He turned the folder over and inside out, as if the papers would miraculously appear.

"This is what was filed with the county," Luke said,

holding out his blue copy. "But there should be a longer report, with soil samples with the final feasibility study, erosion and sedimentation controls, earthwork volumetric calculations…"

Ken looked at Luke like he was speaking French. "All that stuff was done and filed, right down to the alphabetical letter, I swear."

Except this office didn't look like the workplace of anyone who did or filed anything to any letter.

"How about the samples?" Arielle asked. "Can we see them?"

"Those are in storage," Ken said. "Come this way."

He tossed the file onto the pile of other junk and marched toward the door. Arielle followed, but Luke lingered long enough to pick up the business card. *Duane Dissick, Owner, Southwest Masonry.* Of course, the only decent sub on the job.

Ken led them back down the hall to the entrance, outside, and around the back of the building to what looked like a temporary storage pod. As they got there, the front door whipped open, and Michelle walked out, drawing back when she practically slammed into her boss.

She reeked of the bitter smell of fresh cigarette smoke, pausing to stare at Arielle again. And not in any way that could be considered friendly.

"What were you doing in there?" Ken asked.

"I found the reports you should have had but didn't," she said, an edge in her voice. "They're on top of the job box, last row on the left." She let out a loud put-upon sigh and held the door open for them, then she gave Luke a dry smile. "Sometimes it's hard to be the only brains in the operation."

Which made Ken laugh, surprisingly enough, and he shook his head while she walked away. Inside, it was far more organized than the office, with stacks upon stacks of labeled, clear storage bins, each full of plastic bags stuffed with soil, rocks, sediment, and dirt samples.

Ken made his way through the maze of bins to the back, tapping one with satisfaction. "Well, I'll be damned. I did leave the full reports here with the samples." He gave a grin over his shoulder and waved them closer. "She's a bitch on wheels, and I know it, but the whole business would collapse without that girl. Don't know how I got so lucky when she applied for a job."

Luke ushered Arielle through the boxes, the lingering smell of that bitch on wheels' cigarette already giving him a headache. But he'd give her this: If she was in charge of this area, she was better organized than her boss.

"Here's the whole thing," Ken said, slapping a stack of documentation into Luke's hands. "Every single one of those things you wanted."

Luke glanced at the paperwork, then at Ken, who seemed strangely unfamiliar with the common terms in his business. "Did you do this core sample, Ken?"

"Me? No, I hire out with my own subs. I'm just the middleman."

"Can we get in the box?" Arielle asked. "I really want to see the actual samples taken from that property."

"Sure thing. Grab us some gloves." He nodded toward a box of latex gloves hanging on the wall. "Michelle's a freak about cleanliness and safety."

Arielle snapped some gloves from the dispenser, handed them to Luke and Ken, and took another pair for herself. After she'd put hers on, Ken unlatched the box and pulled out one of the bags, full of finely ground pieces of cream and brown rocks and shells.

"Are these from the actual hill in front of the house?" Arielle asked.

"I hope so," Ken admitted with a self-conscious chuckle. "'Fraid you're asking the wrong guy."

At Arielle's soft breath of exasperation, Luke stepped closer. "There's a number on the side of the bag," he said. "And a list of contents in this report. We'll have to go bag by bag and check the numbers against the contents."

She turned and caught his eye. "Would you do that?"

"Of course."

"Well, I won't," Ken said, backing away. "I have a meeting and another client to deal with."

"Can we stay here and do it ourselves?" Luke asked.

Ken's brows knit together. "Why? It's crushed rock and seashells, and the reports are filed with the county, approved, and finalized. What are you looking for, anyway?"

"Peace of mind," Luke said without thinking.

Ken lifted his shoulders in a huge shrug. "I guess. I'll be out, so let Michelle know when you're done, and she'll lock up after you." He held up his hands in resignation. "Not sure what else I can do for you."

"Nothing," Luke said, offering his hand. "Thanks for your time."

"Yes, and for the access," Arielle added. "Very kind of you."

"Not a problem." He walked away and stepped outside. "Gets pretty hot in here, so I'll leave the door open."

When he was gone, Arielle reached a hand out and put it on Luke's shoulder. "Thank you for being so nice about this."

"I'm pretty sure we're looking at bags of shells," he said, holding her gaze. "But I really do want you to feel like we've done everything on the up-and-up, we're not destroying a burial ground, and..." He grinned. "Dinner's on you."

Chapter Eleven

After opening the third bag of ground-up shells and rocks, Ari ripped off one of her latex gloves.

"This is not working." Tossing the glove on the floor, she burrowed her bare hand into the bag and closed her eyes. Nothing.

"Be careful," Luke said, reaching for her hand. "Those are sharp. You could cut yourself."

"But I can't feel anything with that glove on."

"What do you need to feel? They're seashells and stones, Arielle. And they're all broken. You're not going to find ancient artifacts in here, and honestly, I hate to be gross, but if there are bones, we wouldn't even know it."

"I would." She set the bag down and leaned back against the box behind her, frowning at him. "I'd sense it."

His eyes widened enough for her to know he was fighting the urge to laugh or make a very sarcastic remark. To his credit, he did neither, so she felt encouraged to underscore her point.

"I have intuition, Luke," she said softly. "You can ask your sister. When the Barefoot Brides get a new client, the first thing Gussie and Willow ask me is how I feel about them. And they don't mean do I like the bride or not. I

111

have...intuition." She didn't have any better word for it. None that he'd understand, anyway.

"And your intuition is telling you there are no bones of dead people in these bags?"

She relaxed into a rueful smile. "You don't have to fight so hard to keep the incredulity out of your tone."

"There's no incredulity—"

She raised her hand to stop him. "I don't have to hear it, Luke, and that's my point. I feel it. Your utter disbelief for what I'm saying is rolling off you like physical waves, and I can feel them."

"Like a disturbance in the Force?"

"Your joking about it doesn't make it go away."

"So you have, like, ESP?"

"No." She shook her head, looking down at the bag. "There's nothing supernatural about my powers of perception any more than your...your..." She searched his face for an answer, but her gaze fell to his chest and shoulders. She gave his bicep a squeeze. God, it was hard. And fine. And...hard. "Your strength."

He didn't answer, but he might have flexed a little bit to impress her. It worked.

"I assume you developed these muscles with hard work and repeated activities," she said.

"Not in a gym," he assured her.

"But the ghost was in the machine, as they say. Just like my powers of perception are...here." She tapped her chest and then her head. "And here. You were born with the genetic stuff to make these muscles, like I was born with whatever it takes to fine-tune well-developed intuition. Does that make sense?"

His expression answered for her: no.

"I can read people, and sometimes, I feel things."

He searched her face, the humor and doubt fading as he listened, holding back his opinion.

"For instance, I got some really strong vibes—and I don't mean that like a psychic—from our friends Ken and Michelle."

"Don't tell me," he said. "Your powers of perception tell you that Ken's a slob who doesn't care about his environment but has the hots for his assistant, Michelle, who thinks she's smarter than her boss."

She rolled her eyes.

"So I'm right."

"You're not wrong," she said. "But I got a little more than that surface, obvious business."

"Like what?"

"Ken is a good guy." She nodded, looking out the open door, thinking of the honest aura he emitted. "He didn't tell us a single lie, he has no agenda where you're concerned, and he has feelings for Michelle, but my gut says they are more paternal and sympathetic than sexual."

He leaned back against his own plastic backrest, taking that in. "Really. And what about her?"

"She's hiding something."

"Other than the fact that she smokes in the storeroom?"

"I don't know," Ari answered. "She's not honest, though, and I'm sorry if I sound weird, but I can smell that on her."

He let out a little snort. "So dishonesty smells like Marlboro Lights."

"How do you know that's what she smokes?"

"They were the Legion-imported cigarette of choice. I never smoked, but I was around them enough."

She looked down at the gallon-sized plastic bag on her lap, hoping he'd be as understanding about other weirdnesses she had. Like knowing when she's meant to be in love with someone.

"My grandmother had this gift to the point that it might be considered supernatural," she said softly. "She was legions beyond me, but she did teach me a lot."

When he didn't answer, she looked up, meeting his intense gaze.

"Like what?" he asked.

"Like how to touch something and get a sense of…history." She exhaled slowly, choosing her words with care. "I don't tell a lot of people about this. It's too easy to make fun of."

"You can say that again," he said quietly. "But I'll restrain myself, even if I don't quite grasp it."

"I don't expect you to restrain your jokes or understand this," she replied. "What's real to one person isn't always real to another."

His brows furrowed. "Real is real, Arielle. Something either is or it isn't."

"I guess that's a question for philosophers," she agreed, not really wanting to get into a faith debate right here and now, especially one she had in her own head often enough. "But you asked, and I'm telling you what my grandmother could do. I picked up a little bit of it. I haven't really tried to perfect or even use the skill because, frankly, it's not part of my daily life of designing sets for weddings. But when I found those pearls…" She let her voice fade off. A pragmatic person like Luke would never understand.

"Tell me," he urged. He put his hand on her arm and added enough pressure that all her nerves started doing their happy dance again.

She gave her head a tiny shake.

"Arielle. What did you feel when you found the pearls?"

"Like the universe wanted to tell me something important about that place."

He took a slow breath, still studying her. "And what did it tell you?"

"I don't know. You knocked me right off my feet before I could take my next breath."

Inching back, he gave a quick laugh. "I showed up right then?"

"Scant seconds after I found the pearls." Unable to resist, she turned her hand over and slid it down his arm a few inches to capture his fingers in hers. She could feel his pulse, his heat, his strength, his aura.

His aura that *still* told her he was The One.

"My timing is always impeccable," he said. "I shut the universe up."

"Unless you were what the universe was trying to tell me." She swallowed at the admission, feeling warm and close in the small space.

"What do you mean?"

"Either the universe was warning me that you were heading this way to destroy something important." With her other hand, she lifted the bag to show him what she meant. "And you have to be stopped."

"Or?"

"Or you were heading this way to..." *Change my life.* She felt herself inch closer to him. "To..." *Take my heart.* And closer. "To..." *Be The One.*

The door closed with a bang, making them both jump.

"Aren't you two almost done here?"

Luke let out a soft grunt only Ari could hear. "We were just getting started," he whispered.

She smiled and pulled back. "Nearly," she said, turning to watch Michelle on the approach. "Do you need to lock up?"

"I want to go to lunch." She put a hand on her hip. "Find everything in order?"

"We did," Luke assured her, standing and reaching for Ari's hand. "And I think we're done, right, Arielle?"

She let Luke pull her up, then zipped the bag she held. "Were there any other samples taken from the property?" she asked.

As Michelle got closer, Ari could smell that acrid odor of cigarettes, but a cloying scent of something else nearly covered it. A flower, like honeysuckle, but not as pretty. Jasmine? Or maybe Ari was smelling dishonesty because it emanated from this ragged, unhappy woman.

"That's all Ken gave me," Michelle said. "That don't mean that's all there is, but I do my best, you know?"

No, she didn't know. "Why wouldn't he give you everything?"

Michelle looked from one to the other, lifting a narrow shoulder, then sliding her fingertips into the slit pockets of her jeans. "He's Ken."

"What does that mean?" Luke asked.

"Nothing."

They both looked hard enough at her that she took a slight step backward, her shoulders hunched. "He likes shortcuts, is all. He might not be, how do I say it, afraid to shade the truth to save or make a buck."

"Then why do you work for him?" Ari asked.

She shrugged again. "He goes out all afternoon and I can take three-hour lunches. So..." She flicked her fingers to dismiss them. "Let's get you guys out of here so I can start one now, okay?"

Ari started to replace the bag in the bin, but Luke stepped closer to the woman. "You must be really efficient if you can take three-hour lunches and keep this room as organized as you do."

Her eyes widened as she looked up at him, no doubt feeling the same impact anyone with a couple of X chromosomes would feel. "I am," she said. "And you're cutting into my work time."

She tempered the smartass comment with a smile. "Hey, I don't mean to be a bitch. It just comes so naturally." She gave a self-deprecating laugh, which felt oddly honest coming from her. "And, listen, I don't mean to run you two out of here, but let me help you out. Take a bag from that box. Go get it tested or whatever. All we got is Ken's word that he tested these, but if you take them somewhere else, you can be sure that's the truth."

Luke gave her a long, hard look, then nodded. "All right. We'll do that."

She pushed past them and chose a bag from the box. "Here you go."

Luke took it, handing her the paperwork they'd found on top of the bin. "You might want to file this in the proper place, in case someone needs to look at it again."

"I'll do that," she said, taking it and stepping to the side to let them pass. "After my three-hour lunch."

Luke put his hand on Ari's shoulder and led her out, but when she passed the other woman, their arms brushed and something pinged in Ari's head.

Might have been a warning, but it could have been the sickening smell of her perfume. The thing Ari didn't tell Luke about her intuition was that sometimes...she was wrong.

"Whoa, Mr. Fancy McFancyPants."

Luke speared the twelve-year-old doing homework at Gussie's kitchen table with a look. "You've spent entirely too much time with my sister, Alex."

The girl grinned and pointed her pencil eraser at him. "Any chance you understand algebra? Because my soon-to-be Aunt Gussie couldn't solve for X if it bit her."

"Hey." In the kitchen, Gussie tapped a wooden spoon on the side of a pan. "I did that word problem for you."

Alex rolled her eyes with true preteen precision. "You gave me a story about a guy who met a girl on a plane to St. Louis. The question was, how many hours did it take the plane to get there?"

"Long enough for him to get her phone number." Laughing, she turned to look at Luke. "Whoa, Mr. Fancy McFan—"

"Shut up, Auggie. Am I overdressed to have dinner with Arielle?"

Gussie lifted a brow and put her hand to the side of her mouth, directing a stage whisper to her soon-to-be niece. "Should I tell him no one calls her Arielle?"

"Or you Auggie," Alex said. "Auntie Auggie!"

Gussie pointed her spoon at the girl. "Don't make me wash your mouth out with soap." Then she turned back to Luke. "Where are you two going?"

"She said she'd take me to Junonia."

"The restaurant at the resort?" Alex asked. "Wow. No wonder you're dressed up."

"She lost a bet with me this morning," he told them.

Gussie came around the kitchen counter, openly assessing his button-down white shirt and sharp, khaki pants. "When she loses bets with me, I get Pixy Stix. You get filet mignon in melted butter as only Chef Ian can make. It explains a lot."

"Like what?" he asked.

"Why she was so…fluttery when she got to work at almost two o'clock in the afternoon. Where did you two go, anyway?"

"On a wild-goose chase," he said, remembering the morning. "Didn't she tell you?"

"No," Gussie said, tapping the spoon on her cheek while thinking. "As a matter of fact, she didn't talk much at all today. Was on the computer for hours, made some quiet calls, seemed very…preoccupied. With you?"

"I doubt it."

"Then she tore out of there early, saying she had to run over the causeway for something and get home in time to get ready to go out." She eyed him again. "But she never mentioned your name or that you'd been together all morning. Curious."

"What's curious about it? Does she tell you every time she goes out with someone?"

"Yes." She looked at Alex as though seeking confirmation. "Ari tells me everything."

"Has she told you she has some kind of sixth sense that makes her think she knows things about people?"

Gussie laughed. "She doesn't have to tell me, brother dear. She proves it every single day. She's like a human barometer, and if I were you, I'd pay attention. What did she tell you?"

"Not much." He shrugged and tugged at his cuffs, then rolled one up a few times. "Better?"

Gussie smiled. "You look good no matter how you dress, Luke. What has she told you? She's quite…canny. Is that the right word? I mean, she told me I was hiding something with my wigs the second time we were together, and she had no idea about my scar." She reached up and touched the back of her head. "It was weird how she knew."

"That didn't take a psychic, Gussie. She probably made the correct assumption that you wore a wig to hide what was underneath."

"She's not psychic," Gussie replied. "She's just…"

"Intuitive. She told me." Irritation snaked up his back. "How do you know if she's making something up or she's a lucky guess? People can do that, you know."

"Not like Ari does," Gussie said. "I had her meet Tom. Remember, Alex?"

"Of course I do," Alex said, clearly a long way from algebra now. "That was when I convinced you to come to France so you'd fall in love and marry him." She grinned. "My evil plan worked."

"That was not your plan," Gussie said. "But I wasn't sure about him, and when that happens, I turn to Ari because she knows."

She knows *what*? "What did she say about him?"

Gussie's smile grew. "I wanted to kill her that night. She was all over the France idea because she basically said, 'He's the one for you,' and I didn't want to believe it."

The one. Luke rolled up the other cuff, thinking of how she'd used that phrase while talking to him, too. "She says that sometimes…'the one.' I'm not sure what she means." When he looked up, Gussie was staring at him.

"Holy, holy shit." She slammed her hand over her lips. "Whoops. You didn't hear that, Alex."

"Oh, yes, I did."

"It's *you*!" Gussie said, her eyes widening in shock and no small amount of happiness. "You're The One. The One, with capital letters."

"What are you talking about?"

"She said she'd met him, but...*wow*." She slapped her cheek in wonder. "How did I not see this?"

Alex was up from the table now, joining them. "What? What is it, Gussie?"

"Good question, Alex," Luke said. "What the hell"—he glanced at Alex—"*heck* are you talking about?"

"You, my brother, are Ari's one true love, her destiny mate, her future..." Gussie's voice faded as if she couldn't say the word, and Luke was glad of it.

"Cool it, Gus," he said, a slow burn of discomfort building in his chest.

"I will not cool anything." Gussie insisted. "I remember, now. She said something to me the day of Willow's wedding. But wait. She hadn't met you yet. She hadn't even seen you. We were in our office and..." She scowled at him. "*Did* you meet her before the wedding?"

"We met up at the property, hours before the wedding. Didn't she tell you?"

"No. She came flying into the office that day all flustered and flushed and announced she'd met..." Gussie dropped into one of the kitchen chairs like this new revelation made it impossible to stand on two legs. "Well, that's it, then. You're going to marry her."

"*What?*" The question came from Luke and Alex in perfect unison and harmony—Alex with a shriek of excitement, while Luke's voice rumbled with raw, unfettered shock.

"I've known her less than forty-eight hours," he managed to say, thinking about sitting down himself at the certainty in his sister's voice. *Marry her?* "That's freaking crazy, Gus."

"She's *always* told us about this 'one true love' that she believes in. I mean, she truly believes it. She's sent a few good guys packing because her intuition said she'd know

'The One' the minute she met him, and that's who she'd marry." Gussie laughed softly, shaking her head. "Ari as my sister? That's—"

"Ridiculous!" he shot back, a strange white heat burning in his chest. "I must have totally misunderstood what she said."

Even though, he could still see her ripping drywall down and saying she thought he was "the one." When he'd asked her to explain…she never really did.

"I don't want to talk about this anymore." He grabbed his keys from the table and marching to the door.

He slammed it behind him and looked down at his hands. Hands that killed…they couldn't love her. Because these hands had killed the one and only woman he'd ever loved.

He wasn't about to take that chance again.

Chapter Twelve

It didn't take any special empathetic sensitivity powers to figure out that Luke McBain wasn't entirely comfortable at dinner. Oh, he did everything right. He'd held Ari's chair, kept up a lively conversation, shared stories about his childhood, listened to Ari talk about her life and job, and wouldn't let her pick up the tab even though they were both fairly sure she'd lost the bet.

But under the surface, everything about him was taut. A few glasses of wine seemed to have no effect on him, though Ari had relaxed as the evening unfolded.

After dinner, they took a crème brûlée out to one of the wooden benches tucked between palm trees in a secluded section of the Casa Blanca grounds. There, they shared the dessert and watched the moonlight on Barefoot Bay, talking. Once, he casually touched her arm, making a point about something, and everything *buzzed* as always at his touch. Would she ever get used to that?

"Then you agree," he said.

She looked over the spoonful of creamy dessert and met his gaze. "I'm sorry, what did I just agree to?"

Looking slightly amused, he took the nearly empty dessert dish and set it on a low cocktail table next to the bench where a Casa Blanca staffer would scoop it up in a few minutes. "You agree that I should take the samples Michelle gave us and have them analyzed by the new firm I mentioned at dinner."

"Yes, yes, of course."

"And if they pass, we'll do a partial grade." He covered her hand with his, the touch warm and inviting. No, it was hot and searing. Would nothing put an end to this crazy feeling?

Yes. *Sex.*

At the thought, she pulled away, maybe a little too fast, because he blinked in response. "That doesn't work for you?"

"No, I think it could work," she recovered. It could work...*nicely.*

"You're okay with a partial testing?" he pressed, obviously all cool business when she was anything but.

She forced herself to focus on what he was saying and not the softness of his lips as he was saying it. "If by partial you mean a foot of land that is examined by a professional, not an acre that is destroyed beyond recognition."

He gave an easy laugh. "You're relentless."

"Add that to my list of qualities you don't like," she quipped.

"Who says I don't like it?"

She glanced at him. "I don't know." She took a moment to try to decide which direction to take the conversation and knew, in her heart, that honest was the only way to go. "Something tells me you're not one hundred percent comfortable tonight, Luke."

"Ahh." He nodded knowingly. "That's right, I forgot. You're the person who can sniff out hidden feelings." He leaned close, way too close. "Except my guess is you're not always right."

She wanted to inch away, but his breath was warm on her cheek. "Why would you guess that?"

"Because you're wrong right now. I'm comfortable," he assured her. "You're the one who jumps a foot every time our hands accidentally—or not so accidentally—brush." He underscored that with a graze of his fingertips from her knuckle all the way up her forearm, leaving a trail of chills and sparks.

He laughed at the explosion of goose bumps, as if the uninvited response simply made his point for him.

"I'm not jumping," she lied. "But I can tell that something has you..." She lifted her hand, determined to touch him and not feel all melty stupid inside. She returned the light graze of fingertips, only she traveled hers along his jaw, down to the muscle in his neck she'd seen tense a dozen times when he'd studied her closely. "Uptight."

He didn't answer, and she took it as assent, so she pushed a little harder, letting her intuition go to work. "There's something on your mind," she said. "Something about me. Something you don't like."

"Something I don't understand," he added.

Ahh. She probably could guess what it was. "Why don't you ask me so I can explain it?"

"I don't want to put you on the spot, Arielle."

Too late. "Let's get a few things straight," she said. "I am not a circus act. I am not a fortune-teller. I am not an empath, or a shaman, or a soothsayer, or a freak."

"I know." He scooted a little closer on the wooden bench, putting his hand along the back, but not around her. "Why don't you tell me exactly what this...this *aptitude* of yours does? How it works and how accurate you are. I really want to know."

She took a slow breath, getting used to his body warmth.

And wanting more. So much more. He seemed genuinely interested. In fact, he seemed downright determined to get her to talk. And she knew why—because her "intuition" could affect that land and his career.

"You think I'm making this whole thing up so you'll stop what you're doing on that hill?" she asked.

"No. I really want to know what this sixth sense you have is all about. I want to know *you*, Arielle." The way he said it made her die a little inside. She wanted to know him, too. She wanted to know if these feelings were real or imagined, if he really was The One. Sometimes she was so certain, and yet, at other times, she doubted.

Maybe the best way to find out was for both of them to open up, and she'd have to go first.

She swallowed and leaned back against the wooden beams and his arm, hyperaware of his fingertips less than a centimeter from her bare shoulder.

"What exactly do you want to know?" she asked.

"I guess, how has this ability affected your life?"

"That's a good question. In fact, I like that you asked that and not, you know, 'What's the stock market going to do tomorrow?' Like some people might."

"I don't care about the stock market." The rest was implied and clear by the look in his eyes. He cared about *her*.

Emboldened by that, she settled a little closer to him, the hardness of his shoulder and thigh pressing enough against her to make her feel warm and tingly and safe. Safe enough to tell him some things.

"In some ways, it has made my life easier because I can judge people fairly accurately. In other ways, well…" She lifted her lips in a half smile. "It's a burden to be this weird."

"You're not weird, Arielle. Your powers of perception

are what make you *you*. I'm interested in how it, you know, manifests itself."

She liked that he was interested in that. She wasn't sure what brought it on, but just giving credence to her mystical side was a compliment from him. "First and foremost, I don't ignore my gut, my inner voice. When a thought pops into my head, I don't dismiss it like a lot of people do. I listen as if a wise person is sharing worthwhile insights."

"Does that happen a lot?" he asked.

"Enough. Not constantly. I don't hear voices," she said with a laugh. "But, like, when we met Ken today, I felt this inner sense that he's a good guy. Almost like a voice, but not quite. I trust that judgment."

"And what did that inner sense tell you when you met me?"

She breathed in a little sharply, not expecting to get so *personal* so soon. She was ready to tell him about her dreams or how she avoided negative people and how there was another plane of spirituality right in front of them.

But he wanted to talk about...him.

"Did you hear a voice that said I'm a good guy?"

"I told you I don't..." She looked up at him, stunned for a second by how close he was. How real and beautiful he was to her. "Yes," she whispered. "I felt you are good."

"Anything else?"

She smiled. "Well, I didn't need my sixth sense when the other ones were working so well. I could see you're great-looking and...and...nice."

"Nice?"

She laughed again. "What do you expect me to say, Luke?" *That I thought you were my soul mate five seconds after I met you?* She'd sound even crazier than he already suspected she was, but it was almost like that *was* what he was probing for.

"I wondered if there was anything, you know, more than *nice*," he said.

Her heart flipped and flopped and tilted and dropped. She didn't answer, but didn't move her gaze from his, either. Blood rammed through her veins, making her pulse points jump the way that little vein in his neck throbbed right then.

"Do you feel it, too?" she whispered.

He lifted his hand, cupping her cheek and jaw, holding her gaze. "I don't know what I feel, except..." He searched her face, his expression completely vulnerable and open for the first time all night. "I'm afraid you've put a spell on me."

She closed her eyes. "Please don't make fun of me right now."

He stroked her cheek with his thumb, grazing the corner of her mouth and her lower lip. "I'm not." Pulling her close, he kissed her cheek, his lips so soft and sweet she wanted to moan. "That's the scary thing."

With a sexy sigh of resignation, he closed the space between their mouths and kissed her.

Nice. This kiss was all kinds of nice.

And nice is what she'd thought of him when they'd met—not the "forever-and-ever love" that Gussie claimed was going on. Relaxing into that thought, Luke opened his mouth enough to taste more of her, to get the caramel sweetness on her tongue, and to let their lips find the perfect fit.

This was what he wanted, all he wanted. He wasn't

Arielle's "destiny mate," or whatever his sister had called it. This attraction was no more than garden-variety *sexual desire*. And that was just fine. Better than fine.

They both angled their heads naturally, sinking into the kiss and all the sensations that came with it, the world and water and stars and sky fading away as his every sense focused on the touch and taste of a woman he wanted in every way.

That's all this was...not something *more*.

A sweet sound escaped her throat, and his tongue found hers. Arielle closed her hands around his neck, drawing him closer, inviting him deeper into her mouth. And he went, wrapping his arms around her as well, finishing the kiss by nibbling her jaw and throat, counting the crazy beat of her blood under his lips.

"And is this what you thought it would feel like?" he whispered against her skin.

"Better," she confessed, tipping her head back to give him more access to sweet skin. "Much better."

"And you *have* thought about it?" he asked.

"Yes." She sighed into his mouth, clearly enjoying this every bit as much as he was.

He slid his hand under her hair, burrowing up into the thick locks as he closed in for another long, deep kiss that tasted like vanilla and cream and *sex*. Not love. Not forever. But the truth was...

"I've never felt anything like this," he admitted. Oh, *man*. "Your hair," he added quickly, dragging his hand through the length of it, not a single tangle in what had to be damn near two feet of midnight-black silk. "Never felt *anything* like it."

She laughed and leaned her head to the side, tempting him to go right back under her hair for another swipe of the sinfully soft strands. "You've never been with a woman with Native American blood, then."

"Definitely not." He lifted a handful of hair and buried his face in it, inhaling the flowery shampoo and salt air that clung to her. "But you probably already know that."

"I'm not a mind reader, Luke. I don't know much at all about you."

"Then let's change that." He peppered more kisses along her jaw, his hands spreading over her shoulders, aching to slide lower and touch more of her body.

"You want to tell me things I don't know?"

"I want to…" He buried the obvious into another kiss, inching his hand lower to rest on the rise of her breast, and just that little intimacy made him hotter and harder. "I want to go home, Little Mermaid. With you."

He started to stand and tried to bring her with him, but she stayed on the bench, holding tight, refusing to move. She searched his face with her exotic eyes, an expression of vulnerability and fear and uncertainty making her more beautiful.

Completely beautiful. Like no one he'd ever met. Unable to stop himself, he sat back down and closed his hands over her cheeks, holding her face like a precious work of art. "I can't wait to see you naked." The confession, rough and raspy, tumbled out, and she didn't even blink.

In fact, she didn't move or breathe or say a word.

"Too soon?" he asked after a few heartbeats of silence. "Too much? Too—"

She put her fingers over his mouth, the touch so light it tickled his lips. "Stop talking. Just…*feel*."

The order rolled through him like a thunderclap, making him as still as she was. "Feel what?" He didn't want to *feel* anything except her body and her mouth, her hands and her legs—squeezed around him when he slid inside her.

The thought kicked too much blood to his cock, making it harder.

"Come on, Ari—"

"*Feel.*" She insisted. "This." She added some pressure against his lips. "Do you feel it?"

Yes, damn it. He felt it. He felt electricity and desire and some inexplicable deep-seated ache that he assumed started in his balls and wasn't going to end until he had relief. He felt a little brain dead and foolish, and yet as alert as if he were picking up a weapon and heading into battle. He felt physical things he couldn't explain and mental things he tried to ignore and something in the vicinity of where he imagined his soul resided, and he sure as shit did not want to figure out what *that* was.

How the hell did she do this to him? All he wanted was to take her back to her place and do what their bodies had been charged up to do since they met on that hill.

Instead, he felt his eyes shutter closed on a frustrated exhale as he plucked through the minefield of feelings and picked some unloaded words. "I feel completely attracted to you, Arielle, and ready to take this to the next natural place." He kissed her fingers. "If you don't want to spend the night with me, I get that. Won't stop me from asking, though."

"I just wondered if, with me, you feel anything different from, you know, other girls."

Was she asking if he thought they were—or he was—that "one" she talked about? He wanted to know, but then again, he really didn't.

"Luke," she said before he could answer. "I don't spend the night with...anyone." She lowered her hand and tried to look down, but he still had her delicate face in his palms, so he kept her chin raised, and she had to meet his gaze. "I'm celibate," she whispered.

If he hadn't *seen* her say the word, he might not have believed that's what she said.

Celibate.

"Okay," he said slowly, drawing out the two syllables. "That's...good."

She gave him a look, lifting one brow. "Good is not a word I'd use to describe this state of affairs."

That was a relief. "No? I can help you, then." He tried to inch her closer. "I have what you need."

But she didn't move, except for the tiniest shake of her head, which sent a thud of disappointment into his gut. And lower.

"No," she breathed the word.

"Is it...me?" he asked.

Her eyes flashed, and she fought a smile. "I don't know."

Laughing, he leaned back, expecting a sting of rejection, but feeling only...hope. That was weird, but that's what he felt, and she was the one talking about feelings. "Any chance you'll change your mind?"

"Every chance."

Hope, and a few other things, rose. "What'll I have to do? More dates? Flowers? Bared soul? Oh..." The realization hit him. "Stop the building project."

"No!" She gasped a little. "I mean, that's not what you'd have to do. Those two things—the situation with that land and my wanting to be with you—they're separate."

Were they? "But you do want to be with me?"

"Of course," she laughed. "Isn't that obvious?"

Not at the moment. "Then what's the problem?"

"The problem is...well, it's not a problem. It's a promise. To myself and to...no, really, to myself."

He waited, watching the emotions dance over her features, the process of her brain and heart searching for whatever words she needed as pretty as everything else about her.

"What's the promise?" he asked.

"I'm waiting for...someone special."

Exactly what he was afraid of. "And I'm not special."

"You are, but..." He watched her swallow, fighting with a lot of emotions he didn't quite understand. "The next, and last and only, person I'm ever going to sleep with will be the one man I'm destined to...love."

Luke jerked at the impact of the last whispered word. Tried to breathe. Braced for his body to jump and run screaming into the night. He opened his mouth to tell her that he would never, ever use that word with a woman. That he had once and it had ended badly. So, so badly. He wanted to tell her he made a promise, too. To himself. He would never, ever, *ever* go near anything that looked or tasted or felt like *love*.

Instead, he just stood, because this date was over.

Chapter Thirteen

Stricken.

The word had landed on Ari's heart when she'd made her confession the night before, as loud and clear as the universe could be. It had remained there while she'd ended her date with Luke with all the lightness and casualness she could muster.

And no arguments from him. They'd driven home, made small talk by mutual, silent consent, and said good-bye with a chaste kiss at the bottom of the stairs that led up to her apartment.

And all night, alone in bed, she kept hearing the same word in her head.

He'd looked positively *stricken* by the fact that she was looking for love—expecting it, really. And waiting for it.

"Knock, knock."

Ari looked up from her desk in the Barefoot Brides office to see the bright eyes and easy smile of Lacey Walker.

"Good morning, Lacey," Ari said, rising to greet the woman who wasn't her boss, but definitely had the final word on everything that happened at the resort.

"Is it?" Lacey cruised into the office, gathering a handful

of reddish-blond curls as she slipped into one of the chairs at the conference table. "I think I slept two hours last night."

"You don't look it." Lacey somehow never appeared truly exhausted by her giant job. "Did Elijah have a bad night?" Ari asked, referring to the adorable toddler who often visited the Casa Blanca administrative offices, much to everyone's delight.

"Elijah slept like the baby he is," Lacey said with a laugh. "Don't believe people who tell you the little ones cost you sleep. It was my teenage daughter who had me up all night finishing college applications."

"Ashley's going to college next year?"

Lacey looked skyward. "If the apps made it. Of course she was submitting within ten minutes of the deadline." She shook her head and laughed. "That girl will be the death of me." She glanced around. "You all alone today?"

"Gussie's on her way in, and Willow is..." Ari put her hands up and looked toward the heavens. "Cruising around the Keys and the Bahamas on Nate Ivory's yacht."

"Speaking of one of our resident billionaires." Lacey waved a manila file folder. "I see his wedding to Liza Lemanski is on the schedule for spring. Which is why I popped over here."

"Is there a problem with the date?" Ari asked. "He really wants it to coincide with the opening of the minor league stadium."

"No problem at all!" Lacey exclaimed. "It's going to be an amazing, high-profile wedding with all manner of celebrities showing up. The new villas we've added will be done, and we'll need every one, and a ramped-up staff. Honestly, I just came over to sing your praises. The Barefoot Brides is helping this resort be extremely profitable."

Ari beamed. "We're so happy we chose Casa Blanca as

our home base, Lacey. Your staff couldn't be more wonderful."

It was Lacey's turn to grin at the compliment. "When I think that not so many years ago, my daughter and I stood in rubble with no idea what to do with my grandfather's land..." She didn't finish and Ari jumped on the chance she'd been looking for.

"Your grandfather, one of the founders of the island. Along with Balzac Valentine."

She nodded. "They were part of the original settlers of Mimosa Key."

"Maybe not the most original," Ari said, choosing her words carefully. "Surely this island was part of the great Indian nation of Florida."

Lacey's golden eyes sparked. "Oh, I do believe it was, Ari, thousands of years ago."

"Did you grandfather, or his friends, ever find anything to prove that?" Ari asked.

She leaned back, thinking. "The Indian face."

"What?"

"I don't mean to be politically incorrect. That's just what he called it."

Ari waved off the apology, a surprising shudder shimmying through her. "What he called what?"

"He had this...like a face made out of wood."

"A tribal mask?" Ari suggested.

"I guess, I don't know. I remember it from when I was a little girl. The paint was faded and chipped, but it was very authentic looking."

"Where is it?" she asked, unable to keep the excitement out of her voice. A mask like that could help an expert identify the tribe that lived here and prove that Native Americans had inhabited Mimosa Key.

Lacey gave her head a negative shake. "Gone with the wind that swept through Barefoot Bay, I'm afraid. That hurricane was ruthless with our stuff."

Ari tamped down disappointment. "Do you know where he found it?"

"No clue at all."

"Any pictures of it?"

Lacey laughed. "You really want to see that face, don't you?"

"I'd like to—"

"You better be in there, Ari Chandler!" Gussie's voice came from down the hall, along with her footsteps moving at a fast clip. "Because you better spill every blasted detail and not leave out a single thing—" Gussie popped into the doorway, a coffee cup in each hand, a pack of mail under her chin, her green eyes glinting like gems. "Oh, hi, Lacey. Sorry to be screaming in the halls."

Lacey laughed, taking one of the coffees so Gussie could grab the envelopes with her free hand. "Like I don't bring a toddler in here to scream in the halls." She put the coffee in front of Ari. "I take it that's for her."

"Unless you want it," Ari said quickly.

"No, thanks. I better get to a staff meeting." Lacey tapped Gussie's shoulder, offering her the seat she was vacating. "Where I will announce that we're having the Ivory wedding here in the spring, thanks to you terrific bridal consultants. And sorry I don't have more details for you, Ari. I'll ask my mom if she remembers anything about that mask or has a picture. I doubt it, though."

"Thanks," Ari said, giving a wave good-bye. Before she could take a sip of coffee, Gussie practically launched forward.

"I know he's my brother, so I don't want, you know, the

137

goriest of gory details, but you better tell me everything anyway, including…" Her voice faded, thank God. "Why don't you look happy?"

Ari blinked at her. "I don't look anything."

"Exactly. You should be rapturous."

"What are you talking about?"

Gussie looked as confused as Ari felt. "Didn't you spend the night with Luke last night?"

"I did not."

Gussie shook her head, not buying it. "He never came home after his dinner date with you. I wasn't born yesterday, Ari."

He hadn't gone home last night? A slow tendril of dread wended through her. "Where did he go?"

Gussie coughed on her sip of coffee. "I thought he was with you. I thought you guys had—"

"We didn't," Ari said. "We"—*almost did, but then I told him the truth*—"said good night at the bottom of the stairs, and I went up to my apartment. I'd assumed he went to yours."

Gussie frowned. "That's weird. Where else would he stay?"

"Maybe he came and went before you noticed."

"I would have heard him. What did you two talk about?" Gussie asked.

"Oh, the usual. Life, work, the house he's building, the fact that I won't…don't…can't…"

Gussie's shoulders dropped with disappointment. "You turned him down?"

"I just met him," Ari fired back, remembering all too well a similar conversation they'd had when Gussie met Tom. "Do you expect me to fall into bed with him?"

"You said he's The One."

Ari sucked in a breath. "I didn't tell you that, Gussie." Of that she was certain.

"You did, after you met him, you said you'd met The One. You didn't tell me that it was *Luke*. But I put Two and Two together and came up with Obvious."

A slow drain of blood started in Ari's brain, filling her chest with more dread. "You didn't tell him that, did you?"

"I…" Gussie paled, too. "I might have. You know how I, um, don't always filter. Didn't you tell him?"

"No!"

"But why not? If he's the man for you, he should know it." She gnawed on her lower lip, clearly getting the magnitude of the problem from the look Ari was giving her. "Shouldn't he?"

"Yes, exactly," Ari said. "He should know it. He *would* know it. He has to know it or it's not…real." The word fell into the pit of her stomach like a boulder.

Always, always the question: Was anything she felt real? Was this sensation that Luke was different and right and perfect for her real? Or did she just dream it up?

"He's a guy, Ari," Gussie said. "Sometimes they have to be hit over the head with things."

"That's not how it works."

"There are rules for this 'One' thing?" Gussie asked, a hint of sarcasm in her voice.

"Not rules. But as far as my grandmother explained it to me, both parties are instantly aware of the feelings. No one needs to be told anything. And, anyway, he's…"

Gussie moaned softly when Ari didn't finish. "He's what?"

"He's only interested in sex," she said quickly.

"Again, human male species thing, but Luke is a pretty

cool guy. What did he do to make you think that?"

"When I told him I was waiting for..." *Love.* Oh, God, why did she admit that? "Anyway, he couldn't get away fast enough."

"You told him you're waiting for one particular guy, but you don't know who he is, but you think that maybe he's Luke, but you're not sure."

"Actually, yes. But I didn't tell him I thought he was that guy."

"I did," Gussie said, standing slowly. "So, I'm sorry if I screwed things up."

"Nah, I did that all by myself," Ari assured her.

Gussie crossed her arms, thinking. "I guess I really don't know him anymore. I've tried, we've talked, of course, since we reunited, but he's got a guard up around him that I don't remember from when he was young."

"People change," Ari said, wistfully dreaming of a man who'd at least be responsive to the idea of one true love. Not one who shot up and ended their evening when he found out she wanted sex to be with someone special and lasting.

"I suppose." Gussie scooped up her coffee and some of the mail, leaving an envelope hand-addressed to Ari. "Didn't mean to make assumptions, Ari."

"It's okay."

As Gussie walked to her desk, she took out her cell phone and tapped the screen, probably texting Luke. Trying not to be anxious about his response, Ari tore open the envelope with a little too much force, yanking out the single sheet of notepaper.

"Oh, he spent the night at the job site," Gussie said.

Words danced before Ari's eyes, nothing making sense. "*What?*"

"I guess he crashed in that creepy house."

"No, I mean…what the hell is this?"

The words were typed, printed off a computer, in all caps.

PUT THE PEARLS BACK WHERE YOU FOUND THEM

Ari flipped the paper over, but it was blank. No return address on the envelope that was postmarked in Naples, Florida, where much of Mimosa Key mail was processed. Not a clue anywhere, except for the low-grade hum that buzzed through Ari's hand, growing stronger until she had to drop the paper on the desk. A word danced in her brain, but she couldn't quite grab it.

"What's that?" Gussie asked, looking over Ari's shoulder.

"I don't know, but…"

Gussie reached for it, examining the paper, squinting at the words, reading them out loud.

Ari closed her eyes, trying to remember how Grandma Good Bear taught her to listen to the universe. *Go still. Block out all sounds. Focus on the word.*

"What the hell does that mean?" Gussie asked, looking at the paper. "This is—"

"Shhh!" Ari tapped Gussie's arm, frustrated to be so close to hearing something but not quite getting it. "Greed." There. There was the word. Greed. *Greed?*

"Weird," Gussie finished.

"I know, it is."

"I meant you're weird, but I love you for it." She tossed the paper back. "And that's probably from some psycho bride. Check the Casa Blanca lost and found and you'll find plenty of forgotten pearl earrings."

But Ari didn't think this note came from a bride. "I will," she said, even though that wasn't necessary. She knew which pearls this was about, and she was taking that necklace to a safe-deposit box today.

Chapter Fourteen

Ari finished wrapping the five samples she'd decided to take to the archaeologist who worked at the Mound House museum up in Fort Myers Beach and carefully placed them between layers of bubble wrap and tucked them into the top of the crate. She was finally finished going through everything, certain she had some real artifacts. Some shells, some coral, but some pieces with real value, though she couldn't be sure until she got a professional assessment.

Pouring a second glass of pinot noir, she carried it to the sofa where her MacBook was open to the map and directions to a place less than an hour away, known as the Mound House archaeological site.

Curling into the corner of the couch, she sipped wine and clicked through the pictures of the museum and Case House, a structure that had been built more than a hundred years ago on land that once teemed with Calusa Indians.

They were nothing like the Miwok of California, but Ari found the basic Native American similarities in beliefs, clothes, and customs in this tribe that lived off the sea rather than the land. Everything she discovered was familiar, recalling her long, lazy summers of traipsing along next to

Grandma Good Bear on various sojourns to festivals, protests, craft events, and museums.

As Ari thought of those days, a palpable pain squeezed her chest, trying to fill the hole left by her grandmother.

She reached to the table, cupped the wine glass, and lifted it to the air. "To you, Grandma," she whispered. "I have no doubt what you'd tell me to do: the right thing for the people…even if it costs me The One."

Or would Grandma Good Bear's old brown eyes pop with horror at the thought of giving up—

The knock on her apartment door was so sharp and loud, Ari startled, spilling a drop of wine on her sleep pants and sending her heart knocking just as loud. For one crazy, stupid, blasted second, she imagined Grandma Good Bear was at the door to tell her what's what.

"Arielle?"

But it was Luke, and that did nothing to slow down her heart rate.

He knocked again, with a little impatience. What the hell? He was the one who'd gone MIA all day. Not that she'd expected a word from him, or even a phone call. And definitely not a late-night visit.

She glanced at the computer clock as she got up. Did nine thirty qualify as a booty call?

Only if there was booty involved.

She brushed her hands over the thin cotton T-shirt she wore, tugging the material so it almost reached the top of her flannel sleep pants, imagining him seeing her dressed like this. A bolt of anticipation slammed her whole midsection, then tumbled lower. She still wanted him, and maybe she should let go of archaic promises and see what happened if she got him.

There was always the possibility that sex would clear up

the question of whether he was The One or she'd just made that up. And it sure as hell wouldn't feel bad to try. Maybe he was here to give it another go. Everything tensed at that possibility and how much she wanted that. Wanted *him*.

"Arielle, I know—"

She opened the door, silencing him.

"We should talk." He looked down at her, a day's worth of beard darkening his hollow cheeks, his never-the-same-color-twice eyes locked on her, the rise and fall of his Adam's apple a visible sign of a man who'd gulped. Hard.

"Luke, I—"

"Please, Arielle. I need to tell you something."

She didn't even hesitate, opening the door wider and gesturing him in, taking the time to let her gaze slide over his black T-shirt and faded jeans, a little mud around the bottom and on his work boots.

He looked down, tapping one boot on the other. "Sorry for the mud. I've been at the job site," he said. "I'll take them off." He toed off one boot, revealing a thick white sock, then the other.

She stepped away, rooting for the right small talk that didn't include, *Gee, your stockinged feet are sexy, too! Imagine that!* "You want a drink?"

He frowned a little, letting his gaze slide over her, making her crazy aware of how little she wore. "If you're having something."

"Pinot noir."

He made a face. "Any chance you have a beer?"

"Yes, of course." She went to the fridge, grabbing a bottle of Amber Bock. Without turning, she was somehow aware of him moving through the apartment, taking the very seat on the sofa where she'd been.

"Researching the Calusa Indians?"

And, obviously, reading her laptop screen. "I'm going up to a place called Mound House tomorrow to take the crate to an archaeologist there," she said, fishing through the utensil drawer for the bottle opener. "He'll be able to look at the artifacts we found and, with some study and tests, determine their age and authenticity."

She snapped the top off, making the beer hiss while she waited for him to reply. Finally, she turned, expecting to find him focused on the laptop. Instead, he was watching her from the sofa, his eyes narrow. Intense. Inescapable.

A million fire flashes fired through her veins, sharp and hot and...annoying. How the hell long would she have to *feel* all this?

"Can I come with you?" he asked.

And she damn near dropped the beer.

Corraling control, she went back into the living area and handed him the bottle over the back of the sofa. "Sure, but why do you want to?" Their fingers brushed, and of course it felt like she'd touched a lightning rod in a storm.

"More information. You're not the only one doing research on this land." He held the bottle up in a toast. "Did you know that up in Mound Key, which is another place believed to be inhabited by the Calusa and was, in fact, the home of tribe headquarters, that they have not found a single burial mound?"

He looked a little too smug. And cute. A lot too cute. "They're shell mounds," she said, knowing this already.

"Exactly." He let the word fall between them as she rounded the sofa and took a seat not quite on the other end, not quite next to him, but close enough to reach her wine.

She lifted the glass and touched his bottle with a soft clink. "Is that what you came here to tell me?"

He shook his head. "I came here to tell you I acted like an ass last night."

The honesty in his voice caught her off guard, and she tried to cover with a sip of wine. Setting the glass down, she inched back into the sofa. "I wouldn't call it an 'ass.'"

"What would you call it?"

"A guy." She smiled. "A normal guy, even. A guy who wants to, you know, fool around and have fun and not be bogged down by some woo-woo shit about fated destiny."

"You're being too easy on me," he said with a soft laugh of appreciation. "You don't have to do that."

"Yes, I do. I'm the one—"

"No, apparently, *I'm* the one, Arielle." He pinned her with those green-gold eyes again, holding her, no accusation in the expression, just...understanding. Which just about did her in.

"Well," she said quickly, reaching for the laptop, hoping if she ignored the whole thing, he would, too. "I have learned an awful lot about the Native Americans who lived here, and I'm more certain than ever that we found at least some worthwhile—"

"Arielle." He put his hand on her forearm, capturing it the very way he did the moment they'd met. And nothing since then had changed—she was still electrified.

"Don't change the subject," he said.

"Don't embarrass me," she replied.

"You? How do you think I feel?"

She choked in disbelief. "Are you serious?"

"Listen to me." He put the beer bottle on the table with a thud, still not taking his eyes off her. "'Cause I'm here to tell you, you..." He blew out a breath as though it pained him to finish. "You picked the wrong guy."

She didn't *pick* anyone, but obviously he didn't get that.

"I...I can't be that person for you," he said.

A little light popped in her head, and this had nothing to do with the Great White Lights of attraction. "Luke, I haven't asked you for a thing," she said. "I haven't made any pronouncements about who or what you are to me."

"I know that—"

"You don't know anything," she shot back. "You've jumped to conclusions, and you're basing them on two things—the fact that I told you I wanted to have sex only with the man I'm destined to love and the assumption that I have some kind of supernatural ability to know that man when I meet him."

He still didn't take his eyes from her. "Are those conclusions or assumptions wrong?"

No. "It doesn't matter. You've made them, and it's embarrassing, as I said, and none of this really matters because—"

He kissed her so hard she gasped, the contact hot and fast and unexpected. She tried to back away, but he came with her, intent and serious.

"What are you doing?" she asked.

He stayed perfectly still for a moment before whispering, "I feel it, too."

What? She mouthed the word, but she was certain he got the idea.

After a second, he dropped back on the sofa, clearly bewildered. "Are you sure this isn't just plain old run-of-the-mill lust?"

"No, I'm not sure of that. Not sure of anything," she admitted. Except that kiss was perfection and not nearly long enough. "What did you feel, Luke?"

"When I kissed you? All kinds of stupid things that I never felt before. Snapping, popping sounds in my head. An ache in my…my…here." He tapped his chest hard, as though the feeling angered the shit out of him. "My arms are, like, weak." Disgust darkened his voice. "And what the hell is that buzzing in my head?"

She couldn't help it. A laugh slipped out.

He glared at her.

"I'm sorry, I know it's not funny, but…" *It's real*. She almost jumped up and danced around the room and reached up her hands to thank the universe. "I know how you feel," she said instead, unbelievably calm on the outside considering what was going on inside.

Very slowly, he started shaking his head. "I don't do love."

She let that new information settle over her like an itchy, uncomfortable drape of mohair. Who didn't "do" love?

Reaching for the wine, she took another deep drink, fortifying herself. He did the same with his beer, probably because this was a really weird conversation to have with someone you've known for only three days.

Except that it wasn't, which made it weirder.

"Okay, I'll bite… Why don't you 'do' love?" She couldn't help mocking the word. Who "did" love? It just happened. Or not.

He rubbed his lips together, as if he had to taste the beer on them again. "I'm going to tell you what I can. There's a…code, for lack of a better word, that prevents me from telling you more."

A Foreign Legion code or his personal code? Better not to ask, at least not yet. "Okay."

He finished the beer in another slug, then dropped back to recline on the armrest, where it would be so damn easy and fun and nice to…join him. Climb on top or next to him. Stroke his rough whiskers and rub his big chest and touch his—

"I had a bad experience with love."

She coughed softly. "As excuses go, that's pretty crappy."

He closed his eyes, so she used the freedom to drink in the length of his torso, his narrow hips, angled as he half-sat, half-lay on her sofa. He lifted his arms and locked his hands under his head, the position accentuating his sizable biceps and giving her an uninterrupted view of his chest.

Had she really promised herself celibacy? Couldn't that promise be broken...*just this once*?

"I was in love once," he said, ripping her lusty thoughts from his body back to his words. He lifted his head an inch, looking at her from under thick lashes. "Have you been?"

Did *this* count? No, of course not. She shook her head, and he let his fall back. "Well, I'm here to tell you that it's painful when it ends"—he rooted around for a word—"*unpleasantly*. Viciously painful." His voice cracked as if he felt that pain right now, and Ari's heart tipped from side to side as she imagined what kind of woman could inflict pain on this special man.

"I learned that you can love someone with your entire heart and soul and still not trust them." His words were rough, as though they shredded his throat on the way out. "And that makes me wonder if there really is such a thing as love. Because I thought it was love, but it wasn't...real."

Welcome to my life, she thought wryly. "So what happened?"

For what felt like five minutes—but was probably less than one—he didn't move. His chest didn't rise or fall, his pulse didn't appear to beat, his jaw didn't tighten or relax. He stayed still.

And then he sat up enough that she could see the

moisture in his eyes, and when he blinked, a single tear meandered from the corner of one.

Instantly, her heart folded, because she just knew. That look could mean only one thing. Without thinking, she crawled right over that torso she'd been studying, reaching up to him, lying on top of him, needing to do everything to comfort him.

"Oh, Luke. She died?"

"Yeah."

"I'm so sorry."

"Don't be. It was…" He swallowed again, clearly fighting tears. "Don't be sorry for me."

And then she realized what was wrong. He was The One for her, but he'd already met his destined love…and lost her. "Sometimes the universe isn't fair." This time, it was her throat ripped by the words.

"No shit."

Just letting the story out—a bit of the story—should have made Luke feel better, but his body betrayed him. Every cell was on fire for Arielle when he should be at least *remembering* Cerisse.

He sighed into the pressure of her body, the softness of her breasts right there under a flimsy top, her nipples practically screaming, *Touch me!*—all of it making him feel like shit. After Cerisse, he'd sworn off relationships, especially with incredible women who had love on the brain.

"Trust me, I'm not cut out for what you have in mind," he said.

"I think we've established that you don't know what I

have in mind." Arielle tried to sit up, but Luke instinctively snatched her back, wrapping both arms like steel bands around her, refusing to let her go.

He lifted his legs from the floor, grateful to have ditched his shoes, and stretched out on the sofa, getting her right where he wanted her, where he *needed* her. Because he'd never needed anything so much as the womanly curves of her body on his, crushing out his admissions and making him remember how good a female could feel.

Really good.

"No," he agreed. "But if what you're thinking has anything to do with *love*, it's not going to happen." He kissed the top of her head, as if that could take the sting out of his words, and slid her an inch to the left so she wasn't directly over his dick, which might decide it didn't care a bit about love or loss or *what she had in mind.*

"You need to tell me more," she said, leaning up enough to look at him. "And quit moving. Or...not."

He smiled at the bit of innuendo. "I'm sorry, I can't."

She narrowed her eyes to near slits. "There has to be more you can tell me."

Maybe he could tell her some, but not all. He couldn't tell her what happened, or how it ended. Mostly because he couldn't stand to relive the moment and watch the sexy compassion in her eyes fade to horror and disappointment when she learned the truth about him.

He brushed some hairs off her face, stroking the strands he liked so much, taking a few seconds to let his knuckles brush her cheek. He had to take this conversation in another direction...the obvious and only direction. "God, you're beautiful."

"Thank you. Good delay tactic."

"It's not." But it was. "You *are* beautiful." He wrapped a

long, silken thread of hair around his finger, searching her face, looking for a flaw that wasn't there.

"Was she?"

He swallowed. "Very."

"You're not over her."

"I'm over her," he assured her. "It's been four years." He pulled her closer. "Four long, dry years." Oh, shit. Why did he tell her that? Now she'd think he was some kind of weird monk desperado.

She blinked. "You haven't been with anyone since then?"

"Is this the celibate girl sounding shocked?"

"But…but…you're…"

"A guy, I know."

"And a hot one."

His mouth softened into a grin. "You're hot, too, but it hasn't made you go out and get lucky."

"I'm serious." She tried to sit up again, but he refused to release even an inch of her. "What are you waiting for?"

"Not what *you're* waiting for," he said dryly.

"Then what is it?"

He couldn't answer that without telling her the whole story. So he didn't answer, playing with her hair some more, liking the way it tickled his neck as it tumbled down.

"Luke?"

He met her gaze. "I don't know what I'm waiting for," he said. "Just being careful, I suppose."

She eased herself to the side, laying a hand on his heart. "Is that all?"

Oh, of course. She could *read* him. So he better be honest. "It hurt a lot when it ended." Now, there was an understatement for the excruciating pain that had torn through his heart and soul in the months after he left French Guiana. "Enough that I don't want to risk anything serious again."

She settled closer to him, and he turned so they were face-to-face and body-to-body along the length of the sofa. "Who was she? Another soldier?"

He shook his head. "No women in the Legion. Her father was an important government official in French Guiana, and I was assigned to be his bodyguard."

She frowned slightly. "Not what I thought the French Foreign Legion does."

"There's a lot of things the Legion does that no one knows about, but that was a particularly dangerous part of the world."

She gave him a sharp look. "French Guiana? Why?"

"Not going to say." The fewer people who knew about the illegal gold mining in Guiana, and the Legion's dark and dirty efforts to stop it, the better. Plus, it felt like he was betraying...someone who'd already suffered enough because of what happened.

"I can see you as a bodyguard," she said, trailing a finger over his chest.

"Best job of my life," he said. "Fit like a glove on me, with none of the stupid effing red tape of being a contractor."

She looked up. "So, why don't you do that instead of building houses?"

He lifted a shoulder, feigning casual. "They like a law enforcement background."

"You were in the Foreign Legion, for heaven's sake. I would think that qualifies." As he started to reply, she put her hand on his mouth. "And don't give me this 'people don't respect that operation' business, because Gussie already told me that, and I'm not buying it. If you want to work in that field, why don't you?"

"I tried," he said. "Good friend of mine I met on a

mission in Somalia comes from a family who have a security business up in Boston, so when I was up there with Gussie, I went to their offices in Back Bay."

"And?"

His friend's cousin was some badass former Army Ranger with an eye patch, and that guy would have no sympathy for what happened on Luke's one and only legit bodyguard assignment. "When I got there, I just didn't feel it, you know?"

She gave him a look that said she didn't know, but let it drop. "What was her name?"

He couldn't tell her anyone's name. "Classified," he murmured.

"Funny name."

He gave her a look. "It is and it will stay that way, okay?"

She blinked at his tone. "Okay, but can you tell me what happened that made you swear off all women?"

"I did tell you. She...died." A bloody, brutal, unforgettable death.

"And so you'll never give anyone else a chance?" The question was soft, not much more than air.

"I don't deserve it." He ground out the words, hating the sound of them. The truth of them.

"Love or sex?"

He looked at her. "You don't think there is a difference," he said, a slight tone of accusation in his voice. "Am I right?"

"We're not talking about me, Luke. We're talking about you."

Touché. "I swore off heartache and misery, which turned into swearing off sex for a while. A long while." Just saying the word sex made him a little harder, and his body totally betrayed him by rocking ever so slightly into her. "Too long of a while," he admitted on a sigh.

She sucked in a soft breath as if he'd actually touched bare skin.

"We're like a couple of firecrackers with short fuses," she said.

"How long for you?"

"It had been a while since I'd been seeing anyone seriously before Grandma Good Bear died and I made her that promise, so almost three years total."

"Shit," he murmured softly. "That's seven years between us. That's crazy."

"Four years for you?" Her voice rose in disbelief. "That's insane."

"Probably not healthy, either."

She gave him a slow smile. "We might be killing ourselves and not even realize it."

"I'm sure we are." Because this conversation was killing him. Along with her body and hair and the hungry look in her eyes. "Arielle, we should…"

"Masturbate."

He choked out a belly laugh. "Trust me, I do."

"Me, too. But it'd be more fun with a partner." She leaned up to look at him. "I'm torn, Luke. I want to wait for that…that person. And I want to have sex with you. And I want those two things not to ruin each other."

Her eyes were damp with tears, raw and honest tears. "What should we do?" she asked.

Oh, the answers he had to that question. "We could…do other things than sex."

She laughed. "I think we've been doing that for a few days."

"No, I mean…" He moved his hand over her body. "Not everything. Some things." God, he was as bad as a teenager begging for a blow job.

"That might work." She didn't say anything for a long time, but very slowly, so slowly he wasn't sure what was happening, she slid her leg over his calf, and his thigh, straddling him. "Or it might make things worse."

"Let's find out, Little Mermaid." He couldn't take his eyes from her, but moved his hands along her arm, over her shoulder, sliding down to her breast.

Her lips parted with a soft, soft inhale, her nipple budding against his fingertips.

Neither one of them said a word or kissed or moved with any kind of fierce, frustrated anxiousness. Everything was slow and still and silent and…almost secret.

Using two fingers, he picked up the cotton of her T-shirt, piece by piece, lifting it higher and higher. While he did, she spread her fingers over his hip then slowly slid her palm down until she…

Oh, God. Covered the bulge in his jeans.

He touched her nipple. She stroked the denim. He palmed her breast. She rocked her hips against him. They both melted a little deeper into each other, lost.

Her skin was so soft. So damn smooth. She pressed again, harder, until he rolled on his back and brought her with him, putting her body on top so she could rub his full erection.

He almost howled when she did, bowing her back, giving him access to her breasts. She closed her eyes and let out a whimper that fell somewhere between satisfaction and frustration, riding him harder as he lifted his head to suckle her.

Her hair tumbled everywhere, her hips moved faster, and his erection slammed against his pants, dangerously, dangerously close to detonation.

Moaning, she dropped onto his chest, still writhing on

him, kissing and kissing until they were both breathless and lost, until he felt her whole body jerk with a wicked, fast orgasm that ripped a groan from her throat.

His dick pulsed against her as she rested on him for a second, silent but for ragged breaths.

"That was better than my vibrator."

He managed a laugh. "Talk about damning with faint praise."

She finally lifted her head. "Thanks for not making fun of me having a vibrator."

"Hey, I use my fist."

The corners of her mouth lifted. "I have one of those."

He almost said, *Use it.* Almost. But something stopped him. He didn't want to jack off in her hand. He didn't even want her mouth on him. Not the first time.

No, he wanted to be inside her, all the way, buried. Deep. Lost. Complete. "Let's wait," he said, almost disbelieving that the words had come out of his mouth.

"For what?" She sounded equally disbelieving. And disappointed.

He kissed her nose, then cheek, and finished with his lips over her mouth. "For next time."

"Nothing's going to change, Luke. I still want The One, and you…you are fighting some mighty powerful demons."

Damn it. Slowly, he untangled them and eased her off his aching body, silent because what could he say to that allegation? Other than, *The truth hurts.* And he hadn't really told her anything. Those demons were way darker than she knew.

"Can I ask you a question, Luke?"

"Sure."

"What did it feel like? With her? The French woman who broke your heart."

Of course. The woo-woo girl would want to know about the feelings. "You mean the sex?"

"I mean…when you met her and touched her and kissed her. How did you feel?"

He thought about it for a second, then shrugged. "Not like this," he admitted. "None of the…"

"Lights, buzz, and heart expansion?"

He smiled. "No, none of the special effects."

"So, then, maybe it wasn't real."

He looked at her for a long time, the possibility so new and untested, he wasn't sure what to make of it. Except… "Maybe it wasn't," he agreed.

Chapter Fifteen

Luke took the scenic route to Fort Myers Beach, wending up the coast past shops, hotels, and a preserve. Once they were on the grounds of Mound House, Ari was relaxed enough to let the history of the place wash over her like a waterfall on a summer day. She wasn't imagining that; the awareness settled deep in her bones, filling her heart.

She should have made this trip sooner; the whole place felt *right* to her.

And Luke McBain felt right, too. He'd left last night, after a few more long—and longing—kisses and come back bright and early for the trip to Mound House. He'd insisted he wanted to go out of interest and curiosity, but something told her he wanted to spend time with her.

Which was just fine.

She'd had a restless night, with a lot of replaying of every word, kiss, touch, and...possibilities. She'd awakened with a zillion questions about the "classified" woman, even though her intuition told her loud and clear not to go there. Maybe ever.

But that left Luke off-limits, at least emotionally. He could probably be on-limits for sex, based on the crazy connection they'd had on the sofa last night. Would she settle for that? Could she not? How long could they keep their hands off each other? she wondered.

"Do you feel that?" He stuck his hand out the window.

He felt it, too? "That's history in the air," she told him.

He threw her a look. "Um, I meant the humidity. It's going to rain today, and that always delays construction. I hope Duane finishes getting the silt fence up."

She shook her head, laughing. "Always the pragmatist."

"Always," he agreed. "But since you mentioned it, what does history feel like?"

"It's hard to explain." She looked out her window at the emerald foliage of Florida dotting the sides of the road.

"I won't make fun of you, Arielle," he promised after she didn't answer for a few seconds.

"Why don't you call me Ari, like everyone else?"

He grinned at her. "How many times do I have to tell you I'm not like everyone else?"

And how many times did she have to tell him she knew that the minute they'd met? But she didn't remind him now. They'd talked enough about it, and today she wanted to relax, meet with Dr. David Marksman, give the archaeologist some of her samples, and enjoy the museum and the beauty of the place.

"Really, I'm curious and not being the least bit facetious," he said. "How does one 'feel' history?"

His question, and the look that came with it, felt genuine, so she nodded, gathering her explanation so she used the right words. Honest words.

"There's a certain pressure that I feel sometimes," she said, tapping her chest. "My grandma used to call it tribal compassion."

He shot her a look, the hint of a smile on his face. "I'm sorry," he said instantly. "I swear I'm not laughing. It's your voice. It's cute when you're so serious."

She narrowed her eyes. "I'm a lot of things, Luke, but 'cute' isn't one of them."

"Note to self," he mumbled. "Arielle isn't cute. Gorgeous, sexy, kind of adorable, but not cute."

Her heart tripped. Why did he do that? And how? "We'll see how adorable I am when Dr. Marksman confirms that my samples are priceless treasures."

"Why would that make you any less adorable?"

"Because it will make me fight harder for not flattening that hill in North Barefoot Bay."

He shook his head, rounding a wide bend in the road. "If you've unearthed priceless treasures in that house, you have my word I will not demolish one inch of the house until it has been thoroughly and completely searched for more. But that has nothing to do with the land Cutter Valentine wants leveled. If that's made of crushed shells, like we think—and I told you I'm having the sample checked again—then we can level it with no harm done."

His words—and all the sense they made—hung in the truck. But something didn't feel right to Ari.

"Did you bring the sample that Michelle gave us?"

"I have it in the back and an appointment to take it to another geological firm. Why?"

"Would you be willing to leave a small bit with Dr. Marksman, for his opinion?"

"Of course. Hey, look at that." As they turned the corner into the acreage that surrounded Mound House, the trees opened up to show sloping grounds, emerald green and lush with palm trees and brightly blooming hibiscus. Atop the hill was the restored mansion, the cream stucco gleaming in the sun with balanced balconies and floor-to-ceiling windows giving the instant air of a Southern plantation house.

It all looked out over a vast view of Estero Bay, an expanse of deep blue under a cloud-scattered sky.

"They call it Case House," Ari said. "Lots of history, changed family hands, and recently renovated to match what it looked like in 1921."

"Built on an Indian mound."

"It was a different century," she reminded him. "And the estate has given a ton of money to re-create parts of the actual village that was here thousands of years ago." She gave him a nudge. "Maybe Cutter would go for that."

"Doubtful."

"At least the current owners and curators have tried to honor the history and heritage over the years. But back when it was built, they hadn't had too many concerns about history, which is the way it is all over this country. Oh, and"—she smiled—"they say it's haunted."

He snorted softly and pulled into the lot, parking next to a school bus. A group of kids were standing on the lawn, being talked to by a tour guide or teacher, and another group of older tourists piled out of a minivan.

"We're early for our meeting with Dr. Marksman," Ari said. "Want to take a tour?"

He eyed the house and students, then shrugged as he came around the truck to join her. "Sure." He slipped his hand into hers. "If you do."

Still holding hands, they bought tickets and joined a small group of retirees, listening to a museum docent recite the history that Ari had read about the night before. The house had changed hands, been through hurricanes, undergone multiple restorations, but in the past fifteen years, the focus shifted from the history of the families who lived here to the archaeological treasures below ground.

As the small group rounded the outside of the building and walked down a set of stone steps to the underground exhibit that had been built into the mound, Ari experienced a powerful wave of déjà vu.

She hadn't been here before, but she'd been to so many similar places with her grandmother, who was often moved to tears before they'd even entered the sacred sites.

"You okay?" Luke whispered as they reached the bottom.

"Yes, why?" Could he tell how this affected her?

"You just shivered, and it's about a hundred and fifty degrees in the shade."

She smiled, leaning into him for the sheer pleasure of feeling his muscles. "You know, for a hardheaded realist who doesn't believe in anything he can't see or touch, you're pretty intuitive."

He gave her hand a squeeze. "Only when someone has my full attention."

The tour guide cleared her throat and started on the next segment of her speech, but Ari and Luke held each other's gaze for a long beat. When the doors opened to the exhibit, he slipped his arm around her and kept her tucked into his side as they walked by murals depicting the tribe's simple, fish-centric life.

Ari tried to think about the Calusa, how they were like and, in some ways, unlike the Miwok blended in her blood. But her body betrayed her and she forgot about everything but the strength and size and heat of Luke, the woodsy, masculine smell, the timbre of his voice when he whispered a comment or laughed.

He might want to "wait" for them to be physical, he might think he was the wrong choice as The One, and he

might truly be planning to desecrate land she'd fight to save...but all of that disappeared every time she looked at him and melted a little.

For someone who claimed to be intuitive, she sure was having a hard time figuring out who this man was and what he meant to her.

"...as you can see from the timeline." The tour guide's words drifted in and out of Ari's ears, much of the information lost to far more personal thoughts. She shook those off and stood before a timeline along the wall, trying to follow the history that stretched back thousands and thousands of years.

"The great Calusa disappeared in the late 1700s, after Spanish settlers forced them to spread and, sadly, die off," the tour guide said, "but not until this glorious tribe left their mark on the land."

"A mark that needs to be honored," she whispered to Luke.

He gave her a look she couldn't quite read and guided her deeper into the exhibit until they reached the archaeological section, which showed the layers of shell, fish bones, earth, and pottery shards that formed the foundations for temples and homes, and, of course, burial sites. In the paintings, she saw some of the very tools she had packed in the crate in Luke's truck, making her certain that she had found something valuable.

While they were given time to look at things alone, Ari took a moment to admire a mural that showed a Calusa family fishing and cooking while children played and another depicting a man painting a mask probably like the one Lacey's grandfather had found. Of course these people could have taken a boat down the coast to Mimosa Key and created a settlement there.

Luke stayed close, silent and serious, as they studied the artwork. "A lot of history here," he said.

She looked up at him. "If my grandmother were here, she'd be crying."

"Why?"

"She was a big mushball who cried over everything, especially when she discovered something about a new tribe. I don't ever remember her talking about the Calusa. They weren't famous like Cherokee and Sioux, but I can feel how much they mattered." She rubbed her bare arms. "Powerful," she added softly.

He angled his head, enough uncertainty in his eyes to break her heart. "Arielle, this building was constructed in the year 2000 to replicate something that has been gone for centuries. How can you feel anything?"

"I understand your skepticism, Luke, but the aura is here." She didn't want to argue the point, and it was nearing the time for her meeting, so she gave him a soft push toward the door. "Let's get the crate and take it to Dr. Marksman's office."

They slipped away from the group and headed back to the truck. Luke also opened the samples from GeoTech, carefully transferred a small amount of the shells into a spare plastic bag that Ari had brought, and carried it all with great gentleness and care to the small office complex.

Doubtful one minute, respectful the next. No wonder she was confused about this man.

The Wayampi.

Memories swamped Luke as he strode toward the

building where the archaeologist worked, vaguely aware that Ari was a few steps behind him. He was surprised by how the murals and museum pieces had affected him, yanking him back to the sights and sounds of Camopi, a village just outside a malaria-infested jungle along the northeast corner of South America.

The Wayampi believed the land, and the gold, belonged to them.

The country of France felt differently, of course, and that's why they sent platoons of Legionnaires to make sure the Wayampi knew it. But they were people—with feelings and customs, and a deep-seated spirituality not unlike what stirred Arielle's soul. They were families, just like the one in that mural. They were children who should run and play. But there was one who never would again.

And that's why he needed to work—here or across the Atlantic. He had to have a constant stream of income. *Had to.* He swallowed hard, sweat stinging his neck.

"You can wait here," Arielle said, yanking him from his thoughts as they reached a wraparound wooden porch. "I'll just…" She frowned at him. "Are you okay?"

Shit, was he that transparent or could she really read minds? "I'm fine," he lied.

"You don't look fine. You look upset."

Taking a deep breath, he set the crate on the ground, using as much care as possible. "It's hot as hell out here, Ari."

"No, it's not," she said. "You're upset about something. It's coming off you like bad cologne."

He couldn't help smiling. "Bad cologne? Is that how you read people's thoughts?"

"I'm not reading your thoughts, Luke. I'm watching your expression."

He shook his head. "I'll stay here with the crate. You go in and find your doctor. Then come and tell me where he wants me to take this stuff."

She disappeared inside, and he dropped onto the top step, looking out over the grounds and hills, all the way to the gulf. He closed his eyes for a moment, all the images and stories from the tour they'd just taken playing with his imagination, making him wonder what life was like here fifteen hundred years ago.

God, he was as bad as Arielle now.

He leaned back against the railing post, one hand protectively on the crate, the shade of the overhang welcome. His mind drifted far from Florida, across the world to another swampy, hot place, the smell of the jungle, the distant splash of a pirogue making its way down the river, the realization that he'd been set up, the certainty that the woman he loved was a cold-blooded murderer.

Everyone's on the take, Ricard! It's gold! Gold! He could still hear her screaming in French, using his fake name. He was transported to that moment when he realized she didn't even know his name, so how could she love him? That moment when it hit him that Cerisse didn't love him at all…she loved gold more. That moment when he had to make a split decision about who to kill.

Not whether he *should* kill, but who would die? What right did he have to make that decision in the span of a single heartbeat?

He could hear that young boy's voice, a mix of French and unintelligible ancient Wayampi words. He had to do something. He had to—

"Luke? Luke?"

He shook off her touch, jerking to sit straight.

"Luke, are you all right?" Arielle leaned closer, concern

in her eyes but fire in her touch. Always, always warmth from her. "Are you crying?" She whispered the last word, with shock.

He swiped at his cheeks. "Hell no. Sweating my balls off."

She fought a smile. "Dr. Marksman wants to see the samples," she said, her hand still on his arm. "He's right here."

Luke rose immediately—too fast, actually—but managed to shake off the momentary blackness around his vision. He peered at an older man with a deeply lined face and rimless glasses over kind blue eyes.

"David Marksman," the man said, extending his hand. "Nice to meet you."

Luke went through the motions of the introduction, still a little stunned at how the memories had crept up and attacked him. Because he'd been thinking about Cerisse last night, remembering why he couldn't give his heart to this awesome woman. Because he'd done that once, and his bullet had gone right through her heart.

"Why don't I bring this inside?" Luke suggested.

But the older man had already crouched down and looked at Ari for permission to open the crate. She nodded and got next to him, while Luke accepted the fact that he wasn't going to get air conditioning any time soon.

"This one on top"—Arielle reached in and lifted the first item, slowly unwrapping the tissue—"I think it's a gorge."

She revealed a narrow shell less than two inches long, worn to a point on either end. Luke had probably stepped on a hundred things that looked like that on beaches around the world. What made her see—

The older man's eyes lit up. "I believe you're right!"

Whatever it was, the elderly archaeologist saw the same

169

thing. He lifted the shell with care, placing it in his palm as if he'd been given the Hope Diamond. "They'd tie a string around the center and drop it in the water. The points would get trapped in the fish mouth." He chucked a little. "Turkey bone, I'd say, but we'd need to do more research. What else do you have?" he asked, his voice rising with excitement.

"Wait until you see this." Arielle chose the next wrapped item, a look of expectation dancing in her eyes as she revealed it. "A hammer stone?"

He took the round rock, rubbing his thumb over an indentation. "Or a mortar. Did you find something that fit inside that could have been a pestle?"

"I did, covered in coral shells." She lifted a few more packages and produced another with the flair of a magician. "Look at this one."

Dr. Marksman's eyes widened, and he actually gasped. He *definitely* saw something a layman would miss. The archaeologist's hands trembled as he reached for the clump of brown stones that looked like they'd been glued together in the shape of a small ice cream cone. "Where did you get this?"

"I told you, in the house that—"

"This, too?" He looked at her with something close to rapture in his eyes, a touch of a mad-scientist thing going on. "They were all in the crate together? Are there more like this?"

"None exactly like that," she said. "But plenty of others."

He nodded, spotted hands lovingly caressing the coral-encrusted piece. "This is…amazing."

"I know, right?" Ari beamed at the man, then up at Luke. "I told you!"

Luke smiled back, her enthusiasm infectious.

Dr. Marksman finally stood, wiping his hands together

excitedly. "We'll do carbon dating on these and some microscopic examinations. These could be thousands of years old, or as recent as a few hundred. We can probably narrow some down to within a century, I think." He put a fatherly hand on Arielle's shoulder. "Miss Chandler, this is truly an extraordinary find. Please tell me I can set up an archaeological team to investigate further."

Whoa. *Whoa.* "You're turning the property into an archaeological dig?" Luke asked.

"If that's where these samples came from, how can you do anything else?" the man asked.

"Because someone owns the property and wants to live there," Luke said, knowing already that this was probably a lost cause. *Shit.*

He gave a look to Arielle, seeking support. They'd agreed he'd save the house and have the other company look at the samples, but they'd never talked about an archaeological dig.

"You are aware of the laws surrounding this," Dr. Marksman said, obviously unaware of any of those arrangements. "Under the Native American Graves Protection and Repatriation Act, private-property owners are not forced to turn over land for archaeological inspection unless actual remains are found in the ground or the artifacts are considered sacred."

"A mortar and pestle are sacred?" Luke asked. "A fishhook?"

He shook his head. "No, they would not qualify. The decision to turn over the land and, point of fact, the artifacts, is up to the owner. Is that you?"

"No," Luke said. "I'm the builder."

For a moment, none of them spoke, but the gazes of the other two were firm on him, as if to say, *Well, you know the right thing to do.*

His life and situation didn't matter, not as much as a little boy who now had only one leg because of a decision Luke had made on one dark, dark night.

Blowing out a soft breath, Luke looked down at the bag from the core sampling. Wordlessly, he picked it up. "Why don't you take some of this, too, and run your tests on it? We need to know if these are just broken shells or something...sacred."

Arielle looked up at him like he'd hung the moon and painted her name across it. "Oh, Luke."

He gave a quick *it's nothing* wave. He didn't deserve her admiration or her affection or her hero worship. He was no hero. Quite the opposite, in fact.

Chapter Sixteen

They didn't exactly avoid each other for the next several days, but Ari and Luke managed not to tempt fate by spending any time alone. Their meetings were still charged with an undercurrent that Ari was only starting to get used to, but with friends and family around, they managed to keep their hands off each other and their conversations light.

Ari tried to throw herself into work, even going in to catch up on e-mails and correspondence on a Sunday morning, like she was now.

But no matter how busy she kept herself and how casual she kept the conversations when she saw Luke, her feelings only intensified. Along with her questions. Was this real or imagined? Was he The One or just a hot guy who stole her attention? Would she go through with trying to stop the work at the property and ruin his chances of building a career here? And if he left, would she lose Gussie's friendship, too?

Ari pondered the questions over and over, but the only answer she got was the loud rumble of hunger in her stomach reminding her she'd missed lunch.

"I could fix that."

She spun in her desk chair toward the sound of Luke's voice, startled and stupidly happy to see him.

"How about a picnic up on Barefoot Mountain to silence your starvation?"

Speaking of starvation. One look at him, at his slightly sly smile and slightly crooked nose and not so slightly sexy body, and she was...hungry. And not for a picnic.

"I'd love that." She was up and snagging her handbag in a flash. "What's the occasion?"

"I've spent the last few days on the mainland, in offices, meeting with subs, and haven't been to the property in quite a while." His smile deepened his dimples. "And I haven't been alone with you for two, no, make that *three* days."

He was counting. "Is that a long time?"

He slipped an arm around her and led her out the door. "Interminable. Plus, I lost a bet with myself."

Laughing, she let him lead her out. "Who does that? Bets himself and loses?"

"Apparently, me."

"What did you bet?"

He grinned as he opened the door for her and leaned close to her ear to whisper, "That I could make it four days without kissing you."

She almost melted. "I meant, what was on the table?"

"Oh, you'll see. I brought the winnings for you. But I don't have lunch, which is a key part of any picnic. We can stop at the convenience store and get sandwiches, okay?"

She'd probably have agreed to eat leaves at that point. "Sandwiches and a nice grill from Charity, the owner of the Super Min."

He gave her a questioning look. "There's a grill in there?"

"Not the kind you're thinking of."

They chatted about nothing on the way, but every word felt weighty. Everything he said seemed to matter, regardless of the topic, and when she replied, he appeared to hang on whatever she said. Why was everything so intensified with him? Was it always like this, or just because they hadn't been alone in several days?

Who cared? Right now, she just wanted to bury her unanswered questions and enjoy Luke.

At the convenience store, he parked and got out, coming around as always to open her door, a spark in his eyes as he let his gaze travel over the simple T-shirt and jeans she'd chosen for a no-meeting day at work.

"Is it ridiculous to say I've missed you?" he asked.

Not in the least. She took his hand and climbed down to the cracked asphalt parking lot, stealing a whiff of his familiar, masculine scent. "I missed you, too."

Satisfied with that, he walked her inside, the welcome bell dinged, and they got the usual stare-down from Charity Grambling, as Ari had expected. The older woman's steel-gray gaze shifted to Luke and stayed there, curious and questioning, also as expected.

Charity lifted a heavily drawn brow, making Ari smile as Luke guided her toward the cold drinks and wrapped sandwiches. At the refrigerated case, Luke leaned closer to whisper, "Why does she keep staring at me?"

"Because you're new in town and she is the nosiest and most opinionated person on the entire island," she replied under her breath. "She wants to know your name, occupation, closest relative in Barefoot Bay and, most importantly, who you spend nights with. Be prepared, that information will be filed, evaluated, and shared with the next six customers."

His lips drawn into a tight line, he nodded. "Good to

know." At the counter, he set down the purchases and finally met Charity's exacting gaze.

"Luke McBain." He reached his hand out. "Brother of Gussie, and"—he glanced at Ari and grinned—"my overnight company is still TBD." He leaned over the counter and winked. "Can I let you know tomorrow?"

Charity was not amused, but Ari's stomach took a drop down an imaginary roller coaster.

"You forgot your occupation," Charity said dryly, then pierced Ari with a look. "You whisper quite loudly, you know."

"You'll have to guess," he said.

She curled a lip, looking him up and down. "Well, you're not one of the high-flying billionaires, obviously. And not built like a baseball player, so you can't be one of them. Military? Friend of that Navy SEAL trying to pound out the great American novel?"

"Not a billionaire, baseball player, or current military. I'm a builder."

She adjusted her glasses, showing mild interest. "Whatever you're building, it better be to code or you'll have the town council to answer to. And by that, I mean me."

"Trust me, if there's a hoop, I'm jumping through it."

"What are you building?" she demanded.

He stared at her, and Ari laughed softly. "She won't ring us up until she knows, Luke."

He angled his head in acknowledgment. "A house. In North Barefoot Bay."

"On the old Valentine property?" The woman's many wrinkles deepened as she frowned. "You're not the builder."

"New builder," he corrected, nodding to show he was impressed by her skills. "The last one was fired."

Charity's jaw dropped with a soft gasp. "What? No one told me."

"And that's a felony, I bet," Luke joked.

But she refused to laugh. Instead, she leaned forward, her silvery eyes tapering to slits as though the whole challenge of the game turned her on. "Man died up there. You know that, Mr. Smartass?"

"I've heard." Luke slid a look to Ari as if to plead for help. She shrugged. There was no getting around Charity Grambling. If you wanted to buy something at the Shell Gas Station and Super Mini Mart Convenience Store, you had to go through interrogation by either Charity Grambling or her sister, Patience Vail, and neither one was charitable or patient.

"I met that man," she said, sounding miffed that the previous builder hadn't reported in to tell her he'd lost the job. "He had a nasty black tattoo on his shoulder." She almost smiled. "I nailed him but good."

"How so?" Luke asked.

She folded her arms. "His tattoo read, 'Only God can judge me.' And I pointed right at the words and said, 'Yet, here I am.'" She laughed, but it dissolved into a smoker's wheeze.

"Clever," Luke said.

"Been a lot of action up there, I hear," Charity said when her cough ended.

"Not enough," he replied.

"Then maybe you don't know your own job, honey. Because there was some other guy in here at the crack of dawn yesterday on his way up there to do work."

"I think you're confused."

That got him a deadly look. "I might be old and ugly, Green Eyes, but I am not confused. Guy stood right here, bought a Red Bull and a *Mimosa Gazette*, and asked if I knew any way up to Barefoot Mountain other than the road that goes past the resort."

"Is there?" Luke asked.

"Sure, if you're crafty and lived here long enough." Apparently satisfied, she tapped fiery-orange nails on the cash register, and then held out her hand, demanding money.

"To pay for the privilege of being cross-examined," Luke joked as he handed her a twenty.

She snapped it out of his hand. "I prefer to think of it as small talk," she said. "What military?"

"'Scuze me?"

"You said 'not current military.' So, what branch of the military were you in?"

He didn't answer, but stared at her as if he resented the question. But Ari knew him well enough to know he just didn't want to answer it.

"I think you've interrogated this poor man enough for one day," she said, the need to protect him strong and sudden. "And you haven't even asked me about Willow's wedding. Don't you want to hear who got sloppy drunk?"

"No one. I already had five people in here telling me it was all classy and upscale and la-di-dah. Also heard that the other bridal consultant"—she pointed a talon at Luke—"your sister, roped that big-time photographer into marrying her." Charity crossed her arms, swimming in smug. "Guess who introduced those two right here in the Super Min?"

Ari snagged the sodas while Luke took the bag of food. "I'm sure they'll want to get married here," he said. "And you can officiate."

For a moment, Charity almost smiled, but then caught herself. "I like the way you think, Green Eyes."

Ari gave Luke a light push toward the door. "You never know, Charity. We plan all kinds of weddings."

They were out of target range and in the parking lot a few seconds later.

"Is she for real?" he asked with a mix of humor and dismay.

"She's a fact of life around here."

Luke held the truck door for her and offered his hand to help her climb up, but Ari didn't move. "Can I ask you a question, Luke?" She punctuated that by putting her hand in his.

"I feel like I've been asked enough." But he closed his fingers around hers, and his eyes registered the same bolt of electricity that she felt every single time they touched. "Go ahead," he said.

"Why are you so hesitant to tell people you've been in the French Foreign Legion? I mean, really, I understand you think it's not super all-American and people don't really understand what it is, but it feels like it's more than that."

He puffed out a breath that billowed his cheeks and darkened his eyes. "I don't like to talk about it to anyone."

She smiled. "I think we've been over this. I'm not anyone."

"I know." He looked long into her eyes, taking a slow breath and squeezing her hand. "You're right."

"I'm right that I'm not anyone, or I'm right that it's more than that?"

"Both."

The fence had been installed around the property, an ugly

yellow plastic thing that ran around the perimeter and emphasized how sizable the land Cutter Valentine had inherited really was.

"Maybe he doesn't need all this space," Ari mused as the truck rolled up the dirt drive. "He could have a small house and put a little museum up there on the hill, like they did at Mound House."

Luke didn't answer, frowning straight ahead. Which wasn't too hard to understand, considering she was cavalierly making building and design plans where she had no business making them.

"I'm sorry. I've done nothing but make your life more difficult and miserable since you got here," she said softly.

But he stayed frowning, and staring, silent.

"Luke?" she asked after a beat.

"Those are weird tire marks, aren't they?"

Pulled from her admission, she followed his gaze to the wide tracks in the dirt. "Probably the trucks from when they put the fence up."

He shook his head. "No one should have been here."

"Except the guy Charity mentioned."

"I figured she had her days mixed up."

"She's definitely over the top, but she doesn't mix things up."

He grabbed the handle and threw the door open, but stilled before getting out. "And you're wrong, Arielle."

"No, I've known Charity since I moved—"

"I mean about making my life miserable and difficult since we met."

She sucked in a breath, not expecting the honesty in his voice or his eyes. "I...well, I'm glad of that. But I still feel like I've been nothing but one big, fat roadblock for you."

"You're not a big, fat anything. You just...get me." He

shook his head and slipped out to the ground, closing the door and leaving her to sit and wonder if he meant she "got" him or "got to" him or…what.

This time, he didn't round the truck to open her door. Instead, he strode toward the house with purpose, leaving Ari to sit and watch, with a slow sense of dread crawling up her back.

She took a second to let it settle, cold on her heart, then pushed the door open, picnic lunch forgotten as she followed him.

"Someone's been here," he said, still a few feet from the front porch.

"I know." She glanced around, looking for clues, seeing nothing, but feeling something. She couldn't pinpoint what it was.

"The porch boards are lifted. Holy shit, they're gone." He gestured toward the window. "And what was left of the glass is gone. There used to be a big shard sticking up from that picture window."

"Would your demo crew have started early?"

"I met with them yesterday and put them on hold. Stay here." He held one hand up, and the other one almost automatically reached for his waist, then he seemed to remember he wasn't armed.

Squaring his already square shoulders, he walked over the dirt foundation revealed by the missing porch boards, and his whole body stiffened in reaction. "What the hell?"

"What is it?" she asked, coming closer to the porch to see if she could peer around him.

"What the…" His voice faded, but not the sentiment, as he stepped inside the house. "Do not come in here until I check the place, Ari!" he called, halting her progress.

Torn between curiosity and fear, she stayed rooted, trying

to squint into the shadows of the house. It did look different in there. It looked…bare.

He came back to the doorway, filling up the space, his expression pure shock. "Everything is gone."

"What?" She came closer. "What do you mean?"

"I mean, everything is gone. Every wall, every door, every window, every cabinet. Every inch of this place has been torn out, down to the studs and foundation."

The foreboding pressed on her chest, a word taking shape. Greed. Exactly the vibe she'd gotten when she'd read that note about the pearls. But this had the added sense of desperation. Maybe even panic. That's what she felt, the word in her heart, as Grandma used to call it when the universe whispered a message. It made no sense. Nothing in the house was worth a dime except…except…

Except possible ancient treasures that few people valued in the world. "Everything?" she said, her voice a croak.

In other words, if there had been anything else in this house to find, someone had taken it.

Chapter Seventeen

Nothing made sense. Nothing. Not the way this was done, not the timing, not the work, not the…neatness of it all. Luke turned to take in the destruction, which looked like it had been done by a surgeon, not a demolition team. At least not any team he'd ever worked with.

Behind him, he heard Arielle's footstep and soft gasp of disbelief as she gingerly entered the main room.

"Oh, Luke," she sighed. "Who did this?"

"I don't know." But whoever it was, they were thorough.

The walls—the old-fashioned plaster walls—had been sledgehammered out, exposing the studs of the building. Cabinets had been torn off their studs, the ceiling pounded out to expose the rafters, and every single floorboard ripped up, leaving a concrete foundation and some studs.

Luke blinked as the realization hit him. This wasn't demolition—this was done by someone looking for something.

"Where did they put everything that was here?" Arielle asked.

"Good question. There's no dumpster outside and nothing in the back. But all the trash and furniture are gone." Luke had his phone out, clicking through contacts for the demo subcontractor on the off chance they had subbed out to someone who didn't get the word to hold off.

It was the only explanation, he thought as he tapped the number and watched Arielle slowly walk around the foundation flooring, carefully avoiding the treacherous nails in strips of wood that had secured the floorboards.

Why the hell would they take up the floor?

The demo subcontractor was on the line in under a minute, and after Luke talked to him, it was clear he was just as perplexed. He'd done nothing to the house. Frustrated and not sure who to call next, Luke went to the back bedroom, where he found Arielle in the doorway of a closet.

"Every single wall's been taken out," she said, turning to him.

"It wasn't my demo guy."

She threw him a look. "I never thought it was, Luke. You made a promise, and I believed you."

"Except I promised that this wouldn't happen." And he hated that. Inching by her, he stepped into the long, narrow closet that ran the length of the room, marveling at the work that had to have been done by some kind of professional. "This isn't a demolition."

"Obviously, they wanted what I want, and if it was here, they got it."

He turned to her, frowning. "Arielle, I respect that you think there are things around this property that have some value."

"Things? You heard the archaeologist. Artifacts, tools, weapons, utensils, some dating back a thousand years or more."

He shook his head. "This isn't the way to go about looking for them, even if they had street value."

"I know you think they don't have value, and honestly, they wouldn't get much on the black market, I'm certain, but to some people, those artifacts are priceless."

But to whoever had done this? Not likely. He put his hands on her shoulders, sensing how close she was to tears, feeling her tremble under his fingers. "Those kind of people don't steal and empty out a house in the middle of the night. Someone went to an enormous amount of trouble. And who would know they were here except that archaeologist? Surely he didn't come over here with a sledgehammer."

"You're right." She glanced around. "But I'm right about the value because whoever did this was driven by greed so profound I can practically taste it."

He inched back, searching her face. "What do you mean?"

Her shoulders sank a little, her posture narrow and defeated, as though she knew he wasn't going to like what she had to say.

"I can feel it," she admitted, her tone suggesting she knew exactly how ridiculous that sounded. Except he was starting to get used to it, and damn it, something *was* wrong here. He was just desperate enough to take those feelings seriously.

"What do you feel, Arielle?"

"There's an aura in this place of someone desperate for...money." She averted her eyes from his intense gaze. "I'm sorry. I can't deny what I'm feeling."

"Don't apologize. But those things you found in the crate aren't worth enough to make someone greedy. It doesn't make sense."

"It makes sense to me."

"Because you love and appreciate the historical

significance they have. But if you're feeling greed, then there's real money involved."

She fought a smile, the last thing he expected in this situation. "So you're saying you believe me and my feels, Luke McBain?"

"I want to know who did this. And why."

In the distance, he heard a car engine, a roar of something that wasn't a truck like the one that had left the tracks. The sound grew closer, and whatever it was screeched to a screaming halt outside. Without thinking about it, years of training kicked in.

"Stay here until I know who that is," he ordered.

A bit of fear darkened her eyes. "Why? Should I be scared?"

"Just careful." He put his hand to his waist, then swore softly.

"You're not armed," she reminded him. "Do you feel like you should be?"

"I always do," he admitted as a car door slammed. "Wait here."

With a quick kiss on her forehead, he left the bedroom, every sense on alert. A footstep on what was left of the porch, a man clearing his throat, a scuff of a boot against the concrete foundation.

Luke stepped out of the hallway and came face-to-face with the last person he wanted to see right then.

"Hello, Cutter."

Cutter Valentine? The owner of the property? Ari stepped closer to the hall, her mind whirring. Maybe *he* knew why this had been done. Maybe he'd ordered this without telling Luke. Maybe he knew there was something valuable here—and Native American artifacts *were* valuable, despite what Luke said—and that's why he'd had this thorough demolition completed.

It all made perfect sense. And if he'd found anything, surely he was the kind of man who would donate it to a place where many more people could enjoy it.

It was time to find out who the real enemy was—because it wasn't Luke. But if it was Cutter, she needed to get him on her side. And that wasn't going to be done by stomping her feet and insisting he not build. She didn't know why she knew that, but she trusted her instinct.

"You've made fantastic progress in here, Luke!" a booming voice echoed through the now empty house. "Great to see you."

Ari came around the corner, observing the men shaking hands and doing a bit of an awkward bro hug. Cutter was about a half inch taller than Luke, built like a long, lean ballplayer, and not nearly as muscular as Luke. His chestnut hair was tipped with gold, his face angular and much more classically handsome than Luke's. Even from here, his smile blinded.

Ari took a step forward, and Cutter's gaze instantly shifted, his smile faltering. "Hello," he said.

"Cutter, this is Arielle Chandler. She's—"

"An interior designer," she said quickly.

Luke turned, looking surprised and pleased and relieved, all at the same time.

"I work at the resort with Luke's sister, and he said he needed some design ideas."

"Awesome," Cutter replied, meeting her halfway to shake her hand. Everything about the man was bright—his smile, his Wedgwood blue eyes, and his thick hair streaked by sunshine. Everything about him was positive, honest, and real, which made her a tiny bit remorseful about the white lie.

"Kind of early for a decorator, though, isn't it?" he asked, his grip as hearty as he was.

"We're just getting some ideas and thoughts," Luke said, coloring the truth as easily as she had.

Cutter nodded, putting his hands on his hips in a classic baseball stance and looking around. "Demolition looks...thorough." He beamed at Luke. "I knew this was a good idea, McBain. I had a gut feeling you'd do a fantastic job." He turned that smile on Ari. "I never ignore a gut feeling."

She couldn't help smiling back, at the man and the sentiment. "I know exactly what you mean," Ari said. Would his gut tell him that he was right then staring at the biggest roadblock to his new home?

"I didn't expect you here," Luke said to Cutter. "I thought you wouldn't be able to come down until the holidays."

"I thought so, too, but the team owners had some kind of critical hiring decision and flew me in for a quick meeting tomorrow morning, so I thought I'd use the extra time to check on your progress."

"I've only been here a few days," Luke said, probably as an apology for the "progress," and then glanced at Ari as if to say, *And there is this small problem of a woman who wants to stop me.*

But Cutter ignored the exchange, looking around again. "Shit's gettin' done, and that's good. We're going to make the Feb. one deadline, right?"

"That's the plan," Luke assured him. "All I'm doing now is getting all my ducks in a row before the real work starts."

Cutter nodded again, then pointed his thumb over his shoulder. "What about the hill? Won't that eyesore have to be the first thing to go?"

Eyesore. Ari swallowed her response, trying to see it from his point of view. The hill was gorgeous if you could put a house on it—which, thanks to the mangrove and beach-protection laws, you couldn't. So it was nothing but a view blocker.

And, possibly, a sacred burial site.

"I'm on it," Luke said. "We're finishing up the core sampling and some geological testing that has to be done. To be sure, I'm having two additional experts test the soil." Ari noticed he didn't mention one was an archaeologist.

Cutter grunted and looked skyward. "That's what the last builder said. Everything was wait, wait, wait. I am not a patient man." He huffed out a breath and gestured toward a missing wall. "Find anything interesting in here?"

And everything inside Ari zinged. "Interesting?" She stepped forward.

"You know, anything worth keeping?"

"What exactly are you looking for?" Luke asked.

"I don't know, maybe something of..." Cutter fought a smile. "I feel a little silly saying this, but I will. Have you found anything of value?"

Ari's heart kicked up, and Cutter eyed her as if he sensed her interest. Maybe she'd sucked in an audible breath, but her blood was pumping too loud to tell.

"Maybe you don't know this, but the guy who lived here was my great-uncle," Cutter said.

"I'd heard that," she said. "I'm sorry for your loss."

He snorted. "Don't be. I never met the guy and didn't know he existed until some lawyer handed me a couple of beachfront acres and a cryptic message from my Uncle Balls."

"Uncle Balls?" Luke and Ari repeated the name with exactly the same bit of surprise and humor.

Cutter grinned. "Hey, I'm not being disrespectful of the dead. That's what he called himself. Balls Valentine, short for Balzac. He was some kind of freakish baseball fanatic."

"You didn't know your great-uncle?" Ari asked.

"'Great' is pushing it. He was..." He made a face, thinking. "Let me see, my mother's third cousin's father, which might be some kind of great-uncle a couple times removed, but who the hell knows? He said he was my uncle in the will, and no one has contested that."

"No one in your family knew anything about him?" Luke asked.

"Just that after his wife died, he turned into some weird-ass hermit who lived here all alone. No one on my mother's side ever mentioned the guy, and they all thought he died, or at least they acted like he did. I guess he followed my career and decided I should inherit his land."

"And you think there might be something of value here?" Ari came closer, working hard to keep any emotion out of her voice, but probably failing based on the look Luke shot her.

"That's what it said in his letter in the will. But..." He held out two hands to indicate the house around them. "This is hardly a gold mine, so I was hoping when he said I was sitting on one, he meant, you know, literally."

Luke frowned. "He said that?"

"Yeah, in this letter he wrote, thanking me for making him so proud."

"Did he tell you why he thought it was a gold mine?" Ari asked.

"No, but he said I'd thank him for the rest of my life and wouldn't forget him." He snorted. "Which is pretty ironic when you think I didn't even know him when he was alive."

"It is a valuable piece of property," Luke said. "Waterfront, on an island, and zoned for residential. You know, you could sell this lot alone for an easy million bucks."

"Yep." Cutter took a deep breath and let it out slow. "And I would have, 'cept I got this job with a team down here." He grinned at Ari. "How's that for good luck?"

It wasn't luck, she wanted to scream. But this probably wasn't the time to go into her belief that there was no such thing. She was too stuck on that gold mine. Had Balzac known about the Calusa heritage? Had he stashed away more artifacts? And, if so, *who* got them?

"What exactly did he say in his letter?" she asked. When Cutter seemed slightly surprised by her boldness, she opened her hands as if to apologize. "You know, something that might help with a design of the house that would, um, honor his personality."

"Sorry, no." Cutter looked from one to the other, then sighed. "I haven't been able to find out much about him except he collected weird baseball memorabilia like Cracker Jack boxes and ticket stubs."

"Cracker Jack boxes..." Luke said slowly, his emphasis not lost on Ari.

Cutter gave a self-deprecating laugh. "Oh, I know this place has been looted to hell and back since the storm, and kids drink here, so if anything of real value was here, it's probably gone now. But I couldn't help but hope that..."

When he didn't finish, Ari and Luke both leaned closer. "That what?" they asked in perfect unison.

He laughed, at them or at what he was about to say, Ari wasn't sure which. "Well, he was so certain about it that I thought maybe he'd squirreled away a Honus Wagner card or a signed Babe Ruth jersey. Something like that's worth more than this land, to be honest."

"A baseball card?" Ari asked, her own thoughts so far afield she couldn't keep the incredulity out of her voice.

"Crazy, isn't it? But one of those Wagner cards can go for up to three million, they're so rare. But…" He shook his head. "It was just a thought. I mean, if something had been found, I think I'd have heard through the grapevine when it got sold. So, forget about it."

"Well, if we find anything—"

"It belongs to me," he said quickly, then smiled. "But I'll give you a cut as a bonus, Luke, if you get the house built by February. Please don't make me live in that resort. It's nice, but after all these years on the road, I want to settle in and have a home of my own."

"You will," Luke assured him. "We're right on schedule, I promise."

Cutter nodded and thrust out a hand for another shake and manly hug. "Man, I'm so happy we reconnected. It's been too many years." He turned to Ari, slayed her with a smile that no doubt stole as many hearts as his feet stole bases. "Can't wait to see your ideas for my house, Arielle."

"You can call me Ari, and I think my ideas will really capture the true spirit of the land."

Out of Cutter's line of sight, Luke rolled his eyes, but Ari managed to give Cutter's hand a firm shake.

Luke walked him out to the white Mercedes parked outside, leaving Ari inside, considering how she felt about the man who wanted to tear down this house, and that hill. The men's voices floated in through the open doors and windows, and Ari closed her eyes, thinking about Cutter Valentine and the words that came to mind.

Honest. Cocky. And careful. And yet he claimed to be

impatient. She didn't feel that at all. Why would a careful man want to move so darn fast?

She met Luke at the door when he came back, searching his face, which was more quizzical than worried about an unexpected meeting with a client.

"Why'd you lie?" he asked.

"I didn't lie. I told you I'd help you with design ideas if you build this house."

"If?" He choked softly, turning away so that the rest of his reaction was mumbled but not lost when he said, "I love your confidence in me."

But it was confidence in her instinct that made her doubt the house would be built. Something deep in her heart told her that Cutter Valentine was never going to have a house on this property.

"I am building the house," he said. "In fact, I'm having dinner with him tonight to go over plans. And I guess we have our answer."

"We do?"

"Someone must have heard rumors of a Honus Wagner card, right? Makes sense to tear this place apart for a possible three-mill payoff, right?"

It did make sense, but it didn't feel right. "I suppose."

She watched Luke walk outside into the sunshine, which poured over him like liquid gold, touching every inch of him. Oh, to be that sunshine.

He turned and added to the heart-stopping impact of the image by smiling. "I got my appetite back, Little Mermaid. Let's go have our picnic lunch."

Chapter Eighteen

Arielle changed when they reached the top of the hill, relaxing a little, turning her face to the sun, and letting the breeze flutter her hair. Luke threw a blanket he'd taken from his truck over a grassy section, lowering himself while she stayed standing. Well, not exactly standing. More like revolving—her arms extended as she did a three-sixty turn.

"Are you communing with the universe?" he asked.

She smiled, but her eyes stayed closed. "My grandmother believed the wind blows beauty on a person."

"Then you must have been born in a hurricane."

Laughing lightly, she joined him on the blanket. "You're sweet."

"I'm honest. You're freaking gorgeous."

"You're not bad yourself, McBain."

He unpacked their Super Min-bought lunch. "So tell me more about your Grandma Good Egg," he said. "Did she do spells?"

She smiled. "Good Bear. And no, she didn't do spells."

He munched on a chip, then opened his water. "Then how did she convince you to be celibate?"

She coughed on her drink of water. "What makes you

think my dearly departed grandmother has anything to do with my choice to be celibate?"

He tipped his head, eyeing the way the sun made her hair look even blacker, if that was possible. "You're not the only one with intuition, sweetheart. Didn't you say she was a shaman? Wasn't your whole way of thinking about life and...the universe, as you call it, formed by her? So I'm guessing she's who convinced you to wait for..." The One. Damn, he couldn't even say it, let alone *be* it.

Which was exactly why he was eating and talking instead of undressing and—

"Yes, you are correct," she said. "Awfully impressive intuition skills, I might add."

He nodded to acknowledge the compliment.

"When she was close to...the end, I promised her that I wouldn't get intimate with anyone until I was certain he was the man the universe meant for me." After a beat of silence, she grinned. "Something tells me that's a sentence you never dreamed you'd hear from a woman."

And something would be right. He wanted to know more about this destiny love, like the rules and regs, but something kept him from digging deeper. Like maybe he didn't want to know if he was following those rules or breaking them.

"So tell me about her," he said instead.

She let out a slow sigh, twisting the cap to close her water bottle, and then easing herself back to her elbows. Silent, she stretched out, crossing her jean-clad legs, presenting him with an extraordinary profile of elegant cheekbones and a straight, strong nose and well-defined chin. Her hair fell back, grazing the blanket, tempting him to touch it.

While she gathered her thoughts, he took time to appreciate every inch of her. And want her even more, which wasn't helping his determination to keep his hands off her. For a little while, anyway.

"If you really wanted to understand her, you'd have to see Grandma perform a Native American marriage ceremony," she finally said. "It was…" She shook her head as if she couldn't find the word. "Perfection."

"Tell me." He lay down on his side next to her, propping his head on his elbow and plucking a blade of grass to keep his fingers busy with something other than what they wanted to do.

"She'd take a couple up to a hill, maybe one like this, because you had to have an unobstructed view in all four directions." She closed her eyes, making long lashes brush against her smooth cheekbones. "Then she'd make them hold hands and turn east, south, west, and north, asking for special guidance no matter which direction life took them. Then…" She sat up slowly, her gaze fixed on a distant memory. "She'd have them touch their joined hands to the ground…" She clasped her hands and pressed them ground. "And promise Mother Earth that they would respect her and take care of her."

An unexpected chill crawled up Luke's back, settling in his chest, stealing his breath. He lay very still, watching her, transported to an imaginary Native American marriage ceremony, her voice like music, her movements graceful and spare.

"Then they would lift their hands to the breeze." She stretched all the way up, her long arms reaching gracefully to the sky. "And let the wind blow over their partnership, asking that it always be beautiful, alive, and pure."

"Anything else?" he asked, not surprised by the reverence in his voice.

"Oh, yes. She would pour spring water on their heads,

asking that their marriage never go dry, and then, from a flower, she would sprinkle seeds to ask for fertility and many children."

Wow. He just stared at her, as speechless over the ceremony as the woman telling him the story. "And then they were married?" he finally asked.

"Almost. They had to each press their right hand on the other person's heart, of course, and when they did, everyone would be very, very quiet." She extended her right hand, palm flat, toward an imaginary partner. "There couldn't be a single sound, not a breath, so they could actually hear their partner's heartbeat and then become one." She let out a sigh, dropping her hand and facing him. "The ancients believed that in that act, in that moment, they exchanged hearts and then they were one. Not 'the one' for each other, but just one."

"That's it? No rings?"

"No rings, but usually the man would place beads around the woman's neck, with the same idea that they were unending and forever. Oh, and then they'd kiss for a long, long time." She laughed. "Not sure of the legend behind that, but it's everyone's favorite part." She settled back down next to him. "What else do you want to know?"

Everything. He wanted to know about her childhood and family, her dreams and desires, her fears and failures, and favorite song. "What about your parents?" he asked. "The daughter of a shaman married to a minister? That's an unlikely pair."

"Exactly," she said, tapping his arm as if he'd made her point for her. "Grandma used them as proof positive that some people are meant to be together despite the obstacles."

Some people...like them?

"But my mother, especially, doesn't really buy the theory,

but then, she has spent her life trying to 'un-Native American' herself. If she'd just relax and give in to the truth, she'd see that she and my dad were meant to be…" Her voice faded as she searched his face. "Wow, you really hate this topic."

Was he that transparent? "I don't," he said quickly. "I don't understand it, but I don't hate it."

Dark eyes tapered at him as she sat up again. "What are you feeling right this very minute? Quick," she demanded. "One word."

"I'm feeling…" Scared. Alone. Charmed. Beguiled. Confused. So damn confused.

She laughed, giving him another nudge. "Luke, how hard can one word be?"

Hard. "It was the one word that threw me." He reached for her, coming off his arm to sit up next to her. "I'm feeling like you might be wasting perfectly good Native American teachings on a sensible, unfaithful, hard-core must-see-it-to-believe-it kind of guy."

"No teaching is wasted. Someone always learns something, even if they don't want to." She lifted her hand, this time to graze his jaw while studying his face. "And you don't have to hold back on your skepticism or unbelief, although…"

"Although what?" he prodded.

She sighed slowly. "Although if the things I hold true and dear in my heart are meaningless to you, then…does that mean you are meaningless to me? I'm not sure I want to know that yet."

"Yet?" Like him being meaningless was inevitable? "Not sure I want to know that yet, either," he admitted as that possibility crushed his chest a little.

She closed her eyes and puffed out a breath. "I need something sweet," she sighed.

"Then close your eyes." He got up enough to reach into his pocket, making her brows lift in surprise.

"You have something sweet in your pants?" she teased.

"Of course I do." Laughing with her, he pulled out a cardboard package of wax bottles full of sugar juice.

"Nik-L-Nips!" She reached for them. "How did you get them? They're impossible to find."

"Nothing's impossible, Arielle."

Her shoulders softened as she looked at him. "'Bout time you figured that out, McBain." She nodded toward the candy. "I'll share the blue one."

"You have to teach me how to open it."

She slipped the little wax bottle from the case and held it to her mouth. "Put it right here, between your teeth."

Everything, every cell in his body, tightened and squeezed.

"And"—she bit down—"snap it off." She popped the wax top out of her mouth so it bounced on the blanket. "And spit it out."

"That was pretty sexy, Arielle. Except for the snapping-it-off part."

She gave him a slow, sly smile. "Don't worry, I don't bite."

His hormones went wild. Wilder. Wild enough that it took a moment for him to notice the playfulness disappearing from her expression. "What's wrong, Arielle?"

"Look at you, getting all in tune with the feels again. You spend too much time with me, Luke, and you'll be the one communing with nature. Would you like me to teach you how to listen to what the wind says?"

"I'd like you to teach me how to read your expression, which changed a second ago while you were looking at me."

She averted her eyes, as if she'd been caught and couldn't deny it. "Okay," she agreed. "I was thinking, right then when you said wax-bottle biting was sexy, that…"

"That what?"

"That I wish sex with you hadn't taken on all this magnitude because I really want to…" She laughed again, unable to find the word. "I really want to," she finally said.

Thank God, because he really wanted to, too.

"We could…" With a gentle nudge, he eased her to her back, leaning over her. "Let go of the magnitude."

"We could," she agreed on a shudder as his fingers found their way to the bare skin exposed between her T-shirt and jeans.

"What's the worst that could happen?" he asked, stroking the satin of her stomach.

"It could change everything."

"Yeah, we could go from being the world's two horniest people to the most satisfied. That would suck."

"Or we could go from being new friends with a strong attraction to each other to lovers with thoughts of 'forever' dancing in their heads."

And that would suck, too.

Wouldn't it? Every cell—even the ones lining up for a party in his pants—stilled at the unanswered question.

She laughed softly. "And he panics."

"No, not panic." Yes, panic. "Is that what would happen? I mean, is that like a definite possibility if two people are…" He couldn't even say it. But he had to. "Meant for each other?"

She lifted one shoulder. "I don't know. I've never taken on the universe in a full-blown fight. Wouldn't expect to win, though."

For a long time, neither of them spoke. They looked into

each other's eyes while Luke's hand spread flat on her stomach to absorb some of her infallible "gut" instinct.

Barely breathing, he leaned closer, letting their mouths lightly brush, feeling her pulse thrum through her body.

There's no going back. There's no going back.

He closed his eyes, not sure if she said that or he heard it or...it was *the wind*. Either way, right then, he didn't care about anything except how much he had to have Arielle Chandler's body become one with his.

There's no going back.

"I don't care." He murmured the words into a kiss, completely lost under her spell.

"I do." Ari rolled out from under the weight of Luke's body—a move that took superhuman strength, because all she wanted in the whole world was him—and sat up, ending all body contact. "I care very much."

He was next to her in a flash. "I didn't mean I don't care about you. I don't care about...the wind and the woo-woo and The One. I want—"

"I know what you want."

He blinked at her. "Do you?"

Very much. So much she would have forgotten every promise she ever made to anyone just to let him take off her clothes and...get inside. But the look on his face, the uncertainty and confusion, even his jokes, not to mention the voice in her head... *There's no going back.*

She didn't want to lose him. She didn't want to lose the *chance* of him. And she was absolutely terrified that doing more of what they both wanted to do really would crush the possibility of forever. Or it might seal the deal and make her love him forever, even though he didn't "do" love.

She snatched her water bottle, twisted the cap, and took a long drink, aware that he stayed very close, staring at her. She threw a glance sideways, nearly melting at the look in his eyes and the way his lips were slightly parted, his teeth visible. Teeth she wanted to flipping eat her.

Oh, man. Why couldn't sex simply be fun, like it was for everyone else? Why did it have to now come with such baggage?

Because he is The One.

"Shut up!"

"I didn't say a word."

She slid him another look. "Not you."

"Oh, you're hearing voices," he said. "Well, so am I."

"I don't think they're saying the same thing."

"Don't be so sure." He reached under her hair, turning her to him, his hand strong and sure on her cheek. "Let's just kiss," he said, pulling her back next to him. "Lie down, and we'll take it slow. Nothing *too* serious."

But every kiss was serious. How did he not see that?

Because maybe it was all in her head.

The truth was, she still didn't know if he was her one true love or just some crazy-hot, cute, and wonderful guy she wanted to...

His hand stroked her stomach, hot, searingly hot and big and strong against her skin. "Kiss."

Yeah, that.

He covered her mouth, and they were lost again. Blood pumped through her, the beat and heat escalating with each passing second. A minute more, and his rough hands scraped her waist and ribs. She arched to invite his hand higher, his thumb grazing under her bra, making her hiss a breath.

With every kiss, his mouth sought and found hot spots that made her want to writhe and whimper and press harder against an erection growing sizable against her belly.

After a moment, Luke lifted up, searching her face as if he needed to make sure she was okay. "This is not just kissing."

"Says Captain Obvious."

"You okay?"

She was now. Later? Who knew? But now… "I'm good."

"So good." He underscored the compliment with another kiss.

"Don't stop," she whispered.

Taking the cue, he tugged at the hem of her shirt. "Can I?" he asked.

She answered by helping him get it over her head, barely free of it before she gave his T-shirt a yank. With just that much encouragement, he had it off in seconds.

She sighed as he braced himself on one arm and looked down at her, his hungry gaze making her breasts ache and bud even more. "Kiss me again, Luke." She pulled him down, and he covered her mouth, his incredible bare chest pressed against hers, that erection growing even more demanding. He smothered her mouth and tickled her throat and licked her bare breasts, while she did essentially the same, exploring his chest, his abs, the tendrils of hair and cuts of muscle on his incredible body.

Her hands slipped lower, tense with the desire to touch more. To unbutton his jeans and…

His head shot up like a whip, his hand over her mouth as his whole body went taut in a different way.

"What—"

"Shh!" Frowning, he scanned the area, a muscle in his neck pulsing. His eyes narrowed, and his shoulders squared.

Ari couldn't look at anything but him. She was almost scared to chance a glance left or right.

"Here," he whispered, closing his hands over her T-shirt and bra without taking his eyes off their surroundings. "We're not alone."

They weren't? Suddenly more embarrassed than scared, she sat up and pulled the T-shirt over her head, forgoing the bra.

Luke stood, his bare chest rising and falling with careful breaths as he scoped the area.

"Were you expecting a sub today?" She hadn't heard a truck and didn't see one, but she'd been pretty distracted.

"No, but...stay there." Still shirtless, he walked across to the opposite side of the hill, toward the bay. Who would come up from that direction?

Kneeling up but staying where he'd told her, she watched him until he stopped dead and looked up at the shadow of a big bird overhead. A vulture again, like she'd seen the day she'd met him.

In fact, Luke was standing in the exact spot where she'd found the pearls. The weird letter she'd received flashed in her head. She wanted to call out or go with him, but waited for a signal from him.

Luke kept going, not quite disappearing, but making his way down the other side of the hill toward the rocky shore. It wasn't a beach you'd stroll, with sand and shells, so it wasn't like someone would come up here from the water.

So where was he going?

While she waited, she stuffed their trash into the Super Min bag and folded the blanket, hyperaware of every sense and sound around her.

"Arielle!"

She startled at the sound of Luke's voice, popping to her feet. "What?"

"Come here."

Leaving the picnic, she followed the sound of his voice, spotting him almost instantly, on his knees at the easternmost side of the grade. "Is someone here?" she called out.

"No, but you need to see this."

She picked up to a near run, and when she reached him, he took her hand and pulled her down near the ground. "Look at this."

Holes. Someone had been digging, and digging deep. There were five, six, no, seven tunnels burrowed well into the side of the hill, none deep, but all distinctly made by a shovel, not any kind of professional heavy equipment.

"Is this where the core engineer dug for samples?" she asked.

"No. That was about a hundred yards on the other side. This is…fresh. Like it was made today or maybe yesterday."

A chill pirouetted up her back, crawling slowly to settle at the base of her neck.

"And I found this." He held out a can wrapped in a newspaper.

"Trash?"

"Interesting trash." He angled the can so she could see it was a Red Bull, and the newspaper was the *Mimosa Gazette*.

"The guy who was in Charity's store," she said.

He nodded. "Look." A giant red circle had been drawn on the newspaper, highlighting a tiny ad in the classifieds under the label Lost and Found.

Missing: pearl necklace, lost in Barefoot Bay, high sentimental value. $$$ Reward

Chapter Nineteen

Ari heard laughter from the Barefoot Brides offices and nearly broke into a joyous run when she realized that infectious sound of happiness belonged to Willow Ambrose. Well, Willow Hershey, now.

"You're back!" Ari exclaimed when she burst through the open door, arms outstretched. "I thought you had one more day on the yacht."

"Don't worry." Willow returned the hug and added a good squeeze. "The honeymoon will last a long, long time. But Nate and his partners are having some kind of important meeting on board. And that yacht, you guys!" She smacked her chest with a flat hand, dropping her head back with a grunt. "I cannot even describe the opulence of the *N'Vidrio*. I still can't believe a billionaire gave it to us for the week."

"He didn't exactly give it to you," Gussie reminded her. "We're doing his wedding to Liza, remember?"

"Like that was a fair exchange," Ari teased.

"Really, a week on the yacht way outweighs whatever we can do for that wedding, which will have to be a-*may*-zing," Willow said. "Think of what kind of clientele it will bring to us!"

"Lacey is already salivating about the high-end guest

list," Ari added. "But why cut short the trip? Shouldn't you be lounging naked with Nick on the upper deck having him feed you peeled grapes? Yet you're in the office on a Sunday afternoon."

"Trust me, there's been plenty of naked lounging. Nick ran out to stock the house with some food now that we'll have to actually cook instead of having a personal chef, and he dropped me off here so I could dig through the mail and see what I've missed. I found Gussie in here."

"I was looking for you," Gussie explained. "Where have you been, anyway?"

"Up…in North Barefoot Bay."

"What were you doing up there?" Willow asked, pulling Ari toward the round table where they always gathered to chat.

"With my *brother*," Gussie added, slathering on all kinds of meaning to the last word as she joined them.

Willow leaned back, surprised. "Oh? Have I missed something while on my honeymoon?"

"Have you ever, Willow." Gussie pressed both hands on the table, leaning in for dramatic effect. "Luke's The One."

"Gussie." Ari ground out her friend's name and narrowed her eyes.

"What?" Willow practically jumped out of her chair. Maybe her skin. Her blue eyes grew wide as she looked at Ari in shock. "The One? Your The One that you're always talking about? Luke McBain?"

Why had she ever confided her beliefs to her best friends? Because they were her best friends, that's why. Ari shook her head, laughing and sighing at the same time. "You want to know the truth?"

They both gave her their versions of a *get real* look. As if they wanted anything but the truth.

"I don't know," she said on a slow exhale. "I honestly do not know. Sometimes I think he's just a really sweet, funny, wonderful guy, and sometimes I think..." She paused, looking from one to the other. "He's *the* really sweet, funny, wonderful guy. The one and only."

"Oooooh." Willow and Gussie let out the musical exclamation and shared a knowing look and that smug smile that women in love had when they thought their circle was about to get bigger.

"Guys, we're not...nothing's been...anything could..." Ari closed her eyes and sighed.

"Words fail her," Gussie said.

"She's speechless," Willow agreed.

"It's love," they sang in perfect harmony.

Ari opened her mouth, then shut it. Then bit her lip. "Maybe it could be at some point," she whispered, wanting them to be right. "But I really don't know, and that's the hardest part. I thought it would be more obvious, but I'm worried that I'm talking myself into something because..." She looked at their permanent smiles of contentment, their big ol' left-hand jewelry. "Maybe I'm envious of you two, and I want something so much, I wished it into existence."

"You didn't wish Luke into existence!" Gussie said. "And you don't have a jealous bone in your body."

"Does he feel the same way about you?" Willow asked, putting her hand over Ari's.

"He doesn't want to feel anything," she admitted glumly, then looked at Gussie. "He had his heart broken pretty bad. Did you know that?"

She shook her head. "No, he avoids the subject of women when I bring it up. Can I ask him about it, or would that be breaking a confidence?"

Ari gave her a grateful smile for asking. "I'd let it go unless he brings it up."

"Has he talked to you about Ari?" Willow asked Gussie.

"Only enough that I get the impression he's crazy about you, Ari. Which a blind man could see."

"So he feels it, but doesn't say it," Willow surmised. "Which makes him a guy, through and through."

"He's not like most guys, though," Ari said. Most guys wouldn't go four years without sex. "Which is the problem. He's not like any guy I've ever met, so..." She slipped into a loopy grin. "We're back to is he or isn't he The One?"

"Are you seeing him tonight?" Gussie asked.

"No, he's having dinner with Cutter Valentine, and I have a ton of work to do, since we have a couple of major weddings on the docket. Which reminds me, I need to send an e-mail."

She pushed up and went to her own desk, tapping the computer mouse to bring it to life, the address listed with the classified ad still fresh in her brain. She'd promised Luke she'd contact the person looking for the necklace. It was critical to learn where those pearls had come from.

Because if the necklace hadn't been unearthed from the hill, then maybe her whole theory about a burial ground there was all wrong and he really should get on with the building. As Ari slipped into her desk chair, Willow's hand landed on her shoulder.

"What does it feel like?" she asked, her voice barely above a whisper.

She turned in her chair to meet Willow's gaze, and Gussie came right up to join them.

"Yeah," Gussie added. "What does it feel like?"

"I'm pretty sure you two already know," she said.

"Well, if you think Nick and I were meant for each other,

and Gussie and Tom, then you know it isn't always super easy in the beginning. Sometimes you have to fight a little for love. And make concessions and compromises."

Gussie stepped closer, her hands on her hips. "And you don't ruin his plans, cost him his job, and send him packing across the Atlantic."

"What?" Willow demanded, spinning around. "He's leaving?"

Gussie lifted her brows in question to Ari. "Can I tell her?"

"Of course."

"She's trying to stop him from building Cutter Valentine's house because she thinks it's on sacred Native American ground or that there's a treasure trove of three-thousand-year-old tools under the hill. Or dead bodies."

"Maybe," Ari corrected. "I'm not sure. Something came up today that might set us straight on that. Still, I believe there's something in that land because I can feel it." And someone *was* digging for something, that much was clear. Maybe that was just the missing pearls or even that overpriced baseball card, but she wasn't imagining there was something of value on that land, and it wasn't just the million-dollar view.

"Whatever happens, I don't want my brother to go back to France because he made it clear to me that's the only place he is certain of a steady income."

"Couldn't he do something else?" Willow asked.

"I don't know his financial situation," Gussie said. "But he definitely feels a burn to make money and, really, who can fault him for that? We all have to work."

Ari's cell dinged, and she seized it from the desktop without a second's hesitation.

"The grab of hope," Gussie teased.

"Oh, yeah," Willow agreed. "She thinks it's him."

She flattened them both with a look, even though, damn it, they were absolutely right.

But it wasn't Luke's name on the text screen. The message was from Dr. David Marksman from Mound House.

Can you come out here tomorrow? Must talk. Very important.

She tapped a response into her phone, then turned to focus on sending an e-mail to the address in the classified ad in the local paper. But that was another dead end, she discovered, seconds after sending it. The e-mail of the person looking for the pearl necklace was no longer active.

A strange zing traveled up her back, like a telegram from the universe. Something wasn't right.

Luke let his head fall back on the leather headrest of the limo, grateful that Cutter Valentine had the foresight to have a car and driver at the ready after their dinner. Had Cutter been that huge a drinker in high school?

After more than ten years in the Legion, Luke could hold his liquor. Hell, getting stupid drunk was actually considered part of active duty in the Legion, and Luke had done his part in many hellhole bars around the world.

Maybe Cutter just had better whiskey. Whatever, Luke was definitely well past mellow and into toasted as he sat alone in the limo, headed south to Gussie's apartment.

Where Arielle would be sleeping one short flight of stairs above him.

Just the thought of her in bed fired his body with a gallon

of blood, making him shift uncomfortably against the luxurious leather.

He was not going to show up at her door half-drunk and hard up. No way. Fighting the idea for the rest of the ride, he thanked the driver and made his way to the back stairs that led up to Gussie's apartment, the buzz in his head still pleasant enough to slow his step and let him take a minute to appreciate the nearly full moon spilling light and shadows over Mimosa Key. Along the walkway, he sniffed some honeysuckle, a smell he usually found cloying, but tonight it seemed...intoxicating.

Or *he* was intoxicated.

He plucked a few white flowers and stuck them under his nose as he headed up the stairs, unable to stop himself from looking up to the third floor to see if there were any lights on. Because they could talk...

Like hell they'd talk. He'd have his hands up her shirt and down her pants in ten minutes, and she'd hate that.

Except she didn't hate it on the hill this afternoon. And they'd been interrupted, so maybe...

He closed his eyes and almost swayed, more from the memory of her bare breasts in the gleaming sun than the top-shelf whiskey Cutter had been sharing.

At Gussie's door, he was about to knock or reach under the mat for the key, like she'd been leaving it since he arrived. But then he spied a little sticky note on the door handle. He ripped it off and turned toward the moonlight to read it.

Gone to Tom's. Left my key at hardware store to get one made for you. Ari has a spare.

With a damn winky face. Evil little thing—as if she didn't know exactly what she was doing. As if you had to leave a key overnight to get a duplicate. He knew Gussie.

All those questions she'd asked him before he left for dinner, all the insinuations that he might be "the one" for her best friend.

Huffing out a breath, he started up the stairs, trying to decide if he loved his sister for this or might have to kill her. Either way, this was not a booty call. Not a booty call. Not a booty call.

Not. A. Boo—

The door whipped opened before he knocked, sending him back a shaky step. "It's about time."

He opened his mouth to speak, but nothing came out, because her eyes were hooded, her hair messy, and she wore nothing but a longish T-shirt, her legs bare.

Oh, shit. Maybe it was a booty call.

"I've been asleep for two hours, Luke."

"Sorry, I…" He had to touch her hair. Had to. Lifting his hand, he grazed a few strands before she jerked back.

"Here." She held a key out. "This is what you want, right?"

No, he wanted to push her up against the wall, rip that shirt off, and make love until they both howled and cried and couldn't see straight anymore. "Yep, key."

She searched his face again, as if trying to gauge how drunk he was. Pretty drunk, but he'd faced worse scrutiny from a CO after a bender. He met her gaze and didn't flinch.

"Gussie could have put it under the doormat," she said. "But I think she thought she was being oh-so-sly getting you up here."

Arielle could have put it under the doormat, too. But she hadn't.

"That's my Auggie. Sly." His hands hurt, like always, dying to get into her hair. And his chest ached, and every cell in his body—even the ones that had been numbed by

Jameson's—started to do the whole tingle thing they always did when she was around. "Booze didn't kill it," he murmured, almost shaking his head in disgust.

"Good to know. I'd considered trying that, but...I'm not that much of a drinker."

"You know what I'm talking about?"

She laughed easily. "Of course I do, Luke."

"Damn." He put his hand on the doorjamb, not asking to come in, not even getting any closer, but still...there. "You're good. A regular mind reader."

"I told you I'm nothing of the sort." She crossed her arms and looked up at him. "If you think you're coming in here, you're wrong."

"It's not a booty call," he said, the words still a little singsong in his head.

"No kidding."

"It's not even a 'good night, I'll see you tomorrow' call."

"I know that."

He inched closer. "But can I kiss you?"

She leaned right into him. "No."

"'Cause you think I'm drunk?"

She didn't answer right away, but held his gaze. "If I kiss you, Luke McBain, you know exactly what's going to happen."

Everything. "Why don't you tell me?"

Very slowly, a smile tipped her lips as she lifted her hand and put one finger on his chest. He braced for the nudge backward, ready for her to give him an easy shove out the door. But instead, she started drawing a slow, slow line down.

"We'd kiss for twenty seconds, and you'd be up my T-shirt."

Exactly what he'd been thinking. How did she do that?

Her finger traveled an inch lower. "Then you'd walk me

backwards into my apartment, and we might make it as far as the sofa." She made a little circle over one of his ab muscles. Then another circle. Then another.

Every circle made him a little…bit…harder. "And then?" he croaked.

"Then I'd probably start dragging your pants off, because I'm kind of tired of imagining what's in there."

She was…imagining? Her imagination made him grow two inches.

"And then…you know."

"No." But, holy hell, he wanted to know. Had to know. "What?"

By now her finger was over the top of his zipper. A hair's breadth from his engorged cock.

"I'd probably want to…put you in my mouth."

His knees practically gave way. "In your…" His voice sounded like sandpaper. Desperate, anxious, horny sandpaper. "Mouth." Please. He swallowed against his desert throat, not wanting to beg. At least not yet.

"And then…" Her finger pressed on the head of his dick, and he almost exploded at the pressure.

"Then?" He fought the need to rock into her, to kiss her quiet, and get this scene she was describing underway.

"Then…you tell me. Are you leaving? Are you staying? Are you scared? Are you ready? Can you handle it, Luke McBain?"

"Hell yes, I can handle it."

"You can handle sex, I have no doubt." She opened her hand and pressed it against his erection. "But what if it's more than that? What if you really are The One?"

He didn't answer, staring at her, no blood in his brain, no sense in his heart, nothing but her hand and her question and her right to know.

"And what if..." She continued, stroking over his pants, slowly. So, so slowly. "What if I am The One for you?"

Everything froze. Her hand. His heart. His cock. And time...that stood still, too, while she waited for an answer.

An answer he didn't have.

She moved her hand away, torturing him with the sudden loss of pressure. "When you're ready to answer that question, I'm ready to make love to you." She stepped back into the shadow of her apartment and closed the door in his face.

No, it was not a booty call. It was a call to action...but was he man enough to accept it?

Chapter Twenty

Montgomery Land Technical Services couldn't have been more different from GeoTech. The company was housed in a ten-story office building in Naples, with a clean and spacious reception area decorated with sleek works of art and a professionally dressed receptionist who offered Luke a cup of coffee while he waited to meet with Sam Montgomery, the VP of engineering he'd been e-mailing about his samples.

Sipping the hot brew to work off the remnants of a hangover and a very uncomfortable night of cold showers and hot thoughts, Luke picked up a geotechnical trade publication and flipped through the pages, but the articles and ads faded as he pondered Ari's question over and over again.

What if I am The One for you?

What if he didn't believe in that shit, he thought, letting his throbbing headache answer for him.

But what if she was? What if there was something to her crazy, woo-woo intuition? Then shouldn't he know for sure?

"Mr. McBain?" A tall, blond woman in a form-fitting gray suit approached him, her heels snapping against the polished oak floor, her hand extended in a warm greeting.

"Sorry to keep you waiting. I'm Sam Montgomery."

Really. He set the magazine down and stood to greet her, taking in exquisite cheekbones carved under smoky blue eyes, deep-red lipstick, and the wink of a sizable diamond floating over the hollow of her throat.

Holy fracking shit. It was like Cerisse had come back to life and shown up at an engineering firm in Florida. He swallowed hard, the banging in his head like a steel rod against a lead pipe.

She gave him an easy smile as she must have read his surprise. "My father is the other Sam Montgomery," she said with the slightest Southern drawl. "I mean, if you were expecting someone more seasoned. And male."

He laughed softly. "Not at all. You look like…someone I know."

Her smile said she wasn't buying it, but with a smooth gesture, she ushered him through an etched-glass door that led back to the offices. She wasn't quite as tall as the woman he'd once guarded—and loved—and her hair wasn't the same natural color of wheat in the sun. But this lady certainly reminded him of Cerisse, and looking at her brought up a million unhappy memories.

Her laugh, her eyes, her look of sheer shock when the bullet—

"I feel like this analysis took longer than it should have since you paid for a rush," the woman said.

"Not at all," he replied, forcing himself to think of the business at hand and not the coincidence that the engineer was a dead ringer for his ex-lover. "But I am anxious to see the results."

She turned and gave him an unreadable look, her expression so much like Cerisse's he almost stumbled. What a coincidence. Except…was there any such thing as a coincidence? Was this the universe sending a message to him?

The universe. Good God, he was turning into Arielle.

"It was a small sample but not quite an easy job. We worked all weekend." She gestured toward a sun-washed conference room, where several files spread across the center table, along with a sleek laptop and the bag of shells he'd left to be analyzed.

"But the results are fascinating," she added as she took a seat and indicated he should do the same. "How did you manage to gather such an eclectic mix of soil and shells?"

"I didn't gather it, exactly," he said, glancing at the files and the brightly colored computer-generated images on the screen. "The original core sampling was done by GeoTech, hired by the previous general contractor."

"Ahh," she nodded knowingly. "We've had to step in on those cases before." She gave an apologetic tilt to her head. "I mean no disrespect to the firm, but they are not as thorough as some of our clients would like, though I understand their prices are quite, well, competitive."

In other words, the work by Ken Waggoner's shop was of piss-poor quality and cheap.

She waved a hand toward the computer. "So it's very smart of you to spend the money for a second opinion and to use our thermal dyna analysis technique, which I am fairly certain GeoTech has not incorporated into their systems yet."

He smiled, thinking of the warehouse, and Michelle, smoking up a storm around the samples. They didn't have thermal anything. "Not yet," he agreed.

Her eyes twinkled with shared humor and no small amount of flirtation. Which only made him feel a little sicker than yesterday's whiskey.

"But since they ran the core sampling and know exactly

where this source material came from, I have no doubt they were able to find out how interesting this particular sample really is from a geotechnical standpoint." A little color rose in her cheeks as she held his gaze, direct and warm. "Which, I'm going to admit, turns me on. But I'm just your average geotech geek."

She wasn't average anything, and she knew it. Standing to open one of the files, she leaned down, affording him the slightest glimpse of her cleavage. He took a millisecond to appreciate the view, then looked down at the file, surprised at how little interest he had in checking the woman out.

And not because she reminded him of Cerisse. He simply wasn't interested. He wanted…someone else. And, hell, someone else was all he wanted.

Why didn't he have the nerve to tell her that last night?

"I guess I misunderstood when I got the assignment, though," she said, yanking him back to the moment. "I was under the impression this land was in Florida, in Mimosa Key, right off the coast here."

"That's exactly where it's from."

A frown tugged at her pale brows as she glanced at a file, then back up at him. "Then are you certain these were properly logged at the GeoTech lab?"

The trailer lab? Michelle had handed him the bag right out of a bin at GeoTech. Could it have been something from the wrong job? Misfiled? Mislabeled? Misplaced? All of the above were possible at that place. "Why don't you tell me what you found?"

She turned the computer so he could see the screen. "These are shells, every one of them from the East Coast of the United States."

"That's good."

She gave him a questioning look. "How's that?"

"I want this to be a shell mound," he said honestly. "Anything else and I might have some environmental issues. You are certain that nothing in this sample could be"—he had to say it—"bones?"

"One hundred percent certain," she said, unfazed by the idea. "We can immediately recognize the difference in the molecular structure and by the calcium carbonate deposits. These are seashells, but they did not come from Mimosa Key."

"How can you tell?"

"The computer analyzes shell consistency and a number of geographical 'fingerprints,' if you will, such as the residue of water, the amount of salt, and the dirt included, and of course currents and general shapes of the shells."

"I realize dirt can be different from various parts of the world, but shells?"

"Oh, shells are like little GPS trackers in the sand everywhere," she told him. "Again, calcium, water deposits, even the organic parameters of the exoskeletons tell us where the tiniest shell came from."

Organic parameters of exoskeletons were making his headache worse. He indicated the computer. "So what did you find?"

"That the farthest south this sample could have come from is Maryland."

"You're sure?"

"Absolutely. What's more interesting is that this sample included shells from Canada and Maine and quite a few from the New England coast. It was a veritable geographic potpourri."

And none of it had come from Mimosa Key, Florida. *Damn it.*

He leaned back, trying to digest this information. Either

GeoTech made a mistake and he had to go back and get another sample, or he needed to order a whole new core sampling.

"How long would it take to get you guys out there to do the whole job over again?"

"Oh, not long at all." Her eyebrows flicked with interest, making him wonder if it wasn't only rocks and shells that turned on Sam Montgomery. Maybe the owner's daughter got a commission for new business, too.

And maybe that's why he was getting a song and dance about shells from Maine and Maryland.

For one crazy second, he wished Arielle were right here beside him, using her keen intuition to tell him whether he should trust this woman.

"Would a week throw off your construction schedule?" she asked.

"Yes, it would," he admitted. "Let me give it some thought."

She stood, closing the file. "This is your copy. Compare it to the report from the other firm and let me know how you'd like to proceed, Mr. McBain."

"Luke," he corrected, taking the file. Their hands touched, but he felt nothing other than a vague sense of disloyalty. Not like with Ari, when he crackled like he was licking live wires every time they barely brushed each other.

"I have to say, you look surprised at all of this," she said.

At some of it. "It's the usual can of worms no builder wants to open." But he had to have answers. He couldn't start without answers.

What if the other firm was completely bogus, and the core sampling was wrong, and there really was an Indian burial mound under that hill, and Cutter didn't give a shit?

Then what?

Then he could kiss Arielle good-bye. And all he wanted to do was kiss her…more.

How did that happen? He didn't know, but he had to find out.

A kindly old museum docent led Ari to Dr. Marksman's lab, which ran along the back of the Mound House business offices, surrounded by books, art, tools, and multiple computers all running different analyses and date-testing software. He was on the phone when Ari arrived, but he eagerly gestured her in and to a chair and mouthed for her to give him a second.

While he finished the conversation, taking rapid notes, Ari looked out the open sliding glass doors that let in both breeze and sunshine, but her attention shifted immediately to the Cracker Jack crate, open and empty, on the archaeologist's desk. She couldn't wait to hear what he'd found.

As soon as he finished and signed off the call, he stood and held out a hand to greet her, his bright blue eyes practically electrified with excitement. "Miss Chandler, I'm so glad you could come."

"I take it you found something important?" she asked.

He seemed to fight a smile, fidgeting and glancing down at his desk. "You might say that."

"Where are the artifacts I left?"

"Oh, they're being cataloged and examined by some others, down the hall. I can tell you this, they are Calusa tools, and at least one is more than twenty-six hundred years old."

"Wow! Really?" No wonder he was excited. "That is great news."

"But it's not the most important discovery."

"It's not?"

He came around to the front of his desk, leaning on it as he took his glasses off, cleaning them with a handkerchief. "How well did you examine everything in the box you found?"

She felt scrutinized and a little thrown by the question. "I've been through every piece. Why?"

"Frankly, I was curious if this was a test."

"A test? Of your capabilities?" She gave an easy laugh. "Your credentials are impeccable, so what would I be testing?"

"My trustworthiness."

She shook her head, confused. "What could I possibly not trust you with?"

s

A sense of frustration and impatience wended through her. "Know what?"

"I found something of…incredible value."

"It all has value—"

"Financial value. Extreme financial value."

No matter how historically priceless she considered a Calusa stone hammer, it wasn't of extreme financial value. "Really?"

"It's possible you don't even know its real worth."

Then it hit her. The rare baseball card that Cutter had talked about! "Was it hidden in the crate?"

"Hidden completely," he said. "It is small, but worthwhile."

"Three million worthwhile?"

"At least." He lifted his eyebrows, a coy smile wrinkling his face. "There has to be more."

"There might be," she agreed, standing so the older man

224

didn't have the height advantage anymore. Surely he didn't mean to keep the card that belonged to Cutter Valentine. "Apparently, the former owner was aware of its worth. He told his relative, who is now the official owner, that the house was sitting on a gold mine. So, yeah, there could be more."

His old eyes widened as he slipped on his now thoroughly cleaned glasses. "If history is anything to go by, there is more."

"Except someone might have beat us to it," she told him. "When Luke and I were there last, someone had already been there. But if you found something valuable, then Cutter Valentine will be thrilled."

His eyes dimmed. "Yes, I imagine he will. It is on his land, but what will he do? Sell it? Look for more?"

"I have no idea," she said. "But maybe it will buy us time to persuade him not to rip everything down. I'm still convinced that mound could be a burial ground."

"Or that's where the rest of the treasure is."

She blinked at him. "Buried underground? Who would do that?"

"Anyone who wanted to protect it, who thought it could be stolen, and then died before they could retrieve it. You said he died quite unexpectedly."

She angled her head, studying him, not getting what he was saying. "You think that old man buried a bunch of baseball cards in that hill?"

His furry brows shot up, then he laughed softly. A little louder. He actually belly laughed, throwing his hands up to his cheeks as if trying to keep himself from literally laughing his face off.

Ari just stared at him, starting to wonder if Dr. Marksman wasn't a lunatic.

"A baseball card?" He choked the words between snorts of laughter. "A baseball card?"

"Or...something like that. Babe Ruth's jersey or...or Shoeless Joe Jackson's missing cleats?" Exasperation tightened her voice, especially when the old doctor had the audacity to wipe a tear of laughter from his crinkled cheek. "Whatever it is, Cutter's great-uncle told him the house is valuable."

"There's an understatement."

"Why?"

"Because there's rarely only one." He stepped aside and gestured toward the crate. "I put it back in there after I cleaned off the coral that was all over it. I simply didn't know where to put it that was safe. Go ahead, take a look."

A slow, icy chill worked its way up her spine, settling in the nape of her neck, pinching her hairs as they stood on end, like wee antennae on her body. The tingling always meant something major was about to happen.

"Look...at what?" she managed to ask.

He turned to the desk, lifted the lid, and made a grand gesture for her to look inside. There, resting on the bottom, was a rectangular object no longer than her index finger, so shiny, so bright, so...gold.

"That, my dear, is a bar of pure gold, stamped with the king's seal, circa 1544. Do you have any idea what you've stumbled upon?"

A gold mine.

Chapter Twenty-One

For the tenth time in an hour, Luke wandered to the front of Gussie's apartment to check the driveway for Ari's car.

"She's not home yet," Gussie called from the kitchen. "Trust me, she has to pass this kitchen door to get up to her apartment."

Blowing out a breath, he took a swig of beer and wandered back to where the rest of them had gathered. Tom was at the country-style table, quizzing Alex for tomorrow's history test, while Gussie stirred a pot of pasta, her nesting and cooking and homemaking skills growing stronger with each passing day. Clearly, she'd been born to have a family.

The thought kicked a little guilt through him as he remembered how his teenage decisions had cracked their perfect childhood in two. But she'd forgiven him and put that dark incident in their past.

If only he could put other dark days in his past. If he could, then maybe—

"You look pensive, big brother."

"Just thinking," he said, purposely vague.

"Ari's going to be really happy about this new development, don't you think?" she asked.

"I think she'll be pleased to get another shot at testing out her burial-ground theory."

"Are they going to find skeletons?" Alex asked, her twelve-year-old face morphing into sheer disgust.

"Don't worry, Alex," Tom said. "If there were people buried there, it was thousands of years ago."

"Then why is she so worried about them?" Alex asked.

"The same reason you need to know about the Civil War." Tom tapped the study sheet. "Because history matters."

"And it especially matters to Ari."

"Why?" Alex asked.

"She's part Native American," Luke said. "Have you learned about what we did to the American Indians yet?"

"A little," she said sheepishly.

"Let her tell you. Let her tell you about her grandmother and the way she marries people in the wind and…" His voice faded out as he realized all three of them were staring at him. "It's cool," he added.

"What's cool is how in love you are," Gussie said.

"I'm not…" Shit. "I hardly know her."

"I think that's the beauty of her whole fated-love thing." Gussie abandoned her pasta, picking up a glass of wine and coming out of the kitchen. "It's like auto-love."

"There is no such thing." Luke lifted his beer to his mouth, watching Gussie and Tom share a look that said there most certainly was such a thing. Damn it.

Taking his drink, he left the room to look out at the driveway again. The empty driveway. Where the hell was she, anyway? Gussie said she'd left the office at three to run errands on the mainland.

"It's not the worst thing in the world, you know," Gussie whispered behind him.

He turned. "What?" Except he knew what. He knew exactly what.

She crossed her arms and smiled at him. "Being happy. Giving your heart to someone. Finding love."

Done, done, and done. No, thanks. Not again. "It sucks too much when it's over," he said gruffly.

"It doesn't have to end."

"Everything ends," he said, turning back, the memories suddenly powerful and raw.

"I'm taking it you had a bad breakup in France."

"It wasn't a breakup, and it wasn't in France," he said. "And do you forget that I spent almost fifteen years running, fighting, trying to forget real life?"

She had her hand on his shoulder instantly, forcing him to face her. "We've been over this. I'm the one to blame for what happened that night on Cape Cod. You are completely vindicated."

"I know." But did he?

"You might have thrown a bottle rocket that scarred me, but I put myself in a dangerous place."

Which was exactly what Cerisse had done.

"Forgive and forget, Luke. I've done both."

He didn't need forgiveness for what happened with Cerisse, but, man, he sure as hell would like to forget. Because until he did, he didn't stand a chance with Ari.

She put a hand on his back. "Look." She turned him around to see the little blue Mazda pulling into the driveway.

"Oh, thank God, she's here."

"You should see your face," Gussie said with a laugh.

"What about my face?" he asked as he watched Arielle climb out of the car, walking quickly—damn near running—toward the back stairs.

"You're crazy about her."

Arielle's hair swung over her shoulders, a simple yellow sweater and pale slacks looking amazing on her. "Maybe I am," he admitted. "But maybe it's just lust and sex and physical desire."

Gussie snorted. "Hey, big bro, hate to break it to you, but lust and sex and physical desire are just step one."

He almost smiled, watching Arielle disappear at the side of the house. "And we haven't even taken that step. But if we do..." He looked at his sister, knowing he couldn't lie about these feelings and didn't want to. "Then we've crossed some kind of line and..." He listened for footsteps on the outside stairs, hoping, waiting. But she passed the door and went up to her apartment. Shit. "There's no going back."

She looked up at him, her wide green eyes honest and, for once, not twinkling with a joke. "Going back to France?"

"Going back to normal."

"Is it normal to be alone?"

"I don't know what's—"

A scream, shrill and long and coming from the apartment upstairs, cut him off. Luke shoved his beer into Gussie's hand and ran like hell.

Ari slammed her hand over her mouth to contain her shriek, dropping her handbag to stare in utter disbelief at the destruction of her apartment. Every...single...inch was wrecked.

"Arielle!" Luke flew up the last few steps and launched into the entryway, grabbing her. "What's...holy shit."

"Someone's been here." Which was like saying Vesuvius had a little bubble. Everything—every cushion, cabinet, and

230

cranny—had been taken apart, turned inside out, and…searched.

A wave of violation so strong she could practically taste it rolled over Ari, making her stumble backward into Luke. Instantly, his strong arms wrapped around her, turning her away from the mess, holding her, and squeezing her right back into sanity and safety.

"It's okay," he whispered, a catch of real fear in his voice.

But it wasn't. It wasn't okay at all.

"Come with me." He pulled her toward the door, but she didn't move.

"I have to see…"

"Shhh. Get out of here. Come to Gussie's."

She turned her head to look over her shoulder. "But I have to—"

"No, you don't. Not until I go through this place. Armed." The word hit her heart, weakening her enough to let him step her outside as Gussie and Tom and Alex came up the stairs, feet and questions flying.

Luke took over everything, moving them aside, getting them to go back down to Gussie's place, keeping everyone calm and under his orders. He ushered them into Gussie's kitchen, and when Ari was in a chair, he disappeared into the back, reappearing while Gussie and Alex peppered her with questions.

Holding a gun—a gun!—he went outside, his footsteps audible as he ran back upstairs. Tom followed, but Gussie grabbed Alex's sleeve when she tried to do the same.

"You stay right here, missy," she insisted, pushing Alex into the chair next to Ari. "I can't believe you were robbed!" she exclaimed. "Why your apartment and not ours? What did they take? Was your laptop up there? Any jewelry? TV?"

"They didn't want my TV," she said dryly. "Except to break it and look inside."

"What?" Alex demanded. "Who does that?"

Ari didn't answer, closing her eyes as puzzle pieces snapped into place. "They wanted the crate."

"The one full of seashells?" Gussie choked out the question. "I hate to break it to you, hon, but no old tools are worth that much."

But gold is. She thudded her elbow on the table, covering her mouth with her hand. She had to tell Luke first.

"Besides, it doesn't matter," Gussie said, picking up her cell phone. "I'm calling the sheriff."

"Wait." Ari put her hand on Gussie's arm.

"For what? You were robbed! They have to dust for fingerprints and take pictures and do…whatever sheriffs do."

"Wait for Luke." Already impatient to talk to him, she stood. "There's more to this than a simple robbery." So much more.

Gussie blinked at her, but Ari managed to escape when she heard a man's footsteps on the stairs. It was Tom.

"There's no one up there," he said, then put a hand on Ari's arm. "But it's pretty bad."

"I need to talk to Luke," she said, slipping out of his touch, and then throwing a warning look at Gussie. "Don't call anyone yet, okay?"

Gussie agreed with a single nod, and Ari darted outside, running up the stairs to see Luke in the doorway, stuffing a gun in the back of his jeans.

"Did you send the e-mail about the necklace?" he asked.

She came up the last few steps. "It came back as a nonexistent address."

"Do you still have that message?"

"Of course. But, Luke, this isn't about a necklace." She

reached for him, aching for those strong arms around her again.

"They were searching for something, Arielle." He wrapped her in another embrace, and she hugged him back, looking over his shoulder into her demolished apartment. At the sight, her stomach turned. Sofa cushions sliced, all her art off the wall and cut up, every book torn from the shelves, and even her coffee table had been smashed with a hammer and taken apart.

"Luke, they wanted…gold."

Luke drew back, looking at her. "What do you mean, gold?"

She sighed, not even sure how to tell him. "I'll tell you inside." She gathered up her strength, taking a few steps, but keeping one arm around Luke for support.

"Be careful," he said. "There's some glass and shards of wood."

She stole a glance at her kitchen, letting out a little moan at every open, broken cabinet. They'd even gone through her dishwasher.

"Tell me about the gold. Did you have valuable jewelry?"

"Remember when Cutter's uncle told him he was sitting on a gold mine?" she asked.

"Yeah."

She swallowed and picked up a broken mug. "Well, he is. At least, he's sitting on some gold that was apparently taken off a ship that wrecked on that coast in the 1500s. A Spanish galleon called the *San Pedro*, which had been in Mexico and the Caribbean, loaded with gold and pearls. It was in a battle with a French ship, and they both sank."

At Luke's silence, she turned, seeing him as slack-jawed as she'd been when Dr. Marksman told her the story.

"It's been rumored for years in the archaeology world,"

she told him, all the information she'd been given spilling out faster than he could likely process. "The ships are still out there, but have never been discovered. But there's folklore, and possibly some archaeological clues to support it, that when the *San Pedro* was going down, the sailors managed to get some of the gold off the ship and drag it through shallow waters to a small island. A small island, Luke."

"Like Mimosa Key."

"Yes. An offshoot tribe of the Calusa lived here, as proven by many of the artifacts in that box. They may have hidden the gold."

"That's insane."

No kidding. "Speaking of insane, Dr. Marksman was out of his mind with excitement. This would be a monumental find, obviously. He called it the Lost Gold of the Calusa, and he said archaeologists and even treasure hunters have been looking for it for years, but much farther north. No one ever thought there were Calusa Indians living this far south until we found all that stuff hidden in the house. Oh, and Luke, that core sample? It's not even from Mimosa Key!"

"I know," Luke said gruffly. "And Marksman thinks this legendary 'lost gold' is on Cutter's property?"

"Some of it, at least. The rest is at sea. But, Luke, if there's gold on that property, it technically belongs to Cutter, although I suppose there are legal hoops to jump through." She managed a smile. "But I have a feeling he won't be too upset about the delay."

But Luke didn't smile. If anything, he looked angry.

"Don't you believe me?"

"Of course I believe you, Arielle, look at this place. Someone is willing to go to a lot of trouble and"—he practically growled with anger—"I don't want you anywhere near it."

"I won't stay here tonight," she assured him. "We need to report this, and we have to tell Cutter. He's going to want to search the land, and once this gets out, we can expect Barefoot Bay to be inundated with treasure hunters."

He wasn't even listening. He kept looking around the room, as if thinking, a storm brewing from the inside out. "It's always like this," he mumbled.

"What?"

"People lose their wits, their ability to think." He sliced her with a gaze darkened by a world of hurt. "Gold makes people stupid and dangerous and deadly."

Maybe it did, but something was making him furious. "Deadly?"

"Where there's gold, there's…murder. Always."

A chill crawled up her back, a menacing ice pick of a sensation that matched the tone of his voice. "No one's been murdered, Luke." She said it almost to reassure herself because he looked so certain.

"And no one's going to be. Not on my watch." He put his hands on her shoulders and gave her a nudge. "Let's go. And not a word about gold, Arielle. Not to the cops when you report this robbery, not to my sister, not to anyone. Do you understand? Has Dr. Marksman told anyone?"

"I don't know. I don't think so…" She slowed her step and took a moment to feel the low level of something dark and scary, not just in his words, but all through the apartment. It wasn't like the greed she'd felt at the house on the hill, though it was similar.

No, this was deeper and darker and far more sinister. This was more like…desperation. Extreme desperation.

Chapter Twenty-Two

It was late and Luke was starving by the time they finished with the two deputies from the Collier County Sheriff's Department who took a report and walked through Arielle's apartment. Gussie and Tom had whisked Alex off to Tom's house, both of them wanting her as far away from the robbery as possible. Of course, they'd insisted Arielle and Luke stay with them for the night, but Luke had a few things he wanted to do first.

He whipped his truck into the Super Min's parking lot for errand number one.

"Why are you stopping here?" Arielle asked.

"I need to talk to the lady who owns the place. Does she work nights?"

"Sometimes, but if Charity's not here, someone can find her. Why do you want to talk to her?"

"I want to know more about that guy who said he was going up to the property," he said vaguely, climbing out. "Come with me."

She didn't ask any more questions, but then Arielle had been pretty quiet for the last few hours, answering the deputies' questions, staying close to Luke, barely talking to Gussie as the evening's events progressed.

He hustled around the truck to help her out, but when she slipped her hand into his, he felt an involuntary shudder. There was a time when he would have thought that little shudder was the impact of their mutual chemistry. Now, he saw fear in her eyes.

And all he wanted to do was erase it.

A teenage girl looked up from the counter when the bell dinged to announce their entry, her age making Luke wonder how difficult it would be to get information out of her, but Arielle instantly smiled.

"Ashley, I didn't know you worked here."

"Oh, hi, Ari. I come in every once in a while when Charity is in a bind." She leaned forward and whispered, "She can't keep good help. Shocker, huh?"

"This is Lacey Walker's daughter," Arielle told Luke. "Ashley, this is Luke McBain, Gussie's brother."

Luke didn't wait for the introduction formalities to be over. "Do you know how we can reach your boss?" he asked. "I need to ask her a few questions."

"She's in the back doing the books." Ashley pointed over her shoulder to a locked door. "And if I know Charity and her closed-circuit cameras, she'll be—"

The back door popped open. "What do you want from me?" Charity wasted no energy on a friendly smile, which, at the moment, suited Luke just fine.

Ashley bit back a smile and shared a look with Arielle, but Luke walked closer. "Do you remember you told us about a man who was going up to the North Barefoot Bay property the other morning?"

Her brows furrowed, but she nodded.

"Did you get his name or personal information?"

"Why do you need to know?"

"None of your business," he shot back. "But I know you

like to gather personal information, so don't even try to tell me you didn't."

An eyebrow—well, a dark line painted to look like a brow—arched up over her reading glasses. "Everything is my—"

"Not this," he said, cutting her off. "This is a matter of grave importance. Did you or did you not get his name?"

She crossed her arms and narrowed her eyes, meeting his gaze in challenge. But he flattened her with one of his own, knowing the power of how important this was coming through every cell in his body.

"No," she finally said. "He was a miserable prick who wouldn't tell me his name." She threw a look at Ashley. "Sorry, kid."

Ashley shrugged. "Believe me, I know what a miserable prick is."

"Can you describe him in more detail?" Luke asked. "Clothes, hair, size, anything distinct about him?"

"If I know why you need to know."

Arielle stepped forward. "My apartment was broken into this afternoon, Charity. We think that man who you said came in here and bought Red Bull and a newspaper might be able to help us." She reached out and put a hand on Charity's arm. "I feel so violated," she admitted softly. "And I want to find out who did this to me and my apartment."

Her technique worked better than his, making Charity soften visibly.

"Bastard," the woman mumbled with another apologetic look at Ashley. "I suppose you know what that is, too."

"All too well," Ashley said.

"No, I didn't get his name," Charity told them. "He was big and husky, talked on the phone the whole time."

"I thought you said he told you he was going up to the property," Luke said.

She managed to look sheepish. "He said it into his phone, not to me."

Irritation rocked him. "What else did he say into that phone?"

"Nothing I remember," she said. "But his fingernails were filthy."

"His fingernails?" Arielle asked.

"Like he'd been digging in dirt?" Luke suggested.

"Exactly," Charity said. "Stubby, dirty nails and a big hairy chest. Sorry, but that's all I got. And next time y'all are pickin' at me for asking questions"—she pointed one of her long nails at Arielle, then Ashley—"remember that some people want answers."

Luke thanked her and put his hand on Arielle's shoulder to guide her out, aware that she was looking hard at him. "What is it?" he asked.

"I totally forgot to tell you about the weird note I got in the mail."

He blinked at her. "What weird note?"

"A couple of days ago I got this typed note in snail mail that said"—she frowned, remembering—"'Put the pearls back where you found them.'"

He drew back, not even sure where to begin with that information. "Why didn't you tell me that? Who knows you found those pearls? And where are they now?"

She stopped the onslaught with a raised hand. "I said I forgot. I didn't think anyone was looking for pearls in my apartment because I was focused on the gold. And you're the only person who knows about the pearls."

"Did they take them?"

She shook her head. "I put them in a safe-deposit box after I got that note."

He guided her up to the passenger seat in his truck. "I have a bad feeling about this."

"And here I thought I'm the one with all the feelings."

"Not anymore, Little Mermaid."

Ari curled into the overstuffed guest chair in the corner of the Barefoot Brides office, watching Luke silently tap away at her computer. He was searching for a tech trail on the e-mail that she'd sent to the person who'd run the ad looking for the pearl necklace. On the conference table, she'd laid out the unsigned note and envelope she'd saved.

Threads of thoughts, knots of possibilities, and a few loose ends threatened to tangle in her head as she went through what they knew and didn't about this situation. There was gold, there were pearls, there was land, and her apartment had been trashed. The pressure of stress, exhaustion, hunger, and worry made her close her eyes and drift off.

Footsteps in the hall, fast and light, followed by a soft shriek startled her back awake.

"Elijah! Get back here!"

Suddenly, a tiny strawberry-blond head appeared in the doorway, almost immediately followed by Lacey Walker, who snagged her son.

"Oh, hello!" She choked out the greeting and scooped up the toddler, who shrieked again with joy. "I'm afraid our game of hide-and-seek got out of control."

"Hi, Lacey," Ari said, sitting up and fighting a yawn while Luke greeted her.

She looked from one to the other, shifting Elijah's weight to her hip. "What are you two doing here so late?"

"Just some research," Luke said quickly.

"My apartment was broken into," Ari added glumly, knowing Lacey would find out soon enough. The news elicited a gasp from Lacey. "No one was hurt," Ari assured her. "But Luke's helping me."

Lacey shook her head. "I hate to hear about any kind of crime on Mimosa Key. It's always been such a safe place to live, but we're growing. The resort, now the baseball team, and a lot of expansion and change happening in a few years."

"I don't think this had anything to do with the resort or the Barefoot Bay Bucks coming to town," Ari said.

"Still." Lacey shifted the child in her arms, but he arched his back, ready to run again. "Did you call the sheriff?"

"Oh, yeah, and we're not staying there tonight."

"Where are you staying?"

Luke gestured to the overnight bag of clothes they'd brought from home. "We're bunking at Tom's house with Gussie and Alex."

"I don't think so," Lacey said quickly. "Acacia is empty." She glanced at Luke. "It's one of our villas, right on the water. You should stay there. It's not huge, but you'd be so much more comfortable, and honestly, it's not booked for a few more days. You're welcome to it."

The thought of a whole night in the villa with Luke sent an unholy heat through Ari.

"That is so generous of you," he said before Ari could answer. "We'd love to take you up on that offer. Right, Arielle?"

As if she could refuse. "If it's not a problem, Lacey."

"None at all. Have you had dinner? We can get something sent over from Junonia."

Gratitude washed over Ari, making her stand and fight back the burn of unexpected tears. "Oh, Lacey, that's so sweet of you."

"Of course, no problem." Lacey tipped her head and patted Elijah's back with a slow, motherly beat, a hand that could somehow calm anyone and anything. Instantly, Elijah dropped his head on his mama's shoulder. "You've been through a trauma today."

"We have," Ari agreed, remembering how so many of the Casa Blanca employees commented on Lacey's maternal streak. Right now, being mothered felt as good to Ari as it must to Elijah. "And not having to sleep in a guest room or on a sofa at Tom's house is a blessing."

"Well, it's one of our smaller villas, but I'm sure you'll be comfortable," she said. "And the chef has a pasta special tonight that I've heard is getting rave reviews. We'll send it over with a bottle of wine." She lifted an eyebrow, taking in Ari's face. "Or two."

Ari laughed softly and reached out, giving Lacey and her son a hug. "Thank you. This has been a wretched day."

"Then get some rest in Acacia and enjoy a good dinner," Lacey said. "In the meantime, I hope they find whoever did it and throw them in jail. Did they take anything super valuable?"

In truth, they'd taken nothing. Not so much as a piece of costume jewelry. And, somehow, that was even creepier than if she'd been cleaned out. "Just my general sense of security."

Lacey looked sympathetic. "I'm so sorry, Ari. Not feeling like you're safe in your own home has got to be the worst part. At least tonight you'll have a safe place to stay and a very strong man to protect you."

Ari smiled. "True. Luke was a bodyguard in his previous job."

Lacey lifted her eyebrows, interested. "That's a handy kind of man to have around. I've been thinking about beefing up resort security. Maybe I'll pick your brain one of these days."

"Anytime," he said. "Consider it payback for the villa."

"Great plan. I'll call the front desk, and they'll have a key to Acacia ready for you in a few minutes."

Elijah wormed and wiggled as Lacey blew a kiss and left them alone. Luke turned again, half-smiling. "Why'd you tell her I was a bodyguard?"

She waited a minute, then answered honestly. "Because you were, and I think it's cool."

He pushed away from her computer, standing slowly. "You don't know the whole story."

"Then tell me."

"I'd rather not."

Bristling, she looked hard at him. "I'd rather you did."

"Why?"

"Because you're..." She swallowed hard. "You're important to me."

He looked down, avoiding her eyes. "You think that, but—"

"I know that," she fired back. "I feel that, and I know that doesn't always mean much to you, but it's powerful to me, Luke. I feel that you're important in my life, and I care about your past and what you did and how it happened and how it formed you into the man you are today."

He suddenly looked...pained. His eyes grew dark, his lips tight and grim, his jaw clenched.

Why did he hate it so much when she cared? What was he afraid of?

He finally lifted his gaze to meet hers. "I'm not qualified to be in security—"

"Come on, Luke. No one cares that you were in the Foreign Legion and not some more 'respected' organization. You did it. You can handle a gun. You worked as a bodyguard."

"Not a very good one."

She opened her mouth to launch the next argument, but instead said, "What?"

"You heard me."

"What happened?"

"Short version? The person I was protecting died."

"How?"

"I killed him."

"Oh." She took a slow breath, not sure what to say to that.

"And when I did, the bullet also went right through the heart of the woman I loved."

She just stared at him.

"So, bottom line, I'm a shitty bodyguard. Drop the subject, okay?"

She mouthed the only possible answer. "Okay."

Chapter Twenty-Three

There were a lot of things Luke liked about Arielle Chandler, chief among them the way she looked as she walked around the back patio of the villa after dinner, pausing to sip her wine, or gaze at the moon over the bay, or dip the very tip of her toe in the bubbles of the Jacuzzi in the corner of the pool.

Her hair glistened in the ambient light from beyond the French doors, and her body, dressed in a gauzy long dress that hinted at the curves underneath, was high on his list of favorite things.

But the thing he really appreciated—especially tonight—was that she wasn't a demander. He'd dropped a bomb what was now hours ago, telling her something he'd never even told his sister or parents, and she hadn't once insisted he say more.

Most women would be, *You killed him? And her? Why? What happened?* But not Arielle. They had walked along the stone path to the small villa centrally located at Casa Blanca, and while he opened the wine, she'd showered and changed. After a drink, they shared a delicious dinner.

All the while, they talked about the robbery, the pearls, the mysterious message, and the shipwrecked gold that might or might not be hidden somewhere on Cutter Valentine's property.

They asked each other questions, they posed possible answers, they strategized about their next move and how they would tell Cutter. After dinner, they took their wine glasses poolside, to the patio that offered a gorgeous view of the gulf and the moon-drenched sands of Barefoot Bay.

But not once did she ask him why he killed two people he was supposed to be protecting.

Maybe she didn't want to know. Maybe she didn't believe him. Maybe she hadn't quite understood.

"I assume at least one of those deaths was an accident."

The question slapped him. Or maybe she'd been waiting for the perfect moment, which, evidently, had arrived.

She stood at the edge of the Jacuzzi, her toe pointed so she could let the bubbles tickle her toes but not wet her dress.

"You should get in," he said.

She flicked some bubbles with her toes. "I thought we were camping at Tom's house tonight," she said. "I didn't bring a bathing suit."

A slight smile pulled. "Like I said, you should get in."

"Excellent subject-changing technique, Luke." She lifted her foot, precariously and perfectly balanced on the other one, perched like a flamingo holding wine. "But getting me naked and in the Jacuzzi will not stop me from wanting to know."

"And here I was admiring the fact that you hadn't asked."

"Why would you admire that?"

"I was adding it to the list."

"What list?"

"Of things I really like about you."

"Flirting won't get me to stop asking, either." She

lowered her foot and put it back in the water, closing her eyes and sighing with pleasure and want. "I've waited long enough. And I know you want to tell me."

Damn it, why could she read his thoughts? He *did* want to tell her, but he hadn't realized it yet.

"Hang on." He pushed up from his chair and went inside, hearing her deep sigh when he left. In the master bath, he gathered the fluffy white robe hanging on the back door and brought it back to the patio. On the way out, he touched the electronic pad of light switches, one by one turning off every light in the villa and the soft blue beams in the pool.

"Dark out here," she said as he stepped out.

"That's the plan."

"You think I'll strip in the dark with you watching?"

"I think"—he held up the robe like a curtain—"that you can slide into this, take that dress off, and slip into the hot tub, where you will be shrouded in darkness and a thick coat of bubbles. And by doing so, you will be comfortable, safe, and happy."

"And you will have me at a naked disadvantage while you spill your secrets."

He just smiled, because what else could he do with a woman who knew him better than he knew himself?

"Turn around," she ordered as she tugged at her top.

He lifted the robe higher and turned his head away, listening to the rustle of her dress, a whisper of air as it hit the cool bricks that surrounded the pool.

His blood stirred as he thought about how easily he could turn and admire her some more. The brush of silk against skin made him imagine her stepping out of panties. Oh, man. She grabbed the robe from him, but he stayed turned, eyes closed.

"Go over to the chaise," she ordered.

He did, sitting back where he had been and not looking until he heard a sigh of utter contentment over the rumble of the bubbles.

"Oh, this is heavenly," she said, nothing but a dark head visible over the dancing bubbles. If he peered harder, once his eyes adjusted to the darkness, he might be able to see the watery view of her breasts, but not much else.

His mouth went bone dry as he prayed for that night vision to come to life.

But first he'd have to make some confessions. He took a deep drink of merlot, bracing for the inevitable demand to—

Something soft hit him in the face. A black thong.

"Are you going to tell me now?"

He closed his fingers around the tiny piece of silk, the faintest whiff of woman way more of a hit to his brain than the wine. Threading the material through his fingers, he set the thong on his lap and smiled at her.

"Only because you asked so sweetly."

He drank again, draining the glass, considering going inside to open the second bottle, but she'd left her glass on the table, half-full, and he didn't need to be drunk to do this. Did he?

"Luke?"

He nodded, waving the underwear in a half-hearted plea for a minute to at least start the story right. "My job was to guard the family of the prefect in French Guiana."

She sat up enough to show the rise of her breasts, momentarily forgetting her nakedness. "Why exactly did they need to be guarded?"

"Because of the gold."

"What?"

He nodded, understanding her surprise. "There's an illegal and highly dangerous gold trade in Guiana. The

French think the gold belongs to them, but the locals, the Wayampi, feel differently. It's complicated. And deadly for so many people."

Neither of them spoke while he took a few seconds to accept that he was going to do this. He was going to tell her *everything*.

"Prefect Georges Pacquet was appointed by the French president to more or less keep order in the country. Madame Pacquet chose to remain in France in their Paris apartment, but Cerisse accompanied her father to the rough and tumble jungle of French Guiana."

"Cerisse? That's a beautiful name. Was she beautiful?"

He smiled at the interruption and nodded. "She had blond hair and blue eyes and a nice body." *Nice* being the understatement of the year.

"You like that type?"

"I found her to be attractive in a California-girl way, yes."

"I have California in my blood," she said with a slightly teasing tone. "Miwok are from Sacramento."

He looked through the bubbles and steam, took in her wet hair, some strands sticking to her face, which was flushed from the heat. She looked like a witch, all right, a beautiful, sexy, fiery witch bubbling in her own cauldron. And it took every ounce of strength not to leap up, strip down, and climb in.

"Let's just say my type has recently changed."

He saw her close her eyes and fight a smile.

"But, yes, she was quite beautiful and a bit impetuous." He wasn't sure why he included that character trait, except that maybe it let him off the hook a little.

"And you said you loved her."

"I...thought I did. Yes," he corrected. "I did." So, so

249

much. Crazy, hard, achy, mood-altering love. But after she died, that just felt stupid and foolish, so over the years, he'd convinced himself he couldn't have loved her. Because that would just make him a blind idiot.

"What happened?"

"Her father was on the take in a big, bad way," he said simply. "He had everyone in his pocket. The *garimpeiros*, mostly."

"The whatempeiros?"

"The Brazilians who came illegally over the border to steal gold from the mines. There were others from Suriname, too. And, of course, the Wayampi."

She sat up a little. "Natives?"

"Native to that region of French Guiana, but they are actually French citizens. Not a huge tribe, just a few thousand villagers, but they have a lucrative business supporting the Brazilians and Surinamers in the mines, paid in gold."

"How did they support the miners?"

He gave a dry snort. "All kinds of ways, but one of them was to let the smallest children into the tiny crevices to dig for gold."

She made a face, and his heart dropped. She didn't know the half of it.

"Anyway, the prefect was paid to keep his mouth shut and let them do their thing."

"And why is the Foreign Legion there?" she asked.

"To stop the gold mining, to tear down the little villages that popped up around new mines, to confiscate tools, and arrest anyone caught mining. That's what my regiment was doing while I pulled the prefect guard duty."

"And fell hard for the prefect's daughter," she surmised. Correctly. "How old was she?"

"Twenty-four," he said.

"Did the prefect know about your relationship?"

"Most certainly. And used it to his advantage." Tried to use it to save his own life, in fact. Luke pushed up, repositioning himself as if he could get away from the uncomfortable memories. But he couldn't.

"How so?"

"He needed me to do a job for him," he said, a low grade of heat rising as he thought about how heinous that job was. "You see, he was a double-, triple-, even a quadruple-dipper, and those kind of people generally meet their untimely demises. Essentially, he'd been caught taking far more than his share of gold profits, and one group of the more aggressive *garimpeiros* had a plan to do something about it."

"How?"

"Kill him."

"Whoa."

"Yeah, whoa." He puffed out a breath. "He knew what was going on and got Cerisse to convince me that he needed help. He knew where they were mining that day and decided he'd kill them before they killed him." He closed his eyes, remembering the hole in the ground and how they'd lowered kids—the smallest but strongest—to do the dirtiest of work. "He sent me to do the job."

"To kill the gold miners?" Her voice rose in disbelief. "Why?"

"Because I was his bodyguard, Arielle. My job was to stop any threats to the prefect or his family."

"By killing them?"

"Well, if someone lunged at him while he was making a speech or raised a gun to assassinate him, I sure as hell would have shot to kill."

"But that's not what happened."

No, it wasn't. "The man I was protecting demanded that I drop a grenade into a hundred-foot-deep mining cave, where about eighteen illegal miners—including at least six very small Wayampi children—were working."

She sucked in a breath loud enough to hear over the bubbling of the Jacuzzi.

"And his daughter, terrified for her father's life, agreed that I should." No, she demanded, screaming that if he loved her, he would do this.

"Really? I mean, wasn't there an answer other than killing innocent children?"

"You'd think." He shifted again, then stood to stretch his legs. "I'll tell you, Arielle, gold makes people lose their shit." He turned from her, walking toward the wrought-iron railing to look out at the water. "Did you know that the nucleus of the gold atom is larger than most elements? There's something about the chemistry of gold, I once read, that when light hits it and then bounces back to the human eye to strike the retinal wall, there is a pleasure message sent to the brain."

"And here I thought it was because gold powers our economy."

"Other way around," he corrected. "Gold has no intrinsic value except what we place on it, and ancient alchemists believed that it was part of heaven. Did you know that?"

"Careful, Mr. Rational. You're starting to sound like me."

He gripped the railing with one hand and balled up the silky thong he still held with the other.

"Finish your story," she prodded.

"I couldn't do it."

"Of course you couldn't. So what did you do?"

"I sneaked out and warned the miners. I drove out to the mine at night, when I knew they were working. I knew it could cost me my bodyguard position if I got caught, maybe even get me kicked out of the regiment and off to a shittier assignment."

"Would that have been so horrible?"

"I didn't want to leave Cerisse," he confessed. "And, I really liked the job, best I'd ever had in the Legion...until this turn of events."

He grew quiet, thinking of the night not unlike this one. Cool, moonlit, the jungle floor reeking of earth and trouble. He'd found the mine and sat in his Jeep, waiting for one of the miners to climb out and approach him.

He'd heard the engine of another vehicle and turned, catching Cerisse's shiny blond hair reflected above the headlights.

"They came after me, Prefect Pacquet at the wheel and Cerisse next to him, eyes blazing and...and...a grenade in her hand."

Behind him, he heard another soft intake of breath and a splash. "What?"

He didn't turn, not wanting to see her disgust and disbelief that he could love a woman like that. Because he had loved her. He really had.

"She jumped out of the Jeep and ran to me, holding out that weapon like Eve offering the apple."

"Did you take it?"

"Of course." He fisted the silk thong again, remembering the feel of that deadly device against the palm of his hand. "I didn't want her to throw it in the mine."

Would she have? He'd never know.

Another splash. "And?"

"And her father came at us with a .357 Magnum in his hand, demanding I throw the grenade."

And then the sound of a small voice, Taka's voice,

calling out in the chopped sounds of the native language, his little hand appearing at the top of the mine. He could hear Cerisse's French demands, shrill and relentless.

Tu veux que mon père te tue?

Yes, at that instant, he *did* want her father to kill him. Death would have been better than making that decision. Much better. But, then, she might have thrown the fucking grenade in the hole after he was dead.

He closed his eyes, the whole scene playing over and over in his head. Cerisse rushing back to get closer to her father. The flash of light. The explosion. The shot. Taka's scream and...

"And there was a little boy coming out of the mine."

He heard Arielle's soft gasp, and nodded as if to echo the sentiment.

"I knew someone was going to die. Me. The kid. The old man. Cerisse. Someone." He grunted softly when two hands landed on his back.

"What happened, Luke?"

"I threw the grenade in the opposite direction, hoping it would divert everyone and stop the madness. But the prefect raised his gun at me, and I moved on instinct, going for my weapon. As I pulled it out, he fired and I fired back, but..." He couldn't finish.

"But what?"

"But the old man grabbed his daughter to use her as a human shield, so fast I didn't have time to stop my trigger finger, and the bullet went through her and into his chest. They both died almost instantly."

He let his head drop, the shame and anguish and self-loathing that eroded his soul on a daily basis burning in his gut right now.

"Luke." She tried to turn him around, but he stayed stiff,

refusing to meet her gaze. "Luke, you saved those children and those natives."

He squeezed his eyes, not surprised they stung. "But the prefect's bullet hit the boy just as he emerged from the mine, a five-year-old boy. A boy who will never walk again," he ground out, hating the tears that stung his eyes. "So I killed the two people I was supposed to be protecting and ruined a child's life."

"Luke!" She tried again to force him around, but he couldn't stand to look at her right then. "That man wanted to kill children, and she was going to help! And the boy lived."

"Fortunately, that's how the Legion saw it, too," he said. "France wanted to keep it very quiet. So there was no recrimination for me, but I quit the Legion the very day I could." He sighed. "And I haven't stopped working one minute since then."

"Working?" Her voice rose with confusion. "To take your mind off it?"

"To make money. I have to have a steady, constant income, Arielle, because I support Takalawe and his family. I moved them out of the gold mines and set them up on a small farm just outside the village. Taka has a wheelchair and..." Behind him, he felt her shudder.

Turning, he saw her face wet with tears, her lip quivering as she fought a sob. "You're doing that?"

"Of course," he said. "He would have died without help, and the family—"

"And that's why you have to have a job."

"Always. I will never let that family want anything, regardless of where I live. I didn't know any other trade or business but building because it's pretty much half of what Legionnaires do. Anything else would take too much training or education, and I don't have time or enough savings because…"

"Because you take care of…Taka?"

He nodded, fighting a smile. "He's a great kid, too."

A little whimper escaped her throat as she wrapped her arms around him and pressed her tear-soaked cheek against his shoulder and her dripping wet body against his clothes. "Grandma Good Bear would love you."

He smiled against her hair, the compliment like balm on his wretched conscience. "I don't see it that way."

She looked up at him. "Which is the most awesome part." She gave him a squeeze. "I'm really sorry you had to make that decision and those people died, and sorry that soured you on trust and love, and sad that little boy is in a wheelchair."

He was glad there was no but. "Thanks, I am, too."

"And I'm really glad you haven't been with a woman since then."

"I'm not," he admitted. "But I didn't trust myself or my judgment after that. I don't have your intuition for what's right and wrong, what's good and bad, who's meant for me and who's not."

"I have enough intuition for both of us." She smiled up at him. "You are a hero." She lifted on her toes and put her mouth over his, the kiss tender and full of promise and healing. "And you know why you saw that woman's true colors and you had to stop her from killing children and wait and wait and wait to be with another woman? Do you know why?"

"Because I was meant to find you?"

She sighed and smiled and closed her eyes. "I wish that hadn't been a question but a statement."

So did he. "How can we know for sure?"

"I already do."

He felt his heart skip around, wanting so much for her to be right. "You know."

She nodded. "I've never been more sure. Luke, I am The One for you, and you are The One for me, and right now we are going to make love, and it will be absolutely laden with significance and wonder, and the universe will sing for happiness because we found each other or…"

"Or what?"

"Or we'll just have the best damn sex of our lives."

He felt his mouth kick up in a smile. "Let's find out."

Chapter Twenty-Four

They kissed with purpose, and that purpose was connection. Not sex, not pleasure, not the desire that sliced through them. They needed each other in a way that...well, that Ari had never felt before.

That need had her shaking as she balled up his T-shirt to get it over his head, but his hands were sure and steady, already exploring her naked body. When his chest was bare, she splayed her hands over his pecs and rubbed each cut and angle, loving the heat, the hair, the slamming heart under her fingertips.

And the dear, good heart that pounded underneath that sexy male flesh.

He cupped her breast and feathered kisses down her throat, bending to taste her. She reached to his jeans, easily unbuttoning and unzipping, her hand instantly filled with his engorged erection.

"Arielle," he murmured, his kisses stalled while he found his footing and let her stroke the length of him. "I love when you touch me. It's perfect."

It was. He was. This was. She kissed his chest and shoulders and mouth, while they took a few steps away from the railing. He stopped where her clothes were lying and scooped up the bathrobe.

"The bed is on the other side of those French doors," she said.

"Too far." He spread the robe on the cushions of the double-wide chaise. "We'll go there for round two." Standing next to the chaise, he stripped off his jeans and boxers with lightning speed, leaving her on her back, looking up to appreciate…everything.

He was enormous, defined, dusted in dark hair, and as manly as anything she'd ever seen. Still standing, he reached down and stroked her hair, a far more gentle touch than she expected with a man whose gaze was anything but gentle.

She closed her fist around his hard-on, making him hiss in a noisy breath.

"I want to touch your hair," he said. "I want to get lost in it."

"I want to touch this," she said, giving him a squeeze. "I want to get lost in it."

He laughed softly and finally gave in, joining her on the cushion that easily accommodated both of them.

"Out here?" she asked.

"Under the three-quarter moon," he whispered, settling mostly on top of her.

"That sounds like a song."

"I thought it sounded like an Indian legend. Making love under the three-quarter moon guarantees a lifetime of endless, fruitful couplings."

She tried to laugh at his joke, but her heart tripped her up. A lifetime? Fruitful? "You better be careful, Luke McBain. You're starting to sound like Grandma Good Bear."

"I know. I need an Indian name like Moonraker or…" He

stroked her from collarbone to hip, going slow at strategic places in between. "Little Mermaid's Bighorn."

She giggled at that, letting him touch her, finding her perfect place with him, the fight about whether he was The One completely over in her mind. It had evaporated as he told his story, and she understood him so much better now. Understood and appreciated him.

"Hey, you stopped kissing and started thinking," he noted, traveling a finger around her nipple until it budded in near pain.

"I was thinking about all that you told me."

He closed his eyes. "Funny, I was forgetting about it."

"But you can't."

He answered by lowering his head and replacing his finger with his mouth, kissing, then sucking on her breast. Fire licked her veins, his mouth searing her skin. "I have to," he insisted, making her wonder for a second if he meant he had to forget or he had to suck. Harder.

She arched her back and tunneled her fingers into his short hair, pushing his mouth harder against her.

"I have to forget," he murmured as he trailed kisses over her stomach. "I need to...I need to." He punctuated each word with another kiss, moving lower, over her belly, over her navel, lower to lick the tuft of hair between her legs.

She gripped his head and pulled him up. His expression was pure bewilderment. "Let me taste you."

"Then we have to go inside," she said.

"Why?"

"Condom?"

He smiled, slow and easy, reaching around to grab the edge of the robe. He slipped his hand into the large tufted pocket and pulled out a foil packet.

"You brought that out here?"

"Either that or there's one in every bathrobe in this resort. That'd be a good amenity for this place." He grinned as he set it on the armrest next to them. "Now where was I?"

She pushed his head, and he followed the order, kissing his way back to her hips and thighs, using his tongue to tease and torture her, curling, kissing, licking, and making her moan and fight for every breath through every second of pure pleasure.

"Please, Luke." She pulled his shoulders, wanting him back on her, wanting the weight of him on top of her, wanting to spread her legs and take him in.

He complied with one, long, lingering kiss on her tummy, then lifted her legs to kneel between them and roll on the condom.

While she watched, Ari's heart hammered and her hands shook. As always, her heart ached with that feeling of…making room for love. Her limbs were numb with need, her head light with love.

So maybe it had been lust when she first laid eyes on him, but it wasn't now. Despite what they were doing, how utterly lusty it was, this wasn't just lust. The certainty of that washed over her, as warm and exciting as his hands and kisses.

He braced himself over her, positioning his body to enter hers. His jaw was slack with short, pained breaths, his chest heaving with the work of taking each one. But his eyes were soft, unfocused, and full of the same love she felt.

Lowering himself, he eased into her, both of them gasping at the contact, freezing for a moment, then easing into a natural rhythm that rocked the chaise in a *tap tap tap* against the bricks.

Ari closed her hands over Luke's shoulders and pressed her cheek against his, their mouths so close to each other's ear, they could whisper. Words like yes, please, good, more…floated into her head. And phrases like touch me, don't stop, too much, and I can't…all sang in her ears. She couldn't tell what was her imagination, her voice, his voice. What was her body, his body, their connection, and their release.

Her orgasm happened fast, at almost the same time as his, with whip-crack intensity. And more words played around her head. Beautiful. Amazing. Perfect. Sweet.

And…*I love you.*

She wasn't sure if she said it or he did, or if she imagined it or he did. Someone said it. And even if it was only the universe, truer words were never spoken.

He'd never really believed her. Not once, not really. This business about "the one" was merely nonsense. Silly. Ridiculous musings no different from some fairy tale.

Except nothing felt nonsensical right this minute. Or silly. Or ridiculous. In fact, every inch of Luke felt whole and complete, at peace and still.

And not just his body, which was relieved and satisfied. No, this peace was deeper. In his heart. In his soul.

"Luke?"

"Yeah?" Should he tell her? Should he admit that he'd been playing along, not believing anything, until—

"I'm freezing."

He lifted his head to look at her, rubbing his arm over a billion chills. "Let's go inside."

"No, in the hot tub." She gave him a little push. "It's warm, and I don't want to leave the moonlight."

He got up and brought her with him, both of them taking quick steps to the edge of the hot, bubbling water. Holding hands, they stepped over the side, instantly blasted with heat. He sat on the ledge, up to his neck in water, and pulled Arielle onto his lap, tucking her down so she was blanketed in bubbles, too. She wrapped her legs around his waist and settled her bottom on his lap, smacking their bodies as close as they could be.

Her hair drifted around the water like black seaweed, her eyes glistening, her lips a little swollen from their kissing. And his whole being just…melted.

Smiling, she laid her head on his shoulder and let out an audible sigh of contentment.

"I never believed you," he whispered into her ear.

She answered with a tiny squeeze of her legs, not lifting her head as if she sensed it was easier for him to make this admission without looking into her eyes.

"I don't believe things easily," he said. "I mean, I need proof. I need something tangible. I need…" He caressed her back, up and down, memorizing the gentle curves of her body, a little overwhelmed by how she felt to him. "You."

"You've got me."

"Mmm." He kissed her hair and ear and temple. "How'd I get so lucky?"

"There's no such thing as luck. Or coincidence. Or chance. Or random anything." Her voice was filled with such conviction, it nearly took his breath away.

"You really believe that."

She laughed softly, lifting her head. "I really believe it. The same way I really believe you are The One meant for me."

He waited for the punch of fear, the squeeze of nerves, the low-grade headache of *holy hell, this can't end well.* But all he could do was fall into the depths of her eyes and wonder if he would ever breathe again without wanting her.

Damn it.

She laughed again, tapping his nose. "Why does this man look horrified?"

"Not because of what you said," he assured her. "But because…" It can't last. He knew that, because…because nothing lasted in his life. Not his great childhood, which went up in flames when he threw a bottle rocket at his sister. Not his badass military life, which lost its appeal when he killed two people with one bullet. And not this next phase. "Nothing lasts for me."

"What about that little boy, Taka?"

"What about him?"

"He'll last because of you. Don't you see, Luke? All this pushing and pulling we've done with me trying to preserve the ancient history of a long-dead tribe and you saved a family that is alive today. I'm almost embarrassed at my obsession with the past when there are people living like that right now in places I didn't even know existed."

"Don't be, but if you ever want to go down there and meet him…"

"Can I?"

He smiled, the words he wanted to say bubbling up like the water around him. *I love you, Arielle.* But he tamped them down. "I'm sure we can arrange something." He played with some wet strands of hair, stroking her shoulder, the rise of her breast, up her throat. "When did you absolutely know for certain?" he asked.

"About you?"

He nodded. "I mean, I'm guessing you're pretty sure about this."

"I wasn't positive until now. But, really, when I look

back over the past few days, I think I knew when you touched me the first time on the hill. Didn't you feel anything that moment, when you wrapped your hand around my wrist and helped me up?"

"I felt…" He closed his eyes and traveled back to the moment. "Stunned."

"And yet I was the one knocked off my feet. Literally."

He remembered the look on her face, wide-eyed and, yes, stunned. "What was your very first thought?" he asked.

"I was so wrapped up in that necklace, I didn't see you. I heard a bird, a big vulture, and I thought your footsteps were another one flapping its wings." She smiled slowly. "Then you came up the rise of the hill, all sweaty and bare-chested, and I…couldn't breathe."

"Really?" He shook his head. "I slammed into you and felt so bad and stupid, and then I thought you were…perfect." Not gorgeous, which she was, but perfect. "I remember thinking that distinctly. But I thought it was hormones, not my heart."

"Have you ever felt it with anyone else in your life—like that? Like this?"

No, not for one second, not even remotely. "I've felt sexual desire."

"Does it feel like this?"

Not even close. "But what happens when it's over?"

She laughed softly. "Not to freak you out or anything, but it isn't ever going to be over. Can you handle that?"

He closed his hands over her shoulders, gripping her, feeling the realness of her. "Arielle, could you handle if it ever *was* over?"

She didn't answer, but for a long time, they looked at each other, and suddenly, the bubbles stopped, surrounding them in an unexpected silence.

"'Cause it could end," he said. "Exactly like the Jacuzzi timer."

She reached over his shoulder, pressing her whole body into him, then standing a little so her breast was centimeters from his mouth. And suddenly, the bubbles started up with a noisy splash.

"Then we'll turn everything right back on again." She deliberately let her breast brush his lips. "Like that." And let him taste the other. "And that." Very slowly, she rose from the water, her feet on the ledge where he sat, letting every inch of her glorious body pass by his face until his mouth was right against her thigh. "Maybe just like that, too."

He groaned into the kiss, nibbling the soft skin, tasting heaven.

Reaching down, she wrapped her hand around his wrist and gave a tug.

"Looks like I rang your bell, McBain." The words, so like the first ones he said to her, made him smile.

"So, now what, Little Mermaid?"

"Now we go inside and see how we do on a real bed."

"I have a feeling we're going to do great," he said.

She laughed. "You and your feelings."

Chapter Twenty-Five

"I'm about to hand you a few million dollars and more trouble than you probably ever want."

The words, whispered into Ari's right ear, pulled her from a deep sleep and a sweet dream.

Her eyes opened, and reality hit. She was in bed with Luke, under a gauzy canopy with early morning light streaming in through plantation shutters. Very slowly, she turned to face the man who had her curled into his chest and belly, sighing sleepily at the sight of his green-gold eyes and unshaven face.

"Excuse me?" she said.

"Or I could say, 'Hey, Cutter, I got good news and bad news. Which do you want first?'" He smiled and kissed her nose. "I'm practicing for the meeting I called with him this morning."

She leaned up. "You have a meeting with him today?"

"I e-mailed him from your office last night, and he's still in town, so we're meeting at the property in"—he lifted a cell phone from the nightstand and checked the time—"a few hours. Enough time for a proper good-bye." He dropped the phone and wrapped an arm around her, pulling her in for a kiss.

She drew way back.

"Don't tell me you're a 'have to brush your teeth first' girl. I did already while you were sleeping. If you want to—"

"No. I mean, yes. I don't know." She choked softly in exasperation. "I'm not an anything kind of girl because I don't spend the night with guys. Remember? Celibate?"

"Celibacy has ended." He underscored that with a bold stroke over her belly, then lower.

She shuddered when he stroked between her legs. "Yes, it has. But tell me why we have to say a proper good-bye."

His fingers glided over her. "It can be improper." And slid inside her. "Feels like you'd enjoy that."

"I…would. I am." She closed her eyes and dropped her head back on the pillow, letting him explore her. "I don't know why we have to say good-bye. Can't I go…*oh*." Sparks collided inside her as he worked more magic.

"No." He leaned over and suckled her breast, using his thumb to drive her crazy and his tongue to make her want to scream.

"But I want to." She rocked once.

"Then go ahead," he teased, slipping another finger into her, rubbing and thumbing and bringing her right to the edge before she was even fully awake. "Come."

"To meet Cutter."

"In my hand."

She couldn't argue, not then, at least. Instead, she fisted the sheets and writhed under his palm and lost her breath and her mind and her ability to speak until she came, as he demanded, hard and fast.

"How…did…you…do…that?" she managed.

He laughed. "Want me to show you again?"

"Later. I won't be able to walk today as it is." She opened one eye and peered at him. "And I will walk…up the hill when we meet with Cutter Valentine."

"I don't know if it's safe, Arielle. I'd rather you were here."

"I'm safe with you," she said softly, stroking his cheek. He looked doubtful. "I am," she whispered. "I trust you completely to keep me safe. I think that when Cutter decides not to build that house, you should start some type of bodyguard business right here, close to me, because I want to stay with you." Forever.

He just looked at her. "I love how straightforward you are."

"And I'll be straightforward with Cutter." She closed her hand around his morning erection and stroked slowly. "When you take me with you today."

"You're manipulating me."

She smiled, sliding under the covers. "I'm about to."

An hour later, they were in Luke's truck, gobbling up the gravel and dirt on the last bit of road before the turn to North Barefoot Bay.

"What do you think he'll want to do?" Ari asked, taking a sip of the coffee they'd brought with them from the resort.

"Hard to say," Luke mused, his eyes narrowing behind sunglasses. "Why is that freaking fence down?"

The bright yellow plastic fence, the silt fence, as he'd called it, was flattened at the place where they usually had to get out and unhook it.

"Cutter?" she asked.

"I doubt it. He's not supposed to be here for a while."

"Then who's in that big truck?" A mud-splattered white truck with writing on the side blocked the view of the house.

"I don't know. But Cutter's Mercedes is next to it." Luke swore softly. "I'm not late. I hate to be late."

"No, he's early," she assured him as they pulled up. "And

he's..." She looked up the hill and sucked in a breath. "Digging for something at the top."

Luke's eyes popped at the sight. Someone had planted stakes about halfway up the hill and strung an orange rope, and about seven No Trespassing signs decorated the grass. At the top of the hill, Cutter and two other men, both in matching khaki shirts and pants, were talking. One of the men was leaning on a shovel.

Cutter turned and gave a sharp, quick wave, and even from this distance, Ari could see the face of an unhappy man.

"Looks pissed," Luke said as he turned off the truck.

"Maybe the news that he's sitting on millions of dollars will cheer him up."

"Maybe." He put his hand on the door and gave her a warning look. "Don't tell anyone, Arielle. Whoever those guys are, whatever they're doing, don't tell them. It'd be asking for a shit ton of trouble."

She nodded, turning to get out, when her gaze fell on the writing on the side of the truck.

United States Army Corps of Engineers.

Luke saw it, too, but stayed silent as they rounded the other vehicles and headed up the hill together.

"Morning, Cutter," he called.

"Not a good one," Cutter said. "These gentlemen seem to be bringing all work to a stop. Not that it was exactly flying forward."

Ari felt Luke bristle as they reached the others, extending his hand. "Luke McBain."

"Bill Cullen, with the Corps, and this is Matt Prawl, our bone specialist." He turned to Ari and smiled. "You must be Arielle Chandler. We can't thank you enough for filing this report, ma'am."

Her jaw dropped, the words so unexpected and…wrong. "Pardon me?"

"You are"—he pulled out a paper and tapped the top— "Arielle Chandler? Am I saying that right? Do you go by another Native American name, ma'am?"

"Yes, I'm Arielle Chandler, but…" A slow roll of heat crawled up her chest. "What report are you talking about?"

"This one, filed last Monday. Says this building is likely an infringement of NAGPRA. As you see, it's not something we take lightly."

"NAGPRA?" Luke asked, his gaze confused as he turned to her.

"Native American Graves Protection and Repatriation Act," she said, the words barely coming out as anything but a whisper, she was so stunned.

"Passed in 1990," the other man said. "It's something any builder in this country should be quite familiar with."

The subtext of indictment wasn't lost on anyone. Defenses rising, Ari took a step closer. "Just to be clear, I didn't file that report."

Bill snapped the paper officiously. "Your name's on it, ma'am. You called the office and gave the details of this property's location and, according to our notes, said you have reason to believe this mound is a Native American burial site. Are you denying that?"

"No." Damn it, she *had* called last Monday. Before everything started. "I left a message and…was just trying to get more information." Even as she spoke them, the words sounded hollow. And Luke looked like she'd hit him with one of the stakes in the ground.

"Well, thank you for the tip," Bill said. "We do have reason to believe it's a native burial site, so we appreciate you filing the report."

"But I didn't—"

Cutter held his hand up. "I don't give a crap who filed the report. Luke, why didn't you know about this?"

All eyes were on him, but Luke chose to meet Cutter's. "I knew there was a possibility, and I've retained a different geotechnical firm to perform a second core sampling and determine what materials are under this grass. That'll happen next week, and then I'll have two analyses that confirm—or not—that this hill is nothing but a shell mound, which is not protected under any act."

Ari breathed a sigh of relief, so happy he had the right answer.

But he still didn't look at her, and didn't appear to be happy at all. Had he believed her when she'd sworn she didn't file that report? Did he trust her?

Or would she be another woman who took the wrong side against him?

"How long will that take?" Cutter demanded.

"Doesn't matter," Bill interjected before Luke could answer. "Once a report's been filed, we don't use the core sample analysis. According to the law, we have to investigate ourselves, and that means surface digging and even something more aggressive. Whatever we find has to be analyzed at our labs up in DC, and honestly, that's going to take a month or two, maybe even more."

Cutter grunted softly, then slid a dark look to the man with the shovel. "Then get moving."

The man walked away and stuck a shovel in the ground about ten feet away.

"So he's arbitrarily digging around?" Luke asked. "With no plan or purpose?"

Bill snorted a laugh. "Welcome to the US government, son."

They all waited an awkward beat as the shovel thudded into the ground. Ari looked at Luke, hoping to share a secret message—if they found gold, that would shut them all up—but he was watching the engineer, his face the image of unhappiness.

It didn't matter that she hadn't officially filed any reports. She'd called to get information and, yes, she'd mentioned the location on the off chance that someone else had already looked into the possibility this was a burial mound. But that long explanation seemed wrong now. She'd tell him later.

But he wouldn't even look at her.

Biting back the hurt, she followed his gaze and watched the man dig, then closed her eyes as something curled through her. A word she couldn't quite grab. It wasn't frustration or sadness or surprise or any of the things she expected to feel at this moment. It was…

Buried.

Something was hidden. She balled her fists at her sides, keeping her eyes closed, concentrating on the word that somehow was being screamed in her head. Something was buried…*there.*

She turned and looked at the spot, maybe twenty feet away, and recognized it instantly by the foliage around the area. The spot where Luke had knocked her over. She took a few steps toward the place, trying to let her feelings take over any thoughts or memories.

Buried.

She tried to swallow and failed, wondering how she could explain to these men that she felt something was hidden here. Only Luke would understand. She glanced over her shoulder at him, but he still wouldn't look at her.

She refused to let that distract her, turning back to where her intuition led her. What was buried? Treasure, of course.

Gold bricks stamped with the Spanish king's seal. More pearls. Maybe rubies and diamonds.

The *San Pedro* had been loaded, Dr. Marksman told her.

And something was right here. Right on this very spot a foot from a scrubby pygmy palm she distinctly remembered when she'd found the pearls.

It was as if the pearls had *marked the very spot.*

"Right here!" Her voice rang through the open air, making all four men turn to her. "It's right here." A zing of certainty snapped her elbow as she pointed furiously to the very spot.

The bone specialist, Matt, was next to her in a flash, shovel extended.

"What's right there?" Cutter demanded as the man broke ground.

She looked at Luke, and he gave his head an infinitesimal shake. She swallowed hard and managed a shrug. "I'm not sure, but my guess is that it's"—gold—"valuable."

"What makes you think something's there?" Bill asked.

"I…" Feel it. Know it. Believe it. "I found something up here a while ago, and it was right there."

"What did you find? A bone? A skeleton?" Bill asked.

"Whoa!" They all turned to the man with the shovel, who thankfully saved her from answering.

Matt flipped a load of dirt, then froze, inching backward, then kneeling very slowly to the ground. Inexplicable fear pranced up Ari's back. Terror, actually. Horror. Nothing she would expect to feel when they were about to discover The Lost Gold of the Calusa.

"Not a skeleton," Matt said quietly. "This guy's only been dead about a week."

Ari gasped, sucking in air and getting a lungful of wretched stench.

"What?" Cutter practically leaped to the hole in the ground, and Luke came from behind, pulling her away.

"There's a body?" she managed to whisper. That's what was buried.

"Yep," Matt said. "Easy to ID, since he's got a tattoo."

Ari leaned over, the foul smell assaulting her as she peered at the body, dark ink visible on his left arm.

Only God can judge me.

"Holy shit." Cutter peered into the ground, his hand over his mouth and nose for protection. "That's Jim Purty, the builder I fired."

Chapter Twenty-Six

"Luke wants you to ride back with me." Gussie put a comforting arm around Ari, whispering the words.

Ari turned to her, not answering right away, digging for the right response. "Okay." It was the best she could do. She was talked out, anyway, having spent hours and hours with law enforcement, doing interview after interview, telling them everything, starting with the pearl necklace she'd found.

Luke had done the same, separate from her for most of the day, though they'd never left the property. It had all been exhausting and stressful, leaving Ari too wiped to even consider why Luke wouldn't want her to ride with him after they were finally given permission to leave the crime scene.

She knew why, though. And simply couldn't think about it right then.

"Where are we going?" Ari asked as she let Gussie lead her to the car.

"Lacey's house."

Ari palmed her forehead, squeezing her temples to ward off the throbbing headache that had started sometime after they found the corpse but right before the Collier County

Sheriff's Department arrived in full force. Had there ever been a murder on Mimosa Key before? Ari didn't know, but they sure sent out every deputy they had, plus forensics specialists, investigators, photographers. Luke had patiently talked to everyone.

But he'd never talked to her. That's why Ari had called Gussie. She had to have someone to talk to.

"Why are we going to Lacey's house?" she asked, slipping into the passenger seat of Tom's SUV, which Gussie had borrowed to come up here.

"Well, we can't go home, at least not to your apartment, because it's still a crime scene."

Of course, they'd made the association between the robbery and this murder. They'd even sent a sheriff's deputy to the bank to retrieve the necklace from her safe-deposit box. "But why Lacey's house? Can't we go to Tom's? I need to veg and not talk to any people right now."

"Because when there's a crisis at Barefoot Bay, that's where we go."

"There's a crisis?"

Gussie shot her a look, a little sympathy in her eyes, but plenty of *get real*, too. "A dead body is a crisis. My brother's involvement, and yours, is a crisis."

"You mean our involvement with each other? That's over." Even as she said the words, she knew they were true. It shredded her heart, but couldn't be denied.

"I meant your involvement with the property and the robbery at your apartment." She turned the wheel and rolled over the dirt road. "What the hell do you mean it's over?"

"Gussie, he thinks I called the Army Corps of Engineers and filed a violation of NAGPRA."

"Well, you told him you didn't, right?"

"But I did call, but only to leave a message and dig

around for information. I didn't officially report anything. If that's all it takes for Luke to write me off, then, sorry, we won't last."

Gussie waved her hand at the soft break in Ari's voice. "You'll tell him, and then he'll know. That's a misunderstanding, is all."

Ari turned to look at the scrub-lined road, gauging the time to be very late afternoon, based on the light.

"He couldn't talk to you," Gussie said, her voice rising in defense. "You're both suspects."

"That's ridiculous." But she knew it was true. She didn't even own a gun, but Luke did.

And Jim Purty, Luke's predecessor on the job, had been shot in the chest.

"I know that, you know that, and, hell, I think the sheriff guys knew that, too. But they had to follow protocol and keep you separate."

"He never even looked at me." She cleared her throat, because her voice cracked again and she so didn't want to cry over this. She blinked back a tear, knowing it was too late. "We slept together last night."

Gussie didn't say anything, but reached over and put her hand on Ari's arm. "It's going to be okay, sweetie. I'd bet on it. I got a Curly Wurly bar I'd wager."

Ari couldn't even smile, and the foliage grew blurrier.

"So you actually think my brother would have sex with you and then dump you the next day because he mistakenly believes you called the authorities to stop his work?"

"It doesn't matter."

"Like hell it doesn't!" Gussie shot back. "You can't give up that easily, Arielle Chandler. If he's worth loving, then he's worth explaining it to."

"I can explain it, and he might believe me," she said.

"But the damage is done. He assumed the worst. I saw it on his face. He's not The One."

"Oh, screw that 'he's The One shit.'" Gussie repositioned herself in the driver's seat as emotion got hold of her. "You either connect with him or you don't. You had amazing sex or you didn't. You have a chance at a future or you don't. Yes or no?"

"I don't know," she said glumly. "And I should. Listen, take me back to the villa where we stayed last night. I don't feel like going to Lacey's house."

"Luke will be there. You could talk to him."

"Please, Gussie. It's been a helluva day. I want to go take a shower and go to sleep. Luke can stay with you at Tom's house." She turned and seared her friend with a look. "Please make him stay with you at Tom's house. I need to be alone."

Gussie let out a frustrated breath, quiet until they reached the resort. "Running away from him isn't going to solve anything," she finally said. "I know that from experience."

"Tom came back to find you."

"Not until he killed his own demons, and let me tell you, those weeks that I waited were sheer hell." Her touch was gentler now. "Don't put up a wall, Ari, and get all caught up in whether or not the universe decided he's the one for you. Go talk to him and decide for yourself."

Ari didn't answer, biting her lip. "I'm sorry, Gussie, but if this was real, he wouldn't doubt me."

"The guy had your name on a report. He made a fair assumption, but you can set him straight."

"I shouldn't have to set him straight. Not if we're the real thing."

"You're being stupid and stubborn," Gussie said.

"I'm being cautious and self-protective." She grabbed the door handle and pushed. "I just need to think this through."

"Okay. You know where I'll be."

Ari blew a half-hearted kiss and slipped out of the car, practically running down the shadowy path to Acacia. Thankfully, she and Luke had each taken a key, so she could get into the villa, shower, change, and cry.

As she stood at the door, key poised, she closed her eyes against the tears that had decided they couldn't wait for a shower. God, how she wanted him to be here, waiting, open arms, open mind, open heart.

She unlocked the door and stepped into the dark villa. Tapping the light switch, she looked around the small living area, which was completely empty. Walking in, she headed into the hall and looked at the bedroom, all evidence of their lovemaking cleaned up by the efficient housekeeping staff. The bathroom was empty, the patio dark, the Jacuzzi quiet.

She listened for a sound—a message from the universe. But all she could hear were the wise, wise words of her dearest friend.

You're being stupid and stubborn.

Damn it, Gussie was right. What was she going to do here all alone except feel sorry for herself and miss Luke with every bone in her body? They needed to talk. Even if he didn't want to, she had to have a chance to tell him she'd never filed a report. How did the Army Corps of Engineers even know what land she'd been talking about, anyway? They needed to talk.

He needed to believe her.

She grabbed the key and her bag and ran back down the path to the employee parking lot to get in her own car, the decision so right she almost laughed out loud.

She stopped at the four-way light, peering into the brightly lit Super Min. She could see Ashley talking to a customer, obviously roped into working again, and missing the gathering at her mother's house. It certainly wasn't a party under the circumstances, but Ari still felt she should take something to Lacey's house. Especially to say thank-you for offering the villa as a safe place to stay.

She made a quick turn into the lot, parked next to the only other car in front, and hopped out to reach the door just as a customer inside came out.

"Oh, excuse..." Ari's voice faded as she did a double take, recognizing the woman from GeoTech, her name not instantly coming to mind.

The lady had her head down and brushed by, not looking at Ari. As fast as they bumped into each other, the other woman was gone.

"Oh my God, Ari!" Ashley called from behind the counter when Ari walked in. "That's so weird. That lady was looking for you."

"What?" She turned to see the woman getting into her car, and now she was staring straight at Ari. "She was looking for me?"

Ashley frowned and leaned all the way over the counter, trying to catch the woman's attention by waving. "Yeah, she was asking me if I knew you."

Ari turned again, but the headlights came on, blinding her until the car whipped out of the spot. "Why would she ask you?"

"Because the Super Min is generally the center of all information on Mimosa Key."

Ari stood frozen in the doorway, part of her wanting to run out and stop...*Michelle*. The name popped into her head, but something kept her rooted to the spot, staring at the car as it pulled away.

"Weird." Which was exactly how she felt inside. Finally,

she stepped all the way into the store. "Did she say why she's looking for me?"

"No, but—"

"You didn't tell her about what's going on in North Barefoot Bay, did you?" It was only a matter of time until the media got this news. In fact, if people were asking about her, then it had probably hit the Internet already. They'd told the deputies about the gold. It had probably leaked already, and the gold-rush craziness was bound to start.

What had Luke said? *Gold makes people lose their shit.*

Like shoot a man and bury him on a hillside. Or sow seeds of doubt with your lover.

"I didn't tell her anything," Ashley assured her. "I'm not Charity. Anyway, my mom said mum's the word until we have to deal with the media." Her pretty features melted a bit. "Are you okay? I heard you found the body."

"Not exactly, and I'm fine." She passed the counter and headed toward the wine cooler. "I'm going to your mom's house now. Do you know what kind of wine she likes?"

"Red. White. Pink." She grinned. "My mother likes wine."

"Who doesn't?" Ari grabbed a chilled bottle of chardonnay and paid for it, still glancing out to the parking lot. "I know her," Ari said. "Her name's Michelle, and she works on the mainland. I wonder if she lives here on the island."

"Doubtful. I know everybody." She gave Ari change and the wine. "If she comes back, should I tell her where you are?"

Why would Michelle be looking for her? True, they hadn't returned the core sample they'd borrowed, but was she so efficient at her job that she tracked down clients where they lived and demanded missing bags of seashells?

"No, don't tell her where I live. I'll call her at work tomorrow."

"'Kay. See you soon, Ari. I'm done here in an hour, and I'm hoping there's food at home."

"I'm sure there will be. See you there." Holding the wine, she walked out to her car, the real reason Michelle wanted her all too clear. Word must be out about Jim Purty's death and, no doubt, the possibility that there was gold hidden in Barefoot Bay. That would bring all kinds of weirdos out of the woodwork, and maybe Michelle thought she had a leg up or something since they'd met.

There were so many things she hadn't considered this afternoon, she thought as she got into the car. So many things to talk to Luke about. For that reason alone, she was—

"I want the gold."

Ari jumped at the voice, shrieking softly. Then she saw the gun in the rearview mirror, the barrel pointed right at her head.

"And I know you have it."

The place was overrun with billionaires. Three, at least, and Cutter Valentine, who was clearly at home with the men who'd hired him to manage their minor league team. Clay Walker seemed comfortable with the rich company, too.

Luke stood on the outskirts of a conversation circle, listening to Cutter relive the day's events, one eye on the door. His conversation with his sister had been enlightening, and a little frustrating. How could Arielle think he wouldn't believe her? He hadn't been allowed to talk to her all day, all personal conversation forbidden while they were being interviewed. Under the circumstances, he could definitely be a suspect in this killing.

But they could talk now, so why hadn't she come?

And he didn't care that Gussie told him she was determined to stay in the villa. He knew her; Arielle would get to that empty villa, instantly realize how foolish she was being, and jump into her car and drive here. He knew it in his gut. And if there was anything that woman had taught him, it was to listen to his gut.

"You were military, Luke." Clay Walker came around the large glass table that filled much of his patio, obviously wanting to bring him into the conversation. "Would you say the wound that killed Purty was from a rifle or close range?"

Luke managed a shrug. "Hard to say, but whoever pulled the trigger had good aim. It was dead center to the heart."

"I didn't know you were military, Luke." Nate Ivory, one of the most visible members of the large, moneyed Ivory clan, turned in his chair, training lion's-gold eyes on Luke. "What branch?"

He didn't answer immediately, not relishing the expected response. The barely hidden curled lip or the raised eyebrows of disdain.

"Luke was in the French Foreign Legion," Cutter answered for him. "I think I told you we go way back to our high school days before that."

"Really?" Nate looked more intrigued than disdainful. "That must have been interesting."

"Not always," he said.

"What did you do?" Zeke Nicholas, the hedge fund whiz who'd famously married one of the Casa Blanca maids, also turned to Luke with interest.

"A lot of things," Luke said, purposely vague.

"Like what?" The question came from a tall Texas-sounding man who'd been introduced as Elliott Becker. "I think of the Foreign Legion as a bunch of guys in the deserts of Africa."

"I did some time in Africa, but also South America. French Guiana." He cleared his throat and barreled on to say what he so rarely admitted. "Worked as a bodyguard."

Now, eyebrows shot up. "No kidding," Nate said, throwing a look at the other two men. "We were talking about getting a couple of them down here."

"We sure were," Zeke agreed, standing to make his point. "Don't suppose you'd like another job?"

Luke laughed a little and then stole a glance at Cutter. "I probably won't be building anything for the foreseeable future."

Cutter held up his hands in resignation. "I may be renting, man. Had no idea my Uncle Balls left such a hot mess in his will. I'm bringing in lawyers, not builders."

"If they find who did this and locate that gold," Luke said, "I might be able to have something built by summer."

But Cutter shook his head slowly, as if he'd already written off the idea.

"Damn," Clay said. "That's a gorgeous house you're giving up."

"I feel like the land's cursed," Cutter said. "And I know that sounds ridiculous, but—"

"Not really," Luke said. "Sure has a pall over it."

"Then maybe you *are* looking for a job," Nate said, clearly disinterested in building prospects. "I'm definitely going to need security for my wife and son now that I know there's a criminal element on Mimosa Key."

"Whoa, whoa." Clay held up his hand. "This island has

been virtually crime-free for eighty years. I wouldn't call one murder and a robbery a crime spree."

"But if people think there's gold here or even a shipwreck off the coast," Zeke said, "there could be issues."

"There are always issues where I am," Nate admitted. "Money and magazine covers make the people I love vulnerable. I, for one, want protection."

"And the resort should be doubly prepared," Elliott said to Clay. "Your wife might want to beef up security there, too."

"She's been talking about it," Clay said.

"I'm serious about this." Nate approached Luke, his expression underscoring his statement. "If you're not building Cutter's house, come and see me at my office tomorrow."

A low-grade buzz hummed through Luke, a mix of wanting to say, *Hell yeah!* and *You've got to be kidding.* He went with something more benign. "The Legion doesn't give references." *'Cause if they did, my security service record would suck.*

"Screw references," Nate said. "I can see you're built like a mountain, you don't flinch under pressure, and I'd bet a grand you're carrying."

Clay's eyebrows went up in surprise.

"It's in the car," Luke assured his host. "But I can handle a weapon. And a potential kidnapper." Shit, how had this happened? Somehow, he was standing here practically interviewing for a job he really did want.

Arielle would say that was the universe at work. He didn't know, but damn, he wanted to talk to her. He fought the urge to look at the door again, or whip out his phone and call her. He wanted to share this with her. He had to share this with her.

"You have any buddies who might want to come work with you?" Zeke asked.

"I know a few people in the security business." Hell, could he even track down a guy like Gabe Rossi? His whole family was in the business. Maybe he'd have some friends looking to move to Florida for a while. "I could look into it."

"Let's talk," Nate said, putting his hand on Luke's shoulder. "Unless you want to go build houses elsewhere."

He'd rather have his molars yanked out with rusty pliers. Luke laughed softly, the force of the realization hitting him, along with how bad he wanted to tell Arielle and how right this conversation felt. Organic. Natural. Right.

The way things felt with Arielle.

"We can talk," Luke said. "Assuming the Collier County sheriff doesn't think I killed my predecessor on Cutter's job."

Cutter snorted. "I think they have their eye on me."

They all laughed a little nervously. "Who do you think would want that guy dead, Cutter?" Clay asked.

Cutter shrugged. "My guess, based on the excellent investigative work Luke's already done, is that Jim Purty figured out there was gold somewhere on that land, and he made the mistake of telling someone."

Luke nodded. "That's what I told the deputies. His shallow grave was marked with those pearls so, who knows, maybe their forensic people will find someone's fingerprints on them. Someone's other than Arielle's, obviously."

"Where is Ari?" Clay asked.

"Don't know." Luke seized the excuse. "I'll give her a call. 'Scuze me." He started to walk away, then stopped, extending his hand to Nate. "Thanks so much for the offer. I'm extremely interested."

"So are we," Nate assured him. "And you'll probably

need more than one other guy. Hell, start a security business down here. We'll fund a start-up. We live to fund start-ups."

"I will definitely talk to you about that," he said, already hustling toward the front door, threading through a few ladies chattering inside, wanting to get to the quiet driveway to make the call. Or better yet, get in his car and go to her.

"Where do you think you're going?" Gussie snagged the sleeve of his T-shirt.

"To call Arielle and go home."

Gussie grinned. "That didn't take long."

"I told you I believe her and—"

"No, I meant it didn't take long for her to become home."

No, it didn't. But then...he smiled. "She's The One, Auggie."

"Then go find her." She gave him a hard nudge toward the door. "I'll say your good-byes to Lacey."

He gave her a quick kiss on the forehead and stepped outside as a car pulled up, something subcompact, but not Arielle's little Mazda. He swallowed the disappointment and recognized Lacey's daughter, Ashley.

She smiled at him as she got out of the car. "Hi again," she said. "We met at the Super Min when you were with Ari."

"Hi, Ashley."

"I thought you'd be with her," she said. "Is she inside?"

He shook his head. "She's not coming."

She frowned. "Really? She was at the Super Min buying wine to come up to this party. Well, I guess it's not exactly a party, but—"

"When?" Of course he'd known she'd change her mind. He didn't know what made him happier—that she'd decided to come or that he already knew her so well.

"About an hour ago. I'm sure of it, because some woman

in the store was asking about her and then she showed up. It was such a coincidence."

Or the universe at work. "Who was the woman?"

"No clue. She was definitely not a local. But Ari knew her. Said her name was Michelle."

A cold sensation, a low-grade dread, a deep-seated worry, crept through him. He'd normally ignore something like that, but not now. Not now that he'd learned to pay attention to intuition. "And Arielle left the Super Min to come here an hour ago?"

"Well, she got in her car. Maybe she changed her mind."

Or maybe not.

He nodded good-bye and dialed Arielle's number. But it rang four times, and he hung up before it went to voice mail.

Chapter Twenty-Seven

"Luke McBain. We'll ignore that call."

Luke called. Of course he had. Ari had known he would.

Her cell phone hit the floor of the backseat with a thud, like her heart dropping to the bottom of her stomach. Now he'd assume the worst and leave her to stew all night.

No, not the worst. The worst was happening—a slightly crazed, probably deadly, definitely nervous woman had a gun to Ari's head and was demanding something Ari didn't have. And there was no convincing Michelle of the truth.

"We can drive all night, hon." Michelle settled in closer, keeping the gun resting on the back of the seat, visible in the rearview mirror along with Michelle's steel-gray eyes rimmed with smeared mascara and lines. "But eventually I'm going to get tired of holding this gun, and then we'll make this look like some kind of carjacking, and you'll be dead."

"I don't have any gold." Ari had to work to keep her voice from cracking, trying to concentrate on the road but also out-think this woman before she got a bullet in her brain.

"You have the Cracker Jack box, so I know you have the gold."

"How do you know I have that?"

"Because after you left my office I went straight there and it was gone. Pretty obvious it was you and your boyfriend who found it. Now I want it back. And the pearls."

The pearls. The pearls that marked Jim Purty's grave. "How do you know I have the pearls?"

"'Cause they weren't where we—I—left them, either."

We? She wasn't alone in this? "They're in a safe-deposit box," Ari said. "We could get them in the morning." Except they weren't. They were in an evidence bag, but if she could get to the bank in the morning, surely she'd get help. If she could stay alive until morning.

"I just want the box." She ground out the words so hard Ari startled, bracing for the bullet.

None came. She breathed. And re-engaged her fried brain. "I hate to break it to you, but that piece of gold is gone, and there's nothing left in the box, so even if I had it to give you, you wouldn't find anything worthwhile."

"We'll see about that." Michelle snorted. "There's more in there than shells and stones."

"You're right. There are ancient Native American tools and artifacts. Is that what you're after?"

"I'm after what Jim and me—just drive!" She jabbed the gun against Ari's neck.

Jim? *Jim Purty.* Ari closed her eyes and saw the former contractor's corpse. Would Michelle kill over that bar of gold? One glance to the gun at her right gave Ari all the information she needed.

But did she know that Jim's body had been discovered today? If not, Ari had a chance. If so, Ari was as good as dead. She had to get information, keep her talking, and make her think she could take her to the box somehow.

Ari put her foot on the brake, bringing the slow-moving car to a stop. "I know where it is," she said.

Instantly, the gun moved infinitesimally away, the tiniest reprieve, but that filled Ari's heart with hope. There was a person—a living, breathing woman—inside of Michelle, and everything about her was hurting. She'd been hurt, and bad, Ari could tell. And that made her even more dangerous.

"Where?" Michelle asked.

"It's in a museum in Fort Myers Beach." Unless the sheriff took it as evidence. "Why don't we go tomorrow, and I'll give it to you?" And surely a deputy would be there, waiting to help.

"Like you would do that."

Ari blew out a soft breath. "I'm not interested in gold, Michelle. I wanted to save the artifacts inside that crate, and I wanted to be sure that hill wasn't an Indian burial ground, although…"

Michelle looked sharply at her, fear suddenly etched on her face. "Although what?" she demanded.

In addition to hurt, fear and guilt rolled off Michelle in palpable waves. Lots and lots of guilt, confirming Ari's worst suspicions.

Ari took a slow breath, praying hard to the universe, to the gods, and to the one her father so believed in…prayed that she could pull this off and not be killed. She had to be sure that Michelle didn't realize that the body had been found.

"What were you going to say about that hill?" Michelle demanded.

"I think that hill's a lost cause," Ari said, choosing every word as if her life depended on it. Because it sure as hell did. "They want to bulldoze it and get a view for that house."

Even in the ambient headlights, she could see Michelle's color rise. "Trust me, we, er, I've done everything possible to delay that."

"Like file a report with the Army Corps of Engineers and use my name?"

She grunted in acknowledgment. "I couldn't use mine, but after you came to the offices, it gave me an idea. And you'd already called there, so it was perfect. And those guys could delay the sunrise if they wanted to."

But wouldn't she know they'd find the body if they investigated? Maybe in her business she knew that phone call would slow everything and give her time to move that body, and time for her to find the gold.

Ari fought a shiver and managed not to let her gaze shift to the gun. She couldn't let Michelle know they'd found that body. She had to do everything in her power to keep her calm and think she had time to get what she wanted and escape.

Then Michelle would be law enforcement's problem. If only Ari could stay alive that long. Why the hell hadn't she gone with Gussie to Lacey's house? She could have been with Luke right now, safe and happy.

"I need that box," Michelle said, her voice low and strained, through clenched teeth, looking like she'd snap at any second.

"I have an idea," Ari said, wishing she really did have one.

"What?"

"Let's…go get it now."

Michelle's eyes tapered with distrust. "I'm pretty sure a museum is locked at this hour."

"How hard can it be to break into a rickety old office?" The place was freakishly out in the open, as she recalled, with nothing but a single chain around the property. It would be quite easy to at least get to the land where the house and office were. When they broke in, surely an alarm would be tripped. Maybe the universe would look kindly on this effort and make it a silent alarm. Maybe.

Michelle's mouth turned down at the corner. "Why would you do that?"

To live. "I told you, there's stuff in the crate that's important to me. Those shells and rocks are Native American tools, tools from…my people."

"Your people?"

Yes, it was a stretch, but Ari had to think. "I'm Native American. And my grandmother was a shaman." She added that partly to sound legit and partly because she prayed Grandma Good Bear's spirit was protecting her right now.

Michelle's look said she wasn't buying it. "I thought that was a thing you wrap around you in the cold."

Ari bit her lip, grateful her captor wasn't a Mensa candidate. "No, that's a shawl."

She looked embarrassed, closing her eyes.

"A shaman is like a Native American doctor," Ari said quickly, trying to make this murderess feel better about herself. Whatever it took to survive.

"I thought that was a witch doctor."

"We don't really call them that." She gave a little smile. "Can we go up to Fort Myers Beach now?"

"How do I know I can trust you?"

"Because you have the gun, Michelle."

The other woman breathed out slowly and nodded, as if the weight that came with that gun—and using it—pressed hard on her. "Go." But she didn't sit back or take that damn gun away from Ari's head.

Ari didn't move. She had one more piece of her wild-ass

plan, and she prayed Michelle was dumb enough to go along with it. "I don't suppose you'd let me text someone."

Michelle sniffed. "No." Okay, not that dumb.

"If I don't, he's going to call the cops."

She shrugged. "They won't go to some Indian museum."

"No, you're right." Ari squeezed the steering wheel and took a chance. "They'd probably go up to North Barefoot Bay to that property because he knows I've been there a lot, so if I'm missing, I'm sure that's where he'd send the cops...to search...for me."

Michelle paled, silent.

"Just give me the phone, and you can watch me text him," Ari pushed. There had to be a way to clue Luke in. There had to be. Without saying, *I'm on my way to Mound House with a gun to my head. Please save me.* Maybe she could secretly tap 911.

Very slowly, Michelle picked up the phone. "I'll write it."

Damn. "Okay." Which would mean she'd have to put down the gun, right? Would that give Ari a chance to run or fight?

"What's your password?"

"It needs my fingerprint." Big fat lie, but it worked. Michelle handed the phone to Ari, not willing to let go of the gun.

"Let me see what you write," she ordered.

"Okay." Ari's hand was visibly shaking as she thumbed the Home button and brought the screen to life, finding the icon for texting.

Instantly, she saw a string of texts from Luke, sucking in a quiet breath when the name Michelle showed up. How did he know?

Ashley, of course. Ashley must have told him. Her head

grew light with this small victory, and Ari stole a glance at Michelle, who was squinting hard at the screen. Oh, yes, she'd had reading glasses on when they met at GeoTech. God willing, she hadn't been able to see her own name in Luke's texts.

"Come on, type!" Michelle insisted.

"I'm thinking of something he'll believe. If he doesn't, you know, he'll call 911." *And they'll go looking in North Barefoot Bay.* She left that unsaid, but it worked.

Michelle nodded at the phone. "Make it fast."

"Okay." Ari closed her eyes and imagined Mound House, the museum, and Dr. Marksman's office. Could she use the word mound somehow? A combination of marks and man? Would Luke get that?

"Hurry."

What else was up there? The underground exhibits and the Case House. *Case House.* Okay, it was something. Ari started typing.

Sorry we had a fight.

"Did you?" So Michelle could read that much.

"Kind of."

"Keep going," Michelle said.

I'm staying at a girlfriend's HOUSE.

She looked up to see Michelle frowning, probably wondering why house was in all caps. She faked a sigh of frustration. "Damn tiny keyboard."

"That's all you need to say."

"Oh, no." Not nearly. "He'll keep texting if I don't tell him where I am."

"Then he'll go to that house, and you won't be there. You think I'm stupid?"

Hoping you are. "Let me close off the texts for the night, then," Ari said, her quivering finger hovering.

Please don't call. I wanted you to know in CASE—

She let out another frustrated sigh, pretending the cap letters were a typo, then finished with *you wondered.*

She turned the screen to Michelle, who squinted harder, then nodded, satisfied.

"Send it."

She did, along with a heartfelt prayer that Luke McBain wasn't only The One to love, but he'd also be The One to save her.

Chapter Twenty-Eight

Luke marched right back into the Walkers' house, striding toward Gussie.

"I thought you went back to the resort."

He shoved his phone in front of her. "Does this seem right to you?"

Frowning, Gussie read the texts. "Um, Ari does have friends other than the people in this house, but no one I would think she'd stay with and not tell me."

"What about the words?"

"What about them?"

Impatience and worry and a deep, foreboding sense that something was very wrong rocked through him. "Let me see your phone. I want to look at your text messages with her."

Still looking confused, Gussie pulled a cell phone from her skirt pocket, tapping it a few times. "Here are the last few texts we exchanged. Why?"

He skimmed them, looking for random capital letters. Not a one. In fact, she texted with perfect punctuation and capitalization. But not this time.

"House. Case." He murmured the words. Had she gone up to the house in North Barefoot Bay to investigate the case? Or had she really accidentally typed those two words in capitals?

"What was her mood like when she left you, Gussie?"

She angled her head. "I told you, she was upset. She thought you really believed she'd reported the building project as a violation of that law. You hadn't talked to her the whole day, and she was devastated."

"But Ashley said she was on her way here a while ago, and she stopped at the Super Min. And talked to someone named Michelle. Does she have a friend named Michelle?"

Gussie shook her head. "I don't know every single person she's friends with, Luke, but I never heard her mention a Michelle. We had a bride recently named Michelle, but she was from out of town. Why don't you just call Ari?"

"I did," he admitted. "She's not answering."

Gussie took her phone back and tapped the screen. "She'll answer me." As she waited for Ari to pick up, Tom came into the house, walking up to Gussie and wrapping her in his tattoo-covered arms.

"Hey," they whispered to each other in that soft, secret, we're-in-love kind of voice.

Tom and Luke greeted each other, but Luke's attention was riveted on Gussie's phone. "No answer?"

"Voice mail." She held up a finger. "Call me," she said into the phone. "Luke's freaking out. Now he's got me worried. Where are you?"

"What's going on?" Tom asked, concerned.

While Gussie brought Tom—and a few others who gathered, sensing there might be news about the murder—up to speed, Luke stared at Arielle's text message again, willing it to tell him more than it did.

"I'm going back up there," he said.

"Luke, she didn't go to a crime scene in the dark. She's not dumb. There's nothing in that message that said she did."

"Still, she's missing."

"She's not answering her phone," Gussie insisted. "She might have changed her mind and taken the wine back to the villa, and she's in the bathtub drinking it right now. Check there first before going up to the property."

Gussie's idea sounded plausible, but not in his gut. His gut was on fire. "Call this guy." He reached into his pocket and pulled out the deputy's card he'd taken today. "Let him know we don't know where she is. I'm going up there. You and Tom go check the villa."

Gussie took the card and dropped the fight. "Okay."

"Thanks." Luke hustled back to his truck, climbing in and glancing at the phone as if he could will Arielle to return his calls. He almost texted her again with a question about the words HOUSE and CASE, but something stopped him.

What was it?

Intuition. Maybe she wasn't the only one in this relationship who had it. Slowly blowing out a breath, he drove away, seeking out the back road that led to the far less populated section of the island.

Gripping the wheel too hard, he rounded the gardens and drove past the small group of bungalows where some of the resort staff lived, searching the night as if he could actually find this woman he cared so much about.

When did that happen? Not the minute they touched on the hill, he mused. It wasn't instant love. It wasn't even love…yet. But there was something. He'd felt it when they kissed in the closet, when they laughed over dinner, when they made out in the grass, and of course last night in the villa. He'd even felt it when they dragged that box up to Mound House and…and…and Case House.

Case House. Holy shit. Case House! But why?

He didn't know, but he trusted his gut and turned the other way toward the mainland.

Ari was plumb out of grand plans. She drove in silence up Highway 41, skipping the scenic, slow route because she had a better chance of seeing a cop on this boring but busy highway. But none was out tonight.

Michelle grew more anxious with each passing mile, her focus seeming to shift from the road and the plan to Ari.

"How Indian are you?" she blurted out, breaking the quiet of the car.

"We generally say 'Native American' now. And I'm actually only a quarter. My grandmother was a full-blooded Miwok, but she married an Irish guy, and my mom married another non-Native American."

"So, not very." Still leaning into the front seat without her seat belt, Michelle tipped her head as if analyzing or, at the very least, judging Ari. "But I can see it, I guess. You're pretty."

"Thanks."

"No wonder that cute builder likes you. I could tell when you guys came to GeoTech," she mused. "It was easy to give him the fake sample bag, because he was so wrapped up in you."

"The fake sample bag? That wasn't a real core sample from the land? Why?"

"Buying time."

Because she'd left a body buried on the hill? "What did you need time for?"

"To get the…" She shook her head. "Never mind. Not important."

But it was important. "So we still don't know if that land is an ancient burial ground."

Michelle gave her a sharp look, then a sarcastic snort, as if to say, *Not ancient.* But she gave nothing away. Ari's only trump card was that Michelle didn't know what Ari knew.

"Hey!"

Ari blinked, realizing she'd drifted into the other lane, her brain fried from the stress of that gun.

"Please, can you put that thing down?" Ari said. "I'm with you on this. I want to go to this place, and I don't want to die."

"Once I have the…thing I want."

"The gold? There isn't that much," Ari said. "I told you the archaeologist only found one bar."

Michelle closed her eyes for a second. "Just don't talk about it. I'm trying to figure out what to do."

"Are you…in this alone?" Ari asked, ignoring the order not to talk because she could sense it helped calm Michelle. And a calm Michelle was a less dangerous Michelle.

"I am now."

Since she'd shot Jim Purty, Ari thought. "A guy?" she ventured.

"What else?"

Ari nodded, snagging the opportunity to connect with her. "What's his name?"

She shook her head. "Not important. He's gone."

Really gone, if Ari's guess that it was Purty was right. And she was sure she was right, because the idea of *death* was emanating off this woman. Hopefully, not Ari's death.

"Did he…" *Careful, Ari.* "Does he know about the gold?"

"He found some, and then we found…other stuff." She gave her head a hard shake. "Honey, if you want a chance of surviving this, do not say another word or ask another question."

Ari could tell she meant it this time, so she stayed quiet,

concentrating on the road and then the bridge that took them to Fort Myers Beach.

"I'm not sure where to turn," she told Michelle. "You have to put it into your GPS."

"I don't have it. Use yours." She gave Ari her cell phone to thumb with one hand, and the first thing Ari noticed was that she'd missed two calls from Gussie, after the earlier ones from Luke.

But he hadn't called again. So, either he didn't get the text she'd sent, didn't decipher the secret message, or didn't care. No, that last one wasn't an option. He cared, and he'd be there...she believed that. She didn't know how or why, but that's how faith worked.

She found the GPS, and the address for the museum was still programmed in, giving them the directions immediately.

The only sound in the car was the computerized woman on GPS, guiding them to a tiny finger of land that jutted into a waterway. When they reached the end of the street, Ari's high beams bathed the entrance to the circular street that formed the perimeter of the small peninsula.

Access was beyond easy. But then what?

"Where is this office you were talking about?"

"On the property. We obviously can't drive in. We'll have to climb over that chain and walk to the building."

Michelle looked around and made a gesture for her to back up. "Go to the street and park in one of the driveways. I don't want some roving night guard to see your car here." Which was exactly what Ari had been counting on. Crap.

Ari did as she was told, pulling into the last driveway on the residential street that spilled right into the entrance of Mound House. That house was dark, and the driveway empty.

Maybe the residents would wake up or come home and

notice a strange car in the driveway and call the police. Hanging on to one more thin hope, Ari turned off the ignition and waited for the next demand.

"Give me your keys." Michelle held out her free hand and took the keys that Ari pulled from the ignition. Then she opened the back door, keeping that damn gun in Ari's face. She stood far enough away that Ari couldn't shove the door at her, get the keys, and run.

"Lead the way," Michelle ordered.

And now the gun was jammed into Ari's back.

"I need light." Ari slowed her step and pointed to the car she was loath to leave. "I can use my phone flashlight." Maybe she could lean into the backseat and send an emergency 911 call. "Let me get it."

"I have a flashlight on my phone," Michelle said, killing that idea as fast as it came. She added a nudge with the gun, shutting up Ari and her ideas.

They climbed a few steps up a rise to where a thick metal chain hung from white posts that probably encircled the entire property. Why bother, Ari thought dejectedly. Anyone could break in here.

They trudged over grass, then found the paved path that led past the two-story Case House in the middle of the property.

"Is it in there?" Michelle asked, nodding toward the structure.

The truth, the box wasn't in there, and since the building was under a lot of reconstruction, it didn't look like there was an alarm system, or Ari would have lied and said it was. Her best bet was the office.

"No. It's in a small building down around the other side," she said. "Near the water."

As they walked, a plan formed. If she could get away fast

enough, maybe she could find some shadowy place and hide. She'd been through the property and in the underground mound exhibit. She knew her way around this area, and Michelle didn't.

But could she get away without getting a bullet in the back?

They arrived at the small wooden structure that served as the offices, that three-quarter moon she'd made love under last night offering plenty of light. Too much light to hope for a safe escape.

"That doesn't look too tough to break into," Michelle said.

Sadly, it did not. No flashing lights of an alarm system, no padlocks, no guard dogs. What the hell?

Michelle pushed her around the building, toward the back, then closer to a window. Still holding the gun at Ari's back, she guided them to the glass to peer into a darkened room. It was the conference area where Ari had met the first time with Dr. Marksman, empty but for a table and chairs.

Silently, they moved to the next set of windows, which appeared to be a kitchen area. And, last, to the lab that lined the back wall.

"Holy shit!" Michelle exclaimed. "There it is! You were telling the truth!"

The Rueckheim & Eckstein box with the Cracker Jack logo sat right on his desk, empty now, Ari supposed. So the sheriff's deputies hadn't come here yet, or if they had, they'd taken only the artifacts—and the gold bar—and ignored the box they came in. How would Michelle feel about that? Mad enough to fire a gun at Ari?

"There's probably nothing in that box now," Ari said.

"Oh, yes, there is, and we're going to get it right now. The sliding glass door is open."

"It is?" Ari peered at the slider on the other side of the office and, sure enough, Dr. Marksman had been distracted or lazy enough to leave it open an inch. Damn it.

They rounded the back of the building, walked right up to the sliding glass door, and opened it without so much as an alarm beep. Frustration welled up inside Ari, and she dug for another plan.

Except there wasn't one.

Michelle made her slide open the door—cleverly leaving Ari's fingerprints everywhere—and nudged her inside.

"Open the box," Michelle ordered, pulling out her cell phone and flicking on its flashlight.

Ari touched the box and carefully lifted the lid. "It's empty."

"Like hell it is." Michelle came closer, peering over the top into the box. "That's a false bottom."

It was? Ari reached in and tapped the wood, but it felt solid, not hollow at all. "Are you sure of that?"

"Positive. We...I put it there."

She looked up at Michelle, the flashlight making the lines deeper all around the other woman's eyes. "Why?"

"To hide something."

"What?"

Michelle's smile was slow and wry. "You know, if I tell you, I'll have to kill—"

She froze at a sound. Outside. Footsteps.

"In there." She pushed Ari toward the open door of a small powder room. Ari hesitated, squinting into the darkness to see a figure moving, a flashlight cast down. He moved slowly, deliberately, like—

Michelle saw him, too, shoving Ari into the room with her free hand and never once giving an inch with that damn gun. Without making a noise, Michelle shut the door and turned to face Ari, who actually had to bite her lip to keep from screaming the words that ricocheted around her head and heart.

Was that Luke?

"One word, one squeak, one breath, and you're dead."

Ari blinked at her, having absolutely no doubt Michelle was telling the truth. "Why?"

"Because I'll kill you."

"But why? All of this for gold?" Did it really have that kind of power over people?

"For freedom," she mouthed, getting closer. "You know what it's like to be under a man's thumb, under his control, forced to…" She shook her head. "No, you don't. But I do, and I found my ticket out, and I'm…shhh."

A heavy footstep near the slider made Michelle's eyes flash with fear and determination. With the barrel still jabbing her in the back, Ari followed orders and stayed still and quiet.

Except for her brain. Her thoughts were screaming to Luke, hollering for his attention, demanding he come in and save her.

Another footfall, and then the glass door rattled as it slid wider.

Come on, Luke. I'm here. You know it. You feel it.

A footstep on the office floor confirmed he was in. He had to see the box. *Check the bathroom, Luke.*

Silence.

Seconds ticked by endlessly, into two or three long, miserable minutes, maybe more. Finally, Michelle backed away from the door and seemed to breathe for the first time.

"All right," she whispered. "Let's do this." She opened the bathroom door and stepped into the office, and suddenly sucked in a noisy hiss, followed by a dark curse.

Ari looked past her, eyes fully adjusted to the darkness, and stared at the empty desk.

The box was gone.

"Someone's gonna die," Michelle ground out.

Ari had a very bad feeling that someone might be her.

Chapter Twenty-Nine

Luke spotted the Mazda and Arielle's license plate from the corner of his eye. Why would she park in someone's driveway? A hundred different scenarios played out in his mind, none of which made any sense.

Could someone have taken her against her will? Did she have a late meeting with Marksman? Would she have come back to retrieve the artifacts, or the gold? Did it matter to her?

Parking on the street, he stared at Arielle's car and reached under his truck seat, grabbing his Glock. He hadn't fired a gun since the bullet that had killed Cerisse and her father. On his next assignment, he'd never even taken his weapon out.

And now, he almost didn't trust himself. But he took it anyway, along with his flashlight and phone.

He climbed out of the truck and strode to the little blue subcompact, shining a light inside. The first thing he saw was a cell phone that looked like Ari's on the backseat floor and then a small brown handbag he recognized as hers on the passenger seat. She left her car without either one?

He backed away from the vehicle, turning toward the darkened land at the end of the street. That fat, circular peninsula known as the Mound House museum was where the Case House was.

Pointing the gun down, he headed toward the entrance of Mound House, jumping the metal chain fence and peering toward the acres of land.

He turned off his flashlight and easily navigated without it. He'd been there once before, and that was all he needed to find his way. In fact, he closed his eyes periodically to hear better, but the only sounds were critters in trees, the occasional bird, and some crickets.

And a splash.

He stopped dead, turning to his left, recognizing the rhythmic sound of a paddle hitting water on his left. He was immediately transported to the Camopi River, the *splat splat* of a pirogue cutting through the water on a smuggling mission to or from the gold mines. The natives moved like silent night creatures, but a well-trained Legionnaire could hear that nearly imperceptible sound of moving water.

Who was rowing down this canal this late at night?

Someone moving fast, he decided, someone cutting the water with somewhat desperate strokes. Luke hunched down and headed toward the sound, off the path, around bushes to the water's edge, checking out the deserted landscape. It wasn't a likely place to take a late-night canoe ride.

He followed the sound, staying behind a row of mangroves and pepper trees until he had to stop or possibly be spotted, waiting for the rower to appear in the thin moonlight. A man in a dark jacket paddled the boat, steering into a small landing and climbing out with the help of his oar.

He was heavyset and fairly tall, but too far away for Luke to make out any features. The man left an old metal canoe and walked with purpose toward the Case House, a jacket with a hood blocking any chance of Luke getting a read on the guy's face.

Luke hung back in the bushes and watched the man, following at a safe distance.

He passed the Case House and kept moving, headed toward the tiny office building where Luke and Arielle had taken her crate of seashells for examination.

The man walked around the back, and Luke followed, watching him approach the sliding glass door, then he walked right in.

He disappeared into the building, and Luke waited, peering around in the shadows, listening, trying to get close to a window without being seen.

Was Arielle here? Why couldn't she send him some telepathic message, damn it? What had she said she did to get her words from the universe? Close her eyes, block everything out, listen.

But all he heard was the man's footfalls as he left the same way he came in, and Luke backed into the shadows, weapon drawn, ready to do whatever needed to be done.

The man carried a big box, running. No, not a box. *The* box. The Cracker Jack crate. It had to be empty by the way he moved. Luke had carted that box with its original contents, and it had weighed at least eighty pounds. The man moved with more purpose now, following the same path he'd come, heading back to his canoe, carrying the container as if it held…gold.

But that wasn't possible. Surely no one left that single bar in there.

He turned at another sound from the house and saw two figures coming out the back. Two women—and one was Arielle. He opened his mouth to shout, but suddenly she started running full speed toward the man with the box. The other woman held back, but Arielle was determined to get him, her dark hair flying as she ran silently over the grass.

Not silently enough. The man turned, froze, and Arielle kept going straight at him. Every cell in Luke's body went on alert as he watched the scene unfold in slow motion. The man lifting the box, Arielle reaching out her hands, and the woman by the house slowly walking toward them both.

Arielle tried to seize the box from the man, but he yanked it away, and she leaped on him, both of them rolling to the ground.

"You thief!" the man called. "You can't have it!"

Luke started toward the melee, but paused as he saw the woman coming toward them both, a gun in her hand. As that registered, so did her identity. Michelle.

"Get him, Ari! Get the box!"

She was in on this? Part of this? Betrayal, like bile, rose up, taking him right back to that same jungle again, to another moment when the woman he'd thought he could love—he'd thought he did love—proved him wrong.

No, she wasn't like Cerisse. Not even close. What he was seeing was simply…what he was seeing. And that wasn't always *all there was*.

"Get the box!" Michelle yelled.

Arielle yanked the crate from the man's hand, but he gave her a solid push and whipped around. "It's mine!" he growled at her. "You're a thief!"

Behind them, Michelle took slow, measured steps, her hands raised to aim a gun. "Get the box, Ari."

Arielle looked over her shoulder, then back at the man. "Give me the box, or we're both dead." She was right. Michelle's bullet could go right through Arielle and into the man. He'd seen it happen.

Luke had to shoot Michelle.

The man gave Arielle a vicious shove backward, pivoting to run toward the water. As he took off, his hood flew back, and Luke could see his face perfectly. He recognized the mason, Duane Dissick. Of course, a man who had access, time, and tools to look for gold he must have known was hidden somewhere.

"Go get him!" Michelle ordered.

Arielle stayed on the ground, shaking her head.

"Get him. He has the map, the letters, everything. Everything we need to be rich and free."

That's what Arielle wanted? Of course not, but…

Still on the ground, she barely turned, fighting for breath. "You get him. I don't care about any of that."

"Then you're dead."

"No, you are." Luke's voice echoed through the night, shocking both of them.

"What?"

"Luke!"

In an instant, Michelle dropped to the ground behind Arielle, her gun at Arielle's head. "Go get that guy and that box, or I'll put a bullet right through her brain."

"Please, Luke. Please." The terror in her voice sliced right through him. "Do what she says. I don't want to die. Please!"

Wordlessly, a plan forming, he took off toward the water, in the same direction as the mason, slowing only when he was in the shadows, then slipping behind the office building to line up his shot. He didn't give a shit about Duane Dissick, but he'd die before he let anything happen to Arielle.

Leaning around the corner, he saw Michelle force Arielle to a stand, spin her around, and push her about a foot ahead, making her walk toward the water.

Luke's blood turned to ice as his posture mirrored hers. Lifting his gun. Finger on the trigger. Steady. If Michelle took five or six more steps, Luke could shoot her...and his bullet could go through her and right into Arielle.

He had to shoot that pistol out of Michelle's hands.

Off by a millimeter, and Arielle would be dead. But this time...this time...he closed his eyes and believed what he couldn't see. Then he fired.

The sound shocked her, like a cannon in her head. Ari threw her body to the ground, waiting for the agonizing pain of a bullet.

"Arielle! Arielle!"

That was Luke's voice, coming from the darkness, desperate and ragged and drowned out by Michelle's unearthly screams.

"Oh my God! Oh my God!"

"You're not hit!" Luke shouted, the words giving Ari the ability to stop holding every cell frozen in fear. She rolled over, seeing Luke running toward her.

"I'm not hit," she confirmed, more to assure herself than him.

Michelle wasn't shot either, but her screams got louder as she dropped to her knees and held out empty hands. Before Ari could blink, Luke scooped up her pistol with his other hand. He dropped next to Arielle, and she reached both her arms to him and squeezed him so hard she could have cracked a rib.

"Thank you," she whispered.

"For losing the map?" Michelle hollered. "He has the

map, you idiots! Get him! He has it all! The maps, the letters from that Balls guy, everything! It's in the crate!"

"No worries," Luke said, pulling out his phone. "I know who he is. The sheriff will get him, and we don't give a crap about gold."

"Then what about all those bones and masks and thousand-year-old dead Indians buried on that land?"

Ari gasped softly. "What?"

"That hill is full of caves and graves and shit."

"A grave for Jim Purty," Luke said dryly.

Michelle choked. "What? He's dead?" The utter horror in her voice told Ari that her instincts had been wrong. Michelle hadn't killed the builder. "I thought he…I thought he…left me."

"We found his body on the hill this morning," Ari said softly.

"He's dead?" She sobbed the word this time, folding in half. "Who killed him?"

"I thought you did," Ari said.

"Me?" She covered her mouth with both hands. "I love him. Loved him." Another sob racked her. "He didn't leave me. He didn't leave me!"

"Luke, you know that was the mason who just ran off?" Ari asked.

"I know, Duane Dissick."

Michelle shot up. "That bastard! He killed Jim! I know it. He figured everything out and knew we were looking for gold. He killed him."

Luke stood, glancing to the water.

"You can't let him get away, Luke," Ari said. "He's a murderer."

He didn't answer, but handed Michelle's gun to Arielle. "Can you handle this?"

She gave him a look that she knew he understood as *no*, but took it anyway. "Get him, and I'll call the sheriff. She's not going to hurt me. I know it."

"If she does..."

"I know what to do." She elbowed him. "Go."

"I'll be back." He kissed her forehead, turned, and disappeared into the darkness. After a second, she heard the splash of one of the canoes left near the water's edge and a paddle. Ari stood in the silence with a gun, a phone, and a weeping woman.

Keeping her distance and the gun—purely the most foreign thing she'd ever held—on Michelle, she called the deputy on Luke's contact list, told him where they were and why, and then settled down to wait.

Michelle's sobs had turned to shudders.

"You really loved him." It wasn't a question, because Ari already knew the answer.

"He wasn't like anyone I'd ever met. As soon as he came into our offices, I felt something. Like my whole chest would explode."

"He was The One for you," Ari said softly.

Michelle looked up. "Yeah. And now he's dead."

She wanted to say there'd be another One, but Ari wasn't at all sure that was true. One is, well, One. "Can you tell me about the bones and graves in the hill?"

"Jim found stuff in the house," she said, swiping at her running nose. "Letters from the guy who owned it, written to that baseball player."

"Cutter Valentine," Ari supplied.

She nodded. "He was supposed to find them when he took the house down. I guess Balls—that's how he signed his letters, honestly, Uncle Balls—thought the builder would give the whole box of letters to Cutter. But he..." She looked

316

sheepish. "He kept it all when he read about the gold." She sighed hard. "And now he's dead."

The universe had a way of working like that, Ari thought. But she didn't have to tell Michelle. Her expression said she knew all about retribution.

"How did Balls find the gold?"

"His wife found it," she said. "She was some kind of, you know, like you. A Native American. She found all those shells and stuff that you saw in that box, and then she found gold and jewels. Even found those pearls. But I hid them in the kitchen of the house, and that bastard Dissick must have found them."

And he used them to mark Jim Purty's grave. "What about the maps?"

"Oh, they're in the bottom of that crate where Jim and I hid them."

"Didn't you make copies?"

"Jim did and put them in a safe-deposit box, but I don't know where it is or who has a key. I don't have any idea. I trusted him, and then I figured he ditched me—that he wanted the gold all to himself. I helped him fake the core sampling so it looked like there was nothing but shells in the mound. I helped him delay and delay the building. We wanted enough time to find the gold. Then he got fired." She practically spat the word. "And now I know who told the owner that Jim was purposely delaying things."

"Duane Dissick."

"Of course. He figured it out, or maybe Jim brought him in and offered him a cut so he could help us find it. He said he might do that and I told him not to. Then he...disappeared. I thought he'd double-crossed me."

"How could you not find the gold if you had maps?"

"They're not in English, and the pictures are really hard to

317

understand. We tried, and we thought we were following the map, but the gold was never where we thought it would be."

In the distance, Ari heard a siren and breathed easier. But where was Luke? No gunshot, no shouting, no nothing. Where was he?

"Maybe someone beat you to the gold," she suggested to Michelle.

But Michelle shook her head. "I don't think so. The maps of the underground part? They're falling apart they're so old, but they show all these, like, tunnels and graves and shit. The gold has to be buried there."

Red and blue lights cut through the darkness as the sirens grew louder, the cavalry coming to save her.

No, Luke had done that. She stole a glance at the dark water in the distance, still seeing and hearing nothing. For a second, she closed her eyes and listened, trying to hear beyond the screech of sirens to the universe, to listen to the message. Was he successful? Safe? Alive?

But the universe was silent.

Three sheriff's cars thundered over the lawn toward them, bullhorn out, demanding they drop their weapons. Ari waited until Michelle stood and put her hands behind her head, and then she set the gun on the ground and did the same.

She recognized Deputy Brennan from the afternoon and walked to him.

"Duane Dissick killed Jim Purty, and Luke's gone after him on the water."

He drew back, bushy brows cinching together. "Is that so?"

"Yes, it is so." She was too tired to argue and too worried about Luke. "You better go help him because he's been gone—"

"He doesn't need help." His gaze had shifted over her shoulder, narrowing in disbelief. Ari turned and sucked in a soft breath at the sight. Luke had Duane Dissick's hands locked, forcing the man to stumble forward. They were both soaking wet, head to toe. With his other hand, Luke carried the Cracker Jack crate.

Ari let out a soft whimper, pressing her hands to her chest as if that could keep it from bursting apart with so much admiration and joy and pride and love.

Sheriff's deputies came forward in a group, and Luke practically tossed the man at one of them. "He confessed," Luke said gruffly. "Here's the murder weapon." He yanked another pistol from behind his back. "Should match ballistics on Purdy."

"What's in the box?" Deputy Brennan asked.

"Absolutely nothing." Luke turned it upside down and pounded it. "Everything got lost in the water, and it's nothing but shreds of dissolved paper now." He turned to Ari, angling his head. "Sorry, I tried to save it for you."

Sorry? Was he crazy? She practically leaped into his arms, not caring that he smelled like saltwater and soaked her clothes. All she wanted to do was kiss him. Which she did, hard and long.

"Good work, McBain," Deputy Brennan said. "Stick around for a few questions, then we'll let you go."

As the sheriff's deputies went to work arresting and questioning, Luke pulled Ari to the side, away from them, bringing her close for more kisses. But instead of her mouth, he put his lips over her ear.

"Sit on the crate, Little Mermaid. Don't let anyone take it."

She drew back, her eyes wide and jaw loose.

"Shhh." He hushed her with a soft kiss to the lips.

"You know, you're the great American hero, Luke McBain."

He smiled and eased her onto the crate. "Got that right, baby."

A deputy slapped a hand on Luke's shoulder, pulling them apart, indicating Michelle. "Who is that?" he asked.

Ari looked up from her perch. "She's..." Not exactly innocent, but still. "She knows a lot and can help you put Dissick behind bars for good." Maybe they'd cut her a deal.

Brennan nodded, but said something to another deputy who went to deal with Michelle.

"Seriously," the deputy said to Luke. "We could use a man like you in the sheriff's office."

Ari beamed and looked at Luke, not sure if he'd do his I'm-not-worthy business or show real interest. Neither one. He shook his head, smiling. "Thanks for the offer, sir. But I have other plans. Big plans." He grinned at the other man. "I might be the one offering you a job soon."

"Really?" He actually looked interested. "Come on over here, and let's get the questions done then. 'Scuze us, ma'am."

As Luke walked away, he turned and winked at Ari, and that did it. Her chest finally did burst with love.

Epilogue

Luke ran with purpose, his eyes closed, the wind singing in his ears, his feet hitting the earth in perfect syncopation. He sensed her before he actually smacked into Arielle, squinting into the liquid sunshine to see her sitting at the very top of the hill. He stopped, still fifty feet away, to take in the spectacular view.

She leaned back on her arms, her long, black hair hanging like a curtain over her back and shoulders, her legs stretched out in front of her, bare feet crossed, face to the sun. A creamy sundress spread around her, the pale color highlighting her golden skin.

Of course she was surrounded by the maps and letters, the charts and guidelines—copies of them, anyway. The paperwork was everything they'd need when the official archaeological dig started the next day. After weeks of planning, this was the last day their hill would be intact until everything had been excavated, cataloged, and sent to museums.

Once that was done, the Calusa House and Museum

would be built...by someone else, under Arielle's and Luke's supervision. Paid for entirely by Cutter Valentine, in honor of his great-aunt, the wife of Balzac Valentine, and a woman who had apparently had deep emotional ties to the Native American community. Mr. and Mrs. Valentine had left Cutter a rather remarkable inheritance—several million dollars' worth of gold bars they'd buried under the foundation of the most decrepit house in Barefoot Bay.

The maps, which Luke had managed to save in the scuffle with Dissick, had been deciphered by Dr. Marksman, and of course, all the artifacts from the Cracker Jack box had been donated to a traveling Native American exhibit. Eventually, they'd be part of the Calusa House and Museum, when it opened sometime next year.

Luke sighed as a strong northern breeze fluttered the grass and trees on the hill and made Arielle's beautiful hair sway. He wanted to run to tell her his news, since she'd been waiting to hear, but he also wanted to stand there and drink in the woman he loved so very much.

She was definitely The One for him.

"I hear you thinking over there," she called without moving.

"You're lying."

She laughed. "Well, I know you're thinking, and I heard you come up the hill, so not a lie. Educated guess." She turned and let her head rest on her shoulder, watching him. "Take off your shirt."

He smiled. "So demanding."

"Yep. But I want to see you exactly as I did that first afternoon, a great big god from across the sea, barreling bare-chested toward me." She laid a hand on her own chest, as if trying to contain her happy heart. "It was my luckiest day ever."

"How many times do I have to tell you?" He yanked his T-shirt over his head and tossed it to the side, striding toward her. "There is no such thing as luck."

"Just great timing and destiny." She extended her hand toward him, and of course he closed his fingers around her narrow wrist, exactly as he had the day he met her. *Zing.* "How'd the meeting go?" she asked.

"The deed is done," he told her, dropping to sit next to her, to let their bodies touch and get a whiff of her flowery fragrance. "McBain Securities will be handling the entire resort as one of its first clients, and part of our compensation will be a suite of offices in the bungalows at the edge of the resort gardens. From there, we will grow a business that I already heard one smartass call Barefoot Bodyguards."

"It's catchy."

"I like McBain."

"So do I. In fact, I love him." She snuggled into his shoulder. "Congratulations."

He hugged her back, inhaling her fragrance, her hair, and, best of all, her spirit. He couldn't have done this without her. "I have so much to learn about the business," he mused.

"But your friend is coming, right? The guy whose family owns the security company in Boston?"

"Talk about good timing and great fortune," he said, tapping her nose playfully when she rolled her eyes. "Seriously, the chances that Gabriel Rossi, a certified black ops CIA undercover badass to the max, would have time to come down here and advise me on how to run this kind of business…well, that's some serious handiwork on the part of your universe."

"Our universe," she corrected. "And you said he owed you a favor for that mission in Somalia."

"I wasn't even sure he'd remember, but he did, and he's

coming, so I'm grateful. Between us, I think he's getting itchy working for his cousins in Boston. That guy was not cut out for run-of-the-mill security, so I think he hopped on the excuse for a long weekend at the resort."

"Well, this guy is cut out for the security business." She leaned into him and sighed softly. "My guy. My bodyguard guy. You're going to have an amazing new career."

A swell of anticipation for all the possibilities of his new life grew inside him. There was only one more little detail to iron out.

He put his arm around Arielle and gave a squeeze. "You know, Lacey offered me one of the bungalows as living quarters, but..."

"But you'll need all the space for your growing business," she said quickly. "Because you won't only do security for the resort. The billionaires all want some help, and Cutter certainly will need it now, and have you seen the boats out in the bay? Word is out that there are treasure-laden shipwrecks off our coasts. This island is crawling with strangers now."

He let her chatter, wondering when she'd get the real reason he wasn't taking Lacey's offer.

"Yes, I'll need the space, but..."

"Those bungalows aren't that big, even if you reconfigure them into a combination of office and living space, and..." Her voice trailed off. "Why are you looking at me like that?"

"Like you're dense?"

She laughed easily. "Yeah, just like that."

"I don't want to live at the resort, Arielle." He stroked her arm and admired the chill bumps that his touch always left behind. "I want to live with you."

She drew in a soft breath. "Oh. I know we spend almost every night together now, and that it probably makes sense."

Turning away, she looked out to the horizon, silent.

"But you don't like the idea," he said simply.

"Well, I don't hate the idea, but, well, it's not…"

"It's not what you want."

She bit her lip and shook her head. "Not really."

"You want forever and ever. You want the whole enchilada. You want legitimacy and a name change and stamps of official approval."

Each word made her look a little more pained. "Is that so bad?" she whispered.

Very slowly, he slid his fingers under her hair, combing the long, silk strands without answering.

"I mean, I know it's been fast," she said, "and we haven't dated that long, and we really ought to—"

He silenced her with a kiss on her temple. "You think we ought to get engaged?"

She didn't answer, then very slowly nodded once.

"I don't," he said.

Her eyes flashed. "Really? You don't—"

"No," he interrupted. "I want to get married." He stood slowly, bringing her up by holding both her hands. "At least, I want to have the marriage ceremony. Then we can call it engaged and plan something on the beach with white nets and barefoot brides and billionaires and bodyguards running around."

Her dark eyes grew moist as she came to a stand with him.

"But now? First? I want to do this another way, Little Mermaid."

Her frown deepened with confusion.

"Arielle, do you really think there's any doubt you're The One for me?"

"No, but when you said you want to live together, I…"

She released a self-conscious laugh. "I thought maybe you don't really know me at all. Remember, I am the daughter of a Presbyterian pastor."

He threaded their fingers together. "And the granddaughter of a woman who performed some pretty awesome marriage ceremonies."

"Would you like a Native American ceremony when we get married?"

"I would like"—he lifted her hand to his mouth and pressed a kiss on her knuckles—"a Native American marriage ceremony right now. Think Grandma Good Heart is watching?"

She almost lost her balance as emotion washed over her. "I'm sure Grandma Good *Bear* is."

"Great. Then she can officiate." He stood very still and looked down at her. "Arielle Chandler, are you ready for the universe to join us as one?"

Fighting tears, she nodded. "Do you remember?"

"Mostly. You can jump in and help, okay?"

"Okay." She took a deep breath. "First, the four directions."

Clasping her hands, he turned her so her back was against his chest and then circled so they were facing east.

He cleared his throat and started the speech he'd been practicing on the way up there.

"No matter what direction life takes us…" He turned them to south. "No matter how rocky the road to get there…" Then west. "Arielle and I will ask each other for guidance…" Finally, north, out to the expanse of blue water and the sharp line of the horizon. "And will always stay on life's path, hand in hand." He squeezed her fingers. "How was that? Close enough to what she said?"

"Amazing," she whispered, turning to face him and keeping their hands locked. "Can I do Mother Earth?"

"Of course."

She pulled him with her to their knees, placing their joined hands on the ground. "We promise to respect this land and care for it." She closed her eyes for a moment, the power of how much she meant that promise rolling off her and washing over Luke. "This land that brought us together and almost broke us apart." She smiled at him. "This land that meant so much to so many and put us on our journey. This land that will forever honor my people and my promise to my grandmother. We will care for this land as partners."

They looked at each other for a moment, both a little too moved to speak.

"The breeze?" he asked.

She nodded, and they stood back up, lifting their hands in the air, still joined. "Something about beauty," Luke said with a soft laugh. "You've got that covered."

"We ask that our partnership be beautiful and alive and pure," she told him.

"And it will be," he said softly. "You and me, only, forever and ever."

Her eyes glistened at the pledge of his fidelity, and she nodded, almost unable to speak.

"We need spring water for our heads," she said.

He spied a bottled water she'd brought up. "LaVie," he said, making a face. "French, but I guess that's okay." He poured a few drops into the cap and dribbled it on her head, then his. "So we never hit a dry spell?" he asked.

She laughed. "That'll work. Now a flower seed."

"Oh, yes. Fertility." He glanced around and saw a honeysuckle bush and snagged some of the tiny white flowers. "I rub your belly?"

"Why not?"

He placed his whole hand on her stomach with the

flowers in his palm. "Babies, Universe. We want babies. Good ones that don't cry in the middle of the night and definitely get college scholarships."

"Healthy ones as smart and strong as their daddy," she added.

"And as beautiful, kind, and intuitive as their mama."

Her eyes, already damp, nearly overflowed.

"I remember what's next," Luke said, the memory of her explaining this part of the ceremony crystal clear. He lifted his right hand, and she did the same, splaying their open palms over each other's heart.

"Shhh," Arielle said. "Listen until you hear the same heartbeat."

He felt hers before he heard anything. A steady drumbeat, a little faster than normal, pulsing against his palm as if it fed her blood into his veins. His own heart rate kicked up, and her eyes widened as she felt it. Without being told, he closed his eyes and listened.

He heard the wind. He heard a gull squawk. He heard leaves rustle and a soft breath escape Arielle's lips. And then he heard...peace. A completeness, a wholeness, a sense of total...oneness. He heard love. Like someone was whispering it in his ears.

When he opened his eyes, tears were streaming down her face.

"I love you, Arielle," he whispered.

She nodded. "I know. I heard it."

Neither had spoken, but the sounds he'd heard were beautiful.

"I guess the good part is next," she said. "Endless kissing."

He angled his head, frowning as he reached into his pocket. "You forgot a step."

"We're sealing the deal with Nik-L-Nips?"

"Nope." He closed his fingers around the strand of pearls he'd picked up yesterday. Slowly, he pulled them out of his pocket and watched her beautiful face light up.

"Didn't you say the last step is beads for the bride?" he asked.

"Are those the same pearls? They're evidence."

"No, these are your pearls. Cutter let me pick fifty of the best he had from the treasure trove, and I had this necklace made for my bride."

"It's so authentic."

"The pearls are the same, right off a ship that's out there somewhere. Dr. Marksman put me in touch with a Native American artisan who re-created the necklace."

She fingered them as he reached around to latch them behind her neck, looking up at him with tear-dampened eyes. "I can't believe I found you."

He laughed softly. "My girl who believes in things she can't see? Believe it, Little Mermaid. We are one." He tipped her chin and leaned close to her lips. "Let's start that endless kissing now."

"Mmmm. Except I think my grandmother made that part up."

"I love Grandma Good Night."

"So do I," she whispered as their lips met in the first of many endless kisses.

They made love on the grass until the sun touched the water and wind dried their tears of joy, and the only sound on their hill was a gentle flapping of osprey wings as she passed overhead and let out her sweet call of approval.

There's more love on the horizon of Barefoot Bay! Be sure to look for these other stories set on this island.

The Barefoot Bay Brides
Barefoot in White
Barefoot in Lace
Barefoot in Pearls

The Barefoot Billionaires
Secrets on the Sand
Seduction on the Sand
Scandal on the Sand

The Barefoot Bay Quartet
Barefoot in the Sand
Barefoot in the Rain
Barefoot in the Sun
Barefoot by the Sea

A complete list of Roxanne's entire body of work is available at www.roxannestclaire.com/booklist.html

Introducing a new Barefoot Bay Series:

Barefoot Bay Undercover

The sun has not yet set in Barefoot Bay. There are more heart-wrenching love stories, plenty of pages with favorite old friends, and a whole new "mini-series" on its way to you. Roxanne St. Claire is delighted to introduce readers to *Barefoot Bay Undercover*, a new romantic adventure series featuring fearless heroes, strong heroines, a twist of mystery, and a splash of suspense, all set on the sun-drenched shores of Barefoot Bay! Former spy, current bad boy, and eternal heart throb Gabriel Rossi will be at the center of the series, running a covert operation that will save lives and steal hearts. Of course, there will be an exciting build to his long-awaited love story!

Visit Roxanne's website to join the mailing list to receive a brief monthly newsletter with sneak peeks, series updates, and release dates.

Sneak Peek at

Barefoot Bay Undercover

asa Blanca? *Seriously*? Did someone have a Bogart fetish, or had Gabe just landed in Disney Does Morocco, complete with the geometric patterns in the sundried bricks and U-shaped archways? Gabe scanned the sprawling resort tucked into a hidden corner of an island accessible only by boat and one bridge. There wasn't a single high-rise, nightclub, shopping mall, or Starbucks in sight. The only people were the poor slobs who worked for the privileged bastards who flew in on corporate jets and helicopters to demand seclusion, anonymity, and privacy.

The place was fucking perfect.

At least, perfect for what Gabriel Rossi had in mind. And that was so not what his old friend from the French Foreign Legion had meant when he'd called and asked for a little security consulting advice in exchange for an all-expense trip to paradise.

But Gabe would drag Luke McBain over to the right playground soon enough. First, he had to run the final test. Before he could take the next step and kickstart a plan that had been brewing since he left his old undercover life, he had to see just what kind of yahoos worked at this joint.

Time to play a little game.

Standing in the expansive lobby, he scanned his possible targets. A smokin' blonde with fake lashes and real tits at the front desk had already taken note of him. Twice. Farther away, two men, both dressed in custom threads, a Rolex visible on one tennis-tanned arm, talked outside of the spa, probably waiting for their wives. A teenage girl sat on a bench under the mosaic, texting and oblivious.

None of them was right for what Gabe had in mind.

To his right, a couple stood in front of an understated Guest Services desk, deep in conversation. The man was about his own height of six feet and had short dark hair, and while he obviously hadn't done a hundred one-armed pushups at five a.m., like Gabe had, he was buff enough.

Okay. Now we're talkin'.

Gabe took a few steps closer to the couple and their exchange with a sharply dressed concierge, far enough away not to draw attention. He pulled out his phone and pretended to read messages while listening to their conversation.

Tapping the screen, he opened the interceptor software he'd, uh, borrowed when he left the CIA, and tilted his phone toward the woman's handbag.

"All right then, Mr. Carriger," the concierge said. "Your tee time is confirmed, and our driver will pick you up in five minutes at the front door."

The man turned to his wife, a concerned look on a CEO-handsome face. "You sure you don't mind if we forgo the boat trip today, Beth?"

"I'm spending the day in the spa, honey. I far prefer that to getting seasick and looking for dolphins." She laughed and gestured to the concierge. "Married twenty years, you'd think Doug would know that by now."

The concierge gave a warm nod as he picked up his phone, but Gabe filed the man's name, Doug Carriger, and snapped a mental image of how he held himself. He watched the man's facial expressions carefully and pegged an accent someone with a less-trained ear wouldn't even hear. South of Philly, not quite Virginia. Baltimore.

The concierge leaned forward, listening with one ear to the phone. "I'm sorry we can't get you into Eucalyptus until eleven, Mrs. Carriger. But this treatment is worth the wait, I assure you. We are the only spa in the entire state of Florida that offers it."

"I can't wait. In the meantime, I'll go back to the villa and sit by the pool. The housekeeper won't be there, will she?"

"Let me check," the concierge said, glancing at his tablet. "Poppy's doing Bay Laurel Villa in about twenty minutes. Would you like me to reschedule her for later today?"

Immediately, Gabe tapped his phone and did a quick Internet search of exclusive spa treatments available only at Casa Blanca while he walked toward a house phone not too far away. The answer popped up on the screen just as Gabe picked up the phone and asked for the Eucalyptus Spa.

While he waited, the conversation continued, the couple unwittingly making Gabe's mission easier.

"Poppy is a lovely housekeeper, by the way," Mrs. Carriger said. "I was so touched by the rose petals on the pillow."

The concierge smiled as if he'd heard the compliment before. "We do love to celebrate anniversaries here at Casa Blanca. And speaking of the big day, let's talk about tonight's dinner reservations. May I reserve the private booth in Junonia for you?"

"Eucalyptus Spa," a cool voice crooned in Gabe's ear. "How may I help you?"

"I'm afraid I have to cancel my wife's Ayurvedic treatment. I think for ten, maybe nine thirty? She can't remember the time." He glanced at his targets, still arranging their dinner reservations. "She's not feeling well."

"Oh, that's a shame. Is this Mr. McPherson?"

"It is."

Some keys clicked. "Yes, we had her in at nine forty-five so she had a few minutes to prepare. Would Mrs. McPherson like to reschedule?"

"Not right now, thank you."

That business complete, Gabe took a few steps back toward the Guest Services desk, placing himself exactly ten feet away from Mrs. C's handbag as he typed: *We have had a cancellation in the spa for the Ayurvedic Massage at ten o'clock. Would you like this time slot?*

He waited for a phone number to appear courtesy of the interceptor software—a 410 area code, confirming his guess about Baltimore—then hit send. Within a few seconds, Mrs. Carriger reached into her bag and pulled out her rhinestone-encrusted iPhone.

Damn, he was good.

As expected, her face brightened as she read the text. "Well, look at that. They have an opening for me."

Without a second's hesitation, Gabe left the lobby, glancing over his shoulder at the front-desk blonde who was still not so surreptitiously checking him out. *Lose the lashes, toots, and we'll talk.*

Outside, he nodded to the doorman and walked slowly until he saw the limo turn the corner to pick up Mr. Carriger for his golf game.

As the glass doors to the lobby opened, he leaned over just in time to see Mrs. C heading into the Eucalyptus Spa for her overpriced fake Indian alternative massage.

He rounded a lush grouping of palm trees, finding the wide stone path that led to the villas. He'd done just enough research to know where Bay Laurel was, the closest and largest of the villas on the property. And enough research to know that this little resort could be the answer he'd been seeking for a long time.

So far, it certainly had potential.

At a soft hum behind him, Gabe stepped to the side to let an electric golf cart laden with housekeeping supplies roll by. As it passed, Gabe kept his head turned away, facing the sapphire waters of the Gulf of Mexico. He easily snagged a towel from the back, hoping it was big enough. But not too big. That would work better.

When he reached Bay Laurel, he glanced around and slipped into the shadows created by a hedge of hibiscus that ran alongside the two-story villa. Tucking himself between the wall and the hedges, he unbuttoned his shirt and shook it off. Then his pants, stepping out of them and standing bare-ass naked. He rolled the clothes up and hid them, along with his phone, wallet, and weapon under the bushes. Now he was truly naked, which would be the only way this would work.

Opening the towel, he had to laugh. It was oversized, all right, an oversized *hand towel*. Not going to completely cover the Rossi family jewels, but that might make this whole process better and faster.

Wrapping it around his waist, more or less, he headed back to the path, the warm tropical breeze cooling his head. Both of them.

If he could do this easily, he might not have the right place. Whatever McBain had in mind for security, Gabe had to know the place was fundamentally safe for what *he* had in mind. He stayed back until he heard another golf cart and quickly moved to place himself exactly where he'd be if he'd come out in a hurry and locked himself out of the villa. Taking a breath, he closed his eyes, pictured Doug Carriger…and *became* him.

He slumped his shoulders, jutted his chin, and copped the

expression of a man whose plans had been thwarted by his own stupidity.

The cart moved slowly, driven by a heavyset fortyish woman wearing a bright pink uniform, head buds in her ears, belting the holy hell out of *Amazing Grace*.

"Um, excuse me." He stepped into the path, strategically holding the tiny towel.

She slammed on the brakes, ended the tune, and two espresso eyes popped, dropped, and drank him in. Disgust fluttered her lids.

Not the usual reaction he got from women, he'd give her that.

"Can I help you, Mr...."

"Carriger." He gripped the towel in mock modesty and rounded his vowels like a good Ravens fan. "Doug Carriger." And let out the sigh of a true idiot. "Locked-out-of-my-villa Doug Carriger."

Black bushy brows drew closer as she inspected him. "You look different."

No doubt Doug didn't have any ink. "Naked'll do that to a man, Poppy."

She eyed him, fighting the urge to look down, already pulling out a cell phone. "I'll call security—"

"No, please. Don't." He took a few steps closer and nearly dropped the towel. "I don't want my wife to know I got locked out, and they'll call her and make her leave the spa. She's having one of those Ayu...Aruvu..."

"Ayurvedic treatments," she supplied, still frowning at him. "Why are you out here?" she asked, the musical Jamaican lilt in her voice going cold with the question.

"I thought the flowers were being delivered, and I wanted to be sure I got them." He gave a sheepish smile. "Twenty roses for my years with Beth."

She wasn't buying it. Probably could tell he would have had to waltz down the aisle at sixteen to be married twenty years. Points to Poppy for keen observation.

"I got the idea from the petals you left on the pillow, so I guess I owe you." He winked and tipped his head to the door. "Can you please let me back in?"

"You don't have any identification?"

With each little roadblock, his respect ratcheted up a notch. "Can't say I regularly stuff my wallet in my backside."

She wasn't amused, but lifted her cell. "Well, I stuff my phone in my pocket, so I can call security every time I see a man locked out of his villa." She finally smiled, a flash of white teeth that didn't match the serious look in her dark eyes. "Casa Blanca policy."

Every hotel's policy, except when he was the one charming the housekeeper. Then again, he hadn't run into Poppy before.

Voices came from around the bend, the sound of two women chatting, who might swing the momentum in his favor. "Is it Casa Blanca policy to allow guests to stumble upon a naked man on their way back from the beach?"

"Those bridesmaids for the Stanley wedding? Trust me, they won't mind." She dialed. "And I could lose my job if I don't call security. We have a new man on board."

He knew the man. Luke McBain was his host for the weekend.

As the voices came closer, Gabe stepped out to the path and lifted one brow, opening all his fingers but the two that held his hand towel in place.

Poppy barely acknowledged the threat. Damn. Veins of ice. He liked that. A lot.

"Poppy," he said firmly, pulling her attention. "Just pull

out the passkey, and you will not have to be responsible for embarrassing the guests. Not the bridesmaids—*me*."

She slid another look up and down his body. "You got nothing to be embarrassed about, child."

Child? "You mean 'honey child,' right?"

"Nope." She tapped the phone screen.

Well, what do you know? Casa Blanca just might be passing the final test. The out-of-the-way location, the privacy, the anonymity, and the transience of the place was sheer perfection, not to mention the possibility of a "security firm" as cover.

But a staff that had its shit together? Priceless.

"You know it'll take security ten minutes to get here," he said.

"I can give you a bigger towel." She shrugged, dialing.

"How about a Benji or two for your trouble?" Surely some crisp hundreds could buy Poppy's sympathy.

She threw him a look. "Do I look like a pushover?"

"Jesus Christ," he muttered.

"Hey!" She rocked forward, black sparks in her eyes. "What did you say?"

"Jesus—"

She held her hand up. "I heard you." She flipped her fingers over, palm up, outstretched as she hoisted her not insignificant backside out of the cart. "That'll be ten dollars."

Whoa, that was easy. What a shame. Hard-Ass Poppy had a price, and it was low. "Let me inside, and I'll double it."

She flattened him with a look as deadly as any he'd seen in a Pakistani torture cell. "Ten dollars, no more, no less."

"As soon as you open that door and—"

"Oh. *My*." A woman's voice interrupted him.

"Wow," said another.

Two twentysomethings—one blond, one brunette, both interested—stopped dead in their flip-flops to stare.

"I call dibs if he's one of Robbie's groomsmen," one of them whispered.

"He's not," Poppy said, phone to ear, hand out. "He's just a nuisance, and *I'm* calling security. Move along, ladies."

Gabe gave them a pleading look. "I'm locked out."

The blonde smiled, raking him with a look. "You can come to my villa."

Poppy snorted. "I wouldn't invite that kind of trouble, ma'am."

"I like trouble," she replied, stepping closer, taking Gabe in like he was a fucking zoo animal.

"I'm calling security," Poppy repeated.

"No need. I've got handcuffs in my room." Blondie winked.

Poppy waved them on. "To your villas, ladies. Show's over."

They obeyed her—it was kind of hard not to, Gabe thought grudgingly—but not without passing close by.

"*Are* you one of Chris's groomsmen?" the blonde whispered.

For Poppy's benefit, he sighed and looked skyward. "Sorry to disappoint, ladies, but I'm here with my *wife*, Beth, to celebrate our *twentieth* anniversary of wedded bliss."

The two women's faces dropped, but Poppy marched closer, a warning on her face. "Our new head of security is on the way," she announced.

The girls kept walking, and looking over their shoulders.

Gabe returned his attention to the Nazi housekeeper, trying one last tack to see how tough the woman was. "You still have time to save your job, Popcorn," he whispered. "Open the door, and I'll deal with Mr. McBain when he arrives."

Her brows sneaked up. She was impressed or surprised that he knew the name of their brand new head of security. But not worried. Because this woman did the right thing, no matter what, and Gabe could practically kiss her for it.

"Well, shit, Pop—"

She shoved her palm out again. "That'll be eleven."

"Eleven what?"

"Dollars. Ten for the first offense of taking my Lord's name in vain, and another dollar for that latest S-word."

"S-word? Poppy, hon, let me inside, and I got two hundred that'll probably buy you a nice new…handbag."

"I don't want a handbag," she said humorlessly. "You swear, you pay into the Jamaican Children's Fund."

"The *what*?"

"The Jamaican Children's Fund that's going to bring my three nephews right here to this country. Every time someone curses in my presence, they pay accordingly. Those li'l four-letter ones, a dollar. The D-word is three. Five for F or anything I don't like that starts with C. You blaspheme my Lord and Savior's name, and it's always ten. Now, you started with ten, then added one. So, that'll be eleven dollars."

His jaw loosened. "Why is D so high?"

She looked appalled. "Don't you read the Bible?"

"I assume that's a rhetorical question."

She actually smiled, surprising the shit out of him. "Never mind. You owe me eleven dollars, and I'm that much closer to seeing those boys."

"Two hundred wouldn't help?"

She angled her head as if she was just plumb tired of him. "I don't take bribes or ill-gotten gains, Mr. Baby Blues." At the sound of another golf cart, she turned. "Here's your ride, sir."

The cart rounded the corner, and Gabe instantly recognized Luke, who'd changed a lot since his days in the French Foreign Legion, but still sported sizable guns and rugged features.

"What the hell?" Luke muttered.

"Does *he* owe you a dollar?" Gabe asked.

"Do you know this man, Mr. McBain?"

"I sure do." Luke was off the cart, hand extended, looking a little leery about the expected man hug since one of them was butt naked. Still, Gabe gave a smug look to Poppy.

"But you ain't Mr. Carriger," she shot back.

"No, he isn't," Luke confirmed. "This is Gabriel Rossi. He's a legend."

"In his own mind." She stepped back to her cart while Gabe just laughed.

"What are you doing out here in a towel, man?" Luke asked.

"Testing your security systems," he said, giving Luke's back a whack with one hand. "Which are impressive," he added, gesturing to the woman with an angled head. "Dude, you got eleven bucks?"

Luke inched back and reached into his pocket. "I think so. Why?"

"I owe this woman."

A row of blinding-white teeth popped from her dark, coffee-colored skin.

Luke, a mix of amused and confused, pulled out the correct amount and gave it to her. "Thanks for whatever it is you did, Poppy."

"My job." She took the money and stuffed it into her pocket.

"And did it well," Gabe added. As she started to walk

away, he pointed at her. "You should get a promotion to the security department, Pop Star."

She looked him up and down, a woman who took no shit from no one. Gabe could use a person like that on his team. Someone who would keep her mouth shut when she had to, which, with what he had in mind, would be always.

"Why would I do that?"

"Because if you spend enough time with me, you'll have those boys in your arms in about a week." Gabe rubbed his fingers together in the universal gesture for cash. "My loose lips sail lots of ships."

She gave a grudging laugh and passed by him. "'Scuze me. I got a villa to clean."

As she disappeared through the entrance of Bay Laurel, Gabe turned to Luke, who was cool enough to not ask questions, but smart enough to look like he sure as hell wanted some answers.

"Let me get dressed," Gabe said.

"Good call."

Gabe slipped down the side of the house, then returned to where Luke waited in the golf cart. As Gabe slid onto the bench, he slipped sunglasses on, folded his arms, and leaned back. "You don't need to give me the five-dollar tour, dawg. This place is exactly what I want. I'll take the job."

Luke's jaw completely unhinged. "What are you talking about?"

"I'm your partner in the new business we're starting." He gestured for Luke to drive. "Head north. There are nice ladies up there, and I hear they have handcuffs."

Luke didn't move. "First of all, I didn't offer you a position as my partner in the security business I'm starting. Second, I'm engaged."

"I'm not the least bit interested in a security business,

McBain. I'm part of one now, with my family in Boston. I'm so bored I'm counting the hairs on my balls for fun. Mazel tov on your engagement."

"Thanks, but if you're not interested in the security business, why would you even consider coming here and working for me?"

"*With* you," he corrected. "And, no worries, I don't want any part of your bodyguard gig. You can keep the guests of Casa Blanca safe from the baddies all by yourself."

Luke bristled as he started the cart and rolled down the paved path.

"We're just based here," Luke said. "I'm overseeing resort security as a favor to the owner, who gave me offices on the property. But I'm hiring a team for protection and security all over the island. There's some big money down here, a new baseball team, and a mother lode of cash offshore from some shipwrecks attracting all sorts of trouble. That's why I need some of your expertise."

"Perfect." Gabe nodded. "A security company as a front could not be better."

"A front?" Luke threw him a look, and Gabe braced for a barrage of questions. "Now you sound like the spook I met in Somalia."

"Good times, eh, *Ricard*?" Gabe grinned, remembering the hairy-ass mission he'd been on with the group of Legionnaires where he'd met, and respected, McBain.

Luke's lip curled. "Hate that name."

"Oh, yeah, I remember. But everything's cool now?"

"Completely. And I'm happy here. Happier than I've ever been." He turned onto a dirt path that ran alongside a farmette that Gabe assumed helped feed the guests. "Correct me if I'm wrong, but what kind of trouble are you in that you—a freaking renowned spy with an undercover career that reads like a Tom Clancy novel—would consider working at a resort in Florida?"

"No shit, man. What the fuck is wrong with me?" Gabe grinned and elbowed his friend. "Look, my novel-worthy UC career isn't over, hoss. I'm starting a new phase. What's this?" He gestured toward a small compound of small stucco buildings, built to blend with the style of the resort, but far more understated.

"These were built as staff housing, but I'm going to take over at least three of the bungalows for offices."

Gabe hopped out of the moving cart. "I like the one on the end. I can live there and have offices, too. Maybe I'll convince Nino to come with me, and Chessie, too. Except Vivi and Zach will string me up by the 'nads if I steal from the Guardian Angelinos." He threw a look at Luke. "I should have known I couldn't work there when my cousins told me the mind-numbingly stupid name they picked for a security firm."

Luke climbed from the cart, following Gabe. "What don't you tell me exactly what you have in mind?"

Gabe assessed him again. Luke was trustworthy. He'd proved that. And Gabe needed at least a few people to know what he was up to. Hell, he already had two clients lined up and had to move quickly. "I'm have an idea I have for a business that will make bank. And I'll share that bank if you'll give me a front for the operation."

"A front." Luke came around the front of the cart and narrowed his eyes. "Is it legit? Legal? Safe?"

"Legit? Legal? Safe?" Gabe snorted. "It's badass, brilliant, and lucrative." At Luke's hardened look, Gabe added, "And yes, it's...pretty safe. Mostly legit. Legal"—he shrugged—"enough."

Luke shook his head. "I can't let something or someone

onto this property that will jeopardize any staff or guest."

"No jeopardy," Gabe assured him. "All I need is a place where it looks like I'm working, and I can run my own little setup, invisible to all."

Luke just stared at him. "Not until I know exactly what your 'little setup' is."

Gabe blew out a breath, sliding his hands into his pockets as he walked closer to the bungalows, choosing his words carefully.

"There are people who need protection, a place to hide, even a new identity, and they don't always qualify for a legit government program like witness protection."

"What kind of people?"

"Good people," Gabe insisted. "Potential kidnapping victims, abused wives, the poor schmuck who got mixed up with the wrong crowd. Many of my cousins' clients need more than basic security. They need a safe place that is off the grid but still in plain sight." He glanced at Luke to see if he was getting it, noticing the other man nodding. "That kind of 'private witness protection' is pricey, dawg. Hard to find and harder to keep a secret. That's where I come in."

"What exactly will you do?"

Gabe grinned. "Shit no one else can. Bro, I know how to run, hide, transform, and show up as another person on a different continent better than any other spook out there. Why not put those skills to good use and make serious cash from people who are willing to pay for that kind of überprotection? Sometimes, a bodyguard isn't what they want. They need more than standard security, and that's where I come in."

"Will they stay here, or is this 'überprotection' some kind of a pit stop on their way to another place?"

He shrugged, knowing he didn't have all the answers yet.

"Depends on the case. Most will move on, staying here only long enough for me to do the legwork to get them a new identity and home. Some might stay. We'll have to take each deal as it comes."

Listening, Luke crossed his arms and looked toward the bungalows as if trying to picture this whole thing unfolding there. "Why not use that Guardian Angelino business as a front?"

"In Boston? Too easy to find people, too many access points, no control. I have been looking for a place just like this. More or less in the middle of nowhere, where the 'guests' can become anyone, and with a front business that's legit." He unlatched his hands and leaned forward. "With a partner I can trust."

Luke eyed him for a long time. "I didn't want a partner."

"And neither do I. It's a cover, man. And a damn good one. You do your security thing, and, yes, I can give you a metric buttload of advice on how to run that business with my eyes closed and my dick in a sling. In exchange, you just tell people I'm your silent partner or consultant or whatever. I don't go out on security calls, and I don't expect you to help with my cases." At the flicker in Luke's eyes, he added, "Unless you want to. We'll work out the money, and it'll be good."

"How are you going to find clients?"

Gabe just laughed. "Dude, they find me."

Luke still wasn't convinced, Gabe could tell by the dubious look in his eyes. "Who's going to believe that you, Gabriel Rossi, has decided to move to an island in Florida and live the quiet life as a partner in a security firm?"

Gabe put a hand on Luke's shoulder. "I can make anyone believe anything. You just have to go along with it, and you will take a nice cut of the cash for your trouble, and I won't take a penny of yours."

"You didn't make Poppy believe you were a locked-out guest," Luke challenged.

"Which makes me certain I picked the right place. I told you, it was a security test. If the basics weren't here, I couldn't make this my home base. But they are, and I can." He tightened his grip. "Gimme a chance, and we'll see how it works out. I think this place is ideal for running, hiding, and reinventing."

Luke didn't answer for a long time, his eyes narrowing. "You know what I think?"

"That your fairy fucking godfather just landed with a pot of gold?"

"I think you're the one running, hiding, and reinventing, Rossi."

Gabe didn't even flinch, but turned away to be sure his eyes didn't give anything away. "Just say yes or no, bro."

Luke waited a long time. Too long. Then he smiled. "Hell, yeah. I'm in. I gotta believe anything with you is going to be…interesting."

"As fuck." Gabe grinned and smacked Luke's shoulder. "Now show me the new offices. Time for a little action in…what's the name of this hellhole again? Bare-Ass Bay?"

Luke laughed. "Barefoot Bay."

"Cute. Shit's about to get real in Barefoot Bay."

"Real what?"

Gabe slid into a sly smile. "Real…*different*."

BAREFOOT BAY UNDERCOVER
Launching Spring 2015

Other Books by Roxanne St. Claire

The Guardian Angelinos (Romantic Suspense)
Edge of Sight
Shiver of Fear
Face of Danger

The Bullet Catchers (Romantic Suspense)
Kill Me Twice
Thrill Me to Death
Take Me Tonight
First You Run
Then You Hide
Now You Die
Hunt Her Down
Make Her Pay
Pick Your Poison (a novella)

Stand-alone Novels (Romance and Suspense)
Space in His Heart
Hit Reply
Tropical Getaway
French Twist
Killer Curves
Don't You Wish (Young Adult)

About the Author

Roxanne St. Claire is a *New York Times* and *USA Today* bestselling author of nearly forty novels of suspense and romance, including several popular series (*The Bullet Catchers*, *The Guardian Angelinos*, and *Barefoot Bay*) and multiple stand-alone books. Her entire backlist, including excerpts and buy links, can be found at www.roxannestclaire.com.

In addition to being a six-time nominee and one-time winner of the prestigious Romance Writers of America RITA Award, Roxanne's novels have won the National Reader's Choice Award for best romantic suspense three times, and the Borders Top Pick in Romance, as well as the Daphne du Maurier Award, the HOLT Medallion, the Maggie, Booksellers Best, Book Buyers Best, the Award of Excellence, and many others. Her books have been translated into dozens of languages and are routinely included as a Doubleday/Rhapsody Book Club Selection of the Month.

Roxanne lives in Florida with her family (and dogs!), and can be reached via her website, www.roxannestclaire.com or on her Facebook Reader page, www.facebook.com/roxannestclaire and on Twitter at www.twitter.com/roxannestclaire.

CPSIA information can be obtained at www.ICGtesting.com
Printed in the USA
LVOW07s1136260415

436146LV00005B/687/P

JUL 1 3 2015